A NOTE ON THE AUTHOR

HELEN SIMONSON was born in Buckinghamshire and spent her teenage years in a small village near Rye, East Sussex. Her debut novel, *Major Pettigrew's Last Stand*, was an international bestseller, a Richard & Judy Book Club pick, and was translated and published in twenty-one countries. A graduate of the London School of Economics, Helen is married, with two grown sons, and currently lives in Brooklyn, New York. This is her second novel.

helensimonson.com

BY THE SAME AUTHOR

Major Pettigrew's Last Stand

The Summer Before the War

HELEN SIMONSON

BLOOMSBURY

LONDON · OXFORD · NEW YORK · NEW DELHI · SYDNEY

Bloomsbury Paperbacks
An imprint of Bloomsbury Publishing Plc

50 Bedford Square   1385 Broadway
London   New York
WC1B 3DP   NY 10018
UK   USA

www.bloomsbury.com

BLOOMSBURY and the Diana logo are trademarks of Bloomsbury Publishing Plc

First published in Great Britain 2016

This paperback edition first published in 2017

British Library Cataloguing-in-Publication Data
A catalogue record for this book is available from the British Library.

ISBN: HB: 978-1-4088-3764-1
TPB: 978-1-4088-7202-4
PB: 978-1-4088-3766-5
ePub: 978-1-4088-3765-8

2 4 6 8 10 9 7 5 3 1

Typeset by Integra Software Services Pvt. Ltd.
Printed and bound in Great Britain by CPI Group (UK) Ltd, Croydon CR0 4YY

MIX
Paper from
responsible sources
FSC® C020471

To find out more about our authors and books visit www.bloomsbury.com.
Here you will find extracts, author interviews, details of forthcoming
events and the option to sign up for our newsletters.

To my parents,

Alan and Margaret Phillips

Part One

It was in the first place, after the strangest fashion, a sense of the extraordinary way in which the most benign conditions of light and air, of sky and sea, the most beautiful English summer conceivable, mixed themselves with all the violence of action and passion . . . Never were desperate doings so blandly lighted up as by the two unforgettable months that I was to spend so much of in looking over from the old rampart of a little high-perched Sussex town at the bright blue streak of the Channel.

HENRY JAMES, 'Within the Rim'

CHAPTER ONE

THE TOWN OF RYE rose from the flat marshes like an island, its tumbled pyramid of red-tiled roofs glowing in the slanting evening light. The high Sussex bluffs were a massive, unbroken line of shadow from east to west, the fields breathed out the heat of the day, and the sea was a sheet of hammered pewter. Standing at the tall French windows, Hugh Grange held his breath in a vain attempt to suspend the moment in time as he used to do when he was a little boy, in this same, slightly shabby drawing room, and the lighting of the lamps had been the signal for his aunt to send him to bed. He smiled now to think of how long and late those summer evenings had run and how he had always complained bitterly until he was allowed to stay up well beyond bedtime. Small boys, he now knew, were inveterate fraudsters and begged, pleaded and cajoled for added rights and treats with innocent eyes and black hearts.

The three boys his aunt had asked him to tutor this summer had relieved him of half a sovereign and most of his books before he realised that they neither were as hungry as their sighs proposed nor had any interest in *Ivanhoe* except for what it might bring when flogged to the man with the secondhand bookstall in the town market. He held no grudge. Instead he admired their ferret wits and held some small dream that his brief teaching and example might turn sharpness into some intellectual curiosity by the time the grammar school began again.

The door to the drawing room was opened with a robust hand, and Hugh's cousin, Daniel, stood back with a mock bow to allow their aunt Agatha to pass into the room. 'Aunt Agatha says there isn't going to be a war,' said Daniel, coming in behind her, laughing. 'And so of course there won't be. They would never dream of defying her.' Aunt Agatha tried to look severe but only managed to cross her eyes and almost stumbled into a side table due to the sudden blurring of her vision.

'That isn't what I said at all,' she said, trying to secure her long embroidered scarf, an effort as futile as resting a flat kite on a round boulder, thought Hugh, as the scarf immediately began to slide sideways again. Aunt Agatha was still a handsome woman at forty-five, but she was inclined to stoutness and had very few sharp planes on which to drape her clothing. Tonight's dinner dress, in slippery chiffon, possessed a deep, sloppy neckline and long Oriental sleeves. Hugh hoped it would maintain its dignity through dinner, for his aunt liked to embellish her conversation with expansive gestures.

'What does Uncle John say?' asked Hugh, stepping to a tray of decanters to pour his aunt her usual glass of Madeira. 'No chance he's coming down tomorrow?' He had hoped to ask his uncle's opinion on a smaller but no less important subject. After years devoted to his medical studies, Hugh found himself not only on the point of becoming primary assistant surgeon to Sir Alex Ramsey, one of England's leading general surgeons, but also quite possibly in love with his surgeon's very pretty daughter, Lucy. He had held rather aloof from Lucy the past year, perhaps to prove to himself, and others, that his affection for her was not connected to any hopes of advancement. This had only made him a favourite of hers among the various students and younger doctors who flocked around her father, but it was not until this summer, when she and her father left for an extended lecture tour in the Italian Lakes, that he had felt a pleasurable misery in her absence. He found he missed her dancing eyes, the toss of her pale hair as she laughed at some dry comment he made; he even missed the little spectacles she wore to copy her father's case files or reply to his voluminous correspondence. She was fresh from the schoolroom and sometimes distracted by all the pleasures London offered bright young people, but she was devoted to her father and would make, thought Hugh, an exceptional wife for a rising young surgeon. He wished to discuss, with some urgency, whether he might be in a position to contemplate matrimony.

Uncle John was a sensible man and through the years had always seemed swiftly to understand whatever difficulty Hugh stammered out and would help talk the matter over until Hugh was convinced he had resolved some intractable problem all on his own. Hugh was no longer a small boy and now understood some of his uncle's wisdom to be the result of diplomatic training, but he knew his uncle's affection to be genuine. His own parents' parting words, as they left for a long-awaited year of travel, had been to apply to Uncle John in any case of need.

'Your uncle says they are all working feverishly to smooth things over, before everyone's summer holiday,' said his aunt. 'He tells me nothing, of course, but the Prime Minister and the Foreign Secretary spent much of the day closeted with the King.' Uncle John was a senior official in the Foreign Office, and the usually sleepy summer precincts of Whitehall had been crammed with busy civil servants, politicians and generals since the Archduke's assassination in Sarajevo. 'Anyway, he telephoned to say he met the schoolteacher and transferred her to Charing Cross to catch the last train, so she'll be getting in after dinner. We'll give her a late supper.'

'At such a late hour, wouldn't it be kinder to deliver her to her rooms in town and maybe have Cook send down something cold?' said Daniel, ignoring Hugh's proffered dry sherry and pouring a glass of Uncle John's best whisky. 'I'm sure she'll be horribly fagged and not up to a room full of people in evening dress.' He tried to keep a neutral face, but Hugh detected a slight moue of distaste at the thought of entertaining the new schoolteacher his aunt had found. Since graduating from Balliol in June, Daniel had spent the first few weeks of the summer in Italy as the guest of an aristocratic college chum, and had developed a sense of social superiority that Hugh was dying to see Aunt Agatha knock out of his silly head. Instead Agatha had been patient, saying, 'Oh, let him have his taste of the high life. Don't you think his heart will be broken soon enough? When Daniel goes into the Foreign Office this autumn, as your uncle John has taken such pains to arrange, I'm sure his friend will drop him in an instant. Let him have his hour of glamour.'

Hugh was of the opinion that Daniel should be made to understand his place, but he loved his aunt Agatha and he thought any continued argument might lead her to think he resented Daniel being her favourite. Daniel's mother, Agatha's sister, had died when Daniel was only five, and his father was a strange, distant sort of man. Daniel had been sent to boarding school a month after his mother's death, and Agatha had been his refuge in the Christmas and summer holidays. Hugh had always been torn about Christmas. He spent it at home in London with his parents, who loved him and made a great fuss of him. He would have preferred if they could have all gone down to Sussex to Agatha's house together, but his mother, who was Uncle John's sister, liked to be among her friends in town, and his father did not like to be away from the bank too long at Christmas. Hugh had been happy in the midst of piles of striped wrapping paper, huge mysterious boxes and the dishes of sweets and fruits set all around their Kensington villa. But sometimes, when he'd been sent to bed and the music from his parents' guests drifted up to his room, he would lie in bed and peer out of the window over the dark rooftops and try to see all the way to Sussex, where no doubt Aunt Agatha was tucking Daniel in with one of her wild stories of giants and elves who lived in caves under the Sussex Downs and whose parties could be mistaken sometimes as thunder.

'Don't be silly, Daniel. Miss Nash will stay here this evening,' said Aunt Agatha, bending to switch on the electric lamp by the flowered couch. She sat down and stretched out her feet, which were encased in Oriental slippers embroidered, rather strangely, with lobsters. 'I had to fight to bring the full weight of the School Board to bear on the governors to hire a woman. I mean to get a good look at her and make sure she understands what's to be done.'

The local grammar school was one of his aunt's many social causes. She believed in education for all and seemed to expect great leaders of men to emerge from the grubby-kneed group of farmers' and merchants' boys who crowded the new red-brick school building out beyond the railway tracks.

'You mean you want her to get a good look at you,' said Hugh. 'I'm sure she'll be suitably cowed.'

'I'm with the governors,' said Daniel. 'It takes a man to keep a mob of schoolboys in line.'

'Nonsense,' said Agatha. 'Besides, you can't just drum up teachers these days. Our last Latin master, Mr Puddlecombe, was only here a year and then he had the nerve to tell us he was off to try his luck with a cousin in Canada.'

'Well, school had almost broken up for the summer, Auntie,' said Hugh.

'Which made it all the more impossible,' said Agatha. 'We were fortunate that your Uncle John spoke to Lord Marbely and that Lady Marbely had been looking for a position for this young woman. She is a niece apparently, and the Marbelys highly recommended her; though I did get a hint that maybe they had an ulterior motive for getting her out of Gloucestershire.'

'Do they have a son?' asked Daniel. 'That's usually the story.'

'Oh no, Lady Marbely took pains to assure me she's quite plain,' said Aunt Agatha. 'I may be progressive, but I would never hire a pretty teacher.'

'We'd better eat dinner soon,' said Hugh, consulting the battered pocket watch that had been his grandfather's and that his parents were always begging to replace with something more modern. The dinner gong rang just as he spoke.

'Yes, I'd like to digest properly before this paragon descends upon us,' said Daniel, downing the rest of his glass in a swallow. 'I assume I have to be introduced and can't just hide in my room?'

'Would you go with Smith to pick her up, Hugh?' said Agatha. 'Two of you would probably overwhelm the poor girl, and obviously I can't trust Daniel not to sneer at her.'

'What if Hugh falls in love with her?' asked Daniel. Hugh was tempted to retort that his affections were already engaged, but his matrimonial intentions were too important to be subjected to Daniel's disrespectful teasing, and so he merely gave his cousin a look of scorn. 'After all,' added Daniel, 'Hugh is so terribly plain himself.'

Beatrice Nash was quite sure she had a large smut of soot on her nose, but she did not want to take out her pocket mirror again in case doing so roused the inebriated young man opposite her to further flights of compliment. She had checked her face soon after leaving Charing Cross, and he had taken the tiny gold mirror as some recognised signal of coy flirtation. Her book had been further cause for conversation, though he did not seem to recognise the Trollope name and then confessed he had no use for reading. He had even proffered the use of his small bag for her feet, and she had tucked her ankles hard back under the seat, fearing that he might whip off her shoes.

She had scolded him severely when they changed trains in Kent and he followed her into her chosen compartment. He had backed away, laughing, but the train had already started. Now they were stuck together in a compartment without access to a corridor. He was sunk into the appearance of a petulant doze, and she sat rigid, her back straight against the prickly fabric of the bench, trying not to breathe in the stench of stale liquor or feel the insolent proximity of his outstretched legs in pressed white flannels and shiny, buckled brown shoes.

She kept her face turned to the window and let the image of wet green fields run freely across her eyes until the sheep, grass and sky blurred into painted streaks. She wished now she had not refused the Marbelys' offer to send a servant to accompany her. She had been tormented by Ada Marbely's long discussion of what conveyance might be available to reach the station and who might be spared. She had been made to understand that her transfer was a very, very large inconvenience and that of course they could not offer to send her in the car, or send anyone from the permanent household staff. She had hidden her humiliation behind a firm claim of independence. She reminded them that she had travelled widely with her father, from the American West to the kasbahs of Morocco and the lesser-known classical sites of southern Italy, and was perfectly capable of seeing herself and one trunk to Sussex, by farm cart if needed. She had been adamant and now understood that she had only herself to blame for being exposed to the indignities of travelling alone. She managed a small smile at her own stubbornness.

'All women can be pretty when they smile,' said the man. She whipped her face around to glare at him, but his eyes appeared to be still closed, and his face, round and sweating, remained sunk on its thick neck, wrapped in a greasy yellow cravat. He scratched at his shirtfront and yawned without covering his mouth, as if she didn't exist.

It was the cheapest kind of rebuke, to call a woman ugly, but one to which small boys and grown men seemed equally quick to stoop when feeling challenged. While she had always playfully dismissed her father's insistence on calling her his beauty, she believed she had a pleasant, regular face and took pride in a certain strength about the chin and a straight posture. That such an insult was a lie never seemed to reduce its effectiveness, and she could only bite her lip not to give him the satisfaction of a response.

The train slowed in a great hissing fog of steam and she felt a flood of relief to hear the stationmaster calling, 'Rye. Rye station.' She jumped up to take down her bag, lowered the window, heedless of the threat of flying cinders, and had her hand on the outside doorknob ready to open it at the earliest moment.

'Now the stars align,' said the young man, coming to press her towards the door, his bag against her leg. She almost wept to feel him breathing on her neck. 'If you're staying in the area you must allow me to call on you.'

She opened the door and stepped from the carriage, nearly falling to the platform as the train gave a last lurch.

She hit her left ankle with her bag and felt at least one hairpin come away from the side of her head. Not caring for her appearance or the pain, she fled towards the baggage car to retrieve her trunk and ran right into a man standing enveloped in the steam. She could not prevent a cry of fear as he grasped her elbow to stop them both from falling.

'Are you all right?' asked the man. 'I'm terribly sorry.'

'Let go of me,' she said, and she could hear her voice fierce with suppressed rage.

The man, a young man, stepped back, raising his hands in submission. 'I meant no offence, miss,' he said. 'I'm terribly sorry.'

'I saw her first, Grange,' said the man from the train.

'Please leave me alone,' said Beatrice, holding her hand to her face. She was suddenly too exhausted to fight any more. Her rage drained away, and she could feel her limbs tremble as if the light breeze were a winter squall.

'Wheaton, you're an ugly drunk,' said the young man in a voice so calm he might have been talking about the weather. 'Can't you tell a respectable young woman from one of your floozies? Behave yourself.'

'Didn't think you were much for the ladies, Grange,' said Wheaton with a sly chuckle. 'Or is that just your pretty cousin, Daniel?'

'Don't be a bully, Wheaton,' the young man replied. 'Go home before I'm obliged to make you go. No doubt you'll pound me into the ground, but you'll ruin those perfectly good clothes doing it.'

'I'm going; expected home for the fatted calf by my sobbing mother,' said Wheaton, unruffled by the veiled threat of physical harm. 'You can have the schoolteacher.' He staggered away, and Beatrice felt her face flush.

'Are you Miss Nash?' asked the young man. She looked at him but could not trust herself to speak. 'I'm Hugh Grange. My aunt, Agatha Kent, sent me to meet you.'

'I think I need to sit down,' she said. She could tell the young man had kind grey eyes, but she saw nothing else as the whole station began to slowly spin. 'Please don't allow me to faint.'

'Here's a bench,' he said, and she felt his hand tugging urgently at her elbow. She sank down. 'Good. Hang your head below your knees and breathe,' he added, and she felt her head pushed down towards the dusty bricks of the platform. She breathed deep, slow breaths and relief came as a light sweat on her forehead.

'Sorry. Ridiculous of me.'

'Not at all.' She could see only a pair of country boots, well oiled but creased and scuffed with age. 'I'm sorry Wheaton upset you.'

'He did no such thing. I just – I should have eaten more lunch, that's all. I usually eat very well when I travel.'

'It's important to keep up one's strength,' he said, and though she could not detect any note of sarcasm, she felt the anger she had held in all day return. She shivered again, and the young man, his fingers on the pulse in her left wrist, added, 'Shall I go and ask the stationmaster for some water, or do you think you can make it out to the car? We really should get you to my aunt Agatha's right away.'

'I'm perfectly all right,' she said, standing up slowly. 'I must see to my trunk and bicycle.'

'Smith will arrange to fetch them later from the station-master,' he said. 'Let me carry your bag.'

Beatrice hesitated, but there was no hint of condescension in the young man's tone, and his blunt face showed worry in a single vertical crease between the eyes. He was trying to treat her well. She understood that not just in the past couple of hours, but in the past few months, she had lost some trust in how people would treat her. She blinked her eyes and handed him her bag without a word. He took it and hefted its unexpected weight.

'Sorry,' she said. 'I packed too many books as always.'

'That's quite all right,' he said as he took her arm and steered her out through a side gate. 'Though I hate to think how heavy the trunk must be. Maybe I'll ask the station-master to telephone for a cart and save the car from breaking an axle.'

On the ride up the hill away from town, the young woman kept her face averted and her gaze fixed on the passing hedges and cottages. Hugh contemplated the curve of her long neck with the thick brown hair loosely bunched at the nape. She must have been tired, and yet she did not have the rounded slump of permanent defeat that seemed to Hugh to be the hallmark of the schoolteachers he had known. Even his professors at Oxford, many of them secure in family and finances, had seemed to bow over time as if under the perpetual onslaught of student ignorance. The woman's summer travelling coat was made of thick, supple linen that seemed of some quality, and her trim jacket and skirt were fashionably narrow, though unadorned. He judged her to be almost his own age; perhaps twenty-two or -three to his august twenty-four.

While she was not a tremulous girl fresh from the school-room, she was far from the dull spinster he had been expecting. He acknowledged a flicker of interest best investigated and fanned by conversation.

'I apologise again for poor Wheaton,' he said. 'He's perfectly gentlemanly around women when he's sober, but when he drinks he sort of launches himself at any female in the vicinity.'

'Don't apologise,' she said. 'Obviously it was my fault, then, for occupying a railway carriage in which he wished to ride?'

Hugh found himself flushing under her stare. 'Not what I meant at all,' he said. 'But men like Wheaton . . .'

'Are there different kinds, then?' she asked.

'Different kinds?'

'Of men? Only, the majority seem prone to some similar lapse of manners under the influence of alcohol.' She pressed her lips together, and Hugh began to wonder how to get himself out of the conversation.

'Do you wish me to apologise on behalf of us all?' he asked, quietly.

'I would prefer you did not apologise for anyone else,' she said. 'My father always says that if we were as quick to own our own faults as we are to apologise for those of others, society might truly advance.'

'I'd say he's right, but woefully optimistic,' said Hugh. 'Very religious man, is he?' He had a vision of a purse-lipped temperance type with thin fingers tapping the cover of a Bible.

The girl gave what could only be described as a snort of laughter and then covered her mouth with her gloved hand and seemed to struggle with her emotions.

'Sorry,' said Hugh, unable to bite back the word.

'Thank you,' she said at last. A smile transformed her face and set her brown eyes alight. 'He died a year ago, and I didn't think it would be possible to laugh about him again.'

'Not religious then,' said Hugh.

'No,' she said. 'Not exactly. But I do hope you won't repeat it to your aunt. I'm sure schoolteachers are expected to have irreproachable parents.'

'I'm sure they are,' he said. 'Have you studied their other attributes?'

She gave him a doubtful look.

'I assure you I'm completely qualified,' she said. 'But I've been told I have to work harder to cultivate an appropriate attitude of grateful subordination.'

'Lucky for you, my aunt has taken such a stand with the school governors that she would be loath to tell them her candidate was unsuitable,' he said as they drew up on the broad gravel forecourt of his aunt's comfortable villa. He meant it in fun, but he noticed the young woman looked worried as Smith opened her door. As she preceded him in to meet Aunt Agatha, he wondered if he should also have mentioned to her that she was in no way as plain as his aunt would have preferred.

CHAPTER TWO

BEATRICE LIKED THE HOUSE straight away. While its design conjured up a medieval hall bred with a couple of thatched cottages, its large, commodious rooms, electric lights and bright floors spoke of commerce and energy, not a household turning into stone under the geologic pressure of its own lineage. Lady Marbely had moved with the slow drag of a woman waiting her interment in the family crypt, her life and home dusty with protocol and made reclusive by walls of superiority. Beatrice did not know how Agatha Kent and her husband really stood in the world, but she did not think they were likely to pounce on all the flaws in her bloodline before the soup was on the dinner table.

'You must be Beatrice and you must be hungry,' said a plump woman in a slippery Oriental gown, coming out of the open glass doors leading to a living room with many lamps. She was of that certain age when the bloom of youth must give way to strength of character, but her face was handsome in its intelligent eyes and commanding smile, and her hair retained a youthful spring as it threatened to escape from its carefully pinned rolls. 'I'm Agatha Kent, and this is my nephew, Daniel Bookham.'

'How do you do,' he said without even a conventional trace of interest.

Though she had chosen to put the romantic notions of the schoolgirl behind her, Beatrice was not yet immune to a handsome face. With carefully dishevelled brown hair falling into blue eyes, the sharpest of jawlines and an almost downy moustache, Daniel Bookham was a very striking young man. Though she told herself that he was absurd in his carelessly tied cravat and generally bohemian affect, she was forced to squash a brief disappointment that he was younger than her.

'And you've already met my other nephew, Hugh Grange,' added Agatha. Beatrice turned and reconsidered him in the bright light of the front hall. He was taller than Daniel by a head, and plain in a way that might be considered handsome when not compared directly to the almost classical form of his younger cousin. As his aunt dispensed him to see to the luggage and called for the maid to show her to her room, Beatrice decided it would be prudent to keep her eyes firmly in Hugh Grange's direction.

It was probably the third-best guest room, thought Beatrice, small and furnished with a narrow oak bed and a simple writing desk, but pleasantly decorated with blue striped wallpaper and flowery chintz curtains. A lace-skirted sink, with running water, occupied one corner, and a large window stood open to the night and the fragrance of the garden. In the distance, a shimmer of silver indicated the moonlit sea. Across the hall, the maid had proudly displayed a bathroom containing an enormous tub with a frightening array of brass taps and an ornate mahogany throne, the raised seat of which revealed an indoor water closet. A carved mahogany tank set high on the wall and a long brass chain gave it an almost ecclesiastical air.

'I know how to operate it, thank you,' said Beatrice, forestalling the maid's instructions.

'There's no other guests in this wing,' said the maid. 'So you'll have it to yourself.'

'Are the gentlemen not staying?' asked Beatrice.

'They like to stay in their old rooms on the top floor,' said the maid. 'Can't imagine how Master Hugh manages to sleep in that little bed of his, scrunched up like a hedge-hog I expect, but he won't hear of moving, and Master Daniel tried the green room at the front for a while, but Master Hugh teased him something dreadful and Mrs Kent wouldn't let him smoke cigars because the curtains were all new, so he was pretty soon off upstairs again.' Her voice softened as she hurried on, and Beatrice thought better of the young men for inspiring such affection.

She remembered her father and the fierce loyalty he had commanded in the many servants who had looked after the two of them. How sweet, and yet how bitter the many partings. How many times had she been pillowed against the bosom of a sobbing housekeeper who had stroked her hair and begged her to write? Once they had taken a maid with them, to Italy, and the maid had been almost prostrate with grief at letting them down, but found it impossible to accustom herself to foreign parts. Beatrice could summon too easily the cold railway platform, the tearstained face of the maid in the train window, and herself, a thin child, controlling a wave of shivers and resolving to keep the next maid at more of a distance. Each kind servant – and they were all employed by her father for their kindness rather than for any great skills in cleaning or cooking, it seemed – was held a little more distant than the last, until she could look now at Agatha Kent's maid with a completely dispassionate appraisal.

The breathless girl was struggling to remain haughty. No doubt the servants all knew Beatrice was a schoolteacher, and it was a funny thing about those in service, thought Beatrice, that they could be as rude as revolutionaries to those just above them while remaining unconditionally loyal to their masters. The girl was clearly friendly at heart, a stout worker, and had a local accent that probably made her suffer the condescension of others. Beatrice gave her a broad smile.

'Thank you for being so kind, Jenny,' she said.

'I'll fetch you some supper up right away,' said the girl. She smiled back, and no trace of haughtiness remained.

Coming downstairs in a fresh blouse and a shawl, Beatrice met Daniel crossing the entrance hall.

'Ah, wait here one minute and I'll ask Aunt Agatha where she wants you,' he said, disappearing through the living-room doors.

Beatrice paused on the bottom stair, gripping the banister until her wrist ached. She murmured, very fast, 'Humiliation is the sport of the petty,' an admonition of her father's that she had found all too useful this past year.

'Shall I put the schoolteacher in the small study?' she heard Daniel ask.

'Oh, heavens no, there's no fire in there and it's distinctly chilly after dark. Ask her to come in here.'

Daniel appeared in the doorway, a frown marring his classical features, and waved at her. 'In here, miss. Don't be shy, we're very informal.'

'I assure you I was not raised to be shy,' said Beatrice, her voice sharp. 'A country living room holds no terrors for me.'

'Do you hear that, Aunt?' said Daniel. 'Not everyone is terrified of you.'

'I should hope not,' said Agatha, reclining in one corner of an overstuffed sofa. 'Why, I am the mildest mannered of women and I get on with everyone.'

Hugh, sitting in a wing chair by the fireplace, seemed to choke on his own laughter and took a swig from his glass as he got to his feet.

'See, even Hugh will tell you my aunt is a most formidable woman.' Daniel smiled at Beatrice, but she was now immune to his charms, inoculated by his casual arrogance.

'You boys are very rude,' said Agatha. 'Why don't you offer Miss Nash a drink, Daniel? Do come and sit by me, Miss Nash.'

'Nothing for me, thank you,' said Beatrice, who would have loved a small glass of port but knew better than to ask. It had taken several weeks for Lady Marbely to stop commenting on how unusual it was for a lady to be so knowledgeable about port and how sad it was that she had

had no mother to counteract her father's more unusual ideas about what was suitable.

'Did you have enough to eat?' asked Agatha. 'I can ring for some fruit.'

'No thank you, the supper was lovely, and my room is very comfortable. It is so nice of you to have me.'

'Well, I think it's important that we get to know each other, preferably before the rest of the town. We have important work to do, Miss Nash, and it is vital that you and I understand each other completely.'

'I think that's our signal to leave,' said Daniel. 'Hugh and I will go and have that game of billiards now.'

'Hugh must talk to you about the tutoring,' said Agatha, as the young men left the room.

'Tutoring?'

'Some local boys, protégés of mine. I told him you were looking for some private tutoring over the summer, and he was very pleased to pass them on to you. Nothing too taxing is involved – just a little help in the more advanced Latin.'

'I should be honoured,' said Beatrice. 'I tutored the three daughters of a professor at our California university, and it was fascinating to watch how Latin blossomed among such a small and eager group.'

'I'm not sure the boys are such blossoms,' said Agatha, giving her a doubtful look. 'Hugh agrees they are bright boys, and one in particular may prove our efforts worthwhile, but they are somewhat rowdy and defiant.'

'Sometimes the hardest challenges are most deserving of our efforts,' said Beatrice. 'I am very grateful to you and the school for giving me the opportunity.'

'Yes, well, we must make sure the school governors have no grounds to cause you trouble.' She hesitated, and Beatrice watched her struggle to go on.

'They did not want to employ me,' said Beatrice. She did not ask it as a question.

'Well, not exactly,' said Agatha. 'But they will come round as long as you succeed.' She paused. 'I am one of only two women on the Board of Governors, you know. I am in a very delicate position, in which I must temper my impatience for reform and choose my battles with care. We have women teachers, of course, to teach appropriate subjects. But in this case, we had some difficulty in finding a suitable replacement for the head Latin master, who left us so abruptly, and your qualifications so exceeded the usual applicants' that I— Well, I did all within my power to push your consideration.'

'Thank you.'

'Of course, you are not quite what I expected,' she added. She did not elaborate, and Beatrice, under the pressure of the silence, tried to breathe in a slow way that might suppress any flush in her cheeks.

'I assure you my university and teaching certificates are quite in order,' she said finally.

'Your qualifications, and Lady Marbely's description of your wide travels and experience, suggested someone older,' said Agatha.

'I put away the fripperies of girlhood some years ago,' said Beatrice. 'I have served as my father's secretary and constant companion for many years. But more to the point, I do not have the luxury of waiting around to mature like a cheese.' She smiled to soften the rebuke. 'I do not intend to marry, Mrs Kent, and now that my father is gone I must earn my bread. Surely you would not deny me the work for which I have studied and trained?'

'I would not,' said Agatha. 'But let's not mention any such awkward necessity. I think we should rely on your connection to the Marbelys, and to the suggestion of teaching as service rather than profession, to carry the day.'

'As you wish,' said Beatrice, trying to keep the dryness out of her tone as she wondered how to ask about her wages and accommodation if she was not allowed to appear in need of either.

'Of course, I was older than you when I married my husband,' said Agatha. She did not phrase it as a question, and so Beatrice, who was tired of people feeling free to interrogate her on her determination to live free of a husband, bit her lip and did not answer. Agatha gave a sigh and continued. 'The world is changing, Miss Nash, but very slowly. I hope that through the work I do, and the work you will do, we may further the causes of intelligence and merit and move our nation forward.'

'Mrs Kent, am I to suppose that you support the cause of women?' said Beatrice.

'Good heavens, no!' said Agatha. 'Such hysteria in the streets is impossibly damaging. It is only through such sober activities as school boards and good works, done under the guidance of our most respected and educated gentlemen, that we will prove our worth in the eyes of God and our fellow man. Don't you agree, Miss Nash?'

Beatrice was not at all sure she did agree. She rather thought she might like to vote and to have been admitted to a university degree at Oxford, her father's alma mater. Even the most educated of gentlemen seemed disinclined to remedy such injustices to women without being confronted. She was not sure that Agatha Kent was in earnest, either. The face, under an arched eyebrow, was inscrutable.

'I only know that I want to teach something other than elementary school,' she said. 'I want to teach and study and write, as my father did, and to have my efforts treated no less seriously just because I am a woman.'

Agatha sighed. 'You are an educated person and can be of use to the country, but women like us need to demonstrate our worth, rather than demonstrating in the streets. Besides,' she added, 'we don't need all the housemaids declaring their independence and running off to join the music hall, do we?'

'Who would boil the tea?' said Beatrice, before she could stop herself.

'You must know, Miss Nash, that you and I will be under severe scrutiny these next few months. I must be blunt in saying that I expect you not only to demonstrate your own superior merit and irreproachable respectability but to protect my reputation too. I have spent many years, in a quiet way, establishing a position from where I can do important work in this town, but I am not without enemies.'

'I see,' said Beatrice.

'I don't think you do,' said Agatha. 'I have never pushed for something as outrageous as hiring a woman to teach Latin, and I am personally responsible for you. Should you and I fail in this task, many other projects may come undone.' Beatrice saw a moment of weariness in the kind face. 'I have put all my eggs in your basket, Miss Nash. Do I make myself clear?'

Beatrice was curious to feel a tiny sense of purpose flowering. It was different from the purpose – the stubborn fury – with which she had pursued her escape from the Marbelys. She had not been needed by anyone for many months. Now Agatha Kent appeared to need her, and Beatrice felt an echo of the same feeling of determination that her father's plans always inspired.

'I will not let you down, Mrs Kent,' she said.

'See that you don't,' said Agatha with a warm smile. She rose to her feet and held out both hands. It was gracefully done, but Beatrice recognised that she was being dismissed.

'Goodnight, Mrs Kent.'

'And just one more thing, Miss Nash,' said Agatha, as Beatrice moved towards the hall. 'I would not be public about any yearnings to write. It would be an absolute disaster for a lady in your position to earn a reputation as a bohemian.'

In the billiard room, Daniel busied himself over the selection of a cue as if he had not been familiar with Uncle John's four old cues since both he and Hugh were in short trousers.

'I do wish Aunt Aggie would stop taking on projects,' he said, sighting along the length of the ebony and rosewood one picked up by Uncle John in Morocco. He began to chalk its India-rubber tip, and Hugh, as usual, was left to turn up the lamps and rack the balls.

'I think her interest in education might be considered a cause,' said Hugh, enjoying the smooth, dull click of red ball against yellow as he arranged them in a triangle.

'The school governors, yes,' said Daniel. 'But then it was the urchins she foisted on you.'

'Alarmed about the rise of the working man, are you?' said Hugh.

'Not at all,' said Daniel. 'It's absurd to think any of them will even make it to factory clerk. It's just that she risks making herself look foolish.'

'And those around her . . .'

'I'm only thinking of Uncle John,' said Daniel. 'And now, championing a woman to be Latin master at the grammar school? It's just outlandish.'

'I believe the other candidates were quite lacking in skill,' said Hugh.

'I imagine one only needs the rudimentaries,' said Daniel. 'The profession is mostly about having a good strong arm to wield the cane.'

'I think Miss Nash believes it will be a pleasure to share Caesar and Virgil with the young,' said Hugh.

Daniel gave a loud snort, and his face, dropping its unpleasant curl of the lip, broke into a grin. Hugh sighed with relief. It usually took Daniel some time to relax into life in Rye. As a young boy he had always seemed to arrive with a scowl, shoulders hunched under some imagined weight, eyes as wary as those of a kicked dog. Hugh, older by two years, would pretend not to notice and busy himself with a book or with helping the gardener pick lettuce for the kitchen, impatient for his younger cousin to shed his outside shell and get back to leading them in crimes and adventures around the woods and town.

It was Daniel who planned the midnight orchard raids, the fishing expeditions, the hikes to the seashore. It was Daniel who could charm the cook into stuffing his satchel with pork pies and hard-boiled eggs, or persuade the milkman to let them ride on his cart into town. Hugh would have liked to be as fearless as Daniel, as filled with ideas and plans, but he was sharply aware that he was endowed with responsibility and a conscience that understood all the potential pitfalls of Daniel's wilder plans. At least that was what Aunt Agatha told him when Daniel got them lost overnight in Higgins Wood; when Daniel broke his arm falling off a tightrope they had strung up to practise for a circus career; when they brought home a sick, three-legged piglet and tried to keep it in an orange crate in the nursery and it deposited dung all over the rug – and frightened Cook with its squealing, rolling escape down the back stairs.

'You are the responsible one.'

'You are the oldest.'

'Daniel doesn't have a mother to tell him these things.' This last admonition seemed slightly unfair to Hugh. It was hardly his fault that he had a mother still living. They both had fathers, though Hugh's father was admittedly a much jollier man than Daniel's. Besides, he was sure plenty of other people, from Aunt Agatha to the Sunday School teacher who clicked his ceramic teeth when he shouted at unruly boys, were available to communicate basic morals to his cousin.

While it seemed unfair to Hugh that he should always be spoken to as if he had been the one to suggest spying on

the Gypsies down on the marsh, or borrowing the neighbour's donkey to re-create an expedition to Bethlehem, he
kept his tongue. Even at a young age, Hugh understood
that, for reasons that were not explained to him, allowances were made for Daniel's wildness as well as his
scowling arrivals.

Hugh had heard his aunt and uncle discuss quietly, on
several occasions, Daniel's austere boarding school, Aunt
Agatha wanting to speak to Daniel's father and Uncle John
urging her not to interfere. Hugh had never thought the
school to be the problem, since Daniel seemed to arrive
equally morose whenever he came from a visit to his
father's London house. As they grew up, Daniel gradually
replaced his brooding with a distant air of cynical composure. He became more popular at school, and Hugh had
the distinct impression that his cousin had studied the art
of society much harder than mathematics or Greek. At
Oxford he seemed to have become quite sought-after by
multiple sets, and Hugh had seen less of him in London or
Sussex as Daniel accepted invitations to visit country
houses, to accompany families to foreign capitals, or to go
tramping in the Dolomites or some such rustic area.

'Speaking of Virgil, how was Florence?' asked Hugh.

'For the most part, filled with a crush of English and
American matrons all doing their best to squash centuries
of history and art into the usual routines of some provincial summer watering hole,' said Daniel. 'No more than an
hour and a half in the Uffizi because of course there is a
luncheon at noon, and then it is too warm in the early
afternoon to visit churches, and tea is at four. And they are
all campaigning to show off their gaggle of daughters and

so the evenings are all dinners and parties.' He took aim at the phalanx of balls and sent them scattering smartly across the billiard table's green surface. 'They worked very hard to make Italy no more exotic than the middle of Surrey.'

'How did you stand it?' asked Hugh.

'I developed a recurring summer cold,' said Daniel, 'so that several whole days were supposedly passed in my room. Soon as the coast was clear, my friend Craigmore and I would sneak off and spend the day in the city by ourselves.'

'Craigmore shares your affinity for poetry?' asked Hugh.

'Oh, God no,' said Daniel. 'He is a rather brutish artist and an athlete of the worst kind. But he is a great walker, and we tramped the whole city and up into the hills. I was in charge of taking in the beauty and the art, and telling him what to record in his travel journal, and he taught me how to kill the opposition at tennis.'

'You don't usually have much patience with philistines,' said Hugh, gripped by a small jealousy that his cousin had so easily traded their summer companionship for another. 'But then I believe he has a title?' he added.

'Ouch!' said Daniel. 'You don't usually go in for such blows of sarcasm.'

'Sorry,' said Hugh.

'But you can always be counted upon to apologise.' Daniel jabbed his cue and sank a red ball firmly into a corner pocket. Hugh felt his face flush at the suggestion that his good manners were a kind of weakness. At least they were sincere. He had heard Daniel make many pretty apologies that were all charm and no substance.

'I'm sorry, Hugh, that was unpardonably spiteful.' Hugh searched his cousin's face for irony but found none this time. 'He is Viscount Craigmore, Lord North's son,' continued Daniel. 'In some romantic fit his mother named him Lancelot, so he always goes by Craigmore, even to his closest friends.'

'I quite see his point,' said Hugh.

'He and I intend to go to Paris this autumn to write and paint. We're talking about starting up a journal that might combine poetry and illustration.'

'How on earth would you get your father to support such a jaunt?' said Hugh. 'I thought you kept your poetry pretty well hidden from him.'

'I keep many things hidden from him,' said Daniel. 'In this case I'll tell him that Craigmore's father has invited me to stay with them in Paris. Father won't mind me playing the gentleman – especially if I mention that Craigmore has a highly marriageable younger sister.'

'Daniel, don't tell me you're in love?' said Hugh. Hope flickered, for if Daniel was in love, he might broach the subject of his own romantic hopes without fear of being mercilessly teased.

'Good heavens, no,' said Daniel. 'She's a poor, pale squab of a thing and she smells like tapioca – but Craigmore feels his father can be persuaded that a few months in Paris, with extra funds for the maintenance of a suitable mistress, is just the gilding a British gentleman needs before settling down to his responsibilities.'

'So poetry will be the mistress?' asked Hugh, as he missed a corner shot and stubbed his cue into the baize. 'Would she not be better served by your telling the truth?'

'Good God, no,' said Daniel. 'Lord North doesn't like me much. I think he's suspicious of people who read.'

'Well, Craigmore's father may deserve to be fooled, but good luck fooling Aunt Agatha,' said Hugh. 'She has expectations that you will now follow Uncle John into the civil service this year.'

'I just have to convince her that I will have regrets for the rest of my life if I fail to grasp this opportunity now,' said Daniel.

'Surely one can write poetry and pursue a responsible career,' said Hugh.

'Perhaps surgery can be a Sunday hobby, but I assure you poetry is life and death for me, Hugh,' said Daniel. 'I simply must write, just as you must apparently peer into people's bleeding bodies on the operating table and pickle chicken heads in Aunt Agatha's largest jam jars.'

'No need to mention the jars. I put them back in the pantry before Cook notices.'

'No need to mention Paris,' said Daniel. 'The new schoolteacher should distract Aunt Agatha. We should take up the poor girl, Hugh, and make sure Aunt Agatha continues to shelter her under her matronly wing.'

'I'm not sure that's a good idea,' said Hugh. 'Miss Nash is no tapioca pudding.'

'She did have the unfortunate air of a bluestocking,' said Daniel. 'You'll have to engage her in scholarly debate, Hugh. But if all else fails, I can always write her a sonnet.'

'A sonnet?' said Hugh.

'No woman can resist having her name rhymed with a flower in iambic pentameter,' said Daniel.

CHAPTER THREE

THE SUN HAD NOT yet evaporated the dew from the lawn, and the scents of honeysuckle and wallflowers rose on the salty breeze. Early morning was Agatha's favourite time, recalling the simple joys of childhood and beckoning one outside, she thought, to walk barefoot on the wet grass. In pursuit of this goal, she finished tying the bows at the neck and waist of her plain cotton wrapper, stuck her feet into a pair of shabby, low-heeled slippers and headed for the back stairs.

Only in the early mornings did Agatha use these stairs, and never did she feel more at home in her own house than when she popped her head into the kitchen to ask Cook for a cup of tea from the big brown pot kept fresh all day for the staff. For a brief moment, in the black-and-white-tiled kitchen, with its high, sunny windows and gleaming new gas range, they did not have to be mistress and cook, ruling separate domains on either side of a green baize door, but could come together as two women, up before anyone else in the family, in need of the day's first cup.

Today there were two bowls of raspberries on the kitchen table, and Cook was busy straining cream from the top of the milk jug.

'I hope it was all right to have them?' said Cook. 'Only milkman had them on the cart and I know how partial Master Daniel is to a few raspberries – and ours still green on the canes.'

'I fear you will never stop spoiling those boys,' said Agatha. 'And how is that granddaughter of yours?'

'Better for the sunshine and fresh air,' said Cook. 'She gets about so fast now.' The small girl wore braces to correct legs twisted and weakened by rickets, a scourge among the poorer classes. Agatha sent frequent baskets of beef tea and butter home with Cook, but the child, now five, remained stubbornly frail and sickly, and caused Cook such distress that Agatha had to choose carefully which days to ask after her.

'I'm glad to hear it,' she said, and sent a silent prayer of thanks for the health of her own tall, strong nephews.

Cup of tea in hand, Agatha passed through a wooden arch in the thick yew hedge, closing the tall, close-boarded gate behind her and rattling the latch loudly just in case the gardener was about early. All the servants had been discreetly made to understand that this quiet corner of the garden was off-limits when the gate was shut. Still, Agatha preferred to announce her occupation rather than be shy about it.

She took a moment to enjoy her own ingenuity in creating this small green box of a room with its chin-high yew hedge overlooking the sea and its taller yew walls on the three landward sides. The plain, well-manicured lawn looked almost smooth enough for croquet, and the single heavy oak bench in the middle gave her much satisfaction in its charming French-blue paint. She set down her tea mug, uncloaked herself from her wrapper, and kicked off her slippers. She was revealed to the sunny morning in a chemise and a pair of short bloomers over wool stockings from which she had cut off the feet. Wriggling her toes in the damp grass, she took two long, deep breaths, stretched both arms above her head, and began to make energetic circles with her upper body and head.

Whenever she exercised here in the garden, Agatha was transported back to the camellia-scented air of Baden-Baden, where she and John, on a short holiday, had gone to hear a lecture on the benefits of strenuous daily exercise. They had gone out of a desire to see the green and white copper and glass magnificence of the assembly rooms by the lake, and to take in the splendour of the summer crowds in their stiff white finery. The Germans seemed to go in for a lot of coloured sashes encrusted with medals, or brooches that resembled medals, so that a summer evening took on the aspect of a military parade rather than a promenade in a provincial lake town. The lecturer, a slight, wiry Scandinavian man, had not seemed up to the task of commanding the large, empty stage, and while he extolled the virtue of muscle development and the healthful qualities of the cold bath, the hall grew restless. But a sudden stripping off of his trousers had a galvanising effect. Clad only in a loincloth, the man proceeded to stand on his head, to fold himself up and over a bar six feet from the ground, to have a man in the audience bounce up and down on his stomach, and to perform the splits. John was of the immediate opinion that neither of these last capabilities would be an asset to any man of gentlemanly rank and would only detract from sales of the poor man's book, but despite the titters of shock from the excited crowd, and some outrage in the local newspapers, the Scandinavian and his exercise regimen became quite the fashion that summer. Both Agatha and John read the little book to be able to keep up with dinner-party conversation, but John had been won over by the common-sense ideas – sleeping with the windows open, daily sponge baths – and six years on, he had developed an admirably slimmed physique. He chose to be modest about it and was a source of frustration to his tailor, from whom he insisted on ordering clothing in his old measurements.

Agatha had regretfully resigned herself to the fact that she did not have her husband's willpower. Her inconsistent use of the programme, combined with her love of cakes, cream and good, thick gravy, had destined her to retain a plump midsection that refused to succumb to exercise or to corseting. A roll of flesh got in her way now as she lay on the grass, feet tucked under the bench's crossbars and attempted to haul herself up to a sitting position twelve times. However, she enjoyed the routine here in her private garden, on a dry, sunny day, and she looked forward to the end of the set, when she allowed herself the prescribed dose of the sun's healthy rays.

Beatrice awoke to sunlight appearing to dance on blue wallpaper and the sound of birds squabbling for their breakfast in unseen trees. Her window was open, and the breeze brought the scent of a hot morning into the slight coolness of the room. For a moment she could not place where she was, and with a brief skip of her heart wondered if she were not still in Italy, in the village above Florence, and her father already at the *pensione* breakfast table on the terrace below, reading two-day-old newspapers and calling for more hot milk. She squeezed down into the pillow and tried to remain in the semi-waking moment that felt so happy.

When she finally opened her eyes, the unfamiliar room swam into focus along with a slow awareness that she had made good her escape from her aunt's family. She was in Sussex, and her room smelled of the garden outside and, faintly, of the sea. At least the grief, which weighted her limbs to her bed most mornings, could not win today against the anticipation of a new beginning. For the first time in months, she almost sprang from her bed to greet the summer day.

Scrubbed and tidy, in a grey cotton dress with a tucked bodice and a wide belt fastened with bone buttons, Beatrice left her travelling bag closed and ready by the bedroom door and descended in search of breakfast. The polished hall was quiet and empty, as were the drawing room and a dining room across the way. Some faint sounds came from behind the stairs, but Beatrice hesitated to penetrate further into the house before being invited. The drawing room's French windows stood open to the breeze, and so, anxious not to be seen hovering, she slipped out onto the terrace beyond.

The stone terrace already looked older than the house, softened to a pleasant mossy grey under the relentless dripping of English rain, its stone balusters pressed by fat shrubs and draped in twisting vines of honeysuckle, wisteria and the teacup-sized pale green flowers of a clematis. White roses climbed up the house from beds filled with brilliant blue agapanthus. Beatrice stooped to cup in her hands a waxy blue flower head as large as a hat and to wonder if plants ever sensed how far they were from home: this African lily carried on ships to England in the time of Henry VIII, rhododendrons dug from the rippled flanks of Chinese mountains, the passionflower twining about itself in air so much drier than the South American rainforest. Beyond the terrace, a croquet lawn fell away on its farthest edge to a lower terrace of rolling grass, hedged above the steep escarpment of the ridge. Below, the stacked red roofs of Rye poked up from its flat skirt of marshes, and beyond, the sea formed a broad, glittering swathe under the wide blue bowl of the sky. On the left, the terrace ended in a thick wall of pine trees that separated the house from its nearest neighbour, but to the right it extended further, beckoning Beatrice along the flank of flower and kitchen gardens to a door in a hedge and old woodland beyond.

Agatha Kent was dozing on the folds of a white cotton robe, on an intensely blue bench, perched on a smooth green lawn – entirely naked. If Beatrice had processed her pinkness as flesh a moment earlier, if she had only registered the rolling expanse of skin instead of the blue paint of the bench, she might have withdrawn before Mrs Kent's eyes snapped open. Instead she froze. She was aware of Mrs Kent, a plump woman, flailing like a landed fish as she tried to collect her limbs, and then the edges of her robe, and attempt an awkward draping of her ample form. Beatrice felt her face flush hot as she cast her eyes around for some other place to focus. The lawn turned blurry under her stare.

'I am so sorry,' she managed. 'So very sorry.' The vast pink landscape still danced before her eyes.

'You weren't to know . . .' said Agatha, puffing out her cheeks as she sought to breathe and tie ribbons at the same time. 'Everyone knows not to disturb me.'

'So sorry,' repeated Beatrice, wondering if she should pick up her bag and head for the station now. 'I didn't mean to spy.'

'I always meant to put a lock on that gate,' said Agatha. 'Only it looks so funny in a garden and—'

'I'm always up too early,' said Beatrice. 'I don't sleep very deeply.'

'I was bathing in the sun,' said Agatha, her breath slowing and her voice assuming a more authoritative air. 'It is prescribed as a vital part of my exercise programme.'

'Of course.'

'You should try it yourself,' said Agatha. 'No girl your age should look quite as drawn about the face.'

'I'm not a girl,' said Beatrice. 'And I wouldn't look so pale if it didn't rain here all the time.'

'All the more reason we have to drink in the sun when we can,' said Agatha. 'Why don't you come and give it a try right now?'

'I shouldn't intrude.'

'Oh, don't worry, we're not going to cavort like wood nymphs. Just come and sit by me. I'll turn this way and we can both get a little sun, if not the whole bath.' With this she moved to the far end of the bench and shrugged her gown down from her shoulders, using a hand to keep it drawn above her large bosom. Beatrice moved swiftly to the near end of the bench and sat down. She unbuttoned the collar of her dress and turned its stiff edges down. She rolled up her cuffs to the elbow.

'You're going to have to shrug that dress right down to get any benefit,' said Agatha, turning her chin up into the sun and closing her eyes. Beatrice undid more buttons and pulled the dress from her shoulders. The breeze breathed across her collarbones and ruffled the edges of her light chemise. The sun felt like a warm hand on her shoulder. It began to heat the smooth rise of her chest and the fragile skin inside her elbows. She felt her nervous breath slow and relax. As she tipped up her face to the sun, she felt the strangest urge to take off her shoes and walk barefoot on the grass.

Hugh was pretending to enjoy a quiet breakfast with one of last week's London newspapers spread carelessly in front of him, but he was listening for noises in the hall which might mean the ladies coming to breakfast. He was aware of a pleasant sense of anticipation at the chance to see the young schoolteacher again this morning and had already run a few opening conversational gambits through his head. A desire for new conversation and companions his own age sparked his eager mood.

A rustling in the hall and a murmur of voices caused him to wipe his hands on his napkin and tweak his collar straight. He did not have time to fold the newspaper before the door was opened by the maid.

'Thank you, Jenny,' said Beatrice, coming into the room.

'I'll just bring some fresh tea for the pot and some hot toast,' said Jenny, whisking the large silver teapot from the sideboard. Hugh could not remember her ever offering to bring him a fresh pot of tea.

'Good morning,' he said. 'I do hope you don't mind an informal breakfast? You are welcome to ask Jenny to bring you something else.' He was pleased at his own cheerful manner and wondered if his newly discovered affection for Lucy Ramsey was already making him easier in the company of all women.

'I am very happy,' said Beatrice, looking at the fruit platter and lifting the lids of the chafing dishes to inspect scrambled eggs, sausages and bacon, warm raisin cakes and kedgeree. The kedgeree was on its second visit from the kitchen, and Hugh wondered if he should mention that it had become more pungent since yesterday, a fact not disguised by Cook's addition of generous amounts of chopped parsley. He decided it was not his place to notice.

'Only we all like to keep our own schedules in the summer,' he added, aware that domestic arrangements did not qualify as scintillating conversation. 'I'm afraid I haven't seen any sign of my aunt yet.'

Beatrice spooned a small mound of raspberries into a dish and added a large dollop of fresh cream from its pitcher. She placed a sausage on a second small plate and brought both to the table.

'Your aunt has already given me a tour of the garden this morning,' she said. 'After breakfast, we are to walk around the town, and then she has kindly offered to introduce me to my new landlady.'

'I should warn you that my aunt knows everybody,' said Hugh. 'She is not in the least stuffy about stopping in the street to talk to them, and so any walk with my aunt is more a series of energetic starts with much lingering about, trying not to shuffle one's feet too much.'

'Oh dear,' said Beatrice. 'I shall have to summon my best attempt at patience.'

'And with waiting to hear if my uncle is coming from London, I'm sure she won't get away from the house until late,' added Hugh.

'What am I to do?' asked Beatrice. She spoke in a light-hearted tone, but Hugh noticed that she stabbed her sausage quite emphatically with her fork. 'The plan was your aunt's, and yet my willing acceptance of her direction has made me a dreadful inconvenience.'

'Oh, not at all,' said Hugh. 'I was only thinking you must be impatient to see the town and . . .' He trailed off as his own vague plan became clearer in his mind and the enormity of suggesting it crushed his recent sense of ease.

'Perhaps she can spare a maid or someone to show me the way,' said Beatrice. 'Though the town seems small enough for me to do very well by myself.'

'My aunt wouldn't like that,' said Hugh. He took a deep breath and plunged in. 'I don't believe I have any definite plans this morning, or at least I could try to change them.'

'Indefinite plans are the worst to rearrange,' she said, smiling over her teacup.

'What I mean is that perhaps you would permit me to escort you on a small tour of the town and then deliver you to your lodgings to meet my aunt at some appropriate hour?' With the offer made in such a stumbling manner, he could only wait and try not to blush.

'I would be delighted,' said Beatrice. 'It's such a lovely day and I would enjoy a real walk. Can I rely on you to set a fast pace, Mr Grange?'

'Oh, do call me Hugh,' he said, his sense of ease return-ing. 'You are a walker then, Miss Nash?'

'My father and I enjoyed nothing better than a tramping holiday,' she said. She did not invite him to call her by her first name. 'Have you walked in the Alps, Mr Grange?'

'I have had that pleasure,' said Hugh. 'There is nothing finer than the snow-capped mountains and dinner in some rustic Swiss farmhouse.'

'Of course, the scenery is possibly more powerful in the American West,' said Beatrice. 'But I agree that nothing beats a stein of homemade dark beer at the end of a day climbing through the passes.'

'Well, quite,' said Hugh, hoping she was not planning on donning a knapsack and hobnailed boots for the walk into town. 'So I can assume you are not afraid of a few briars and that we can go down via the fields instead of the road?'

'Lovely,' she said. 'A little fresh air and no quarter on the pace, please, Mr Grange.'

After breakfast, Beatrice followed Hugh on a brisk descent down a muddy country path to town and then a climb up cobbled streets as steep as any in a Swiss village. At the high street, Beatrice paused, trying not to breathe too heavily as she leaned against a convenient post for a moment's respite. She had matched Hugh's every stride, but as she was to meet Agatha Kent at her new landlady's home, she had been forced to wear her heeled town boots and had pulled her corset tighter than suitable for such exertion. Her face flamed, and despite her light cotton dress, she was conscious of a trickle of sweat down her spine.

'I say, are you all right?' said Hugh. 'You look a bit winded.'

'I'm perfectly fine, thank you.'

'It may not have been quite gentlemanly to take you absolutely at your word on the pace?'

'It is only my attire that can't quite keep up with you,' she said. She reached into a pocket for one of her father's large, plain handkerchiefs and fanned her face as she looked about her. 'Just a moment to take in an impression, perhaps?'

The high street seemed to be a pleasingly crooked collection of Tudor and Georgian shopfronts with bright awnings. Plenty of customers, many overdressed for the day in the cautionary way of rural burghers everywhere, were puffing and fanning themselves in and out of doors. A cart went by, sprinkling cool water onto the hot cobbled street. A large car nosed impatiently along behind it, coughing out the sharp odour of mechanical fumes to mingle with the humid scents of horses, flowering baskets and meat pies cooling in an open shop window.

When Beatrice had recovered, they continued up into the narrower lanes around the churchyard, passing old Elizabethan black-timbered houses with tiny leaded windows, bowed rooflines and bricks mellowed under centuries of gentle English rain, then emerged onto the wide, green lawn of an ancient stone tower, rising far above the flat plain below.

'It's like a painting,' said Beatrice as they took in the tumble of roofs down the steep hill and the full sweep of the marshes, leading to the distant, shimmering English Channel. 'It feels as if the sea should be right below us.' A breeze offered to dry their damp foreheads, and she took off her straw hat to pat back her hair.

'It was, in earlier centuries,' said Hugh. 'Now we are marooned in the marshes, and the boats have a devil of a time getting stuck in the mud.' To their left, a single huge sail seemed to be floating in a field of sheep, its boat invisible behind the grassy dyke. 'That's the Royal Military Canal, built to keep out Napoleon,' he added.

'Hard to picture such a narrow waterway keeping out an invasion,' said Beatrice. 'How far does it go?'

'Runs twenty-eight miles from Hastings to Folkestone,' he said, pleased that she did not seem to mind what Lucy Ramsey had gently derided as his masculine need to burden all pleasant views with boring facts. 'Keeping out the French has been a national pastime for centuries,' he added. 'That castle in the distance was Henry VIII's contribution.'

'Whatever shall we do now that we're so "Entente Cordiale" with Paris?'

'We'll use them as a huge buffer against any unpleasantness in the rest of Europe,' said Hugh. 'And we'll hire French chefs for our dinner parties.'

'Sounds wonderful,' said Beatrice. 'Though I don't think there will be a French chef in my immediate future.'

'No, in my experience landladies tend to prefer mutton chops and gooseberry sponge,' said Hugh.

'You have one?' she asked.

'Yes, a Mrs Rogers. A good woman, but her way of ensuring I and the other three medical students never go hungry is to wrap as many foods as possible in suet pudding or a cold-water crust. Only diligent exercise keeps me from corpulence.'

'You are going to be a doctor?'

'A surgeon, to the dismay of my parents,' he said. 'I've just finished a year of surgical fellowship under Sir Alex Ramsey, and he seemed to like my research, because he has asked me to stay on.' A note of pride crept into his tone, for it was not a small accomplishment to have drawn the notice of London's most respected surgeon.

'Your family disapproves?' she asked. Hugh noted that she gave a wry glance, as if from experience of such disapproval.

'My father has enjoyed a long and distinguished career in banking,' said Hugh. 'I think my parents saw me embellishing the family honour by doing something more gentlemanly and less bloody than medicine.'

'What did they have in mind?' said Beatrice. 'Marrying a rich widow?'

'Rich widows are in short supply, even the ugly ones,' said Hugh.

'Whatever will you do?' asked Beatrice.

'My surgeon does have a knighthood, and a practice at the more fashionable end of Harley Street, so my parents have become more amenable to my career in recent months,' said Hugh. 'But they would prefer to see me a gentleman of leisure.'

'You are a man of action?' she asked.

'We're building flying machines and talking to each other across copper telephone wires, and medicine is moving so fast, the books have to be revised every couple of years.' He stopped, and grinned as if he had once again spoken more than he should. 'I can't imagine just sitting by, playing golf, visiting my club and doing the social rounds.'

'I think that's splendid,' said Beatrice. 'What are you researching?'

'Well, I've been investigating the impact of shock on patients after surgery,' said Hugh. 'It's quite interesting how many patients come through brain surgery without a problem and then just die in the wards.' Fearing the topic too gruesome, he changed the subject to add, 'But of course I'm taking the summer off. My surgeon and his daughter have gone to the Italian Lakes.'

'The advances of a new century must wait while we indulge in cures and sea bathing,' said Beatrice. 'And is the eminent surgeon's daughter impressed by your hard work?'

'Lucy?' he said, and then wished he had referred to her as Miss Ramsey. He feared he might blush as he stammered. 'She's young and much too sensitive to stomach the details of our work. Her father and I do our best to protect her.'

'I never aspired to delicacy,' said Beatrice. 'I preferred to be at my father's side.'

'Well, Lucy is a great help with her father's correspondence, and she is a wonderful hostess,' said Hugh. 'I go to tea several times a week.'

'You must be quite lonely while she is away,' said Beatrice. She was smiling, and he knew she was teasing him.

'I'm keeping busy this summer.' He was flustered by her friendly challenges. Lucy often teased him, but she always maintained a charming deference, and he indulged her from all the advantage of superior age and knowledge. 'I go around with old Dr Lawton some afternoons,' he added. 'There is a whole array of interesting cases among the poorer cottages.'

'I expect the country doctor is suitably impressed?' asked Beatrice.

'Not at all,' admitted Hugh. 'He has known me since infancy and thinks me quite as much a fool as when I was scraping my knees in the orchards with my cousin. But he has forgotten more medicine than I can imagine learning, and I find it humbling to try to be of use to him.'

'If one cannot transform one's age, it is perhaps enough to be useful,' said Beatrice. She sighed, exchanging her teasing tone for sincerity. 'I hope I may aspire to some usefulness.'

'I hope you will be able to be happy as well as merely useful,' said Hugh. 'This town has always been a very tranquil refuge for me, but you may find it quiet after your life of travel.'

'I would settle for being a hermit,' she said. He noticed that her eyes lost some of their light. 'After the past year, I crave only to be allowed my work, and my rest, away from the stupidities of society. I shall be like Charlotte Brontë's Lucy Snowe, content to tend her little school for the children of the merchant classes.'

'Well, I'm afraid there are a number of charitable committees and ladies' groups in the town,' said Hugh. 'I doubt they will leave you alone for long. My aunt has threatened to keep a cricket bat in the front hall to see them off.'

'Thank you for the warning,' said Beatrice, smiling. 'I shall give my landlady instructions that I am never at home.'

Beatrice was sorry that she had left Hugh Grange at the high street, and that upon her arrival at Mrs Turber's double-fronted cottage she had casually declined to wait for Agatha Kent before entering via the larger of the two front doors. She was used to the inspection and approval of lodgings and had many times, and sometimes in other languages, firmly negotiated terms and arrangements on behalf of her father. But whereas the very particular requirements of a well-regarded man of letters had always been treated with respect, if not instant agreement, by landlords of several countries, the simple requests of a tidy spinster did not meet with similar patience or courtesy. Mrs Turber's fleshy, well-fed face had expressed surprise, a not inconsiderable suspicion and eventually an undertone of fury as Beatrice questioned her as to cleaning methods, mealtimes and menus, the delivery of coal and hot water, and the proper airing of bed linen. It was sobering to acknowledge that she probably should not have commented on the smeared window glass. Mrs Turber had become so red in the face that Beatrice had asked if she were quite well and volunteered to look upstairs by herself while Mrs Turber went for a sit-down in her own quarters.

In the tiny bedroom, she rested her head against the cold, rough plaster of the wall and gave herself to the slack-jawed silence of a weary grief. She was conscious of a wish to shout at her father, who had abandoned her so absolutely. He would have found this funny – looking around the squalid cottage with his eyebrow raised as he gently pointed out that death had not been his first choice; that he had, in fact, been called away before finishing several important pieces of work. She imagined he would have a few words to say about her impetuous flight to Sussex and the entirely unnecessary choice to submerge herself in the grim world of salaried work. With her eyes shut, she felt a corner of her lip twitch at her own foolishness. The daughter of Joseph Nash, she reminded herself, did not succumb to self-pity. Her tiredness eased, and she opened one eye halfway and gave the cottage's bedroom a squinty look.

It had a bowed aspect, as if it were a cabin on an old galleon. The walls seemed to lean on each other above the sagging floor, and the ceiling had a slight convexity, like the underside of a large white dinner plate. The window, while smeared, had pleasant old speckled glass in leaded glazing bars and a deep ledge. The furniture was appalling. The bed's posts were spindly and pocked with wormholes. The dresser had lost half a sheet of veneer and two of its blackened brass handles. The rush bottom of the single chair mirrored the sag of the floor. Beatrice stirred herself upright and lifted a corner of the rag rug with the tip of her shoe. It was greasy with dust and smelled of what might have been men's hair tonic. It reminded her that other people had undressed in this room, sweated onto the hard mattress, and used the china chamber pot that sat in a wooden box under the bed. Beatrice felt a twinge of regret for the white-tiled magnificence of the water closet at Agatha Kent's house.

She stood up and gave a small bounce on the floor. At least it did not give. She walked to the window and looked at the deep ledge on the outside, which might hold a pot or two of fragrant mignonettes. The view was of the cobbled street and the front doors of the houses opposite. A pleasant Georgian door with white pilasters next to a low oak-studded Tudor one, black with age against freshly painted white daub walls. A window box of white lilies and a potted bay tree for the Georgian house, and a lead trough of scarlet geraniums for the Tudor, gave the street a gay, holiday aspect. The sun's reflections off red-brick walls and clay-tiled roofs warmed the shadowed street and cast a glow into the room. Outside the bedroom, a small nook on the landing held a window overlooking the rear courtyard. She thought it might be perfect for her writing desk, but she would have to do some work to improve the view, which was of the outdoor water closet shared by both halves of the conjoined cottages, and Mrs Turber's dingy sheets flapping on a line.

She could hear voices from downstairs, and as she descended the squeaky staircase with its sticky banister, she could tell that it was Agatha, speaking in a low, urgent tone to Mrs Turber, whose voice was a suffocated squeak of indignation. Their conversation carried into the small room through a connecting door from Mrs Turber's larger quarters next door.

'All I'm saying is that I run a respectable house. Mr Puddlecombe never gave me no trouble about hot water, and as for opening all the winders to let in the dirt, well . . .'

'I assure you Miss Nash is as respectable as I am, Mrs Turber, and I'm sure she will be amenable to discussing what services can be provided.'

'A bit too respectable for her own good, if you ask me,' said Mrs Turber. 'People will ask what's a girl that young doing on her own.'

'I have every faith that her being sheltered under your own chaperonage will still every wagging tongue, Mrs Turber,' said Agatha. 'Your name can surely never be associated with gossip.'

'Well, that's as may be,' said Mrs Turber, and Beatrice could hear a hint of satisfaction in her voice.

'Who among us would deny a young woman the right to make her own living when she is cast upon the world by the death of her esteemed father?' added Agatha with a catch in her voice. 'Lady Emily and I are so appreciative of your sanctuary, Mrs Turber.' Beatrice thought this was going a little far, but the loud sound of Mrs Turber blowing her nose suggested that some hint of empathy had been elicited. Agatha Kent, she reflected, was quite the politician.

'Well, I can't be asked to bring in hot water more'n once a week,' she said. 'Orphan or no, I've got much to do and my legs won't stand for carrying them heavy jugs all day. Mr Puddlecombe never bathed more than once a fortnight.'

'We will find a way, Mrs Turber,' said Agatha. 'You and Lady Emily and I, together we will find a way.'

As Beatrice stood grinning in the parlour, Agatha Kent appeared against the bright sunlight of the open back door and let herself in. Beatrice went forward into the small kitchen to greet her.

'Ah, there you are,' said Agatha. 'If you're intent on staying here, I do hope you'll try not to ruffle Mrs Turber too much.' She lowered her voice and added, 'She's not the biggest gossip in the town, but she's probably ranked second or third, so best to keep on her good side.'

'I can boil my own bathwater if necessary,' said Beatrice. 'I had no idea I was being difficult.'

'I have arranged to send Mrs Smith, our chauffeur's wife, down to give the place a good scrub,' said Agatha, ignoring her. 'She loves a challenge. Do you have furniture? I fear our lamented former Latin master, Mr Puddlecombe, was not overly concerned with his comfort.'

'I have a small desk that was my mother's and the chair that my father insisted on toting with us wherever we went in the world. I must send for them.'

'Is that all?'

'We mostly rented furnished rooms,' said Beatrice. 'My father was always being invited to lecture at universities or to help collaborate somewhere on a new journal.' She felt herself blushing. Somehow it had never before seemed poor to live in rented rooms. She had always merely seen to the unpacking and shelving of her father's library and stripped the mantels and side tables of excess gimcrack trinkets and doilies. They had lived mostly in Paris, in a succession of rooms near the Sorbonne, but in recent years had also made an extended visit to Heidelberg, spent two years in the romantic decay of a tall merchant's house in Venice, and finally, had inhabited the rambling wooden house of an absent professor in the precincts of a California university. She had understood that their peripatetic life was sometimes dictated by the moderate limits of her father's private income and might be partly the interior restlessness of an exile, but she had always felt rich in both her father's companionship and the fierce life of the mind that they pursued. With his absence, all seemed reduced to meagreness.

'Well, we have a small store of old things in the stable,' said Agatha. 'I've told Mrs Turber I'll be sending some pieces along. You must come and choose whatever you want, and if we are missing something, I'm sure Lady Emily would be glad to look through her attics.'

'Oh, I couldn't possibly trouble Lady Emily,' said Beatrice. Agatha stiffened at the note of anxiety which Beatrice was not able to conceal. Beatrice made a quick calculation and decided to offer Agatha the truth. 'I met Lady Emily's son on the train.'

'Obnoxious young fool,' said Agatha. 'Not half as much a man as my Daniel, or Hugh, but twice the income and prospects. A great trial to his dear mother.'

'So you understand that I'd rather not be indebted,' said Beatrice.

Agatha sighed and took off her hat. 'My dear child, I fear we are all indentured servants of society. There is no escape. In your case, Lady Emily's seal of approval on your employment won over the school governors where I, also an appointed member of that body, could not prevail. I'm afraid your independence, and my efforts in appointed office, both depend on our titled friend and on her little monogrammed invitations.'

'I am grateful to you both,' said Beatrice.

'And we are to you, my dear,' said Agatha. 'You will prove us right and raise the educational efforts of Rye with your superior learning. And we will bask in your knowledge, and your presence will be a tiny move towards a society of merit and honour.'

'Goodness me, that's a lot to expect for thirty shillings a week,' said Beatrice.

'Well, do try your best,' said Agatha. 'Let's show them how much more they can get from a woman – and at less expense to the annual budget. Ah, I hear a cart outside. Must be your things.' She bustled out, leaving Beatrice a moment of privacy in which to consider that while she and her father had discussed the more abstract principles behind the pricing of labour, it was not at all pleasant to discover that, simply as a woman, one was to be paid less than Mr Puddlecombe of the sticky floors and cheap hair tonic.

Under Agatha's direction, Beatrice's trunk was shoved and manhandled through the narrow front door and, after some discussion, was placed in the middle of the parlour, on the greasy rag rug, as it was too large to go up the narrow stairs. Her boxes and crates of books were stacked alongside, and Beatrice had to still a quiver of anxiety that she was to live, for the first time, in a place without a single bookshelf. Her bicycle came in last, and as she held the door for the man to wheel it through to the back garden, they all heard a muffled snort from the rooms next door that indicated Mrs Turber was not an enthusiastic supporter of the sport of cycling. Agatha saw the men to the door and then paused, as if reluctant to leave Beatrice alone in the cottage.

'Thank you,' said Beatrice. 'It was very kind of you to come with me, but I shall be perfectly all right now.'

'I am sending Mrs Smith this afternoon, and I don't want to hear about it,' said Agatha. 'And you will come to dinner this evening. Just the family. Perfectly informal.'

'There's no need . . .'

'You won't say that so readily once you've sampled Mrs Turber's rather basic fare,' whispered Agatha. 'Come early and you can get a look at the boys Hugh has been tutoring. I believe they call on him at four in the afternoon.'

'I look forward to meeting them,' said Beatrice.

Agatha gave one last hesitant look around the dingy parlour. 'I am not at all sure about leaving you here. When you come to dinner tonight you will tell me whether, upon reflection, you would not prefer to be found a room with a nice family.'

'Thank you,' said Beatrice. She looked at the two lumpy wing chairs, deal table, and tarnished brass fire screen, which did little to soften the empty room. 'I think I'll be just fine, but I must say this cottage in its current state is almost enough to drive one into marriage after all.'

CHAPTER FOUR

As the heat slipped from the day, Beatrice found Agatha Kent dallying among the thickly planted flower borders in the front courtyard of her house, snipping hydrangeas and tossing them abstractedly into a trug. She wore a loose tea gown and a straw hat.

'Oh, goodness, is that the time already?' she said, waving as Beatrice walked in at the gates. 'I must have missed the dressing bell.'

'I came early to meet the schoolboys I am to tutor,' said Beatrice, enjoying the pleasant cool of Agatha's garden after her stiff walk up the bluff.

'Oh yes, I had quite forgotten,' said Agatha, picking up the basket and dropping several hydrangeas onto the gravel. Beatrice bent to help her gather them. 'It has been a little chaotic this afternoon, as first Lady Emily telephoned and made it quite obvious that she wished to be invited to meet you straight away, and then our man of letters, Mr Tillingham – well, I can't imagine how he even heard – but he wanted to come too, and I am just hopeless at putting people off, so we are extra for dinner and Cook is being wonderful about it, but I needed more flowers and another leaf in the table and Smith was nowhere to be found and . . .'

'You can't mean Mr Tillingham the great writer?' asked Beatrice. Surely the American author widely described as one of the age's leading literary figures could not be coming to dinner with Agatha Kent?

'Well, he would certainly think so,' said Agatha. 'I do hope you won't twitter and gush at him like so many of our ladies? We try to treat him as any other neighbour.'

'Of course not,' said Beatrice, trying unsuccessfully to quell her excitement. She was to meet the master whose work she had studied and even aped at first in her own stumbling efforts towards writing a novel. Even her father, who so despised the novel form that she had omitted to share her efforts with him, had grudgingly admired Tillingham in his peak years. She was dizzy at the sudden prospect. 'May I help you?' she asked Agatha. 'I can trim flowers.'

'Well, if it isn't rude of me, perhaps you can find your own way to the stable house. I think Hugh is up there – he has a workroom upstairs.'

'I think I can manage,' said Beatrice, who could see the stable building visible behind a large hedge at the edge of the courtyard.

'After you've met the boys, do have a good rummage through the box room for furniture. It's behind where we keep the car. The key should be hanging under the stairs and Hugh knows where it is. And if you could discreetly remind him that we are dressing for company tonight.'

Two horses hung their heads over loose box doors and regarded Beatrice without much interest. She ducked into the cool, dark interior of the stable building, where a staircase to her right led to an upper floor. She hesitated, aware that it was silly to be intimidated by a piece of machinery but unwilling to step around the large motorcar. Upstairs looked sunnier, but she was reluctant to just walk up without an invitation.

'Hello? Anyone home?' she called, her foot on the lowest step.

'Who's there?' asked a man's voice, and Hugh appeared at the top of the stairs, a square of glass in one raised hand.

'Your aunt sent me,' said Beatrice. 'To meet your pupils?'

'We are in the middle of making microscope slides,' said Hugh. A scent of formaldehyde wafted down the stairs. 'I believe you said you were not delicate?'

'Oh, I'd love to come up and see,' said Beatrice, enthusiasm overcoming her intention to be reserved and polite. 'My father and I made slides sometimes. I have quite a collection of insect wings.'

'Sectioning chicken heads is quite a bit messier,' said Hugh.

'I assure you I'm not at all squeamish,' said Beatrice, her stomach giving an unpleasant lurch.

'Come up at your own peril,' said Hugh. 'Only if you faint, we won't be able to catch you without smearing brains on your frock.'

The room at the top of the stairs was set under heavy rafters and boasted a bay window overlooking the kitchen gardens. It contained a large worktable and several lumpy armchairs of mismatched and tattered upholstery. The late-afternoon sun was streaming in at the window, and two of Hugh's three pupils were bent with sharp knives over lumps of bloody tissue on the table, while a third was curled up in an armchair, chewing a pencil and leaning on a large book, sneaking glances at the open window. They stood up at her arrival and looked at her with frank curiosity. She smiled to cover her shock, for they were more unprepossessing than she had expected, with all the gangly knobbliness of boys who were no longer children but had not yet solidified into men. Though they were of different heights and faces, there was a uniform ugliness to their large ears, badly cut hair and drooping socks. And despite evidence that they had combed their hair and washed before their lessons, they carried the unmistakable odour of young men, against which a weekly hip bath could make little impression. For a moment Beatrice quailed to think she would soon face a roomful of such rudely gaping mouths. She wondered how Agatha Kent had come to see any promise in three such grubby specimens.

'A splendid room,' said Beatrice, faintly.

'I was exiled here as a boy shortly after my chemistry experiments proved malodorous,' said Hugh. 'Just give me a moment to finish this and I'll introduce you to the boys.'

To adjust her composure in front of her new pupils, she walked along the wall to view the glass-fronted cabinets, and extra shelves propped up on bricks, which contained books, boxes and a lifetime's collection of natural specimens. Skulls, rocks, fossils, feathers, half a dried bat and a stuffed pheasant beset by moths seemed like a lost treasure. Beatrice was struck with a painful pang of jealousy that in this, the home of an aunt, a room bigger than her entire new accommodation would have been set aside for a visiting boy's hobbies. She touched her fingertips to the cool, dimpled surface of an ostrich egg and bent to peer at a tank containing two frogs. One of the frogs swam energetically against the side, and Beatrice could not help but pause to examine his mighty efforts to scrape his way to freedom through the glass.

'That's Samuel and Samuel, miss,' said the boy with the book. He was the tallest and wore boots of enormous size.

'We were going to call them Johnson and Pepys, but Daniel thought it sounded like a grocer's,' said Hugh, carefully plucking something thinly sliced from a cup of formaldehyde and transferring it with tweezers to a slide held close to his face. 'That boy impertinent enough to speak to a lady without being asked is Jack Heathly.'

'Sorry, sir,' said Jack, his ears flushing red. 'Sorry, miss.'

'Jack's father is one of our most respected local shepherds,' said Hugh. 'And Jack's older brother is a sheep-shearing champion.'

'Gone all the way to Australia, he is,' said Jack, who looked both proud and wistful. 'I keep all the stamps from his letters.'

'I think they are upsetting Samuel with their brain slicing,' said Beatrice, smiling at Jack. 'Did Mr Grange section the heads of all his brothers and sisters?'

'Only if they died of natural causes,' said Hugh. 'I'm not too good about killing things up close. Our cook dispatches the chickens.'

'I'd kill stuff for you, Mr Hugh,' said the shortest boy, sitting down at the table.

'Thank you, Snout,' said Hugh. 'This fine if somewhat short fellow is Snout. His father has the forge down by the Strand.'

'How d'you do, miss?' said Snout. He did not look up but continued to slice with slow precision through a chicken head, his thin face creased into a frown and his tongue pressed between his lips.

'And this third fellow is Arty Pike, Miss Nash. No doubt you've seen Pike Brothers, the ironmongers in the high street?'

'Ironmongers and haberdashery,' said the jug-eared boy, coming to attention. '"All your needs and no fancy prices" is our motto, miss.'

'I shall be sure to open an account, Master Pike,' said Beatrice. Her magnanimity was met with a smirk that suggested he had already appraised the modest size of her business.

'Finish up, boys, and I'll introduce you properly to Miss Nash, who is going to be taking over as your summer tutor.' They must have been warned, thought Beatrice, for they managed to keep their groans as low as a mutter. They were not as enthusiastic to be taught as she was to engage in teaching.

'Can I finish up too?' asked the boy with the book.

'Only if you're done with your translation, Jack,' said Hugh. He looked up at Beatrice to add, 'We have an agreement that Latin homework will be done each week if we want to help with the science experiments.' He smiled in a way that telegraphed he might have much more to communicate about the boys were they not in the room. She returned the smile, admiring that he could disguise scientific enquiry as a reward.

'Wot we learning Latin for, anyway?' Jack asked, chewing his pencil. He looked with gloomy despair at three lines of Latin text scrawled by Hugh on a large sheet of brown butcher's paper and returned to consulting the reference book.

'Jack's learning Latin and bowing and scraping so he can be a gentleman,' said Arty. 'They're going to give him a top hat to wear while he's shearing sheep.'

'Better a working man than a sot, my dad says,' said Jack, putting the book away on a shelf as if it was all agreed that he was finished with his Latin. Arty's face went dark at the apparent insult, and Hugh intervened.

'Now, now, boys. Let's behave like gentlemen in the presence of Miss Nash.'

'I don't want to be no gentleman and I doubt a bit o' Latin is going to make 'em let us join anyway,' said Jack.

'I want to be a gentleman,' said Snout, handling his knife with the ease of experience as he sliced the last of his heads paper-thin. 'You don't get laughed at for reading books, you don't have to let no one on your land, and you can kill all the rabbits you want and no one calls the coppers.'

'He's a poacher, miss,' said Jack.

'Say it again and I'll 'ave you,' said Snout, balling up his fists and screwing up his face so much Beatrice began to see the origin of his nickname.

'Come now, Snout, you must not rise to the bait,' said Hugh. 'And, Jack, perhaps you should spend less time insulting Snout and more time learning from his superior

Latin talents?' This did not seem to be welcomed by either boy. They both glared, and Beatrice was glad she had been educated privately and not in their schoolroom, where, she began to understand, talent might bring as much ridicule as respect.

'Latin is not just the language of the Caesars but also the language of the science you are studying,' she said. 'And it underpins all medicine, law and religion, so it's the key that unlocks many fields.' She stopped as they looked at her with suspicion. Her calling to teach was partly inspired by her father's view that education in general, and Latin in particular, should not be kept for the few, that it was wrong to divide the world and keep all success and distinction in the hands of a small elite. But perhaps his leanings towards such new ideas, and his wish to spread classical education to the people, would not be popular in the rural setting of Rye, she thought.

'There you are, boys,' said Hugh. 'Miss Nash intends to make you as erudite and as wealthy as the ancients.'

'May I see what's under the microscope?' said Beatrice, hiding her blushes as she changed the subject. 'I assume it is brain matter?'

'See, boys, Miss Nash really is not squeamish,' said Hugh, and Beatrice felt a flicker of satisfaction at her own stoicism. 'Do come and look. It's a slice across the medulla.'

'*Medulla* from the Latin meaning "pith", miss,' said Snout. 'The black stain shows the paths where the brain sends messages to breathe and things.' He seemed to have forgotten to be shy, and his eyes, now raised to hers, reflected a sharp intelligence. 'Silver chromate, they call it. Very poisonous, but the chicken was already dead, miss.'

'A very fine explanation, thank you,' said Beatrice, feeling slightly more optimistic that at least one boy showed real enthusiasm. She bent over the eyepiece of the large black microscope and squinted at a piece of yellow flesh as translucent as onion skin, swirled with complex black lines like fine calligraphy. 'It's very beautiful,' she added.

'From where did you acquire such fortitude?' asked Hugh, setting all three boys to disinfecting the worktable with strong yellow soap.

'As unfashionable as it is to have a strong stomach, my father developed a fondness for pioneer history while we were in America,' said Beatrice. 'He became convinced that education should not be divorced from basic skills and that it was weakness in the educated classes to affect delicate sensibilities.'

'I hate to think how one proves such a thing,' said Hugh.

'There was a harrowing visit to the university's kitchen yard, where I disgraced myself by running away with the chicken whose neck I was supposed to wring,' she said. She looked up from the microscope and added, 'This is perhaps a more macabre hobby than insect wings?'

'It's not a hobby,' said Hugh. 'It's part of my research. There's a lot to be learned from chicken brains.'

'Only if one is planning on specialising in the brains of clergymen and politicians, that is,' said a voice as his cousin Daniel sauntered into the room. 'Are you coming to dinner smelling like a chemist's shop again?'

'I have plenty of time,' said Hugh.

'Given your perfunctory wardrobe style, I don't doubt it,' said Daniel. 'Goodness me, you'll never make it while the place is still positively pustulating with the great unwashed.' The three boys, who were soaping their hands at a zinc basin in the corner, turned with lowering faces that suggested several blunt responses were being only barely quashed by respect for their superiors.

'If you're going to be rude, Daniel, perhaps you could do it in your own study,' said Hugh. 'Boys, you are dismissed. I want your pages translated back into the Latin for next time.'

There were three sets of groans, made shorter by the boys' eagerness to escape from a room containing a strange woman and the rude poet with the fancy vocabulary.

'I look forward to seeing you at my home for your next lesson,' said Beatrice, hoping her voice projected more authority than she felt. 'No dead chickens, I'm afraid, but lots of exciting stories and discussion.'

'Yes, miss. Thank you, miss.' With the briefest of mumbled answers and nods to Beatrice they were gone, clattering down the stairs and out across the sunshine of the drive.

'I made Mr Grange late,' said Beatrice. 'I'm sorry. I was so interested in the boys and the brains. I'm not sure I will be able to find some task half as compelling to keep their attention.' Though concerned, she was also eager to begin. To bring a true appreciation of Latin to such boys would honour her father. And she was ready to test her talents against the grubbiest and most stubborn, for if she could bring these three to heel, she had an idea the grammar school classroom would no longer fill her with dread.

'Oh, don't listen to Daniel,' said Hugh. 'He's never on time to dinner parties, and when he's there he can't be trusted to be polite. He is to be ignored – on most occasions.'

'Oh, that hurts,' said Daniel, clutching at his chest. 'But I know your anger merely distracts from the fact that you have finally lured a maiden to your lair.'

'Don't talk nonsense, Daniel,' said Hugh. 'Miss Nash is a protégée of Aunt Agatha's and you are not to make her feel uncomfortable. Why don't you take her for a promenade in the garden while I clean up?'

'Actually, your aunt sent me to search the box room for spare furniture,' said Beatrice. 'If you can just direct me to the key, I can amuse myself until dinner.'

'I think the hideous relics in the box room demand a knowledgeable guide,' said Daniel, 'lest the great tower of Kent history topple on one's head.' He flopped into an armchair and took out from his pocket a cigar and a slim volume that looked like a poetry journal. 'I would be a Virgil to your Dante, Miss Nash, but I fear I am not expert enough to steer you away from all the pieces Hugh might have used over the years to dissect or store his bits of animals.'

'Oh please, it was just the one bureau, and only one jar leaked,' said Hugh. 'But by all means let me just wash my hands and I'll show you, Miss Nash. I know there are a couple of nice Georgian bookcases that Aunt Agatha wisely refused to let me have for rabbit hutches.'

'I'll just stay here and have a moment to read and smoke in peace,' said Daniel. 'Aunt Agatha has chased me even from the terrace.' He withdrew matches from his pocket, and Beatrice wondered if he meant to light his cigar right under her nose. However he merely turned the box over between his fingers until Hugh, having soaped his hands at the basin and dried them with a rough towel hanging from a nail, was ready to lead her downstairs. As they left, Daniel, without looking up from his book, added, 'If I don't hear the guests, do come and fetch me, Hugh – but not until the soup is absolutely on the table.'

Beatrice had feared the box room might leave her dirty and covered with cobwebs, but the cleaning abilities of Smith's wife had not been exaggerated, and from the spotless room she had selected a simple green bed and bureau, a small tea table and chairs, and the bookcases, which she felt were far too valuable but which Hugh insisted were just the thing.

'I allow plenty of room for sentimental attachments,' said Hugh. 'But once something is consigned to the box room it is a matter of guilt, not love.'

As she ran upstairs to wash her hands and deposit her hat in the third-best bedroom, to which Jenny directed her as if the room would now always be Beatrice's, she smiled at the realisation that Hugh Grange hid a dry sense of humour beneath his plain scientific demeanour. He was quieter than his dazzling cousin, she thought, but it seemed he was no less sharp-witted.

Beatrice came down to a drawing room lively with voices and the clink of glasses. She hesitated in the doorway, knowing she should be eager to meet her patron, Lady Emily, but instead fluttering with anticipation and scanning the room to see the great Mr Tillingham. All the time in the box room, while she talked to Hugh about the boys and laughed over the fat ottomans and plant stands to which he tried to tempt her, she had been growing more and more nervous. To meet the man whose writing she admired above all others was delightful, yet she feared to seem too eager. She was almost glad that Agatha had forbidden her to mention her desire to be a writer; otherwise she might have blurted out some gauche declaration to the great man.

She noticed that Daniel had decided to be polite and was already present. He stood up briefly as she came in. Agatha, in a pale green dress, adorned with a brooch of silver and peacock feathers, and curly Arabian gold slippers, came forward, glass of Madeira in hand, to greet her.

'Miss Nash, why don't you allow me to introduce you to our little school's most important patron,' said Agatha. 'Lady Emily, may I introduce to you Miss Beatrice Nash?' Lady Emily, despite the warm evening, wore severe, high-collared black silk. She was a study in gaunt angles, her limbs folded carefully onto the least comfortable chaise in the room, chin lifted as if she were about to have her portrait taken. As a concession to the informal dinner, to which she had all but invited herself at the last minute, she wore only a choker of fat pearls.

'Welcome to our little town,' said Lady Emily. 'Agatha tells us we are lucky to have attracted a teacher of your credentials, and Lady Marbely has of course vouched for your character.'

'I am very grateful to Mrs Kent and to you, Lady Emily,' said Beatrice. She knew what it must have cost her aunt to pen a few lines of praise in order to be rid of her and took great satisfaction in not repeating her aunt's name, even though Lady Emily's pursed lips suggested she was waiting for more communication. Beatrice merely offered her blandest and most demure smile.

'And may I introduce you to Mr Tillingham,' said Agatha, sweeping a plump arm towards a heavy-jowled older man, who was struggling to rise from a deep chair. 'Though I'm sure our most distinguished literary neighbour needs no introduction.'

At last the great man was in front of her. With a heave, he popped upright, swaying a little as the bulk of his torso sought equilibrium above two short legs and a pair of dainty feet. He considered Beatrice from hooded eyes under a broad forehead that continued up and over the back of a balding head. She thought at once of a large owl.

'No, indeed,' she stammered. He was less impressive in person than in the photographs she had seen of him in the newspapers, but she was still struck with a childish blush as he took her hand.

'How do you do,' he said.

She struggled for a reply as she tried not to pour out an effusive gush of silly compliments about the beauty of his language, or the elliptical construction of his sentences. She settled on, 'My father, Joseph Nash, was a great admirer of your work.' At least her father's name would signal that she was more than just the ladies' latest educational experiment to be gaped at over dinner.

'Joseph Nash? Joseph Nash?' said Mr Tillingham, his face politely blank as he grasped for some connection to the name.

'*A Short History of Euripides?*' she said. 'You were kind enough to write to him about it.' It was the most successful of her father's modest published works, and he had considered it his finest achievement, in some part because it had resulted in correspondence from Mr Tillingham. Tillingham had written in praise, her father had responded in kind.

Tillingham had written again to suggest that he concentrate exclusively on historical biography and to lament
that so many threw away their talents on cheap journalism
and low criticism. Her father had laughed and written to
thank Tillingham for the advice. Neither had mentioned
the journal to which her father contributed and in which
he had roundly criticised one of Tillingham's first plays.
She still had Tillingham's original letters, along with her
copies of her father's replies. They were wrapped in oilcloth
and tied with a thin leather lace, in a tin box of her father's
papers, a box she had barely managed to smuggle from the
Marbely home. She felt a rising anxiety as everyone wrinkled their brows as if searching for a collective memory.

'Well, I'm sure Mr Tillingham must correspond with
dozens of people,' said Agatha.

'What colour are the boards?' asked Tillingham. 'I have
a good memory for colour.' 'Green,' said Beatrice. 'Rather
slim, with a cream title.'

'Ah yes, I remember now,' said Tillingham. 'A rare
historical work that achieved its own promised brevity,
and one or two moments of surprising clarity within the
pages. I believe I was not unimpressed.'

'Thank you,' said Beatrice.

'I shall look it up in my library,' said Tillingham. 'Perhaps
it will remind me further of your father's correspondence.'
There was a slight easing of tension around the room, as if
Mr Tillingham's recollection of her father's book served as
a password.

'Do sit down, Miss Nash,' said Agatha, indicating a
place beside her on a comfortable sofa. 'You must still be
tired after your journey yesterday.'

'Just a little,' she said. 'The stations in London were very hot and crowded.'

Hugh slipped into the room, his crooked bow tie and damp hair betraying his last-minute haste in dressing. No one seemed to notice him, and Beatrice was deeply aware that they were too busy examining her even as they pretended to look elsewhere.

'I never travel by train,' said Lady Emily, breaking an awkward pause. 'All the soot and such a crush of vulgar humanity.'

'Yes, one may encounter the occasional vulgar person,' said Beatrice. She kept her face blank and did not look at Hugh, but she was satisfied to hear him rattle a decanter loudly.

'Anyone for more sherry?' he called. The maid, Jenny, stood by the decanters with a small silver tray to carry drinks.

'There's no need to be abrupt, my dear,' said his aunt. 'Do pour Miss Nash a small glass of sherry.'

'But, dear Lady Emily, if you never take a train, however do you get to Scotland?' asked Daniel, lolling in his chair with the carelessness of a child.

'Well, of course I do take a private sleeping car to Scotland,' she replied. 'Even so, I have to send two of my maids to give it a thorough cleaning before I go aboard.'

'One would wish to bring one's own linens, I imagine,' said Mr Tillingham, tilting his head to one side and pursing his lips. Beatrice wondered if he was making notes for a future novel. 'And perhaps a hamper or two?'

'Naturally,' said Lady Emily. 'And of course, special cushions for the babies. They used to roll around on the floor and were terribly uncomfortable.' Beatrice lost her firm grasp of the conversational thread at this image and was unable to repress a raised eyebrow.

'Lady Emily raises the most adorable dachshunds,' explained Agatha.

'They travel with me everywhere,' said Lady Emily. 'Except here when you dreadful boys are home.' She shook her fan at Daniel, who broke into laughter, and at Hugh, who looked appalled.

'I say, Lady Emily, that was a long time ago,' said Hugh. 'I assure you your tiny canines would be quite safe.'

'What on earth did you do, you young scallywags, to upset Lady Emily's dachshunds?' asked Mr Tillingham, leaning in conspiratorial manner towards Daniel.

'Well, one time we made a circus and used them as clowns,' said Daniel, in a stage whisper. 'And once Hugh decided we should take them ratting in the woods and one of Lady Emily's beasts caught a sizable vole.'

'I don't think we need to air our youthful delinquencies, Daniel,' said Hugh, and Beatrice was delighted to see from his blush that Hugh Grange had once been less than perfectly responsible. She liked him the better for it.

'Of course, it is long forgotten,' said Lady Emily. 'Though I was sorry to give that one away.'

'You gave him away?' said Daniel. 'The ratter king?'

'Heartbreaking, but I could no longer feel quite comfortable looking at his little teeth nibbling bacon from my breakfast plate,' she said. 'One has to be so careful about disease.'

'Quite understandable,' said Daniel. While he struggled to hide his amusement, Beatrice noticed that his cousin Hugh looked pained.

'Colonel Wheaton likes to complain that we employ half a footman just to brush away the hair,' said Lady Emily. 'But then I find him in his study, reading the newspaper, with a dog under each arm. It takes days to get the smell of his cigar out of their coats.'

'I often think I should get some sort of little dog,' said Mr Tillingham. 'An aggressive terrier, perhaps, to keep away all the unwanted visitors who interrupt my work.'

'I can't abide people who dislike dogs,' said Lady Emily. 'I am especially suspicious of those who prefer cats.' She peered as if Beatrice might be guilty. 'There is something too malleable about them, don't you think?'

'I believe our Mayoress, Mrs Fothergill, has two rather elegant long-haired Siamese,' said Daniel.

'A very pushing sort of woman,' said Lady Emily. 'However, I will hold my tongue tomorrow in order to secure Miss Nash's position.'

'Not that your position in the school is not secure,' added Agatha. 'But Lady Emily hosts an annual tea with the school governors, the Headmaster and staff, and some of our other dignitaries. We thought it would be a lovely Sunday afternoon introduction to ensure your welcome to the community.'

'Of course, we did not expect you to be so young,' said Lady Emily. Beatrice felt a flush spread across her neck and cheeks as the question of her age, which would not, of course, be asked, hung in the air.

'I am twenty-three,' she said, looking directly at Lady Emily. 'I hope I am therefore sufficiently advanced into spinsterhood?'

'I am sure there is no question that you are,' said Agatha.

'Positively ancient,' said Daniel. 'Don't you agree, Hugh?'

'That isn't what I meant at all,' said Agatha.

'A more wrinkled physiognomy and grey hair might have been expected,' said Hugh. 'But I'm sure a few weeks of our local grammar pupils will achieve the desired appearance.'

'I believe the real problem is that Lady Emily and Mrs Kent present such figures of youth that anyone your age must appear a mere slip of a girl,' said Mr Tillingham.

'You are being absurd, dear friend,' said Lady Emily, but she looked a little pinker in the face.

'He is being a writer,' said Daniel. 'All writers must tell truth to beauty.'

'Obviously poets are compelled to produce excesses of hyperbole,' said Hugh. 'I imagine writers merely exaggerate?'

Daniel laughed, and Beatrice saw Mr Tillingham's face flicker with annoyance before he too relaxed into a chuckle.

'And thus, with a blunt saw, we are crudely and cruelly dissected by the medical man,' said Mr Tillingham.

'Well, regardless of age, I am sure Miss Nash will present herself as a modest, dignified woman and show that we have made the right decision,' said Agatha.

'I shall be sure to wear my ugliest dress,' said Beatrice.

'Plain will do,' said Lady Emily, in a severe tone. 'We just don't need another spectacle like our French mistress and her preposterous silk dresses.'

'To be fair, Miss Clauvert is not an Englishwoman,' said Agatha. 'It is our good fortune to have a real Frenchwoman.'

'True,' said Lady Emily. 'But I'm thankful Miss Nash's family is of impeccable English lineage.'

'Actually, my mother was American,' said Beatrice, before she could stop herself. She clamped her lips closed in order to resist adding that her father had been disowned by the Marbelys and had disowned them in return for as long as possible.

'An American?' said Lady Emily, in a tone of horrified surprise.

'How delightful,' said Daniel. 'Lady Emily is a great admirer of all things American, is she not, Mr Tillingham?'

'Of course,' said Tillingham. He did not look terribly happy at being reminded of his own citizenship. Beatrice now recognised that his careful articulation bore deliberately little trace of any accent.

'My father is English,' she said. 'Though after my mother died, he could never seem to be happy here.'

'Ah, the mysteries of the human heart,' said Mr Tillingham. He raised a hand into the air, as if about to conduct an unseen orchestra, and everyone paused, as probably he intended, thought Beatrice, in order to await a bon mot from the great mind. 'For I long ago found a home and a safe harbour in this tiny corner of England and I can never seem to be happy anywhere else.'

'And we consider you quite one of us, Mr Tillingham,' said Lady Emily. 'I assure you I no longer even think of you as American.'

'Mr Tillingham is in great demand among the local hostesses,' said Agatha to Beatrice. 'He is quite pestered with invitations.'

'I must be ruthless in declining or I would never dine by my own comfortable fireside,' said Mr Tillingham. 'The public acknowledgement of one's literary contributions is of course gratifying, but the burden of reputation can be heavy at times.'

'Good thing you don't have to suffer under such a burden with your poetry, Daniel,' said Hugh. 'I shall pray for you to remain unpublished.'

'I have broad shoulders,' said Daniel. 'Bring on the fame and the laurels.'

'You may joke, boys,' said Mr Tillingham, 'but wait until yet another local squire leans across the dinner table to ask you loudly whether he might have read anything you've written.'

'I know something of what you mean,' said Beatrice. 'My father was often asked to explain who he was and what kind of things he wrote. He was always patient.' There was a polite pause, and Beatrice froze, realising with horror that they thought she was referring to Mr Tillingham's earlier failure to recollect her father's name.

'I, alas, am not as patient perhaps as your father,' said Mr Tillingham, and gave her a smile that eliminated any tension. Beatrice could have kissed him for his unexpected graciousness. 'I like to respond that I do not write for the Farmers' Almanac and so cannot dare to hope that the gentleman has read any of my meagre oeuvre.'

'It is far more polite to admit that one doesn't read,' said Lady Emily. 'Who has the time? Of course we have all of Mr Tillingham's works in our library. I always give your latest volume pride of place next to my drawing-room chair, Mr Tillingham. I have a special gold bookmark with a Fortuny silk tassel.'

'I am touched,' said Mr Tillingham.

'If Mr Tillingham prefers to dine in his own home, we should make an effort to invite him less often, Aunt,' said Hugh. 'It would be terrible to think that we distracted him.' He smiled, but Beatrice detected that Hugh was not altogether joking. She wondered why he didn't like the great man.

'I trust Mr Tillingham knows he is at liberty to come to dinner anytime and to decline dinner whenever he feels like it,' said Agatha. 'We do not stand on ceremony with those we consider family.' She turned to Beatrice and added, 'Mr Tillingham is always writing to me to enquire about the boys and has taken a kind interest in Daniel's poetry.'

'To help along the next generation of young writers and poets is a duty I consider both sacred and rewarding,' said Mr Tillingham. 'I'm hoping, Daniel, that you will come to dinner and bring me some more poems to read?' He raised a thick eyebrow and gave Daniel a conspiratorial smile.

'I'm afraid they're hardly in a fit state,' said Daniel, maintaining a languid air of indifference. 'But I'm trying to wrestle some life into one or two pieces.'

'I believe Miss Nash also writes,' said Hugh.

'Oh no,' said Beatrice, flustered by an urgent desire to have the great writer offer a smile of interest towards her and the competing wish to heed Agatha Kent's injunction. 'I mean, I have spent the past year editing my father's personal letters in the hopes of publishing a small volume.' She looked at Mr Tillingham, whose face showed a hint of relief.

'Collecting and sorting such material is an admirable project for a daughter,' he said. 'I'm sure it will be of great interest to your father's friends and family; and at least it is a sober endeavour and not some flighty female novel.'

'Perhaps Miss Nash also wishes to write a novel?' asked Hugh.

'Miss Nash will be fully occupied by her vocation as a teacher and will have no interest in such frivolous pursuits,' said Lady Emily. Agatha Kent looked at Beatrice with an eyebrow raised in mute hope.

'My teaching duties will be all my concern,' said Beatrice, bitterly disappointed but resigned to the practical.

'Thank the Lord,' said Mr Tillingham. 'There is a great fashion for encouraging young women, especially American women, to think they can write, and I have received several slightly hysterical requests to read such charming manuscripts.'

'And did you?' asked Daniel.

'Goodness no, I would rather cut off my right hand,' said Mr Tillingham. 'I delegated my secretary to compose her own diplomatic replies and to consign the offending pages to the kitchen stove.'

'I thought you were great friends with that American woman who insists on writing even though her position and fortune make it quite unnecessary,' said Lady Emily.

'The lady of whom you speak is in a category by herself,' said Mr Tillingham. 'She does possess a fastidious eye for the narrow milieu of which she writes, and I cannot fault her competence nor argue with her considerable success.'

'Plus she's very generous, I hear,' said Daniel. 'Doesn't she come down and take you out in her enormous motorcar?'

'Daniel!' said his aunt.

Mr Tillingham waved his hand to indicate his lack of offence. 'I assure you, dear boy, that I am quite capable of accepting friends' generosity and still telling them exactly what I think of their art,' said Mr Tillingham. 'Indeed I wish it were otherwise, for I have lost friends and chased away a great love or two in my time with what some of them described as my brutish candour.' To Beatrice's great surprise, he pulled out his large silk pocket square and dabbed at his eyes, which were filling with tears.

'I would never describe you as brutish,' said Daniel. He turned to the room at large and added, 'But the last group of poems I showed to Mr Tillingham was so thoroughly and precisely dismantled that all I had left was a single couplet.'

'It is a curse, but I have never been able to speak anything but the truth when it comes to the written word,' said Mr Tillingham. 'I believe your father felt the same way, my dear.'

'You do remember him?' said Beatrice.

'It is coming to me,' said Mr Tillingham. 'Is it possible that he wrote an absolutely scathing review of my very first play?'

'I believe he did review it,' said Beatrice, blushing.

'Well, he wasn't the only one, to be sure,' said Tillingham. 'But I do remember his analysis was astute enough for me to feel unable to write my usual long and detailed rebuttal.'

'Thank you,' said Beatrice.

'I will look for his book as soon as I get home,' added Tillingham. 'And you must come to tea and show me one or two of your father's more interesting letters.'

Beatrice felt tears sting the backs of her eyes, and she dug her fingernails into her palms to keep from betraying her gratitude. Mr Tillingham patted her hand, and Beatrice felt Lady Emily's astonishment.

'Wonderful,' said Agatha. 'Remind me to make sure the Headmaster and the Vicar also extend invitations.'

'It is an act of common decency to take turns in relieving the loneliness of the parish's lady spinsters,' said Lady Emily. 'Whenever I'm home, I have two elderly sisters in for bridge on Tuesdays. Perhaps you play, Miss Nash?'

Beatrice struggled to find an acceptable evasion, as she was rather proud of her bridge skills.

'On Tuesdays, Miss Nash will be tutoring some of the grammar boys,' said Agatha smoothly. 'I had not wanted to impose on you any more, dear Lady Emily, but an invitation to tea from you, issued publicly in the middle of the garden party, would be just the thing to make our little project unassailable and stop Mrs Fothergill's intrigues.'

'Well, if you think it would help,' said Lady Emily, looking somewhat mollified. 'I would willingly endure absolute hardship to put Mrs Fothergill in her place.'

As the dinner gong rang, Beatrice caught sight of Hugh and Daniel exchanging a smothered grin. She suppressed a smile of her own and thought that she would willingly hear herself compared to a hardship just as long as she did not have to join Lady Emily's parade of spinsters.

CHAPTER FIVE

THE GIRL WHO KNOCKED at Beatrice's bedroom door the next morning did not seem strong enough to carry the heavy tray on which rested a cup of tea in a florid porcelain cup and a heavy jug of hot water for the washstand. She was hollow in the cheeks and narrow-shouldered, her hair pulled back mercilessly into a single braid. Her dress and apron hung loosely, and her boots looked comically large laced onto such scrawny ankles.

'Cup of tea, miss,' she said. 'And I'm to tell you breakfast is under a cover below because Mrs Turber is gone to church at eight and she hopes you won't expect her to set God aside for people who use the Sabbath for sleeping late.'

'Why didn't you wake me?' asked Beatrice.

'I tried, miss, but you didn't want to stir and I took the tea away cold.' She put the tray on the floor, transferred the jug to the washstand, and brought the tea, her lips clamped in concentration to keep the cup from wobbling on its gilded saucer. Even when Beatrice took the tea from her, the girl did not look up but merely turned away to the tray.

'I've never failed to wake up,' said Beatrice, taking a long gulp of hot tea. 'I suppose I was tired from travelling.' She was used to the pale dawn hours, the birds' thin choir accompanying her waking thoughts of her father. Curiously, she did not feel guilty for sleeping so late into the hot morning. And if she was tired, from the travel and all the new impressions around her, at least it was a different kind of exhaustion than she had felt all year; more a good physical tiredness and less the enervating lassitude that comes with hopelessness.

'Mr Puddlecombe never got up before noon on a Sunday,' said the girl. She shuffled her absurd boots, and her cheeks flushed an unflattering red.

'What's your name?' asked Beatrice. The girl gave her a sideways glance and seemed to be gathering her courage to speak.

'I'm so sorry, miss. I'll call out louder next time if you want,' she said. 'But if you get up early, Mrs Turber will make me go to church too, and then it's very hard to get to all the polishing done before lunch, and I get Sunday afternoon off but only if I'm all done, and my mum is poorly and needs me and . . . my name's Abigail.'

'How old are you, Abigail?'

'Thirteen, miss. Or almost, but I'm strong for my age.'

'Well, Abigail, I prefer to go to later services anyway, and I'm not going today at all because I'm to be introduced at a garden party this afternoon and I'm being kept quite hidden from view until then.'

'I can bring your breakfast up if you like,' said Abigail. 'It's a hard-boiled egg and toast, some cold bacon and tomatoes.'

'I'd like them packed in a napkin,' said Beatrice. 'I think I'll take a ride on my bicycle and eat my breakfast on the beach.' Abigail seemed too surprised to reply, and Beatrice's smile only served to make her look more alarmed. 'Run along and pack them up for me,' added Beatrice. 'I'll be quite out of your way and you can polish silver all morning.'

'A bicycle, miss,' said Abigail. 'That's a grand thing.'

Sunday dinner, served promptly after the noon church service, was the one meal a week to be taken in Mrs Turber's own dining room.

'I won't be in to tea, Mrs Turber,' said Beatrice, pushing the gristle from a leathery slice of beef under a piece of cabbage and neatly setting her knife and fork down on the plate. She was sitting wedged between the heavy oak table and a large dark sideboard. The sideboard wore a crocheted doily, as did the backs of the dining chairs, a small curio cabinet and several plant stands containing fat ferns and bulbous, rubbery plants for which Beatrice had no name. The table was also decked in a crocheted white tablecloth over a green baize square, which in turn protected a heavy red damask cloth that was never removed. The furniture was further protected by festoons of chintz and pleated muslin over the one small window, and the room was as airless as a vacuum. Beatrice sipped her glass of water and prayed for patience as the gilded parlour clock on the mantelpiece made a tocking sound at agonisingly slow intervals.

'Well, it's a good thing I didn't make the Victoria sponge this morning, then,' said Mrs Turber. 'That would have been a waste.'

'I think Mrs Kent told you that I'm required up at Lady Emily's,' said Beatrice.

'I thank the good Lord that I've never been one for putting on airs,' said Mrs Turber. 'Some people about this town— Well, I don't blame Lady Emily for being taken in.' She scowled, pressing her lips together over an undisclosed record of slights and ringing her little crystal bell for Abigail to come in and clear. The girl came in bearing a steaming jam pudding in a basin.

'Is Colonel Wheaton's house very imposing?' asked Beatrice. She thought she might faint from the addition of steam to a room devoid of oxygen. Mrs Turber got up with some difficulty and went to the sideboard to cut two slabs of pudding.

'I only went once, when the poor Captain was still alive,' she said. 'A meeting of the aldermen. Lovely it was, and Lady Emily admired my hat very much.' She sighed. 'Of course no one wants to invite a poor widow.'

'I think it's mostly the governors of the school,' said Beatrice.

'Oh yes, it's just the governors or just the aldermen or just the coursing club and their wives,' said Mrs Turber. 'I told Mr Puddlecombe, it's enough to make one consider marrying, just to make them come up with better excuses.'

Beatrice looked down at the tablecloth and closed her eyes against the image of Mrs Turber offering such a suggestion to the departed former Latin master.

'I am not looking forward to it,' said Beatrice. 'It will be awful to be stared at.'

'Well, to be grateful is to show proper humility,' said Mrs Turber. 'I hope you don't want anything else, only it would be a shame to keep the girl from her afternoon off.'

In the warm afternoon, Beatrice again walked the road out of town, up the hill, to Agatha Kent's house and reflected on how quickly it had become a familiar way, and how comfortable the small town already seemed. It was no doubt some effect of sunshine, and of the breeze, which always held a hint of salty marsh grass. She had told Mrs Turber she did not relish the coming attention, but now, striding forth, she felt such energy to begin her new life and vocation that she could not wait to join the party. She found Mrs Kent and her two nephews waiting for her in the cool hallway.

'We will watch for one or two carriages to go by and then stroll over at a leisurely pace to the party,' said Agatha, straightening her hat in the hall mirror. It was quietly new, of an expensive glossy dark straw with a moderate circumference and with a wide navy-and-white striped grosgrain ribbon finished with a neat rosette to one side. 'Lady Emily has charged us to be early, but she cannot expect us to be premature.' She gave a last brush to her suit, which was not, to Beatrice's eye, quite as new but was of thick linen, carefully pressed, and bearing fresh strips of ribbon around the cuffs to match the new hat. It was the kind of suit bought to be used for many years – its skirt let in or out, embellishments stitched on or carefully unpicked as fashions changed – and every autumn laid away in a trunk with a sachet of dried orange peel, lavender and cloves to keep out the moths. Her own cotton dress felt insubstantial and girlish by comparison.

'A stuffy marquee and sticky lemonade is hardly the way to spend such a glorious afternoon,' said Daniel. 'I hope we'll be able to creep away.'

'If you attempt to flee, I will be forced to tell your Uncle John that in his absence you proposed the flipping of a coin to decide who should escort us,' said Agatha, pulling on white lace gloves.

'But, Aunt Agatha, that's what you keep Hugh around for,' said Daniel. 'You know he has the better manners.'

'You are such a child,' said Hugh. 'You always complain about going and then you, and Harry Wheaton, are always the last to be dragged away from the champagne tent.'

'I assure you, Miss Nash, that Lady Emily's garden party is always quite lovely and is considered one of the highlights of the summer,' said Agatha. 'And the garden, while impossibly French, offers wonderful coastal views.'

'I hope, Miss Nash, that my aunt has some time allotted for garden viewing and lemonade,' added Hugh. 'Though I fear Lady Emily and she plan to keep you busy with a campaign of introductions.'

'You must each keep one eye on us, boys,' said their aunt. 'When I raise a brow you must come and rescue poor Miss Nash.'

'I'm very fond of garden parties,' said Beatrice. 'People are usually so pleasant out of doors.' The two young men seemed to find this statement amusing. Even Agatha Kent smiled at her.

'The worthies of Rye are much more pleasant out of doors – chiefly because one has more room to manoeuvre away from them,' said Daniel. 'If I were you, I would keep the gates in view at all times and be prepared to run.'

'Well, now that you have demolished any hope Miss Nash might have had of a pleasant afternoon, shall we be getting along?' asked Hugh. 'May I?' He offered Beatrice his arm and they followed Daniel and Agatha out from the cool hall and into the sun-dappled afternoon.

The home of Colonel Wheaton and Lady Emily was not the weathered country seat that Beatrice had expected. Walking through elaborate iron gates, she was presented with an abruptness of red brick: a tall edifice of a house with its edges and principal features all piped, like cake icing, with elaborate white stonework. Two footmen in buttoned jackets and two maids in crisp caps and starched aprons stood sentinel on a smoothly raked gravel forecourt. The forecourt in turn was edged in symmetrical box beds, each clipped to geometric perfection and carpeted with a bright pattern of bedding plants. Severely pollarded lime trees stood in rows along the perimeters of the property.

'What do you think of the Wheaton country cottage?' asked Hugh.

'It is very grand,' said Beatrice, trying to be noncommittal.

'The Colonel has extensive interests in the French brandy business,' said Agatha. 'The house is designed in a thoroughly French style.'

'Heaven forbid that the lines of its beauty be softened and blurred under the pressures of English rain or herbaceous fecundity,' said Daniel.

'There's no need to be droll, Daniel,' said his aunt. 'Lady Emily is allowed her taste.'

But from the way she smiled, Beatrice thought that Agatha Kent was enjoying an unworthy moment of satisfaction that Lady Emily's money and position did not mean she had superiority of taste.

The Wheatons' garden could not be anything but a felicitous scene: the emerald of the lawn, the tightly pitched white marquee made festive with strings of pale blue pennants, the hats, like the heads of summer flowers, nodding above the ladies' linen and cotton dresses. The uniformed servants, a small navy, ferried trays of sandwiches and buckets of ice across a green sea, and the entire scene was sharply outlined by afternoon sun and teasingly ruffled by a light breeze. Beatrice's heart lifted, and she allowed her jaw to let go its determined clench as she smiled.

Some couples were strolling about the stone-walled perimeter of the lawn, but many of the assembled guests had gathered under the slightly steamy heat of the marquee. It was a human condition, Beatrice had often noticed, to hurry under any roof or protective wall, even when the weather was perfect and no danger threatened.

'There you are. We were about to send a search party,' called Lady Emily, who was waving her sunshade from her spot at the edge of the marquee. 'We are all waiting to meet Miss Nash.' With these words, Beatrice felt herself subjected to the bald scrutiny of dozens of faces, all turning in her direction. The buzz of conversation fell a note and then rose in intensity, and she concentrated on trying to keep the fleeting sense of lightness, breathing more slowly, in and out, trying to rise above a small wave of panic that threatened to make her falter. A hand steadied her elbow, and Hugh Grange, frowning, steered her discreetly behind Agatha and Daniel so that they might traverse the swathe of grass between terrace and tent in the protective cover of Agatha's broad back and large, plain sunshade.

'They are not a bad lot,' said Hugh. 'I think you'll like the Headmaster. He always lent me books from his library in the summers. He understands boys very well, and he collects moths.'

'Thank you,' said Beatrice, her throat dry.

'The usual prominent families,' he added. 'I'm afraid they can be quite long-winded about the old family history if you give them the slightest opening.'

'Hugh, we should have a bet as to who manages to communicate the most dazzling ancient connections to Miss Nash,' said Daniel, over his shoulder.

'Daniel, do behave,' said Agatha Kent, moving forward and attempting to embrace Lady Emily without disturbing either of their hats. 'So lovely of you to invite us, dear Emily.'

'Bettina Fothergill is up to something,' said Lady Emily in her abrupt way. 'I don't know what it is yet, but she's cooing like a dove.' She glared across the marquee, and Beatrice tried to follow her glance as unobtrusively as possible.

It was not hard to spot the portly figure of the town's Mayor, who had chosen to wear his chain of office with garden-party flannels. Beatrice assumed the thin woman on his arm must be the much-discussed Mrs Fothergill. She was dressed in a narrow mustard linen suit and was using her free hand to steady an enormous green straw hat covered in red velvet cherries. When she caught sight of Lady Emily and

Agatha Kent staring, she let go of the hat momentarily to offer a smile and a wave that was more a wriggle of the fingers.

'Good heavens, she came as a tree,' said Agatha, waving back.

'Oh, I think she was going for the whole orchard,' said Daniel.

'She brought some nephew or nephew of a cousin with her,' said Lady Emily. They all contemplated the young man in a tight striped blazer who was leaning in to listen to the Mayor speak, an action which seemed unnecessary given the prominent size of the young man's ears. 'Some sort of law clerk; I didn't really pay attention.'

'That is much the best policy,' said Agatha. 'Let's ignore her as long as possible. I really want to introduce Miss Nash to one or two people.'

'Well, here comes our dear Headmaster,' said Lady Emily. 'He is in a hurry to make sure you are just as ordered.' A kind-faced man in crumpled beige linen was carving a determined path between the guests.

'Or maybe he's just after that book with the colour plates that you failed to return to him last summer,' said Daniel, digging Hugh in the ribs.

'Good heavens, you're right,' said Hugh. 'I entirely forgot.'

'If you ladies will excuse us,' said Daniel. 'I had better take my cousin out of harm's way and leave you to your introductions.'

'Headmaster, how delightful to see you in holiday dress,' said Agatha. The Headmaster wore a slightly crushed straw fedora and a cravat tucked into his shirt. He looked, thought Beatrice, exactly like a headmaster on a summer tour of Europe's antiquities. He shifted his shoulders as if feeling the phantom weight of missing academic robes. 'May I introduce Miss Nash?'

'Wonderful of Lady Emily to have arranged for us all to meet in such relaxed circumstances, Miss Nash,' he said, shaking Beatrice's hand. 'One is more at ease outside one's formal setting.'

'I am grateful to you for giving me this opportunity,' said Beatrice. 'I hope to justify your faith in me.'

'Have you met our staff?' asked the Headmaster. He waved a hand towards a small group hovering on the edge of the crowd. A young woman with a lace sunshade and a ruffled silk dress of pink and green panels was chatting to a woman of more indeterminate age, who wore a dark, narrow hat and had added a stiff white collar and cuffs to a dark blouse. An older man in a dusty black jacket was holding forth to a hearty man with a large moustache and striped flannels, strained at the shoulders from a muscular build. 'Mr Dobbins, our most senior master, is mathematics,' said the Headmaster, pointing. 'Mr Dimbly is gymnastics and science, Miss Clauvert is French and Miss Devon is English, history and sewing.'

'I am eager to meet them and to visit the school,' said Beatrice.

'Well, we must arrange something,' said the Headmaster, but he made no move to lead her over to make introductions, and Beatrice found she was not at all in a hurry to join her ill-at-ease colleagues. 'Of course, right now we are in the process of our annual fumigation,' he added.

'What a fine excuse for any circumstance,' said Agatha. 'Headmaster, you are quite the wit this afternoon.'

Under the tent, Beatrice felt a headache tightening its iron band around her brow. She had been introduced to so many people that they had all blurred together. She was asking a servant about the relative merits of the lemonade and the fruit punch, hoping for a brief moment in which no one would ask her another penetrating question about her family or her qualifications.

'I recommend the lemonade,' said a voice, and she turned to find Hugh Grange at her elbow. 'You must be tired of introductions?' he added.

'Everyone has been very kind,' she said. 'But it is a lot of people to remember.'

'How did you find the Headmaster?' asked Hugh.

'We talked about exterminating vermin,' said Beatrice. 'He assured me that they fumigate the school after every term to keep the infestations to an acceptable minimum.'

'I expect that was of great comfort,' said Hugh.

'Not really,' said Beatrice. 'He said Miss Devon would show me how to sew little bags of sulphur into my hems to deter lice.'

'Ah, the realities of modern education,' said Hugh.

'Your cousin was right about the importance of family history in the town,' said Beatrice. 'Some of your neighbours managed to slip in several centuries of family deeds.'

'And did you meet Mrs Fothergill?' he said.

'Mrs Fothergill I will not soon forget,' said Beatrice. 'She quoted Latin at me and then appeared very surprised when I replied. She seems to think I was hired to teach a language I don't know.'

'My understanding is that after Mr Puddlecombe, the upper-grades Latin teacher, left, quite suddenly, the gymnastics teacher, Mr Dimbly, had to fill in, and he's a great chap for football and rope climbing, but I believe he couldn't write a word and will be relieved to have the classics taken away from him.'

'Mrs Fothergill's nephew, a Mr Poot, also speaks Latin, but at least he had the manners not to do so,' she said. 'Mrs Fothergill was at pains to tell Lady Emily how fortunate it will be for both her nephew and Harry Wheaton to have suitable companionship in the neighbourhood.'

'I can't wait to tell Daniel,' said Hugh. 'He will be delighted to know that Bettina Fothergill thinks us delinquent.'

'She is quite the least pleasant woman I have met today,' said Beatrice. 'Despite the fact that she could not seem to keep from smiling.'

'Did you meet Lady Emily's daughter, Eleanor, yet?' asked Hugh. He pointed to where a young woman with a pale, oval face and coils of shimmering fair hair had retired to a wicker chaise under a large tree. She was elaborately attired in a blinding white ensemble of cotton lawn and a tulle-covered hat the size of a cartwheel. Behind her, in deep and cool-looking shade, a severely attired nanny rocked a perambulator so enormous that Beatrice would not have been surprised to find it required a small horse to move it. 'She is married to a German baron,' added Hugh.

'Perhaps you would introduce us,' said Beatrice. 'She is such a confection that I suppose I am a bit unsure of myself. Is she as grand as she is beautiful?'

'If she tries to be, just ask her about the time Daniel and I had to fish her out of the canal as a child,' said Hugh. 'She was always a great scamp, and we make it a point not to let her play the baroness around us.'

The afternoon was going just as planned, but Agatha Kent was beginning to crave one of the large French éclairs that were arranged on an ornate three-tiered stand in the middle of the snowy table piled with silver trays of delicacies. Shiny chocolate glaze dewed with moisture suggesting the chilled cream within, fleshy crusts barely tinted by their brief turn in the oven – Agatha wondered if she might allow herself just one in celebration of how smoothly Miss Nash's introductions had unfolded. It was a satisfaction, as the wife of an important civil servant, to prove one's subtle skills of influence. In a mood of gracious victory, she looked about her for an empty chair at one of the many small wrought-iron tables and, seeing only one, she gathered her skirts with one hand and made her way over to where Bettina Fothergill was seated with her nephew.

'May I sit down with you, dear Bettina?' she asked. 'Only I am in desperate need of some tea.'

Mrs Fothergill, who had three finger sandwiches, two chicken aspics and a separate plate containing a large piece of fruitcake, smiled while dabbing a napkin to her lips. The nephew rose slowly to pull out a chair.

'But of course, you look exhausted,' said Bettina. 'This is my sister's son, Charles Poot. Charles, do run along so that Mrs Kent and I may have a pleasant tête-à-tête.'

'At once,' he said, picking up his plate and almost bowing his waistcoat into his egg sandwich. Agatha disliked him immediately, not for his ears but for his air of oily cooperation.

She could not imagine Daniel or Hugh receiving any such peremptory order from her without a suitably defiant remark.

'A cup of tea and just some plain bread and butter,' said Agatha to the footman. The éclair, she decided with a sigh, would have to be forgone, as to eat one in front of Bettina Fothergill would be a weakness, and Bettina was prone to pounce on weakness like a weasel on a frog.

'Your Miss Nash seems a very pleasant girl,' said the Mayoress. 'Perhaps not of the age and experience that some governors had been expecting,' she added. 'And, if anything, too qualified for our poor little educational efforts?' She continued to exude a smugness that Agatha found almost as nauseating as the green straw hat.

'She is very well qualified and we are lucky to have found her,' said Agatha firmly. 'The Headmaster is quite content in his new appointment.'

'I'm sure he is,' said Bettina and sighed. 'Any whispers of discontent are only that – the merest of whispers.'

'I believe the Headmaster has made an excellent decision,' said Agatha.

'Of course one always desires to stand firmly behind the Headmaster,' said Bettina, gazing with fondness at a cucumber sandwich. 'Though technically you do remember that the governors may exercise a right of approval?'

'So I have been reminded several times this afternoon.' Agatha concentrated on breathing silently in to the limits of her corset. The footman brought her tea, and for once she welcomed the fussing about: the setting down of the elegant porcelain cup and saucer, and the careful aligning of the small plate of bread and butter. 'Is there something I should know, Bettina?'

'I wouldn't presume to say,' said the Mayoress. 'Unlike you and dear Lady Emily, I was not appointed to the Board of Governors.' The school's board was legally required to appoint two female members. In a marvellous sleight of hand, Colonel Wheaton, who chaired the board, had suggested that husbands and wives should not serve together, and then, after Agatha had been confirmed, he had neatly removed himself from the board in favour of his wife, leaving Mayor Fothergill to face the wrath of his own wife. 'Perhaps you should ask Miss Nash to attend the governors' meeting, just in case they wish to examine your choice further,' she added. Then she gathered her skirts, and sacrificing her plate of delicacies for the thrill of the victory, she bid Agatha good day and tottered away across the trodden-down grass.

Eleanor Wheaton's skin was as white as if she had come from a sanitarium, and her dress, viewed from a close angle, was of a quality and subtle sheen that suggested costliness. Her hair was piled in intricate curls, but she carried her head with great ease. She would not have been out of place at a royal garden party, thought Beatrice, and was almost more dressed than even the grandeur of her family home could endure.

'Eleanor, may I present Miss Nash,' said Hugh. 'No doubt you will have heard all about her.'

'How do you do?' said Eleanor, inclining her head before turning to Hugh to add, 'Your cousin has yet to come over and see me. He and Harry are drinking all the champagne, and as you can see, no one has thought fit to bring me any. Fräulein and I are quite parched, are we not,

Fräulein?' She leaned towards the nanny and added, in the loud voice reserved by the English for speaking to foreigners in any part of the world, '*Wir sind* parched, *nicht wahr?*'

'My goodness, your German is appalling,' said Hugh. 'What have you been doing all year?'

'I would tell you, but I may faint at any moment. Do bring Fräulein and me some refreshment, I implore you.'

'I'll be right back,' said Hugh, jogging off towards the marquee. Beatrice wished she had asked for another cup of lemonade, but she did not like to call after him.

'Miss Nash, this is Fräulein Gerta – Gerta, *das ist Miss Nash,*' said Eleanor with the bored air of one used to the flow of smooth and unimportant social niceties.

'*Freut mich, Sie kennenzulernen,*' said Beatrice. The nanny nodded her head and broke into a smile that transformed her from stone to apple-cheeked youthfulness.

'*Ganz meinerseits,*' she replied.

'You speak German?' said Eleanor. Her blue eyes flashed interest at once, and she threw off her air of boredom as she smiled widely. 'Oh my goodness, perhaps you were sent to save me. I have been struggling like the devil to pick it up, but Fräulein speaks no English at all, and it is too exhausting to be always throwing myself across the chasm of understanding.'

'I expect your husband is fluent in both languages?' asked Beatrice.

'Yes, he is, damn him, and he seems to think it should be easy for me to be the same,' said Eleanor. 'Now do sit down here beside me and tell me do you think it at all reasonable for him to accept a summons home and leave me surrounded by a German staff who speak no English?'

'I have often found that necessity does make one pick up languages a little faster,' said Beatrice. She sank cautiously into a canvas deckchair. 'I once had to lease an apartment in Cairo . . .'

'Yes, yes,' said Eleanor, tossing her beautiful head and threatening to dislodge her hat. 'But could he have at least engaged a bilingual nanny or lady's maid? No, Fräulein Gerta and Liesl the maid are from families who have served his family for centuries, and the Baron's family only has one way of doing things.' Here she assumed a slightly deeper voice and wagged a finger at herself. She crossed her eyes while doing so, and Beatrice could not help laughing.

'I hear your husband is young and handsome and that you are both very much in love,' said Beatrice, who had heard the same whispered by several admiring matrons during the afternoon.

'Oh, he is besotted, and I have him twined around this little finger of mine,' said Eleanor. 'But on this one issue he is immovable because his mother insists I cannot be presented at court until I have enough German to answer should their Imperial Majesties stoop to speak to me.' She sighed and kicked off her white, heeled shoes onto the grass. 'With two thousand people circulating in the most complicated of processions, I would be lucky if a footman asks for my wrap.'

'Oh dear,' said Beatrice, trying not to grin.

'And so I am confined to making little signs and pointing like a blind person,' Eleanor complained, leaning down to massage toes encased in white silk stockings.

Beatrice was not quite sure about the analogy, but she lost her train of thought as she saw Hugh coming across the grass, bearing with him not only Daniel but also Harry Wheaton and a footman with many glasses carried on a tray with legs.

'We weren't sure what everyone would want to drink, so we brought everything,' said Harry Wheaton, his face as innocent and unself-conscious as that of a spaniel puppy.

As the footman set the tray table next to Eleanor's chair, Beatrice stood up to make a hasty withdrawal, but Wheaton forestalled her. 'I say, Eleanor, I made an absolute donkey of myself insulting Miss Nash the other day, and I beg you to help me make my apologies.'

'Did you really, Harry?' said his sister. 'Well, you may have to leave immediately, because if Miss Nash is not of a mind to forgive you, I'm afraid I must choose her over you. She is going to teach me German.'

'Really, it was nothing,' said Beatrice. 'But I should find Mrs Kent. If you'll excuse me . . .'

'But we will certainly not excuse you,' said Eleanor. 'We will have my oaf of a brother removed by several footmen. Do pass me some champagne, Daniel.'

'Miss Nash, I really do apologise, most sincerely,' said Wheaton. 'Do stay and have a glass of champagne – or have a glass of lemonade, as I intend to do.' He picked up a glass of lemonade, causing his sister and Daniel to go off into peals of laughter.

'I forgive you, Mr Wheaton,' said Beatrice, 'if only for the sake of your mother, who has been so kind to me, and your sister, who is so charming.'

'I am often so forgiven,' he said. 'I will drink this lemonade in their honour and promise to be a better man hereafter.'

'Good,' said Eleanor. 'Now Beatrice can sit down and we can all be comfortable while Daniel reads us some of his poems.' The footman offered lemonade and champagne, and Beatrice took the lemonade and promised herself it would be the last time.

'I'm an invited guest, not the entertainment,' said Daniel. 'I only show my poems on the most serious of occasions.'

'You used to show me one for a penny,' said Eleanor. 'I have a whole box of ditties tied up with a tartan ribbon from my twelfth birthday.'

'I was less discriminating in those days,' said Daniel. 'Discrimination being less affordable when one is a small boy with no pocket money.'

As the talk ebbed and flowed, Hugh pulled up a deckchair and Daniel sprawled on the grass with no regard for his light flannel trousers. Harry Wheaton perched on the end of his sister's chaise, and there was talk of a picnic expedition to the hop fields and of the new bathing machines at Camber Sands, and then Eleanor was expressing a wish that Beatrice accompany her to bathe, as neither Fräulein nor the maid enjoyed the water and had made such a fuss last time. Beatrice, pleased to be still and cool and among this laughing circle of young people as the shadows lengthened across the lawn, felt for a moment released from care and repeated to herself that it had been a happy decision to come to Rye.

When the time came to leave, Agatha Kent seemed distracted and was still looking about her after she, her nephews and Beatrice had already taken their farewells of Lady Emily. 'There he is,' said Agatha and waved her sunshade quite rudely at the Headmaster, who seemed to be slipping away down a side path.

The Headmaster changed direction and came to say goodbye. 'Lovely afternoon,' he said.

'We have been looking for you everywhere,' said Agatha. 'You have been positively elusive.'

'I have been looking for you, too,' said the Headmaster. 'Quite impossible in the crush, of course.' The small group of guests remaining on the large lawn did not seem to Beatrice to qualify as a crush, and Agatha's pursed lips suggested she thought the same.

'Mrs Fothergill seems to be under the extraordinary impression that Miss Nash should appear at the governors' meeting tomorrow,' said Agatha. 'I am sure she meant no offence to your independence and judgement, Headmaster, but I did suggest it would be the height of rudeness to suggest any debate of your decision in such matters.'

'I appreciate your support, Mrs Kent,' said the Headmaster. He looked uncomfortable around the neck and pulled at his collar. 'I do hope my letter to you, Miss Nash, indicated that a final approval of our Board of Governors was usual.'

'And usually automatic,' added Agatha.

'Quite so,' said the Headmaster. 'And it seems to me that Miss Nash has little to fear from any last-minute candidate.'

'So there is a candidate?' said Agatha.

'Quite sudden and unexpected,' said the Headmaster. 'I assure you I did not suggest nor promote the young man in question, but it has been argued persuasively that should we deny the board a chance to hear from all parties, we may be open to criticism at a later date.'

'Bettina Fothergill's work,' said Agatha.

'Is it that weaselly-looking nephew of hers?' said Daniel. 'He had the audacity to ask me where I purchased my tie and I don't think he meant it as a compliment.'

'That's it,' said Agatha. 'For once you are perspicacious, Daniel.'

'Are you suggesting I am usually a fool?' said Daniel.

'Of course, in the event of an unforeseen decision in the unfavourable direction,' said the Headmaster, smoothly refusing to engage in answering the question, 'I will make myself personally responsible to return Miss Nash to her family entirely unburdened by any travel expenses. So there is no need to worry at all, young lady.' He smiled widely and patted Beatrice on the arm. She fought against the urge to push him to the ground.

Agatha took her other arm and pressed it firmly. 'We shall see you at tomorrow's meeting and will rely on your continued support,' she said. 'I shall be writing notes to some of the other governors, and you can be sure Lady Emily will be doing the same.'

'You can be sure of it,' said Lady Emily. 'We must not tolerate underhanded machinations.'

'Not unless we instigate them, of course,' Beatrice heard Daniel whisper to Hugh. 'We must do something to help Aunt Agatha, Hugh.' She could not help but admire and despair of the family loyalty expressed in his urgent tone, which only highlighted her own lack of any family to stand with her.

'I am sure it is all quite a formality,' the Headmaster was saying, 'but it was not within my power to refuse.'

'I think I would like to go home now,' said Beatrice faintly, the pleasures and potential pleasures of the conjured afternoon falling away like so many blowing ashes. 'Thank you so much for inviting me, Lady Emily.' As she allowed Hugh to lead her away, she gathered up a few thoughts of the lovelier parts of the afternoon and stowed them away in the back of her mind, where they might remind her at some future date that lovely afternoons do not survive the chill of dusk.

CHAPTER SIX

DESPAIR HAD A WAY of making tea taste bad. Beatrice recognised the feeling and knew that the ladies' parlour of the finest coaching inn along the high street was probably not as drab as it appeared to her at this moment. The white wainscoting seemed bright enough, and fresh flowers adorned a low table in front of the fireplace, but the floral upholstery of the chairs made her dizzy, and the sun, lancing in at tall courtyard windows, was painful to her eyes.

A sleepless night counting and re-counting her small stock of money had left her feeling weak. By no creative arrangement or stringent budgeting could she contrive to manage independently on the small allowance under her control. She might have managed abroad, in some small French town perhaps, but her father's family would never advance her the funds to establish herself and she had no intention of humiliating herself by asking. In the dark she had considered writing again to those American friends of her father to whom she had already written, thanking them for their condolences. There had been expressions of concern and support on their part, and perhaps she had been too elliptical in her replies. But in the pale hours of the dawn, she knew she had been clear in her expression of a desire for meaningful work and a productive life. She had all but asked them to find her a position. Only two had found it necessary to reply again, and both carefully worded letters had extolled the virtue of home and reminded her of her father's dying wish to see her safe in the bosom of his family.

She had declined one other teaching offer in favour of Rye. A northern mill town had offered just the productive life, the challenge of public service that she craved, but her heart had failed her at the thought of soot-blackened streets and rows of tenement cottages running across the hills. She had been forced to laugh at her own hypocrisy in choosing seaside Sussex over the surely greater educational impact she might make among the children of factory workers. Now she wondered if she would have time to write again and ask them to reconsider her. If not, she might eke out a few weeks at a friend's home near Brighton, but her chances of finding some other position immediately were not good. She had no romantic notions of becoming a parlour maid or an actress, and she had never had patience with those more literary heroines who solved their problems with a knife or an oncoming train. She would have to write to Marbely Hall at some point and ask to come back.

'Excuse me, miss,' said a serving girl, peering around the door. 'They're ready for you in the Green Banqueting Hall.'

'Thank you,' said Beatrice, rising reluctantly from her chair. She shook out her skirts and smoothed a hand across her hair, looking at her face in the overmantel mirror. She would face the Board of Governors with her very best smile and a forthright presentation of her skills and qualifications. She would not let them see that she knew the answer was already decided. They would pick the man over her, but she would make sure they knew, in their hearts, that she was the better candidate.

Hugh and Daniel were hovering outside the coaching inn, which presented an august Georgian façade to the high street and was the site of many a municipal meeting and festivity. Or rather, as Hugh acknowledged, he was hovering, conspicuous in his anxiety, while Daniel leaned against the inn's front wall, smoking a cheroot and gazing upward in the annoying way he did when he was suddenly struck by some fortunate arrangement of words. Hugh could only hope he would not start pulling out his notebook and a pen when time was so precious.

'He said he'd be here,' said Daniel, still musing. 'I do wish you'd stop fidgeting.'

'And Harry Wheaton is the most reliable man we know,' said Hugh.

'He is most reliable when there's a prank to be played or a girl to be courted,' said Daniel. 'He seemed to regard the removal of Mr Poot as a lark.'

'Well, Poot is sitting in the hallway now, and Miss Nash is already in with the governors,' said Hugh. 'We should go and talk to him ourselves.'

'Poot?' asked Daniel. 'What would we say? "Could you please withdraw so our aunt can beat your aunt?"'

'We have to do something,' said Hugh. While Daniel and Harry had agreed that Bettina Fothergill could not be allowed to usurp both Aunt Agatha and Lady Emily with her machinations, Hugh found himself unusually indignant at the unfairness of Mr Poot snatching away a job from a young woman who so clearly deserved it. As he peered through the inn's open door again to where Mr Poot sat very straight on a wooden settle, looking like a skinny toby jug, he reassured himself that ordinary chivalry demanded action and that his indignation had more to do with Miss Nash being alone in the world than with a pretty face or the intelligence behind her eyes.

'Oh, for goodness' sake, he'll see you,' said Daniel. 'We're trying to be discreet, remember?' Just then an automobile horn gave a loud blast and a large black car swerved to a halt with Wheaton, attired in a voluminous duster and goggles, at the wheel. The chauffeur rode next to him, tight-lipped and gripping the door.

'Am I on time?' called Wheaton. He removed his goggles, wiped his face with a driving scarf, and hopped out of the car. The chauffeur slid over to take the wheel. 'We dropped off my mother earlier and I took the old car for a spin. Still getting the hang of it. Round the corners it's like trying to steer a cow.'

'Ridden many cows?' asked Daniel.

'A few,' said Wheaton. 'At least, that's what they tell me. I can't say I remember clearly.'

'We are too late,' said Hugh. 'Miss Nash is already being interviewed, and they may send for Poot at any time.'

'Well, we'd better get to work,' said Wheaton. 'Daniel and I will lure Poot into the taproom while you slip your aunt a note and ask her to stall as long as possible.'

Hugh hung back as they entered the inn's lobby and asked a porter to bring him a pen and paper. He took a seat at a small table in a window nook and busied himself with turning over the pages of an old issue of the *Racing Times*. Trying to appear absorbed in tables of results from early spring's races and advertisements for stud services and worm treatments, he kept a keen ear on Wheaton's conversation.

'Just telling my friend Daniel here that this town is sorely lacking in congenial chaps on whom one can rely for a companionable talk.'

'I tell him he's too fussy about where he gathers,' said Daniel, shaking Poot by the hand.

'I don't like rubbing up against all and sundry,' said Wheaton. 'I prefer a quiet room and a landlord who knows his regulars. Don't you agree, Pooty, old boy?'

'It's just Poot,' said Poot.

'Have you met Old Jones, the landlord here?' asked Wheaton, stuffing his driving gloves into his coat pocket and shouldering off the voluminous garment. A footman stepped smoothly up to take it from him. Wheaton was well known in half the public houses in town, and while most had had occasion to escort him off the premises for some wild act stemming from drunkenness, they never failed to welcome him with a hopeful deference.

'I have not had occasion—' began Poot. He looked ready to deny any desire to frequent public houses, but Wheaton interrupted.

'What luck,' he said. 'Daniel and I were just stopping in now to ask Jones about hosting a small supper for a few chaps. Come with us and I'll introduce you.'

'Oh, I couldn't, I'm waiting to see the school governors,' said Poot, but Hugh saw his eyes flicker towards the taproom.

'That could take hours, knowing my mother,' said Wheaton. He slapped Poot heartily on the back. 'You come along with us and we'll ask Old Jones to give us the nod when they need you upstairs.'

'When Harry Wheaton introduces you, you're all set in this town,' said Daniel, steering him by the arm now. 'It's a good thing we came along.'

As they disappeared into the taproom, Hugh looked around for someone to take up his note. It took a few moments to find a man and to give him instructions and fish out a sixpence to thank him. When the note was safely on its way upstairs, Hugh shuffled slowly past the taproom door and glanced in to see Mr Jones, the landlord, lead a toast to the King, and a nervous Mr Poot, earlobes scarlet, drink down his glass in one swallow. His eyes closed as if in prayer, but his face did not twist or pucker as might be usual in someone unused to strong drink. Of the four men gathered around the bar, only Daniel gave a smothered cough as the dram went down. At some signal from Wheaton, the landlord refilled the glasses, filling Mr Poot's to the brim, and proclaimed a loud welcome to Master Wheaton's new young friend. Hugh walked away satisfied, wondering only how he might explain to Aunt Agatha why Daniel would need to miss lunch and lie down all afternoon.

In the Green Banqueting Hall, Agatha Kent watched hopelessly as Beatrice Nash gave a good account of her qualifications, her extensive travels and her experience to a table filled with men who mostly did not care. The Headmaster had the grace to look uncomfortable, making copious notes on a paper and fiddling with his collar. The Vicar looked earnestly pious, but his eyelids were drowsy and he was obviously smiling not at Miss Nash but at a mental picture of his lunch to come. Emily Wheaton was just now glaring at Mr Satchell, the shipowner, who was whispering to Farmer Bowen. The farmer, who owned large acreage, from sheep pasture on the marsh to hop fields towards the Kent border, wore his best wool suit and polished boots, and as usual this time of year, he was at the meeting to make sure the school would remain closed for the full period of the hop harvest and otherwise to vote as the Mayor wished him to do. Mr Satchell was very interested in the educational efforts of the school, looking as he was for a steady supply of young clerks for his maritime warehouses. He could usually be persuaded to support new efforts and ideas. But he was immune to the social inducements of Emily Wheaton, so his support for Beatrice was uncertain. Mr Arnold Pike was Arty Pike's uncle. He was a tight-fisted man and suspicious of all change, as if it were somehow designed to strip him of his worldly position. Agatha thought this might be the result of a pricking conscience. He had benefited from the disinheritance of his older brother, Cedric, because their Chapel father had not approved of Cedric's weakness for the occasional tipple. Now Cedric worked in the ironmongery on a store clerk's salary and could not reliably afford his son's school fees. Agatha's and John's little scholarships were supposed to be confidential, but sometimes she thought Arnold Pike glared at her with even more suspicion than usual.

'I believe Miss Nash is not only fully qualified to teach Latin but has even had some work of Latin translation published?' said Agatha, trying to encourage the room at large. She had received a note from Hugh asking her to extend the interview as long as possible, but the frowns around the table did not inspire confidence.

'Just a couple of short Horace poems published in a literary magazine in California,' said Beatrice. 'And I also created a third poem in a similar style as a commentary on the original content and to display its connections to events of our own times,' she added.

'Whoever heard of making up new Latin on top of what already exists!' said Mr Satchell, looking comically alarmed. 'I had enough old Latin beaten into me without trying to expand the stuff.' He stuck an elbow in Farmer Bowen's ribs, and they both chuckled.

'I am sure Miss Nash understands what an effort it is to get our young men to memorise the usual passages of trans-lation,' said the Headmaster. 'We did terribly in last year's scholarship exams, and so we must be sure not to waste a moment trying anything too innovative this coming year.'

'*Repetitio est mater studiorum*,' said the Vicar, who could not resist speaking Latin in the deep tone that he used for projecting sermons to the farthest reaches of St Mary's Church.

'Hear, hear,' said Farmer Bowen, to cover the fact that he had no Latin whatsoever.

'I absolutely agree that repetition is the mother of all studies,' said Beatrice Nash in a firm tone. 'But I do find that the more ways one can vary the necessary practice, the more one can commit to memory not just the text but the story and the meaning.'

'What we need is a master who'll not spare the rod,' said Mr Pike. 'These boys must forget stories and games and bend their backs into hard work if they're to acquire a respectable trade.'

'Well spoken, Mr Pike,' said the Mayor.

'I'm sure Miss Nash is more than able to wield a cane to suitable effect,' said Lady Emily. 'Do you play tennis, Miss Nash?'

'Tennis?' asked Beatrice. She looked bewildered, and Agatha sighed. She was used to the very different paths of logic by which her fellow board members pursued their thoughts, but she realised now that to an outsider the exchange must seem like a chapter from *Alice in Wonderland*.

'It's all in the wrist,' said Lady Emily.

'I do all the serious caning myself,' said the Headmaster. 'I find it adds to the gravity to have the offending child take the long walk to my office. They are usually quite cowed by the time they see me.'

'I understand that you would also like to increase proficiency in Euclidian geometry?' asked Beatrice. 'I have pursued advanced studies in both geometry and the newest algebraic theories.' They looked at her as if she had offered to demonstrate fire-eating. It seemed to Agatha that Beatrice now gave up the fight. Her shoulders seemed to slump, and she folded her hands in her lap.

'We are delighted in all your proficiencies,' said Agatha. 'I believe we can let Miss Nash escape now?'

They agreed, and as Beatrice left the room, Agatha looked over at Emily Wheaton, who was rigid with fury but who gave a small shake of the head. Agatha feared they were defeated.

'Could we ask Mr Poot to come in now?' said the Headmaster to the girl who was holding the door for Beatrice.

'If my wife understood mathematics, maybe she'd keep tighter accounts and not be asking me for dress money every year,' said Mr Pike.

'Perish the thought, man,' said Mr Satchell. 'I'd rather show my books to the excise man.'

Mr Poot sat very stiff on the upright chair and fixed his gaze, carefully it seemed, on the Mayor's moving lips.

'Not because he's my nephew, of course,' the Mayor concluded after a long and enthusiastic summing-up of Mr Poot's career. In the Mayor's telling, the man was something of a legend, thought Agatha. 'But we would also be getting the benefit of his legal experience, and I believe he would be a figure our boys could look up to.'

'We have girls as well, Mr Fothergill,' said Agatha.

'One or two, but they do not count in this case,' said the Mayor. 'They cannot aspire to a legal career, whereas we may have several future clerks among our boys.'

'Mr Poot, may we enquire further about your wish to exchange the law for teaching?' asked Lady Emily. 'What propels you into academia?'

The young man swivelled his head towards her voice and opened his mouth to reply, but his head appeared to continue to revolve past her, and as slowly as in a dream, Mr Poot toppled off his chair and lay in an inert heap on the carpet.

'Well, I imagine that had something to do with it,' said Agatha.

With neither the heart to hope nor the energy to repack her possessions, Beatrice Nash sat with a book open on her lap. She had, however, forgotten her reading and was instead engaged in the important task of staring at a small brown spider which was constructing a lopsided web in the lower corner of the cottage's front window. The spider seemed to lose its footing often and would drop, hanging from its trailing silk and tangling the lines, like an old lady dropping stitches in her knitting. Beatrice wondered how far the world extended for the spider. Did it have a warm spot in the garden to soak up the sun, or was its life circumscribed by the rough oak window frame and a small, dark hole in the painted sill? If it were accidentally dropped into a trunk and transported by ship to the wilds of South America, would it notice or would it just find another sill, another hole, and would the flicking tongue of a predatory lizard be no more a threat than Abigail's broom? Wishing to expand the spider's options in life, she caught up a portion of web and spider on the edge of her book and opened the stiff iron catch of the window to shake him out onto the street.

Shouted calls and the scrape of a horse's shoe on the cobbles made her lean out to look down the steep hill. A farm cart was coming up the narrow street, the straining horse coaxed not just by the farmer driving but by a boy walking at its head while other people pushed from behind. The cart contained a stack of objects wrapped and roped to such a dizzying height that it looked like some strange circus wagon. On top of the heap she could see Daniel, standing like a charioteer, whistling a jaunty martial tune and twirling a broad straw hat.

'You're not actually helping,' came a voice, the narrow houses amplifying and projecting the sound towards her. She saw it was Hugh pushing behind the nearside back wheel.

'I'm directing the triumphant approach,' said Daniel. 'One more push up the middle there, sir.' The farmer gave a crack of his whip, and the cart lurched forward, the load shifting dangerously backwards and left. Daniel whooped but grabbed for a rope to steady himself, and the boy at the horse's head had to step nimbly aside as horse and wooden shafts thrust forward.

'Do be careful,' said Hugh. 'I said we should have done it in two loads.'

'Where's the triumph in that?' said Daniel. 'This is an arrival!'

'This is a spectacle,' said Hugh, raising his hat to three ladies who had wedged themselves into a doorway in fear.

The spectacle was increased by the blast of a car horn as Agatha Kent's car made the turn at the top of the lane and nosed down to the cottage. The horse gave a loud whinny and backed slightly before being wrestled to a stop. The car parked directly outside Beatrice's window and revealed Agatha Kent, sitting amid a pile of brown-paper parcels and a bouquet of roses. Jenny the maid was squashed into the rumble seat clutching a quantity of mops and brooms, and from his perch on the running board, an aproned shop boy sprang down to haul a huge basket from the front seat. Agatha waved as Smith ran around the car to open her door, and Beatrice experienced a momentary desire to slam the window and flee into the back alley as she realised the spectacle was coming to her door.

'We are come with all the spoils of victory,' said Agatha, speaking through the window. She waved Jenny and the shop boy towards the front door, adding, 'Do let's get inside before we disturb all the neighbours.'

'I don't understand,' said Beatrice.

'The position is yours, my dear,' said Agatha.

'But I thought . . .' Beatrice began.

'A mere formality, as I had supposed,' said Agatha. 'Now, Hugh, do have them take great care with those bookcases. They were my mother's.'

Beatrice could only stand back, in shock, as the procession came into the tiny parlour: first Abigail carrying the shop basket, then Jenny and her mops, the farmer and his boy carrying a bookcase, and Agatha, ducking her hat under the doorframe and filling the room with the scent of pink roses.

'Is it true?' asked Beatrice. 'I thought for sure Mr Poot would be chosen.'

'Mr Poot proved himself an – an unsteady candidate, shall we say,' said Daniel, coming into the crowded space carrying a stiff-backed chair.

'We shall not,' said Agatha in a reproving tone. 'Do go through to the kitchen, Jenny, and get those few things put away. The bookcases either side of the fireplace, I think, don't you, Miss Nash? Oh, and these are for you, from the garden. Do you have a vase?'

CHAPTER SEVEN

HER BICYCLE HAD REACHED a speed at which its wheels seemed to spin without effort. The dirt road thrummed beneath her, and a breeze of her own making refreshed her face and kept her cool even as she pumped her legs faster, boots pressed to the hard rubber pedals. Out here on the marsh, there seemed to be no other person in the world, only the flutter of white butterflies among the nodding meadowsweet and tall grasses that edged the green and weedy ditches. The very day seemed to dance within her, and Beatrice Nash hitched her blue serge skirts higher and let out a whoop of joy to have the whole day to herself.

To be established, for a week now, in a freshly scrubbed cottage, to be in possession of paying work, and to have found congenial acquaintances while being under no one's direction seemed to Beatrice fortunate indeed. Even when school began, she thought, there would be both the

satisfaction of noble vocation and evenings free for reading and writing. And today she was a real writer. Her book
was on its way to Mr Caraway, her father's publisher, and
she rode out of town with all the confidence that comes to
a writer from having wrapped a finished work in several
sheets of stout brown paper, secured it with strong twine
and red sealing wax, and handed it in to the man in the
Post Office.

On such a fair day, the summer bank holiday, Beatrice
was inclined to be generous even towards the dark shadow
of Mrs Turber. That very morning there had been a purse-
lipped negotiation over the beef sandwich now in Beatrice's
bicycle basket. It was Mrs Turber's routine, and apparently
much praised by the prior lodger, to provide a substantial
noontime dinner and a cold supper at night. Evening dinner
was offered only on Saturday nights and a glass of wine
provided along with the best china. It was hardly decent,
she said, to expect her to provide portable cold lunches,
nor would a lady of Mrs Turber's standing be caught eating
such a lunch alone along a public road somewhere. Beatrice
had pleaded summer weather and asked for a simple plate
of dinner to be reheated and served on a tray in the
evenings. Mrs Turber had grudgingly called for Abigail to
make the sandwich, but she'd continued to sniff her disapproval, and only a gleam in the eye betrayed a possible
satisfaction that a widow could be forgiven for pocketing
some small savings from this arrangement. Breathing the
fresh air of the fields and basking in the sun, Beatrice
laughed aloud and vowed to treat the widow with such
resolute and kindly respect that her landlady's crusty air of
suffering must eventually give way.

She followed the ribbons of country lanes across vast fields of corn and rye, through coppiced woods, and down the brief streets of thatch-roofed hamlets. She lost track of time, and the sun was over her shoulder before she thought to take stock of her location. Coasting to a stop at a crossroads, she looked about to fix her direction. Without the clatter of her wheels, the world seemed to fall into silence. It was so still, she could hear the slight rustle of dry corn in the field and the lumbering buzz of a fat bee somewhere on the far side of a thorny hedge. No voice or sound of human occupation broke across the sleeping fields. She had travelled further than she had meant, but climbing onto the lower rungs of a five-bar gate, she looked across the marsh and was pleased to see the very top of Rye's hill, just the church tower and a couple of rooftops, peeking above the plain. The coast lay to her south, and the curving bluff of the Sussex Downs formed a continuous wall to the north. Above her head the sky was clear of clouds and seemed to enclose the marsh in a protective blue bowl. There was, she reasoned, no way to be lost. She would eat her picnic and then just meander home, keeping always to the west, until she found herself on familiar pathways.

As she ate, and drank from a glass bottle of water that was still cold to the touch, Beatrice reflected that Mrs Turber's fare might be meagre but that, like all food, it was greatly improved by being eaten outdoors. Fleeting images of other picnics asked to be remembered, and she held them in trembling stillness, waiting for the sudden stab, like that of a toothache, which too often came from remembering her father. No clutch of pain came and so she allowed, tentatively, the memory of freshly caught fish cooked on an apparatus of sticks by a large bonfire on a California beach, her father and two other professors, poking the fish with their knives and telling stories as if they were rough backwoodsmen rather than soft-handed academics with gracious front porches on a leafy campus and tenure. Their wives unpacked pies from towel-lined baskets and passed cold flagons of birch beer and lemonade, and she, next to her father, her back tucked against a warm boulder, was free to listen and to turn her face alternately from the warmth of the fire to the dark, eternal crashing of the ocean surf.

A smaller picnic came to her – just the two of them and a slow walk away from the musk of the sickroom, up a grassy avenue of giant elms like a green cathedral to a stile looking over a valley of neat hedged fields. She had asked the kitchen for two soft bread rolls and hot chicken soup, in one of Lord Marbely's newfangled Thermos flasks, and had slipped into his study to fill her father's hip flask with brandy. She remembered a childlike urge to get her father out of the house, away from the dour private nurse. The walk had been painfully slow, her father's breathing laboured and her own urgency becoming a frustration. She remembered a sudden feeling of anger towards him, as if it were his fault that the sun and breeze did not restore him, and a swift shame in the recognition of her own selfish desire not to have to endure his decline.

They settled on the step of the stile, and her father sipped soup, laced with brandy, from a metal cup held in shaky hands. He pronounced it nectar though he could not drink more than half a cup, and she finished it while he looked at the vale below with the unblinking stare of a statue. She grew frightened and laid a hand on his to call him back to her.

'Father?' He responded with a wavering smile and lifted his arm with difficulty to wave at the view as he quoted,

> Happy the man, whose wish and care
> A few paternal acres bound,
> Content to breathe his native air,
> In his own ground.

It had been their game and a favourite parlour trick since her early childhood for him to startle her with lines of poetry and demand citation. She could remember many social evenings where she had been suddenly called upon and much fussed over by ladies who thought her a clever little monkey.

'Alexander Pope, "Ode to Solitude",' she said quietly. She knew they were both seeing the poem in their heads. Neither of them quoted from the final stanza: 'thus unlamented let me die . . .'

'Of course he quite borrowed the thought from old Horace,' her father said, and it was then that she sank to her knees and hid her tearful face in his lap.

Had her father been Catholic, she was quite sure he would have critiqued the priest during the last rites. He had left with his solicitors a list of hymns and readings for his funeral. However, the list was simply obscure lines from each, and there was a note to 'ask Beatrice'. She smiled to remember Aunt Marbely's growing apoplexy as the selections, each piece more unsuitable than the last, were slowly revealed. She stood up and shook out her napkin, determined not to spoil such a lovely day with angry tears. As she collected her bicycle, the thought came, unbidden, that she might entertain Agatha and her nephews with this story of her father's last instructions. That Beatrice Nash should have new friends with which to share such amusing anecdotes was such a novel idea that she laughed aloud and startled a rabbit from the hedge.

An hour or more later, she had circled back to the very same crossroads. She could see the gate and the dent in the grass where she had sat to enjoy her picnic. She was tired now and thirsty from Mrs Turber's salty beef. The marsh, so flat and open to the horizon, had transformed itself into an impenetrable maze of crooked lanes and dykes with no bridges. In the fields, sheep shaved the grass with their black lips and looked at her with sly eyes. She could now understand how smugglers in centuries past had managed to elude the excise men over this seemingly simple land-scape. Taking a deep breath to quell a rush of anxiety, Beatrice decided not to force her way west but to ride north, towards the bluffs where she remembered the canal and its road, built to defeat Napoleon, which would take her home to Rye. Hugh had told her about the canal, and as she remembered sensible Hugh, she took heart and set off once again with renewed determination.

Fear is a great spur to endeavour, and when Beatrice at last slowed her pace, she had covered some miles and the canal and the main road were just before her, the dark line of trees and cliff welcome after the flat heat of the marsh. Unfortunately, the slackening of velocity revealed a trem-bling in her exhausted limbs. Just before the junction where the lane crossed a small bridge to meet the main road, the bicycle gave a large wobble side to side and then, with the front wheel catching on the dry, rutted surface, it tumbled Beatrice sideways into a bramble-filled ditch, catching her right ankle a severe blow as it fell on top of her.

She lay very still, thinking only that the ditch felt dry and that this was a blessing. The herbal scents of crushed weeds and the woody smell of warm blackberry brambles were thick around her head, and the sunlight was pleasantly fractured and dappled by the canopy of a tree. Rubbing at a small trickle of blood on her neck from a bramble scratch, she searched her pocket, glad once more to be carrying one of her father's sensible handkerchiefs in place of the cambric scraps usually favoured by young ladies. A wood pigeon, always the cello in the orchestra of birdsong, gave out its low double coo from the shade. But for the throb, like a beat from a large drum, which began to vibrate in her right ankle, she thought it would have been very pleasant just to lie there.

Hugh was conscious of the need to keep the horse and trap going at a smart pace if he and his aunt were to reach their final visit and be back for tea. Yet at the same time, his aunt was in some fear of breaking the fresh eggs in their flannel-lined basket and of shaking the milk custard and the jellied beef tea into a puddled mess in their crocks, so he was fully occupied in picking the smoothest parts of the unmade road and in keeping the horse steady through a firm but gentle pressure on the reins. The trip might have been smoother and swifter if they had taken the car, but his aunt felt strongly that sick visiting was not the occasion for ostentation and that she would not remind her poor but proud neighbours of their charity status by sweeping in with motorcar and finery. Indeed, she wore a very plain dress and a beige linen driving duster, and her hat, which she kept for such visiting, was of plain straw and as modest in dimension as Cook's Sunday hat. Hugh wore a more formal suit, as befitted a representative of the medical profession. He had already visited today's patients with Dr Lawton and had been charged with following up on an informal basis as he accompanied his aunt on her rounds. As they bowled briskly around one of the few slight turns of the Military Canal road, his eye caught sight of a female waving a large hand-kerchief from a roadside bench. He was poised to wave back as they drove by when his aunt startled him.

'Pull up, Hugh, pull up,' she said, tugging at his arm in a way that caused him to jerk at the horse's mouth and set the horse swerving towards the nearside ditch. Hauling the reins back, Hugh fought to draw the trap to a stop without causing the horse to plunge and rear.

'It's Beatrice Nash,' his aunt exclaimed. 'I think she's in distress.'

Hugh handed over the reins and leaped down to the road, heedless of the dust. As he hurried towards the bench, he found himself praying that Beatrice had not been attacked on the road. She was dishevelled and scratched, with blood on her neck and a large bruise on her arm. Her hair was tangled with thorns, and her skirt, he could see as he came close, was dark-stained and torn about the hem.

'Miss Nash?' Further enquiry stuck in his throat.

'I fell off my bicycle,' she said. 'Rather a nasty tumble into a ditch.'

Hugh was careful to hide his relief. 'Are you hurt?' he asked. Bones and blood he could bind up.

'My ankle,' she said. 'I don't think it's broken, but it took a blow. I was afraid if I took off my boot I would not be able to get it on again.' She smiled, but her face was pale and he had an urge to gather her up like a bird with a broken wing.

'I'm going to carry you to the trap,' he said. 'And once we have you settled, the boot needs to come off.'

'I think I can hobble,' she said, looking alarmed at his offer.

'I think not, given that the ankle is not yet examined,' he said. Speaking with authority came easily to him in the cottages of farm labourers, but not so smoothly in the face of this young woman's sceptical gaze. 'Now do be sensible,' he begged.

As he hesitated, looking for the most efficient way to thrust an arm under her legs and another around her waist, she wrapped her skirt more closely about her legs, to subdue its volume, and cleared her throat. 'I am not the tiniest of women to carry,' she said.

'And I am not the world's strongest man,' he said. 'But I think I can manage to stagger a few yards.' With that he bent at the knees and gathered her up. The ribbing of her stays pressed into his flesh, and he could feel her back warm against his arm. She was not heavy as long as he pressed her close. He could feel her arms around his neck and smell the faint odour of soap under the more vivid scent of dirt and wildflowers. He resisted an unlikely urge to drop his head to her hair.

'My goodness, what on earth happened?' said his aunt as they approached the trap.

'Hurt an ankle,' said Hugh. His aunt gave him a sharp look, and he might have blushed, but he was fully engaged in trying to figure out how to help Beatrice into the rear bench seat of a trap that had never looked higher off the ground. It required at least two good feet to step up. 'Hold the horse steady, please.'

'However will we manage?' asked Beatrice. 'I think you'd better put me down.'

'No, no,' said Hugh. 'Just be ready with your left foot. I'm going to step up and sort of launch you upwards.' He stared with grim focus at the small, smooth iron step, no bigger than a child's foot, which protruded from the rear of the trap, and tried not to think of them both falling hard into the road should the horse move at the wrong moment.

'It is at times like these that one regrets not owning a landau,' said Agatha. 'Do be careful, Hugh.'

'Yes, do be careful, Hugh,' said Beatrice, and she was laughing, and Hugh was so delighted to hear her call him by his name that he almost lost his footing as he made the upward leap. In a rush of petticoats and a small squeak of pain, Beatrice was deposited on the hard bench, clutching for the railing as Hugh fell away and managed to land without twisting an ankle himself.

'I think we should push on to Little Hollow and get some cold spring water on that foot,' said Agatha, looking back from the front seat. 'Does it hurt much?'

'I'm not sure that's a good idea,' said Hugh, who was now lashing the twisted bicycle to the rear of the trap with a spare leading rope. 'They don't welcome strangers.'

'On the contrary, Hugh,' his aunt said. 'I believe it would be taken as a sign of trust if we ask for help. This is our opportunity to show Maria Stokes that we value her knowledge.'

'But do you wish to shock Miss Nash with such an encounter?' asked Hugh.

'Miss Nash is a well-travelled and stout-hearted woman and will not go into hysterics over meeting a few Gypsies,' said his aunt, but Hugh noticed, climbing up to take the reins, she eyed Beatrice with care for any sign of distaste.

'No, indeed,' said Beatrice. She looked a little concerned, but not as much as he'd feared. Either she was an exceptional young woman or she had faith in his aunt's good judgement.

'On Wednesdays I do my sick visiting,' said Agatha as the trap began to move again. 'Dr Lawton likes me to stop in quietly on some of his more delicate or difficult patients.'

'He's saving them from the Ladies' Church Auxiliary,' said Hugh. 'He told me so quite plainly.'

'It's true that some cases are too delicate to receive the full delegation of ladies,' said Agatha. 'But they do good work and are not to be mocked, Hugh.'

'Last summer, Mrs Fothergill gave her prune jam to a dysentery patient and nearly killed him,' Hugh said with a laugh.

'It might have been the bedside lecture rather than the jam,' said Agatha in an equable tone. 'But without such visits, many a sickly child would go without beef tea and milk pudding.'

'My aunt is ever the diplomat,' said Hugh. 'When she knows you better she will tell you tales to stand your hair on end.'

'Dr Lawton has been visiting old Maria Stokes for several years,' said Agatha. 'She is considered a healer among Romanies in the county, and Dr Lawton sometimes asks me to bring her supplies. They don't trust most people.'

'Dr Lawton is the only doctor for miles who will come to them,' said Hugh. 'And none of the other ladies would stoop to visit.' The small clan of Romanies showed up reliably every summer to camp in Little Hollow and work the various harvests, beginning with strawberries and ending with the hops. Then they left as quietly as they came, and Hugh had often wondered why no one seemed to know what paths they took or to what distant parts they travelled.

'The farmers could not do without their help,' said Agatha. 'But most of the town treats them like thieves and vagabonds.'

'You do not think them thieves?' asked Beatrice.

'Dr Lawton jokes that the Stokeses' annual arrival is the start of the poaching season for locals,' said Hugh. 'He says when they start blaming a Gypsy you can be sure they have a rabbit stuffed down each trouser leg.'

'Hugh!' said Agatha. 'There's no need to be crude.'

'Sorry,' said Hugh.

'The truth is that I would not leave my silver lying about when any stranger comes selling heather at the back door,' said Agatha. 'But they are no less Christian than Bettina Fothergill, and Maria Stokes is a particularly impressive woman. Were she not a Romany she would have made a fine district nurse.'

Little Hollow was well hidden from the road by a slight fold in the cliffs from which the road turned away. Beatrice noticed that Hugh had some difficulty finding the narrow dirt path and coaxing the nervous horse between thick trees and· undergrowth. In a small clearing, two lean dogs emerged barking from under a dark wooden caravan with a black tar roof. A shaggy horse tethered to a long rope looked sideways from one large eye but did not bother to take his mouth from the long grass. The old woman sitting on the caravan steps was as wizened as a dried apple and, though the day was hot, was wrapped in several shawls. Yet her hands were swiftly stripping lavender buds from their stalks into her apron while her eyes, squinting from the smoke of a black pipe, met Beatrice's with a piercing stare. Nearby, an iron pot sat on a tripod above a small, smoky fire and a small child slept on a straw pallet under a primitive tent of canvas draped over bent tree branches. Further down the path, a glimpse of another caravan roof and the smoke of another fire indicated others were nearby.

Calling the dogs to heel by some strange word, the old woman carefully shook the contents of her apron into a basket and stepped forward to meet them as Hugh helped his aunt down from the trap.

'Good day, Mrs Stokes,' said Agatha. 'How is the poor child?'

'Middlin' fair,' said Mrs Stokes. She looked pointedly up at Beatrice.

'Glad to hear it,' said Agatha. 'I have brought you some of my cook's best junket and some beef jelly.' Mrs Stokes said nothing but continued to stare at Beatrice in silence.

'We rescued our young friend, Miss Nash, along our way,' Agatha continued. Beatrice thought she detected a note of uncertainty in Agatha's voice, as if she were conscious that bringing Beatrice might undo some delicate relationship. 'She fell off a bicycle and banged her ankle quite severely.'

'We would be grateful for your assistance,' said Hugh. 'I want to get the swelling down and we are far from home.'

'Best be setting her down then,' said Mrs Stokes. She pointed at a fallen log set beside the caravan. It was covered with a thin cotton rag rug, the colours almost washed and beaten out of it. 'I'll have the boy see to the horse.' With that she set off towards her caravan without a backward glance. Agatha was left to hoist the baskets of food, and Beatrice had to submit once again to the less than dignified operation of being lifted down from the trap and carried by Hugh.

The ankle's throb had merged into a continuous ache, and Beatrice felt her boot like a vice squeezing at the leg. She sat down and bent to undo the long rows of laces, but her ankle was so swollen that the pressure of her fingers on the tight knot made her flinch.

'It hurts,' she whispered.

'The boot needs to come off,' said Hugh. 'Aunt Agatha, hold her comfortably please and I'll do it.' Agatha sat on the log beside her, and Beatrice felt the pressure of her enfolding arms.

'I've got you,' she said. As Beatrice turned her face, like a child, into Agatha's broad bosom, she could not hold back a sudden welling of tears. She could only hope they would think it from the pain and not the exquisite and almost forgotten sensation of being held. It had been so long since her father's last embrace, reduced to a tentative stroking of her hair, his hands papery and blue-veined. In the months since his death, she now understood, she had enjoyed no human touch beyond the occasional shaking of gloved hands.

Agatha supported her while Hugh, with no thought for his clothes, sat cross-legged on the ground and took her foot gently across his lap, stripping off his driving gloves to work the stubborn leather laces through their tiny brass grommets. Beatrice felt pain and then relief as, inch by inch, the boot released its grip from her flesh.

'I'm going to manipulate the foot now to make sure it is not broken,' said Hugh. His voice was low and kind. She could feel his warm fingers through her thin lisle stockings, pressing gently as he moved her foot slowly in multiple directions. 'I don't think it's broken.'

'We'll be needing to get that stocking off,' said Maria Stokes, coming back with a boy who carried two large buckets of water on a yoke as if they weighed nothing. The lean dogs gave him a raucous welcome, and Beatrice recognised, with some shock, that it was Snout, the boy she was to tutor. He seemed not at all pleased to see her. He set down the buckets hard enough to make the water slop.

'I'll want to look at the bruise before we bind it up,' said Hugh.

'I'm sure you will,' said Maria Stokes in a way that made young Snout grin and Hugh Grange turn red.

'Well, perhaps if Snout will see to the horse, I should check on the child,' said Hugh. He handed the boy a coin, and Snout whistled to the dogs and slopped away to the trap with one of the buckets.

Beatrice soaked her foot in the cold spring water and drank strong, hot tea out of a porcelain cup and saucer which, though of florid design, were edged thickly with gold and obviously costly. Maria Stokes preferred to drink from a large tin mug she kept at her belt. When the tea was done, the ankle was examined in Maria Stokes's rough hands and pronounced to be only badly bruised.

'I got a salve for that if 'ee care to take it,' she said.

'Oh, I'm sure . . .' began Beatrice.

'That would be most kind,' said Hugh, as he returned to them and peered at the ankle from a respectable distance. 'Mrs Stokes is famous for her remedies.' And so Maria Stokes produced from her caravan a small wax-sealed jar of a thick, pine-scented salve, spread it liberally on Beatrice's rapidly darkening bruise, and covered it in tidy fashion with rough strips of linen bandage.

'It's quite pungent,' said Hugh, who peered with a frown of professional interest at Maria's ministrations. 'Do I smell rosemary?'

'Maybe you do,' said Maria. 'Be sure to use it dawn and dusk,' she added to Beatrice.

'For how long?' asked Beatrice.

'When the jar be empty you'd best stop,' said Maria. 'And it be good luck to return the jar wi' something in it.'

'Thank you,' said Beatrice.

'How d'you find the babe?' Maria asked Hugh.

'Much improved,' he said. 'The lungs sound quite clear now. I think with rest and careful diet he'll be running around in a week.'

'Thank 'ee,' she said. 'I'm afeared of nothing except when the children get the fever in the lungs, and then I go all to pieces with worry. Tell the doctor I'm grateful he came out.'

'I will.'

'And thank 'ee, ma'am, for coming,' she added, pressing Agatha's hands. 'Precious few ladies would put themselves out for a child o' ours, and us don't forget.'

'We must thank you for helping our young friend,' said Agatha.

'The boy can go back with you and take the machine to his father if you like, miss,' said Maria.

'Oh, I'm sure it's too much bother,' said Beatrice, in a hasty manner she hoped would not betray her reluctance.

'No trouble, miss,' said Snout. 'Bicycle is going to need some hammering out and a new chain.'

'Save 'im a long walk if you've no objection to my great-grandson on your step,' added Mrs Stokes.

'That's settled then,' said Agatha smoothly. 'Mr Sidley is the very best in all mechanical repairs.'

The rooftops of Rye were ahead of them, the sun indicating the lateness of the afternoon, and Beatrice's head nodding with exhaustion when Hugh stopped the trap in a small turning before the river. Snout hopped down from his precarious perch on the rear step and untied the bicycle.

'I'll bring it when I come for me lesson, miss,' he said, and paused before asking, 'No reason Arty and Jack got to know anything 'bout it, though?'

'*Silentium est aureum,*' she said. He was surprised into a grin, by which she knew he had understood her promise to be silent. He tugged at his cap and wheeled the bicycle away.

As Hugh flicked the horse on, Agatha turned to Beatrice and shook her arm. 'I think you'd better come home with us,' she said. 'We have hot water for a bath and Jenny to help you. You have some cuts and scrapes that should be swabbed with iodine.'

'I'll be fine,' said Beatrice. 'I'm sure Mrs Turber can spare me a kettle of hot water.'

'In case you haven't met my aunt, I don't think her invitation was optional,' Hugh advised with a laugh.

Beatrice felt she should further protest, but the thought of Agatha's gleaming white bathtub, the soft bed in the blue room and a freshly cooked hot dinner seemed irresistible after such an exhausting day, and so she agreed with the politest of thanks.

They pulled into the driveway, laughing over the pungency of Mrs Stokes's salve and Hugh's insistence that she also offered love potions, and claimed she could poison a pig without ruining the meat but said she never would. The front door stood companionably open, and a pleasant-looking man in shirtsleeves and tie was somewhat incongruously admiring the front gardens while smoking a cigarette.

'John, whatever are you doing home?' called Agatha. As the horse pulled to a standstill, he stepped to hand her down from the trap and they embraced as if young lovers, he swinging her off her feet while she clutched for her hat. 'Do put me down, for shame,' she said. 'You will throw out your back again.'

'It would be worth it, as ever,' he said. 'But I will settle for a kiss.' She kissed him on his greying sideburns and he kissed her back and then he was shaking Hugh's hand.

'And this is Beatrice, whom you met in London, who has fallen from her bicycle,' said Agatha, and Beatrice found herself given a hearty handshake by John Kent.

'Do you need a hand to get her down, my boy?' said John, but Hugh assured him he did not.

'I think we have this down to an art now,' he said, and Beatrice subjected herself once more to being lifted from the trap and carried into Agatha's front hall.

'It is so good to be home and to worry about something real, such as a lovely young woman's injured ankle and the fact that Cook is not happy to have had no notice about dinner,' said John Kent, following them inside. 'I swear it gives one faith that England will always stand.' He was smiling, but he rubbed his temple as if a very tired man.

'Why, John, it's not like you to wax lyrical in the middle of the afternoon,' said Agatha, taking off her hat and tossing it on a peg. 'Whatever can be the matter?'

'I am just grateful to be home,' said John Kent, catching his wife by the waist and kissing her again on the cheek in a very firm manner. 'You have no idea how grateful.'

Hugh slowly let Beatrice down and held her arm as she balanced as little weight as possible on her bad foot. She was grateful once again for the pressure of his touch as John Kent looked gravely into his wife's face.

'What Uncle John is trying to say is that home and England may not stand always,' said Daniel, leaning against the drawing room doorway, a large glass held in his hand and his tie unacceptably askew. 'So we are drinking to them now.'

'Why is Daniel drinking whisky so early?' asked Agatha.

'Is there bad news from London?' asked Hugh.

'I'm afraid so,' said his uncle. He caught Agatha's two hands in his and held them to his lips.

'Germany has invaded Belgium,' he said. 'Tomorrow we will be at war.'

Agatha Kent tucked a strand of hair back into its roll and wondered if she should call Jenny to come and fix her hair more tightly. But she had declared that they were not dressing for dinner. John was exhausted, and while a note had been sent to Mrs Turber's to bring fresh clothes for Beatrice, Agatha thought it easier not to request evening dress. She added a small hairpin, decorated with an emerald turtle, to the wayward hair and smoothed down the clean blouse she had added, happy not to have to exchange her loose stays for an evening corset. She always enjoyed the peaceful half-hour before the sound of the dinner gong, and at her dressing table, the evening light coming in the window and the companionable sounds of John changing his shirt in his dressing room next door, it was easy to believe for a moment that this evening was no different, that John had not come home for such a brief visit, and to give them such terrible news.

'Can you help me with this damned cufflink,' he said, wandering in with his shirt untucked and his feet in his favourite Moroccan slippers. He sat comfortably on the end of the bed and held out his arm. Agatha turned around on her dressing stool to oblige, and while she struggled with the stiff cuff, John sighed deeply and leaned his head forward onto her shoulder, tucking his cheek against her neck. Securing the cufflink, Agatha placed her hand on his back, and they sat a moment in an embrace of silent mutual comfort, which was, she often thought, the reward of those long married.

'We thought the Kaiser would compel Austria to show restraint in the east,' he said. 'Instead they are turning on France. They are already in Luxembourg and tomorrow they will rip apart Belgian neutrality.'

'You have done all you could, I'm sure,' said Agatha.

'We have been caught flat-footed by Berlin,' he said, raising his head and running a hand over his hair in weary frustration. 'And as we refuse, above all else, to look publicly foolish, I fear they have left us no room to remain outside the conflict.'

'It does seem unimaginable that we would be enemies,' said Agatha. 'What is Emily Wheaton's daughter to do? Her husband is such a lovely young man.'

'If she wishes to join him, she should leave immediately,' said John, standing up to use Agatha's dressing-table mirror as he knotted his blue-spotted bow tie. 'Travel will soon be impossible. All the railroads are to be commandeered for troops, and no one can be sure of having one's bank drafts honoured abroad.'

'But as an Englishwoman, how can she be expected to go to Germany at a time like this?' said Agatha. She reached to adjust the tie with a practised hand.

'Legally German now by marriage,' said her husband. 'She may not find it altogether comfortable here if war is declared.'

'That just proves the whole idea is absurd,' said Agatha. 'And they have a baby.'

'When I get back to London I shall be sure to pass on your opinion,' said John. 'But first may I please have a family dinner at my own table and a stroll in my rose garden with my beautiful wife?' He leaned down to smooth a strand of hair from her face.

'Yes, but just because there's an international crisis, don't think you're coming down to dinner in that awful striped blazer of yours,' said Agatha. 'We do have a guest.'

His old college punting blazer was thin at the elbows, its stripes soft and fuzzy with age, and Agatha waged a quiet but seemingly eternal war over his urge to pull it out whenever she suggested the slightest relaxation of standards. He could usually be dissuaded by reason, and yet on the two occasions she had tried to send the offending coat to the ragbag, John had become seriously angry and had marched down to the linen room to retrieve it personally. None of the servants would now touch the thing, and it hung in the wardrobe attracting moths and brushing its fuzzy sleeves against all the newer clothes.

'But it goes so well with this tie,' said John. 'And you said we're not dressing.'

'I said we would be informal,' said Agatha. 'I did not say we would be eccentric. I'm going to check on our young guest now. Please do not show up in the dining room looking like a carnival barker.'

'I suppose I can't wear slippers, either?' said John.

They did not talk of the crisis at dinner.

'We do not want to excite alarm among the staff nor have gossip spreading down the hill to the town,' Agatha said quietly to Beatrice as she helped her down the stairs. 'In my husband's position discretion is of great importance.'

Instead they spoke of the weather, the progress of the kitchen garden and how Beatrice enjoyed the town. John Kent wanted to know all the details of her arrival and settling in, and no member of the school governors, nor Mrs Turber, was spared in his wife and nephews' retelling of events.

'And can you believe Mrs Fothergill's nephew came inebriated to his interview?' said Agatha.

'It was a complete shock to all of us,' said Daniel. 'The Fothergills are such an unexceptionable family.' Beatrice caught the two cousins exchanging a grin, and Daniel, seeing her stare, opened his eyes in exaggerated innocence so that she realised they had had some hand in the business.

'Well, I know the best candidate won,' said John Kent. He raised his wine glass to Beatrice. 'You are a welcome addition to the town and to our family dinner table, my dear.'

'Thank you,' said Beatrice. She had been grateful to John Kent for personally taking time to see her across London to her train, but she realised now that she had been too tense to see him properly. He was a trim man of middling height and a quiet demeanour, which was perhaps the inevitable outcome of a long career as a civil servant. However, his eyes twinkled in the same devilish way as his wife's. These were people who knew more than they said and who understood more quickly than those who talked more. They communicated to each other without words, and as they laughed and chatted, Beatrice caught the occasional raised eyebrow, quiet incline of the head or tiny wave of a finger that hinted at their secret language. Beatrice had learned to read some of her father's expressions and anticipate his needs, but Agatha and John Kent seemed to enjoy a far deeper, more mutual understanding. Beatrice felt a momentary shiver of loneliness wash over her at the thought that her independence meant she would never know such a bond with another.

'How is the poetry, Daniel?' asked his uncle, changing the subject.

'I was published in a couple of journals,' said Daniel. 'I brought Aunt Agatha some copies.'

'Some of those journals are quite scurrilous,' said Agatha. 'I'm not sure your uncle would enjoy them.'

'It wouldn't be art if it didn't scandalise the average person,' said Daniel.

'Thus we are firmly put in our place, my dear,' said John to his wife.

'I didn't mean you, of course,' said Daniel. 'Mr Tillingham thought my poems moderately promising.'

'Thus are you put firmly in your place,' said Uncle John.

'Indeed,' said Daniel. 'He insists on looking over my newest lines in order to prevent me from making, he says, the kinds of juvenile errors that marred those already published.'

'I believe that is quite high praise from the great man,' said Hugh.

'Miss Nash, I think you said you are also a writer?' asked his uncle, turning a friendly smile to her.

'A complete impossibility, according to Mr Tillingham,' said Beatrice. 'I am to be dismissed out of hand as a female.'

'I think it is Mr Tillingham's opinions that are often impossible,' said John Kent. 'Yet society insists on finding the pronouncements of great men indisputable.'

'If Mr Tillingham likes my newest work, I'm hoping he might be willing to write me a short foreword for a book of poems,' said Daniel. 'I know a small publisher in Paris who might be very interested.'

'Publishers in Paris may have more urgent things on their minds for the next few months,' said John. 'I would not direct any hopes in that direction.'

'Oh, but all will be resolved in a few weeks, will it not?' said Daniel. 'The difficulties surely won't reach as far as Paris?' Jenny came in with a large sherry trifle and Smith followed with a platter of fruit. The family stopped speaking, and an awkward silence accompanied the serving of the dessert – Jenny knocking the large silver spoon against the crystal bowl, the trifle clinging stubbornly to the spoon, Smith offering the fruit in a whisper that rasped like a metal file.

Finally they left the room, and after a moment's pause, John Kent said quietly, 'You will hear many declarations in the coming weeks, most of which are designed to put the best face on the situation and to reflect a proper sense of patriotism.' He paused to choose his words with care. 'You will hear very little more from me, but I believe it will be impossible to travel on the Continent for the foreseeable future.'

'But I'm moving to Paris next month,' said Daniel, his face turning white. 'Craigmore and I are starting a journal.' Beatrice could see from Hugh's reddened ears that he had known of this plan but that it was an unexpected pronouncement to Agatha and John.

'But I have secured you a place . . .' began his uncle.

'Oh, I'm so sorry, dear,' said his aunt simultaneously. The silence resumed, and Daniel seemed to inflate with some combination of anger and disbelief.

'It can't be,' he said in a clipped voice. 'It is all arranged.'

'War does have a way of interfering with one's most closely held desires,' said his uncle. Beatrice detected a note of impatience.

'I'm going to Paris, no matter what,' said Daniel. 'If you will excuse me.' He stood up abruptly, his napkin slipping to the floor unnoticed, and left the room.

'I'm sorry we have not minded our manners better in front of our guest,' said John to Beatrice. 'Please forgive my nephew.'

'Daniel can't help his impetuous nature,' said Agatha. 'He is artistic.'

'He is some combination of artistic and spoiled,' said John in a mild voice. 'We have yet to determine the absolute proportions.'

'You knew of this plan, Hugh?' said Agatha.

'This is where I usually get dressed down more severely than Daniel for just knowing of some nefarious action for which he has been discovered,' said Hugh to Beatrice. He ate his last spoonful of trifle and waved the spoon about. 'This time I draw the line, Auntie. Daniel is a grown man and I am no longer responsible for his scraped knees and wayward nature.'

'I can't imagine his father would have approved,' said Agatha. 'Of course it is the fashion for young men to experience *la vie boulevardier*, I suppose.'

'Boys with more means than sense,' said John. 'These times will call for men of sterner character.'

'I can only hope you are proved wrong,' said Agatha. Jenny came in to signal that tea was ready in the living room, and Agatha added, 'Oh, just bring the tea in here, my dear. The ladies will not be withdrawing early tonight.'

The tea had been poured and the doors were just being closed to the ears of the staff when Daniel slipped into the dining room again.

'I apologise for my abrupt withdrawal,' he said. 'My distress at the thought of Paris and all her treasures under threat required a moment of composure.'

'Do you need some brandy?' asked his uncle.

'I'm sure Hugh would agree it's a good idea, if only for medicinal purposes,' said Daniel. 'Assuming you have more dismal news to share?'

'I can't really say much more,' said John, pouring brandies for himself, Hugh and Daniel. He tilted the bottle towards his wife, but she shook her head. 'There may be yet a few days in which to urge Germany to reconsider, but as you can imagine, military action has its own forward momentum.' He sighed and walked over to stand in the open French window and breathe deeply of the evening's fragrant air. 'With Russia also on the move, I fear it may be like trying to stop a runaway train by putting out one's hand.'

'And we were honour bound to guarantee poor Belgium's safety, were we not?' asked Beatrice.

'There is no honour in diplomacy, Miss Nash,' said Daniel. 'The loud declaring of its violation is usually designed to produce some advantage.'

'Daniel!' said his aunt.

'The boy may not be wrong,' said his uncle. 'Though I have spent many years struggling in its cause, I believe the age of honour among civilised nations may be coming to its end.'

'So we will not defend Belgium?' asked Beatrice. She felt sadly confused, and she was sure one should not be confused about the need for war. 'But we have a treaty!'

'Oh, we will defend them,' said John. 'If Germany were to defeat France and gain a stranglehold on the northern French ports, they would threaten our Channel shipping and our dominant position over the sea-lanes.'

'So we will fight them for our own benefit?' she said. 'Saving Belgium is just a story to tell the humble masses?'

'Quite the opposite,' said John. 'The saving of innocent Belgium is a story for the benefit of Parliament and all the important people who must agree to give us the troops and money to fight. You can't get anything in politics without telling the politicians a good bedtime story.'

'Will there be conscription?' asked Hugh.

'I don't know that it will go that far,' said his uncle. 'We have the Expeditionary Force mustering now. They are seasoned and experienced. We'll ask for volunteers. I think the immediate response will be a rush of the inexperienced but well-connected yahoos, looking for a plum spot from which to help run the proceedings in perfect safety. My own office is already receiving a deluge of letters of introduction and requests for commissions.'

'Now that Paris is out, I hope you'll see that this is the perfect time for you to enter the Foreign Office with your uncle, Daniel,' said Agatha. 'I know your father wishes it.'

'I have no interest in sitting in Whitehall learning to order woollen socks by the bushel,' said Daniel. 'Craigmore and I will just start our journal in London and contribute to the cause through our art.'

'I'm sure a journal containing stirring poetry and patriotic sketches would be a welcome and successful enterprise,' said his aunt. Beatrice noticed her dry tone and was not at all surprised when Daniel took violent exception.

'Good God, that's the worst idea ever,' he said. 'We would surely suffocate under the mudslide of maudlin submissions containing nothing but cheap sentimentality and empty blusterings. No hint of patriotism must be allowed to corrupt the art. If anything, the cause of poetry must always be peace.'

'You may not find many subscribers in time of war,' said Hugh. 'Poets must also eat and pay rent.'

'If necessary we'll run the journal from here,' said Daniel. 'We'll just move into your garage, Hugh.'

'Behind every poet stands not the muse but a well-provisioned aunt with a country house?' said Hugh. He remained deadpan, drinking his tea, and Beatrice hid a smile.

'Exactly,' said Daniel. 'What would I do without you, Aunt Agatha?'

'What should the rest of us be doing, Mr Kent?' asked Beatrice. 'One wants to do one's duty.'

'Keep one's regular routine and refuse to show agitation,' said John. 'It is important that we set a good example, because news of this kind has a way of stirring up the population.'

'I had better get in a few supplies,' said Agatha. 'You know I like to be prepared.'

'Hoarding will be frowned upon officially,' said her husband. 'It produces shortages and drives up prices.'

'Then I will be circumspect about the town,' said his wife. 'But I'll expect you to go to Fortnum and Mason on your way to the office and put in a respectably small order for immediate delivery.'

'I should get a few things for town too,' said John. 'My club dinners are bad enough in time of peace. A stock of Gentleman's Relish and some potted oysters should see me through some months of hostilities.'

CHAPTER EIGHT

Upon reflection during the days that followed, Hugh could see that the gathering storm clouds in Europe had been well reported in the newspapers, but that, like so many, he had failed to notice the goings-on of the Continent.

'I avoid the papers altogether,' said Daniel. 'I'm pretty sure wars would be shorter if we weren't all so eager to read about them.'

'And what are we to do now?' asked Hugh. 'I feel anxious just sitting here.' They were in the garden, Daniel lying in the hammock and Hugh sprawled in an old canvas deckchair. 'My dear cousin, sitting still is quite the best option,' said Daniel. 'Did you not hear Uncle John say we are to carry on as normal and refuse to appear concerned?'

'What is normal when there are soldiers guarding the train station and one can't change a five-pound note anywhere?'

'I should be so lucky as to be in possession of a five-pound note,' sighed Daniel. He let his book fall to the ground and placed his hands behind his head. 'The scent of war does add crispness to the outlines of one's day,' he added. 'I detected a certain urgency of purpose in the gait of the milkman's horse this morning.'

'Oh, do be sensible, Daniel,' said Hugh. 'Between you playing the fop and Colonel Wheaton enlisting every drunken idiot in front of the Town Hall, it's as if the whole world has gone mad.'

'I saw the Finch woman photographing a handsome young recruit draped in the Union Jack, with his mother and three little sisters all weeping into bunches of daisies' said Daniel, sighing. 'I was quite tempted to enlist myself, just so I too could swoon under the flag and send the picture to Craigmore to make him weep for me.'

'Dr Lawton says the recruits are a feeble, malnourished lot and liable to succumb to a chill from the first route march,' said Hugh.

'Are you going to help him fatten up the Sussex youth for the front lines?' asked Daniel.

'I have written to my surgeon for advice as to what I should do,' said Hugh. 'I do not feel able to sit idle if I can be of service in some capacity. I hope to be called to London any day.'

'And will your surgeon's daughter be willing to give you up to some war effort, or will she cling to you in this hour of desperation?' asked Daniel. Hugh frowned, for he was quite sure he had not mentioned her to Daniel, and this meant Daniel had been nosing about his desk again, no doubt stealing all his best pen nibs and laughing at the many drafts it took him to compose a suitably casual note to a woman.

'Miss Ramsey has far too many beaux about her to notice me,' said Hugh. He hoped Daniel would probe no further as he was not about to confide in his cousin and be rewarded with endless gibes.

'Perhaps you should join the cavalry,' said Daniel. 'Women love a man in uniform.'

'And you would stay in flannels and play cricket until the Hun are at the beaches?' asked Hugh.

'I'll have you know I wrote to Craigmore to propose an immediate launch of our journal in London,' said Daniel. 'We shall give our finest young poets and artists a superior forward position from which to defend our nation through art and language.'

'I thought you said patriotism is anathema to art?' asked Hugh.

'I have decided that, like money, it is best considered a necessary handmaiden to the cause,' said Daniel. 'Of course I shall keep all patriotic items to the rear of the journal and smother them with illustrated borders so that no one will actually read them.'

'You are in a practical mood,' said Hugh. 'War has had a sobering effect on us all.'

'And with concrete results,' said Daniel. 'Craigmore writes that he and his parents are coming down to visit.' He reached down for his notebook and pulled some onion-skin pages from the middle. 'Part of some sort of commission to assess local defence arrangements.'

'And does he say his father agrees to your venture?' said Hugh.

'Not in so many words,' said Daniel. 'But the universe brings all together. I am sure Craigmore and I can make an unassailable case for art and poetry as part of our national defences.'

By the last post of the evening, Hugh received a letter summoning him to London, and after some difficulty at Rye railway station, where the ticket office had no change and the stationmaster graciously allowed him to write an IOU, he set off for London the next morning.

The London home of the surgeon Sir Alex Ramsey was a tall Harley Street house of warm red brick, handsomely ornamented with stone and appointed with large windows trimmed with lead window boxes of late-summer flowers. A discreet brass plaque was the only suggestion that the house contained the surgeon's consulting rooms, a small suite just beyond the front door. Behind the gracious façade, the home contained a number of commodious rooms with lofty ceilings and wide hallways. Hugh had seen both upstairs and downstairs parlours, the library and the surgeon's private study. He particularly enjoyed the lower back parlour, which was Lucy's domain, and from which her charmingly arranged conservatory led to an elegant garden with a small carp pond and brick walls lined with espaliered peach and apple trees. Waiting on the front step, Hugh allowed himself a moment to imagine owning such a house, and perhaps a large, well-managed medical practice of similar renown. It would require many years to attain such eminence through his talent and hard work, but he was not afraid of the effort. He acknowledged the flowering of some hope that Lucy Ramsey's affections might smooth his way, but he knew himself innocent of any dark motive. If they were to marry, he thought, any advancement would be mere gilding to the sufficiency of love.

'Come in, my boy, come in,' said the surgeon, waving as the butler showed Hugh into the book-lined consulting room, where only the plainness of the carpet and the slightest hint of carbolic suggested a professional use. 'Lucy has the usual crowd in to tea, but she insisted I must have a few moments' private talk with you alone, Grange.'

'I'm honoured,' said Hugh, sitting in a comfortably upholstered chair in front of the polished mahogany desk. 'How were the Lakes, sir?' They chatted awhile about the hardships of the lecture tour, the crowds at Bellagio and the superior pleasures of the quiet towns of Lake Como's western shore.

'I think Lucy liked the quiet,' said the surgeon. 'A baronet with a phaeton and matching set of white ponies saluted her every day in the gardens, but nothing could turn her pretty head. She's a sensible girl and no mistake.'

'And did you have any trouble getting home?' asked Hugh. 'I hear the European banks stopped honouring our drafts?'

'We got out just in time,' said the surgeon. 'The manager at our hotel cashed a cheque in gold sovereigns and we caught one of the last trains to get through to Paris before the borders closed for good. One or two people were taken from the train, but I'm relieved to say that Lucy did not have to witness any nastiness.' He stroked his beard and added, 'They were warned not to take up arms, these Belgians, but apparently some of them would not follow orders. Of course I share the communal outrage, and I mean to bring all my expertise and resources to aid my country and my King.'

'I wanted to ask how I might be of service in those efforts,' said Hugh. 'I do not wish to offer you any less than my full attention as your assistant, but perhaps on my days off I can volunteer some extra hours in one of the hospitals?'

'That is exactly why I wanted to talk to you, my dear boy,' said Sir Alex. He shuffled some papers on his desk and handed Hugh what appeared to be a list of equipment and staff needed to set up a full hospital with several operating theatres. 'This war is the opportunity of a lifetime to advance our field at a rate unheard of in peacetime.' He rubbed his hands. 'Think of a new specialist hospital and an unlimited supply of wounded, offering us the opportunity to catalogue every possible type and severity of brain injury! I envision a whole battery of the new X-ray machines, the latest in equipment from bone saws to drug compounds, and of course, the brightest of our doctors to work with me on this Herculean task.'

'It would be an enormous advance in the field,' said Hugh. 'Where will it be, sir? I heard they were commandeering an asylum in Chelsea?'

'No, no, my boy, we shall go over there!' said Sir Alex. 'As close to the lines as possible in order to get the freshest cases. Head wounds don't travel well, as you know. I would prefer a seaside location . . .'

'In France?' asked Hugh. He was conscious of a thump of anxiety in his chest. Not fear, he told himself, but just a natural reaction to the idea of going into the war.

'The War Office is proving wary of civilian efforts – too many ladies of the realm wanting to stock a grocer's van and call themselves an ambulance. Then there is always the question of funding.'

'Some significant hurdles,' agreed Hugh.

'They have offered to set up my hospital as a military effort, part of the Royal Army Medical Corps,' said the surgeon. 'I was concerned, of course – military bureaucracy and all that – but they have offered me a commission.'

'Congratulations, sir.'

'Just a colonel rank to start, I believe,' said the surgeon. He tucked a hand in his jacket and straightened his back as he spoke. His contented face suggested he might be contemplating other honours. 'In the meantime I must recruit. I must have the best and brightest, and of course, that includes you, my boy.'

'I thank you for the compliment,' said Hugh, evading a direct response.

'You and Carruthers and possibly that Michaels chap, though he's asthmatic if you ask me; probably won't take him,' said the surgeon. 'Some of you'll have to serve where they need you for the few months until we get set up.'

'It's just that I have only a few months left to be fully qualified,' said Hugh. 'I had thought my place was here.' He had looked forward to assisting the surgeries, to conducting hospital rounds at the side of the eminent surgeon, to working in the clean, tiled laboratories, and to the writing of an academic paper or two. He had planned to continue living simply but to perhaps buy opera tickets and to invite Lucy to an afternoon or two at the British Museum. And he had seen volunteering in the evenings – an extra surgery here and there to save a limb or an eye – looking for no recognition beyond Lucy's admiration for his indefatigable efforts.

'My boy, one month at the front will be worth ten years in the operating rooms of London,' said the surgeon. 'Think of the experience, the papers to be published and the advancement of our scientific understanding.' Hugh might have added the saving of lives to the surgeon's list of advantages, but he understood that the mind of such a great man was all on the science.

'With your permission, I would like to consult my uncle,' he said. 'And I must write to my father abroad.'

'Plenty of time to decide before the autumn term,' said the surgeon. 'I hope you receive their blessing. Those notes you put together for me on the effects of keeping patients warm after surgery were quite well received this summer. I had thought we might consider a paper on the subject?'

'Thank you,' said Hugh. Though he knew the name of a lowly assistant would not appear on any paper the great man published, he was thrilled to imagine his ideas being discussed by influential surgeons on the Continent.

'I would be sorry to lose you,' added the surgeon, giving him a stern look. 'And I know Lucy would be sorry to see you part from us.' Hugh's elation evaporated. He did not know quite how to respond, for it was suddenly clear that the surgeon did not mean to continue to supervise any of his students who did not agree to go to France. It had been one of the proudest achievements of Hugh's life to have been chosen to work with Sir Alex, and he had come to feel secure under his wing. Now he felt, like a blow to the chest, that he might have seen genuine affection in what was, perhaps, merely an affable manner.

'Why don't we go to the parlour and ask Lucy to give us a cup of tea?' said the surgeon gently. 'I know she has been counting the moments to your arrival.'

To walk into a parlour filled with colleagues and friends, with the great surgeon's arm across his shoulders, was to receive such attention, acknowledgement, and not a little envy that Hugh could not but feel comforted. That the surgeon's benevolence might be self-interested did not preclude a genuine warmth, thought Hugh, and he basked in the knowledge that all assembled knew he had just been closeted with the great man.

'Our star brings tales from his country doctoring,' said Sir Alex. 'I hope you've left him some teacakes, Michaels?' Hugh shook hands with his colleagues and was introduced again to several young ladies of Lucy's circle who seemed to delight in coming to tea with the young doctors and then conversing among themselves about all the young men they knew from higher circles. The tea party spilled into the conservatory, where more young people perched amid troughs of fern and glazed Italian urns of aspidistra and rubber plant. Under the slender arms of two tall potted lime trees that shaded the glass roof, he spotted Lucy sitting on a wicker settee, a low table at her elbow containing the tea urn and a large platter of cakes. Two of her friends sat with her, doing their patriotic duty by knitting green wool socks for soldiers. His nearest rival for the attention of both the daughter and the father, Carruthers, had obtained a favoured spot on the settee itself, where he held a skein of green wool for Lucy to wind. As Hugh paused to admire Lucy's white lace dress with its girlish pink ribbons on the tight bodice, and her pale blue French boots propped alluringly on a low footstool, she raised her heart-shaped face from her winding and gave him her most brilliant smile.

'You must cede your place now, Mr Carruthers,' she said in a charming tone that brooked no opposition. 'You have had the monopoly long enough, and I promised our friend Mr Grange a real talk.' As Carruthers got to his feet to shake hands and to make his somewhat grumbling departure, the two knitting girls also made their whispered excuses, Lucy leaning her pale curls towards them and lowering her lashes over her blue eyes as they spoke. Hugh had the distinct impression that she and her friends were fully aware of her father's plans, and he wondered how many of the surgeon's other students had been persuaded with teacake and a private chat in the conservatory.

'Now, Hugh, you look even more stern than usual,' she said, pouring tea into a china cup. 'You are quite the most serious and least charming of my father's acolytes, and yet I must confess it makes me like you the most.'

'I am honoured,' he said, sitting by her side and accepting a cup of tea and a buttered teacake from her long, pale hand. His pulse quickened at the touch of her elegant fingers, and as he felt her breath on his cheek and the slight heat of her body against the coolness of the flowers, he was ashamed of his churlishness.

'Those other boys are so quick to flatter and be silly,' she said, smoothing her skirts across her lap. 'They present no challenge at all.'

'I do not mean to be difficult,' he said. 'Have I been rude?'

'Not at all,' she said. 'But as usual, how to make you smile is a puzzle.'

'I am not good at parlour conversation,' said Hugh. 'How were the Lakes?' She talked at some length about her trip, and Hugh learned that she had noticed the baronet and white horses rather more than her father suspected. But she was charming in her insistence that she had missed Hugh's conversation and when she put her pale hand on his arm, he thrilled again with all the feelings he had discovered in her absence.

'But enough of my silly holiday,' said Lucy. 'These times make light conversation less attractive and I know you might prefer to talk of serious matters.'

'Indeed I would,' said Hugh, wondering how to begin some sort of declaration of his intentions.

'My father is set on going to France,' said Lucy, with a more serious face than he had ever seen. 'I know he has asked you to go with him.'

'Yes,' said Hugh. It was not the opening he wished, but he would follow her lead. 'What will you do when he goes?'

'My father wishes me to go to my aunt in Wales,' she said. 'But it is not a pleasant house, nor as lively a city. I have asked to stay in London, where my friends and I plan to contribute to the war effort in so much larger a fashion.' She paused and gave a pretty sigh. 'But I know I should not worry my poor papa when he is making ready to sacrifice so much.'

'I'm sure he'll be quite safe,' said Hugh. 'He won't be in the front line, you know.'

'I do so hope you'll go with him,' said Lucy. 'I won't flatter you, but only say that it would give me such peace to know he has you.' She looked into his eyes, and Hugh felt a vibration between them that inspired him to be bold.

'I find that I have missed you this summer and I do not welcome the idea of going away,' he declared.

'Why, Hugh, I missed you too,' she said. 'The Lakes were so dull and full of portly old people that I thought of you with increasing fondness.' He thought she was teasing, but her face revealed no irony. That she should so often be unaware of the funny things she said was a contrast to the sharp wit of such women as his aunt, or the schoolteacher, Beatrice Nash, but he thought it a charming symptom of her youth.

'I was afraid my focus on my work had made me a dull companion too,' he said. 'You are surrounded by medical men.'

'They believe they know so much more than they do and yet insist on lecturing me as if I were a child,' she said. 'I like that you always speak plainly.' She glanced towards the parlour, where he noticed Carruthers was frowning at them over his tea. His was not the only glance, and Hugh saw with great clarity that to be at Lucy's side was to be in the very centre of the company. Affection for Lucy and for her father blossomed in his heart. He understood that the tall brick house and the respected consulting rooms might be his. And that Lucy, raised to understand a doctor's needs, would offer him all her pretty freshness now and be eager to mature under his guidance.

The moment hovered in silence while a small fountain plashed in its mossy bowl and a breeze, stirring across the cool, tiled floor, set the flower heads to nodding. At last, Hugh put down his teacup, balancing his large buttered teacake on the saucer. Wiping his hands swiftly on his napkin, he seized Lucy's hand.

'Dearest Lucy,' he said, and now as he looked into her eyes, he felt no hesitation in laying his heart before her. 'For some time I have hoped to speak to you . . .'

'Forgive me, but I must beg you not to,' she said. She did not withdraw her hand, but she turned her pretty eyes away and added, 'You know that I hold you in very high esteem, Hugh.'

'Then why may I not speak?' he asked, pressing her hand. 'Just a brief word no one else need hear?'

'I fear you mean to make some sort of declaration,' she said, and lowered her long lashes to her cheeks. 'But as I told Mr Carruthers only last week, it is not possible for an Englishwoman to entertain any pretty declarations from a man not in uniform.'

'I don't understand,' said Hugh.

'My friends and I have sworn we shall entertain no declarations, no matter how handsome the gentleman or advantageous the match, until he has enlisted,' she said. As she withdrew her fingers and clasped her hands together in her lap, he saw her give the faintest nod towards a large stand of aspidistra. The two girls with whom she had been knitting nodded back.

'Surely love must rebel at such an arbitrary test?' He could not restrain his impatience at what seemed a silly contrivance. 'We are not in some fairy tale where dragons must be slain and golden apples fetched for the princesses.'

'Mr Carruthers swore he would give up his August holiday in Brighton and go straight to the recruiting office,' she said, a pout to her lips and a flush in her cheeks.

'I wish you much happiness with Mr Carruthers,' he said with mock severity.

'In his case I had hoped he would refuse and I would be rid of him altogether,' she admitted. 'But in your case, Hugh, surely you mean to sign up and go with my father? He says it is to be the greatest opportunity for all who follow him.'

'I'm sure your father considers duty above opportunity,' said Hugh. 'I can assure you I do not fault your patriotism or doubt the importance of your father's plans, but I won't join the fools dashing thoughtlessly to the recruiter.'

'I would expect no less from my stern friend,' she said, smiling again. 'I shouldn't say this, but if you decide to join us, you would be well served to let my father know before the first week in September.'

'I have asked for time to write to my father,' said Hugh.

'My father plans to hold a large general enlistment rally during his first lecture back at the hospital,' she said. 'You will be expected to attend, and it would look well to show your commitment ahead of the crowd.'

'A general recruitment of doctors?'

'The Army Medical Corps is found to be much smaller than required,' she said, taking up her knitting again. 'My father has pledged to recruit a hundred men, and I am pledged to attend every rally to hand out hand-painted flag pins to every new recruit.'

'A charming incentive,' said Hugh, glad at last to have hold of an opportunity to return to romantic banter. 'Perhaps I should delay my decision to claim my token from the lady's fair hand?'

'I must warn you that my friends and I will hand the white feather to all who dare leave the hall without signing up,' she said, and though she ducked her head and smiled with her familiar youthful charm, there was a hint of steel in her eye that he had not seen before. 'I have given up an entire swan's wing hat to the effort, and it was from Paris, no less.'

CHAPTER NINE

STANDING IN THE HIGH street, her basket on her arm and her straw hat shading her eyes from the bright August sun, Beatrice could see the striped shop awnings with their hastily produced Union Jack pennants strung from edge to edge, the municipal flower trough sporting stiff paper flags on sticks, and every empty wall and post displaying a handbill urging attendance at this evening's public meeting on the war effort. And yet the town's business went on as normal. A delivery dray off-loaded crates at the ironmonger; a woman swept the pavement outside the milliner; the fishmonger's boy set off at an awkward run, a parcel of paper-wrapped fish under one arm and a large bucket of live crabs on the other. As the boy tripped on a wayward cobble and almost lost a half-dozen crabs from his bucket, England seemed as peaceful and pastoral as the ages.

Beatrice's basket contained a paper bag of broken biscuits, three small currant buns and some elderflower cordial. Her pupils were coming this afternoon for their usual tutoring and though she did not plan to spoil them, their bored and gloomy faces at the first two lessons had prompted her to try these small inducements. The bakery and the grocer had both displayed thin shelves. The big loaves were usually sold out by the afternoon, but today all bread in the bakery was sold and there had been no fancy sugared cakes at all, not even their almond smell, but only buns that looked smaller than usual. In the grocer, all the fresh food was sold, the glass-fronted pie and dairy counter empty, and women were reduced to competing over tins of pressed meat and dried fruit from the uppermost shelves. Honey and sugar being sold, they took black treacle and even brewer's malt.

'I'd like a standing order for a quarter-pound of sugar and a pound of flour,' said the lady being served ahead of Beatrice. She had a long paper list and was accompanied by a stout boy who carried a straw basket of immense size.

'Sorry, madam, I'm not taking any more standing orders,' said the grocer, who looked drawn and nervous, perhaps from delivering such news all day to unhappy customers. 'Even my current orders are being reduced, and likely I won't be able to fill them all.'

'When will you get in more sugar?' asked the woman, and made a written note of the day he mentioned. 'I'll be here first thing and I shall expect to find you have kept some available,' she added.

'I'll do my best, ma'am,' the grocer said. 'But it'll be all cash money, small notes only and nothing on the accounts.'

He mopped his balding brow as she swept from the shop, the stout boy laden with a full basket behind her.

'A bottle of elderflower cordial, please,' said Beatrice. 'And a pound of loose biscuits.'

'Biscuits is all gone, miss,' said the grocer, reaching up high for the last, slightly dusty bottle of cordial on his shelves. Beatrice thought it must have been retrieved from deep in the storage cellars. 'I've only got broken ones.'

'A pound of the broken then,' she said, reluctantly. Shop-bought biscuits might be the necessary compromise of those who lived in rented rooms, but she would not have willingly served broken ones even to servants. However, they might not be frowned upon by hungry boys, and she must have something to nibble on when hunger struck between Mrs Turber's small meals. The grocer shovelled loose, broken biscuit pieces into a bag and quoted her a price that she was sure she had paid a few days ago for intact ones.

'Everything is very dear these days,' she said, counting out her coins.

'And everyone complaining and accusing me of making a tidy profit,' he said. 'No one asks me what I'm being charged up and down.'

'I didn't mean . . .'

'And how I'm to keep the shop stocked and make a living when there's nothing being delivered,' he added, shaking his head. 'I shall be forced to close my doors if things go on this way.'

'It must be very hard,' said Beatrice, noting that his wife, knitting green socks in the corner of the shop, looked very well fed and that she had a large slice of fruitcake at her elbow. 'I am so sorry for your troubles,' she said to the lady.

'Try us tomorrow – might have a crate of tinned pilchards coming in and also some French soap,' said the wife in a cheerful tone.

'That's right,' said the grocer. He laid a finger against his nose to signal the pilchards were a secret. 'But better be early. Be twice the price by afternoon.'

Beatrice did not go in the butcher's shop, but she could see the marble slab in the window was empty save for some dried sausage and a large grey piece of liver. The haberdashery was doing a brisk business, as if people feared a sudden shortage of rickrack ribbon and polka-dotted Swiss muslin by the yard. Beatrice bought the last two yards of some dove-grey grosgrain ribbon to lighten a black mourning dress that had too much wear left to discard. Only the tiny bookshop seemed full of merchandise, and the bookseller stood in his doorway watching the bustle of the high street pass him by. Beatrice would have dearly loved to go in and buy a book, if only to cheer him up, but the increase of prices and the lack of cash in the streets and banks made it prudent to hold on to her dwindling purse. She merely smiled as she passed, and he raised his hat in acknowledgement.

At Mr Samuels's, purveyor of fine wines and liqueurs, an assistant took the last two bottles of Spanish sherry from the window. Through the open door, Beatrice saw Harry Wheaton in the uniform of his father's reserves. He was lounging against the counter with his cap askew and collar loosened, as if he were wearing boating flannels. As the assistant wrapped the bottles for him, she heard him ask, 'I assume my father's account is in good standing in this crisis?'

'On any stock we have, sir,' said the assistant. 'But if you were able to pay in advance in gold sovereigns, my guvnor, Mr Samuels, may be able to procure you some Bordeaux or even some cognac.'

'Please make some specific enquiries and send me a note if you can,' said Wheaton. Beatrice walked on so she would not have to meet him, but before she could reach the street corner, he called to her loudly. Though her ears burned to be so hailed in the public street, she stopped and turned back to greet him.

'Miss Nash, you look the picture of domesticity with your little basket,' he said, straightening his cap and mimicking a formal bow. 'I hope you have been more successful than I in our meagre shops?'

'People with money seem to be enjoying the scramble to stock their cellars and pantries against the end of the world,' she said. 'But I'm afraid the empty shops and high price of bread and meat will be a hardship for many.'

'It's hardship all right,' said Wheaton. 'Not a decent bottle of wine to be had in the county. I took two bottles of sherry but not sure why. Overpriced and I never drink the stuff anyway.'

Beatrice laughed at him. 'If you don't drink it, you have paid too much, Mr Wheaton,' she said.

'You are right, Miss Nash,' he said with a wry grin. 'But if I give it as a gift, in these sparse times it will be worth more than its price.'

'Very true,' she said.

'So please allow me to tuck one of these bottles in your little basket. I know ladies enjoy a spot of sherry now and then.' He made to tuck a bottle next to the bag of biscuits.

'I couldn't possibly,' said Beatrice. But in rescuing the biscuits from imminent crushing, she created just the room he needed to slip in the bottle and step back laughing.

'Now, Miss Nash, I will have to ask my sister to bring me with her when she comes to tea, and you can offer us sherry with our scones.'

'Which I assume you will refuse?' she asked.

'In times like these you should only offer your food and wine to guests you are sure will refuse,' he said. 'My own mother is currently offering all callers gooseberry jam, hoping they will leave hungry.'

'Since to refuse your gift would mean further public tussle in the street,' said Beatrice, 'I shall accept with all proper thanks.'

'Good,' he said. 'I will tell my sister I have made further amends. My sister has been doing nothing but talk of your little cottage. She seems enamoured of playing shepherd-ess, like Marie Antoinette.'

'I am honoured to receive her,' said Beatrice. 'She has been most generous.' In addition to inviting her to tennis games and luncheons, Eleanor had come to tea at the cottage twice, each time bringing some household items of her own to give. A heavy linen shawl embroidered with crewelwork cabbage roses, a quantity of French tulle left over from dressmaking and a silver chocolate pot were among the gifts.

'My old nanny made me the shawl,' Eleanor had said. 'I could never find a decent excuse to part with it, but I'm sure it's much too country cottage for my husband's family.' Beatrice had merely smiled and thanked her, caught between a genuine gratitude at Eleanor's attention and the small creep of humiliation at being treated, however gently, as a charity case.

'Now if I give the other bottle to the German nanny, she might forgive me for dropping the baby on the lawn yesterday,' said Harry Wheaton, stroking an imaginary beard. 'And on the other hand, I am in the middle of pursuing a rather fetching young lady whose widowed mother might think well of a gentleman bearing such a gift.'

'You are a disgrace, Mr Wheaton,' said Beatrice firmly.

'Unless some upstanding paragon of a woman undertakes my reform, I fear I shall remain incorrigible,' he said. 'Will you not save me, Miss Nash?'

'I shall not,' she said. 'Good day, Mr Wheaton.' He raised his hat and went away laughing. Beatrice, looking around, saw two old ladies frowning and whispering about her in a doorway. She straightened her back and walked away at a dignified pace, resisting the urge to scurry.

Beatrice was rearranging fresh paper and sharp pencils on her parlour table and hesitating between passages from Virgil and Horace in a dog-eared anthology of Latin suitable for schoolboys, when a loud knocking on the back door indicated the usual arrival of her pupils via the alley. Abigail came from Mrs Turber's side of the house to let them in, and there seemed to be some sharp discussion in the scullery before Snout shuffled through the doorway alone, cap in hand. As always, he had clearly been subject to the scrutiny of his mother, for he was scrubbed red about the ears and his wet hair was slicked to his head. His clothes, though threadbare, were brushed and ironed, and

Beatrice appreciated such respect and felt it as a quiet rebuke to her urge to warn Abigail about the young Gypsy. He had removed his boots in the scullery and hopped into the parlour, twisting his socks as best he could to disguise several holes. She almost gave him a smile, but the absence of his fellow pupils meant she must not be charmed, but must offer her most severe frown.

'Arty and Jack are awful sick, miss,' Snout began. He looked her straight in the eye as he lied and his face wore an impressive frown of concern. 'Might be the bronchitis again, miss. They both had it bad in the winter.' Bronchitis was a stubborn pestilence in the damp British winters, and her father's family had fussed about it as if it might carry him off instead of the cancer. She was not pleased that Snout would raise such a spectre as an excuse, nor that he would think her so gullible as to accept bronchitis in the middle of one of the sunniest and driest summers on record. But she understood that he was the scapegoat, delivering the message for boys who were no doubt among the dozens of children waving at troop trains from the railway bridge or watching Colonel Wheaton's reserves drilling at their camp out in the fields.

'I hope they do not plan to die just to avoid my lessons,' she said. The gloom with which all three boys obviously regarded the good fortune of having a Latin tutor for the summer was almost comical. She was not surprised that they should attempt to evade her. 'I trust you have no such life-threatening symptoms, young man.'

'A bit of a tickle in the throat, miss,' said Snout. 'Perhaps I should go home and get into bed just in case.'

'Pity you cannot stay to eat up all the buns and biscuits,' said Beatrice, as Abigail came in with a jug of elderflower cordial and a plate with the buns and some lumps of partial biscuit. 'It was to be a treat, and now I'm sure they will go quite to waste.'

'I can stay if it doesn't bother you, miss,' said Snout, his eyes widening. 'I did my homework, and I brought their homework with me too.' He rummaged in a battered leather satchel and produced the dirty, ink-stained copybooks in which they attempted to translate the passages from Cicero or Caesar she set them.

'I would be delighted if you would stay,' said Beatrice. 'I would like to show you a book that is very special to me.' She went to the nearest bookcase and took down the slim leather-bound copy of Virgil's *Aeneid* from which her father had taught her the poetry of Latin. 'Perhaps you can look at this while I mark your work. Start anywhere you like.'

As she marked her changes, she could see Snout munching on biscuits and slurping from his cup. He seemed to become so engaged in his reading that he reached for both without looking, and she bit her tongue and tried not to picture splashes of cordial and crumbs spoiling the pages of her father's precious text. She was surprised to find that Snout continued to display a simple but accurate sense of translation and that his handwriting, while abysmal, showed some laborious care. Arty and Jack made fewer ink blots, but each rushed into easy translation mistakes, and Jack seemed to have a policy of never looking back, because his paragraphs always finished in cheerful incomprehensibility. When she was done, she joined Snout at the table in the window. He looked up from the book, his face sticky with bun, and gave her an unexpected grin.

'It's a grand story, the *Aeneid*, isn't it, miss?' he said, his eyes lit up with eagerness. 'You can smell Troy burning and you think Aeneas must die, but then he comes striding out of the flames with his old father on his back.'

'He is a virtuous son,' said Beatrice quietly. She could not read those books of the epic now without a tear for her own father, who had weighed so little at the end that she would gladly have carried him beyond death's reach.

'He has nothing left, but he never gives up, does he?' said Snout. 'And his men – "One day you will look back on your problems as if they were nothing," he says to 'em. *Forsan et haec olim meminisse iuvabit.*'

'In the future you may be helped by remembering the past,' Beatrice added.

'If you don't die first, of course,' added Snout. 'He lost half his ships just on the way to Italy.'

'I've always thought Virgil's *Aeneid* quite the most exciting of the Roman texts,' said Beatrice. 'Would you enjoy us all reading it together?'

'I'm not sure the others will,' said Snout, wrinkling his nose in doubt. 'Usually, we just read a passage or two and use the dictionary to help us write it out.' Though he did his best to appear uninterested, she noticed he brushed some crumbs carefully from her father's book and closed it with unexpected gentleness.

'Written translation is far too much work for the summer, don't you think, Snout?' she asked and was amused to see how suspicion and interest mingled in his face. 'It's much more entertaining to read the whole story and just argue about it.'

'I'm not sure Arty and Jack'd see it as easier, miss,' he said. 'You'd really have to try and understand what it says, so you know who lives and who's all lying on the ground with his head chopped right down the middle and his cheeks and brains falling on opposite shoulders.'

'It's true the book is rife with bloody gore,' said Beatrice.

'The bit where the Queen of Carthage climbs the funeral pyre and stabs herself with a sword, miss, that's a gory bit,' he added.

'Would it be too much, I wonder.'

As Snout hastened to assure her that they could stomach the full horrors of ancient combat, Beatrice smiled and hid her surprise that the boy had obviously already read the entire epic before.

'Maybe it would help if we acted it out?' she said. A vague plan to excite the whole Latin class with the fun of group performance began to form in her head. 'We could acquire some swords and those round shields . . .'

'And bash each other in the head while we recite?' said Snout. 'I'm all for that, miss.'

'Very well, we are agreed,' she said. 'We will spend the summer enjoying our *Aeneid* again; and in the autumn you three will help me bring the excitement of Aeneas and his quest to the whole Latin class.'

'I'm not sure Arty and Jack are going to like it,' said Snout, frowning again. 'They'll probably work out how to blame me for it somehow.'

Beatrice sighed in frustration. 'Mr Grange informed me that you might have a serious chance at the annual Latin Scholarship if you work hard,' she said. 'If you keep worrying about what others will say, I'm afraid you'll deny yourself a real future, young man.'

'Me, sit for a scholarship?' said Snout. He snorted. 'They'll never give one to the likes of me, miss.'

'It's offered strictly on merit, Snout,' she said. 'No one will be counting the holes in your socks.'

'Sorry, miss.' He blushed, and Beatrice regretted her snappishness. No doubt the boy suffered much at the hands of his peers.

'We can talk more about scholarships when the term begins,' she continued. 'In the meantime, I suggest you grumble loudly when you tell Arty and Jack of my dreadful plans, but be sure to emphasise the cordial and buns.' Bribery might not be financially possible or morally defensible for the Latin class she would teach in the autumn term, but she smiled to know that for the summer she had two she could bribe and one who, disguised as the most prickly and unprepossessing of boys, had the makings of a real scholar.

Mrs Turber, wearing a hat like a cabbage, was crushed into the back row of the Town Hall's council chamber amid a crowd of similar hats while Mr Tillingham sat up front, wearing brown tweeds as if they were a general's uniform. Every one of the small leaded windows in the vaulted chamber had been opened to the evening air, but this merely allowed in the dust of the street and the raucous sound of the town brass band playing down on the cobbles below. Beatrice, who was torn between her moral duty to attend and a healthy fear of being cornered by any number of officious-looking ladies, had almost decided to slip away when Agatha Kent waved her over to a spare seat.

'If the war could be won by the wearing of red, white and blue ribbons on one's hat,' said Beatrice, sitting down behind a lady with a particularly large and festooned example, 'perhaps it would already be over.' She thought her father would have been appalled at the abundance of frivolous ornament detracting from the seriousness of the times.

'I assume that the good burghers of small German towns are at this very moment holding similar hot and crowded meetings,' said Agatha, fanning herself vigorously with a copy of the printed agenda. 'Apparently, we must attempt to create more committees and official titles than the enemy.'

'You are alone?' asked Beatrice. She could not ask directly after Agatha's nephews, but she had not seen them in a few days, and while she would never admit such a thought publicly, her independence did not preclude a lively interest in the young men.

'Hugh has been busy helping Dr Lawton out at the encampment, and Daniel has gone walking the Downs with some disreputable-looking poet friends,' said Agatha. 'So I'm quite alone.'

'Where is Lady Emily?' said Beatrice. 'I expected you both to be in charge.'

'Emily Wheaton is preoccupied with turning a wing of her house into an officers' hospital,' said Agatha.

'That's admirably patriotic,' said Beatrice.

'She hinted that it might forestall the army from taking the whole house and allowing all ranks to run amok in her flower beds,' said Agatha.

'Patriotic and practical then,' said Beatrice.

'Quite,' said Agatha.

On the dais, the Mayor, in full regalia, gavelled the meeting to order. Colonel Wheaton, whose local territorials, it was rumoured, were about to be given official standing as a regiment in Kitchener's new volunteer army, sat to his left. To his right he was flanked by Mrs Fothergill, dressed in full uniform of the Voluntary Aid Detachment with an extra sash of blue-and-white satin pinned with red roses.

The coming of war had given prominence to anyone of official status and in uniform, and so the front rows of the room contained those who had managed to drum up some sort of insignia. They were currently engaged in the tedious process of standing one by one to add their ceremonial notices of support to the afternoon's proceedings.

'The Sporting and Working Dog Association wishes to record its unconditional support of His Majesty's Government,' said Farmer Bowen, wearing the green sash of the Association Grand Marshal. The Boy Scouts, the Fire Brigade and the Merchants' Guild followed suit. Beatrice tried not to feel the dribble of sweat collecting along her spine as Agatha continued to fan energetically and the room cheered and applauded, leaving each speaker pink-faced and very pleased. As the flow of speakers diminished, Mrs Fothergill rose in a great rustling of starched linen and waited, stern-faced, for quiet in the room.

'The Ladies Voluntary Aid Detachment of East Sussex, Rye Chapter, offers its colours to our sovereign,' she intoned. At her words an entire row of similarly dressed ladies stood up from their chairs and processed up the centre aisle carrying an array of crutches, boxes of medical supplies, and flags of the nation and the association attached to stretcher poles. Farmer Bowen looked quite put out, as if he suddenly wished he had thought to bring dogs wearing rosettes.

'Are we all done?' the Mayor asked, as the ladies processed back to their seats. A tall woman in a severe black linen suit and a small hat rose from her chair. She wore only a single lapel button of office and carried a stack of newsletters.

'Who is that?' asked Beatrice.

'That's Alice Finch, a friend of Minnie Buttles, the Vicar's daughter,' whispered Agatha. 'They have recently come from London and opened a small photography studio in a converted stable at the lower end of the high street.' She peered closely at Miss Finch and added, 'I must say that to speak at a public meeting seems a little forward for such a newcomer.' Beatrice smiled to find that Agatha Kent was not entirely immune from the provincial suspicion of outsiders. The smaller the town, the more decades one was likely to be viewed as a newcomer; though in a town like Rye, newcomer was considered a step up from being a summer visitor and totally disregarded by all.

'The Women's National Suffrage Union, East Sussex Chapter, echoes the official statement of its national head-quarters in suspending all suffrage campaigning and declares its sacred duty and intention to support all national war efforts,' said Miss Finch. Her voice was hoarse, as if she were recovering from a bad cold. 'We have more information here if anyone would like a copy of our national directive.' The woman next to her, whose wispy curls and ruffled blouse gave her the look of a wind-tousled chick, stood with a hesitant smile and waved a pamphlet. Beatrice assumed she must be Minnie Buttles. The clapping was distinctly muted and mingled with some low chuckles and whispers. The severe woman looked tight-lipped, while her companion blushed.

'Suffragettes!' whispered Agatha as if communicating a great scandal. 'I'm quite sure invitations to tea are being quietly withdrawn all over the room.' Beatrice, who had some intellectual interest in the question of emancipation, had never met a suffragette in person. She tried to disguise her quickening interest, for it would not do to show any such enthusiasm.

The Mayor banged his gavel. 'The town thanks the ladies for their sensible response,' he said. 'I'm sure my wife, Mrs Fothergill, could use your members' help with her sock-knitting drive.' Mrs Fothergill and the severe woman each looked distinctly alarmed at such a prospect, and Beatrice noticed that Agatha hid a smile behind her printed agenda.

'I intend to offer our services to the Territorial Army in the form of a bicycle- and motorcycle-based messenger service,' said Miss Finch, her tone as severe as her manner.

'Quite so,' said the Mayor. 'All plans will be submitted during tea; ladies' organisations to Mrs Fothergill at the tea table and gentlemen to Colonel Wheaton and myself at the desk down here on the right.'

The Mayor was then induced by Colonel Wheaton to accept nomination as Chairman of the War Relief Committee and proceeded to read a slate of other commit-tee candidates: the local butcher, Mr DeVere, to manage food supplies; Mr Satchell, the shipowner, to coordinate maritime security; the Vicar to manage issues of morale and pastoral care; and Dr Lawton to coordinate medical services and programmes.

'That is a pretty neat coup d'état,' said Beatrice. 'Aren't you going to object? Don't you wish to be appointed?'

'I would never presume to interfere in the gentlemen's sphere,' said Agatha, folding her hands in her lap and assuming a neutral face. 'I will wait with all feminine patience to learn where I am needed.'

'Really?' asked Beatrice.

'No, of course not,' said Agatha. 'But the easiest way is always to work through a suitable man. You see, I already have Dr Lawton in place, which quite puts Mrs Fothergill and her volunteers where I want them. Now there is just the question of the Belgians.'

'As you all know,' said the Mayor, 'the advancing scourge of the German army has been laying waste to poor little Belgium with a ferocity unprecedented in Europe in these many centuries.'

'Well, if you don't count the Turks,' said Colonel Wheaton.

'Precisely,' said the Mayor. 'Such savagery has no place in the civilised countries of Europe or in civilised warfare, and we are called upon to bring relief and succour to the tens of thousands of our poor, innocent Belgian brethren fleeing these atrocities.'

'How many?' asked Farmer Bowen in consternation.

'We thought to fetch perhaps ten or twelve suitable refugees to begin with?' said Mrs Fothergill. 'Our illustrious neighbours, in the town of Bexhill-on-Sea, already claim to have twenty-six,' she added. 'Not that one wishes to accuse them of broadcasting their own generosity.'

'My wife, as you can see, has already devoted some time to the study of this issue,' said the Mayor.

'Oh no you do not,' whispered Agatha Kent, rising to her feet and waving.

'Mrs Kent?' said the Mayor.

'If I may beg the indulgence of the room to hear a word from the concerned ladies of Rye, I would just like to applaud dear Mrs Fothergill, on behalf of all of us, for her leadership in this area.' She paused for a hearty round of applause.

'Thank you, dear Mrs Kent,' said Mrs Fothergill, simpering.

'Mrs Fothergill and I are eager to work on this issue together,' continued Agatha, 'and I believe we ladies have the opportunity to do so under the guidance of a gentleman who not only has been working on this matter locally but has been asked to take a lead on the national stage.'

'Who is she talking about?' said the Mayor in a loud whisper to his wife, who could not answer him through her clamped lips. Her face turned as pale as her dress.

'For the sake of the Belgians and for the opportunity to associate our town with a national spokesman on this issue, I know dear Mrs Fothergill and I will join Colonel Wheaton and Dr Lawton in asking the room to nominate Mr Tillingham by acclamation.'

'I think Mrs Fothergill is quite capable . . .' But the Mayor's voice was drowned out by an enthusiastic round of cheering and clapping, which grew louder as Mr Tillingham stood up from his seat at the front of the room, waving his hat to all sides and bowing modestly under the applause.

'We have our full committee heads, I think,' said Colonel Wheaton. If he had been primed by his wife to act in concert with Agatha Kent, he gave no sign. The Mayor glared and his wife sat down abruptly, but the room was decidedly in favour of Mr Tillingham, who made some show of reluctance before mounting to the podium to speak to the room.

'This small corner of immutable England has been a home and a refuge for this poor wandering scribe, and so I cannot express my gratitude that you would entrust me to represent you in this important cause,' said Mr Tillingham. He held his hat over his heart and looked to the heavens as if asking for divine inspiration. 'In a time of great peril, one cannot but look around this ancient town, filled with generations of stout-hearted, generous English men and women, and know that our Belgian neighbours could not ask a kinder, more welcoming sanctuary.'

'Actually the good people of our town are as frugal and suspicious a group as I have ever met, and they actively dislike all foreigners,' whispered Agatha to Beatrice. 'But we will hope for the best.'

As the meeting concluded, Beatrice looked around to see how she might escape the ladies, such as Bettina Fothergill, who now measured all women by whether one was at leisure to work full-time on the war effort. Agatha, rising to move swiftly to the aisle, took the time to stop and pat her hand.

'If anyone should ask, you are pledged to Belgian Relief full-time, my dear,' she said. 'Direct all further questions to me.'

'Thank you,' said Beatrice, grateful again for Agatha's sharp understanding. As she slipped from the room, she grinned to see Agatha shake hands with Miss Finch and her companion and direct them, deliberately, towards the tea table, where, Beatrice assumed, Agatha intended their enthusiasm to be the final straw in Mrs Fothergill's bad day.

Snout was after rabbits. He had thin wire snares set below two of the many holes in the bank, a small pile of apple skin left a few inches away. He knew the sweet, clean smell was all in the warren, filling the dark tunnels and causing rabbits to flick sleepy ears and snuffle their noses. As he crouched against the high bank of the dirt lane, his back buried as much as possible into a patch of tall, furry nettles, he could smell the bitter, milky sap of the crushed stalks. The flowers of a tall pink mallow trembled over his head, and he smelled his own warm sweat and the sharpness of fallen apples in the orchard above the bank.

While he waited, he pulled from his bag a dog-eared translation of Virgil's *Aeneid*. He had borrowed the book for the summer, slipping in when the school library was empty and dropping the book out of the window into a yew bush to avoid Miss Devon, who seemed to think her job as English teacher included defending the school's books against dirty boys. His fellow pupils would have pilloried any boy for reading a single page more than required, but he had whiled away many a detention in the library breathlessly following the Trojan Aeneas on his quest to found the Roman Empire. At year's end, and halfway through his third rereading, he could not bear to leave Aeneas outside the stench-filled cave to the Underworld, with the hell dogs baying at the dreadful Sibyl's approach. He had resisted the urge to show Miss Nash the book. Teachers enjoyed their godlike powers to toy with him and punish as they pleased, and he had already let slip too much enthusiasm for Virgil. But he had a strange feeling she would have understood.

As he waited and read, he kept one eye on his snares and one ear cocked for any sound of the farmer. Any nailed boots, any cart wheel or snorting of ewes being herded in a mass of hot, oily wool, a collie nipping at their heels. It was not the farmer's time to be in this lane, he was likely harvesting corn in his upper fields, but it was always wise to listen. The farmer had no respect for the track being a public way and would box the ears of rabbiting boys and threaten them with the constable for poaching. Snout could still feel a blow he had once had from the farmer and being held almost to choking, by the collar, until the constable was called and the constable asking for his full name with which he was christened, and the farmer shouting that he was a dirty Gypsy and not deserving of the benefits of Church.

'Richard Edmund Sidley,' he had said, the name almost unfamiliar in his ears. Everyone called him Snout, except his mother, who called him Dickie darling (which was worse than Snout if there were other boys about to hear), and his father, who called him Son.

'Fancy name for a low poacher,' the farmer replied, and the constable arrested him and hauled him away in his dog cart, taking along one of the two dead rabbits. Near town, the constable gave him a half-hearted box on the ear, not half as hard as his sister or mother could deliver, and told him to run home.

'Lucky for you we don't hang poachers no more,' he said.

'Can I have my rabbit?' Snout asked.

'Course, I could send you to the reformatory,' the constable said. Snout took off running and heard the constable calling after him, 'Tell your mother Arnie Sprigs sends his best regards.' His mother had been a beauty in her day, and many a man in Rye still shook his head in disbelief that she had chosen to marry his father instead.

A leaf twitched at the nearest hole. A soft grey nose wriggled and sniffed. Snout held his breath and did his best to quiet the beat of his heart. A bird sang a clear note in the treetops, the leaves of the hedges shivered, and a grey-brown rabbit dashed headlong into the wire noose to fall, writhing in the dirty lane, blood spurting from its neck. Snout wrapped the body as best he could in big dock leaves and put it in his bag. He put the Virgil on top and hoped the rabbit wouldn't bleed all over it.

Part Two

War broke: and now the Winter of the world
With perishing great darkness closes in.
. . .

For after Spring had bloomed in early Greece,
And Summer blazed her glory out with Rome,
An Autumn softly fell, a harvest home,
A slow grand age, and rich with all increase.
But now, for us, wild Winter, and the need
Of sowings for new Spring, and blood for seed.

WILFRED OWEN, '1914'

CHAPTER TEN

IT WAS A LATE August evening when the refugees came. The sun was lying in a low amber shaft along the high street below, the rooftops and chimney pots still painted in glowing colour, but the houses of Mrs Turber's cobbled street were already sunk deep in their own shadows. Beatrice had been called to her door by the train whistle and waited, like other householders, in her own doorway. Mrs Turber stood two doors down with her neighbour, clutching a shawl around her shoulders, as if the arriving refugees had brought the chill of war to the warm evening. Above them, Mr Tillingham, prevented from going to the docks by the sudden flaring of his gout, stood at the open window of his garden room smoking a cigar.

The small group, led by Dr Lawton and the Mayor, came slowly up the cobbles. Despite the doctor's age and the Mayor's girth, they seemed regally upright and hearty compared to the refugees, who climbed with great fatigue, heads down and shoulders hunched under shawls or grey donated blankets. Instead of the apple-cheeked children expected by the ladies waiting at the Town Hall, these were mostly families, the parents and grandparents leaning in one to the other, a hand reaching or a shoulder offered. Three old nuns made a small family of their own in the rear, habits creased and grimy, hands counting their rosary beads. All carried only small, shapeless bundles, as if there had been no time to gather belongings, or as if they had been forced to shed them along the way.

Beatrice had not expected the silence. She heard only the scrape of wooden clogs and the wheezing of breath, the strike of the doctor's cane and a low cough somewhere in the rear. It was the same pressing sense of solemnity as a funeral procession, and Beatrice felt her heart clench. A sob broke the silence, a low and plaintive sob as a young woman carrying a small child raised her face to the brightness above the rooftops. Her shawl fell from her head, revealing a tumble of pale blonde hair and a face as white as bone save for the blue hollows beneath her eyes. Her dress was dirty and torn about the hem, and yet Beatrice saw it was panelled in thick lace down the front, and her boots, now ruined with mud, were of soft leather with an elegant curved heel. The child she carried wore a rough peasant's smock and clogs. His ruddy cheeks announced that he belonged not to the girl but to the large family just ahead of her, the mother already clutching a baby and the father keeping his arm around the back of an old woman, bent low under the weight of her years and suffering. Hugh Grange brought up the rear, supporting the shuffling steps of an older man who kept a hand over his eyes, as if he had seen too much and could no longer bear to look about him.

As they passed, the neighbours seemed to grow conscious of their own staring and called out welcomes in softened voices. But the tired and stumbling refugees only shrank further into their blankets and quickened away up the hill. Hugh glanced at Beatrice as he passed, and his face seemed to brighten as if he were glad to see her. He gave her a small nod.

Beatrice had decided to keep away from the Town Hall. Though she was determined to give such free time as she had to Agatha Kent's committee, there were many more ladies than needed to meet the arrivals, and she did not wish to be among the curious with their pressing enthusiasm. Now, however, she felt an urgent need to follow the refugees and assist as she might in their safe billeting.

The council room was in some state of uproar when she arrived. Urgent discussions bordering on argument seemed to be going on in many corners while the seated refugees were attacked from all sides by ladies swinging hot teapots in reckless arcs and pressing huge trays of sandwiches on people who were already holding sandwiches. The lady pounding spirited music-hall favourites on the piano was blithely unaware that she was merely adding to the general din. Meanwhile a small girl, dressed in Sunday best, much beribboned about the head and carrying a basket of shortbread, offered her treats to the refugees with the trembling timidity of one asked to pass raw meat through the bars of a lion's cage.

Beatrice saw Hugh standing apart, eating two ham sandwiches at once.

'Sorry to be so rude, but I'm famished,' he said by way of greeting. He sounded exhausted. 'A very long day and no lunch.'

'What's happening?' asked Beatrice. 'I see some anxious discussions.'

'We have a number of large families who understandably do not wish to be parted,' said Hugh. 'Meanwhile many well-meaning ladies have made meticulous arrangements to take in one or two guests each. Ironic that families who cleaved together through German brutality may be forced asunder by English charity.'

Mr Tillingham, a frown of concentration on the great forehead, walked towards them, deep in discussion with an agitated Mrs Fothergill. 'One must open one's heart in the face of this scale of human tragedy,' he was saying, a hand patting her arm. 'Would that I had more to offer than the limited scope of a bachelor establishment.'

'We had requested mostly children, but my husband said the people in charge were quite rude about it,' said Mrs Fothergill. She spotted Hugh. 'Mr Grange, you were there. Were there no children to be had?'

'We managed one or two,' said Hugh, 'but as you can see, they came with parents and grandparents attached, and they were unwilling to part with them.'

'One could also have wished for more genteel folk,' said Mrs Fothergill. She frowned at a man who was noisily drinking from a teacup held in both hands and lowered her voice. 'Of course, we will succour all who need us, but it is quite impossible to ask our ladies to take absolute peasants into their own houses, however charming their wooden clogs.'

'I'm afraid it was all desperation at the docks,' said Hugh. 'They just sorted us a group, like cutting out sheep at the Wednesday market, and your husband did not like to refuse. I believe the Mayor of Bexhill was there collecting a second batch.'

Agatha Kent seemed to have quieted most of the arguments and now approached bearing a sheaf of papers, pen in hand. 'The farm at New Road will take one family. They have an empty cottage,' she said. 'Colonel Wheaton has offered a gamekeeper's lodge to hold another, and the Misses Porter will take in the nuns until they can receive assistance from their order. Meanwhile, we will just have to remake the lower street hostel over to accommodate families instead of boys' and girls' dormitories.'

'People will be so disappointed,' said Mrs Fothergill. 'They wished so much to open their hearts and homes.'

'Perhaps you could give up taking in the accountant and his wife?' asked Agatha, indicating a thin refugee couple sitting very protectively either side of a battered brown suitcase. 'You already have so many obligations with the Voluntary Aid Detachment, and there are other ladies wishing desperately to be called.'

'Let me sink from exhaustion, yet still will I do my duty,' said Mrs Fothergill. 'I shall not shirk from the strife.'

'Is that everyone?' asked Hugh.

'I believe so,' said Agatha. 'There may be just a small issue with the professor whom you offered to take in, Mr Tillingham.'

'He's not a charlatan, is he?' said Mr Tillingham. 'I picked him out as a man of great intellectual refinement.'

'It's just that he comes with a daughter,' said Agatha, indicating the pale girl Beatrice had noticed in the street. She was still sitting among the peasant family, holding the baby while his mother drank tea. As her fingers played with a tiny hand and the baby reached for her pale hair, Beatrice saw on her white face the same faint smile as in a Bellini painting of the Madonna. It was a look of grace that Beatrice had always thought came from knowledge of events to come but which she now saw more simply as a temporary moment of quiet solace on a refugee's journey.

'I'm not sure a bachelor household is at all suitable for a young woman,' Mr Tillingham was saying. He seemed quite agitated at the thought, as if a young woman would be sure to leave stockings drying in the parlour and walk about in her chemise, shedding hairpins on the carpets.

'If you wish to withdraw, we have others willing to step in,' said Agatha.

'No, no, I am called to leadership on this issue on the national stage,' said Mr Tillingham. 'I must have my refugee.'

'Well, I'm sure your housekeeper can cope with one extra girl,' said Agatha. 'And Miss Nash is just down the street. I'm sure she would be happy to be invited to entertain the young woman.'

At this suggestion Mr Tillingham seemed to brighten up. 'Perhaps a different solution is before us,' he said. 'Perhaps the young lady can stay with Miss Nash and the professor with me?'

'Again, they want to stay together,' said Agatha.

'But in this case, we are the nearest of neighbours,' said Mr Tillingham. 'Why, we might view Miss Nash's quarters as an annex to the garden, and the young ladies would of course be free to trip back and forth across the lawn as they please.' With a wave of the hand he thus disposed of the twelve-foot-high brick wall that shut all trace of his sylvan landscape from the street.

'I fear I am not the mistress of my own home,' said Beatrice, torn between wishing to chide Mr Tillingham for his high-handed approach and the promise of the doors to his home being thrown open to her at last.

'You and the young lady would also be welcome to the full use of my small library if you so wish,' he said, as if the offer were a casual afterthought. But she knew it was a deliberate inducement, and she also knew she could not resist.

'I would be honoured to do my part, of course,' she said.

'Mrs Turber shall be compensated from my own narrow pocket if necessary,' said Mr Tillingham. 'Though I believe large amounts of funds are being raised?' he added, looking with barely disguised eagerness at Agatha.

'Your generosity will show us all the way, Mr Tillingham,' said Agatha. 'Let us go and talk to the professor.'

'Our Mr Tillingham does like to insist publicly on his own penury,' said Hugh. 'I believe his sighing garners him three or four dinner invitations a week.'

'I suppose the greatest writers are by definition too true to their art to become as wealthy as those who write entertaining rubbish,' said Beatrice. 'Only he does seem to have one of the nicest houses in town.'

'He does not stint himself alone at home,' said Hugh. 'He is as fond of good claret as the next man. Only, when he has guests to dinner, he invariably feeds them mutton and cheap Spanish wine.'

'I look forward to that,' said Beatrice. 'I have a feeling he and Mrs Turber may compete to feed us badly. Perhaps I will start saving my bread crusts.'

'If you become malnourished, I shall undertake to escort you and the young lady to a suitably respectable tea shop and feed you up on scones and cream,' said Hugh.

'How gallant of you,' said Beatrice. 'I imagine the same invitation would be forthcoming even if the young lady were less than beautiful.'

'You must admit she is quite the damsel in distress,' he said. 'My cousin Daniel will no doubt fling himself at her feet, parchment in hand.' Hugh seemed gloomy at this prospect, and Beatrice laughed at him. 'Not to suggest that you are in any way not worthy of a poem or two,' he added. 'I didn't mean to imply . . .'

'I am quite beyond such foolishness and therefore cannot take offence,' said Beatrice.

'Nonsense,' said Hugh. 'No lady is too old for a sonnet, which is why Daniel still writes them to Aunt Agatha's cook and always thereby receives the largest slice of Victoria sponge.'

'Victory is ours,' said Mr Tillingham, returning with Agatha. 'The professor makes no objection to the arrangement.'

'And Mrs Turber is more than agreeable to being compensated for a second tenant,' said Agatha. 'So the burden falls on you, Miss Nash. Are you sure you won't mind?'

'She can sleep in my writing corner,' said Beatrice. 'I can squeeze my desk into my bedroom.'

'I am deep in your debt, young lady,' said Mr Tillingham. 'You must bring your guest tomorrow to see her father. Not too early, of course. I work in the mornings. I think we should meet for tea, and I will make arrangements for the green parlour to be set aside for father and daughter to meet quietly at any hour.' He looked at his watch and repeated, 'Not any hour, of course. I must be able to work.' With that he swept away to carry off the professor. Beatrice watched Mr Tillingham, solicitous, and the professor, a little more cheerful, offer a brief farewell to the girl. The girl said nothing but merely watched her father leave, her hands at her sides, her body leaning slightly, as if invisibly pulled after him, and all the light gone from her face.

As the birds announced dawn, the girl in the upstairs cottage bedroom began calling for her papa. Beatrice woke to find her cheek pressed to a floorboard, her arms and legs stiff from sleeping on the parlour rug. She had given the exhausted girl her own bed, helping to remove her ruined boots and then merely loosening buttons and stays before pulling the clean sheets and blankets over the girl's filthy dress and tucking her in as she might do for an invalid. She had then taken a quilt and retired to the parlour to sleep on the floor. Now the cottage was cold and dark, her quilt warm. It felt easier not to move, but another moan from above led her to unwrap herself and stumble to her feet. She gathered the quilt around her shoulders like a shawl and crept upstairs. The girl was deep in sleep, but twisted in her sheets, moaning and plucking at the covers with her fingers and muttering in French. Abigail the maid was crouched at the bedside, smoothing her hair and trying to straighten the bed linen with one hand.

'There, now, you lie still,' Abigail was repeating quietly. 'You're safe now and Papa's safe too.'

'Does she need a doctor?' asked Beatrice, tiptoeing across the room in her stockinged feet.

'She'll be fine, miss,' said Abigail. 'My mum has bad dreams sometimes. If you just speak to 'em like they're awake it seems to calm 'em right down.'

'I don't know that she speaks English,' said Beatrice.

'I don't think it matters, do it now, miss?' said Abigail, leaning in to pat the girl's shoulder. 'Just a kind voice in the dark is all we want most times.' The girl gave a sigh and settled more peacefully on her pillow, her face relaxing. Abigail patted her hand, and the fingers stopped clawing.

'You have the touch, Abigail,' whispered Beatrice. 'Can you sit with her awhile?'

'I could stay a bit, miss,' said Abigail. 'But I need to get the stove lit soon. I'm thinking you'll be wanting a fire laid under the copper for some bathwater, even though it's not bath day?'

'Yes, perhaps you'd better run along and get the copper going before Mrs Turber wakes up,' said Beatrice. 'That way we don't have to disturb her morning with all this added generosity.'

'I'll bring you some tea, miss,' said Abigail. 'If the lady cries out again, just hold her hand.'

The girl's hands lay on the covers like fledgling birds. Beatrice remembered how her father's hands, similarly naked and blue-veined, had withered under her touch, and how she had felt the warmth retreat from them even before her father took his last breath. It seemed to Beatrice, in the chilly half-light of dawn, that this moaning girl had come out of that same place of death, bringing its smell and its fear with her, and Beatrice shrank from touching her. She slumped to the floor by the bed, drew the quilt tight around her, and looked hard at the window as if by staring she might urge the sun to quicker life.

It was still early when Beatrice went out into the courtyard bearing a large comb, a broad sash of white grosgrain ribbon, and her sewing box. Birds sang in a garden beyond the wall. A white butterfly was looking for milkweed. She could hear the snort and jingle of a horse tossing his head in the street and smell the peppery scent of Mrs Turber's tomato plants wilting against sun-heated brick. Amid the sounds and scents of the hot summer morning, the girl sat on a wooden chair in the small courtyard behind the cottage, head bent, allowing Abigail to vigorously towel-dry her hair.

After a gentle scrubbing with carbolic soap, the girl had emerged from the dented copper hip bath in the kitchen as unself-conscious as a child being bathed by its nanny and allowed Abigail and Beatrice to rub her dry with two of Mrs Turber's rather rough cotton towels. She had one or two large bruises on her arms and a deeply bruised cut on her thigh, which was scabbing over but red and black around the edges. Beatrice sent Abigail for a bottle of iodine and they soaked the wound, the girl crying out only once as the iodine stung. When it was a dry purple stain, they dressed her in a set of Beatrice's underclothes, neither the oldest nor the newest she owned, and in a medium-good cotton tea dress and a pair of embroidered leather slippers which had always been too good to discard but too flowery for Beatrice's taste. Beatrice was sorry to lose the tea dress from her adequate but not extensive wardrobe, but understood that the loss meant she had picked correctly – bestowing a gift rather than the abject charity of handing over something only suitable to be discarded. She was also slightly pained that the dress swam on the girl, and that its cornflower blue, set against the pale skin and hair, made a colour harmony worthy of a painter's brush, whereas it had only ever looked washed out against her own dark hair.

As Beatrice approached, the girl stood and let Abigail gather the back of the dress with a few running stitches and then tie the sash around to hide the makeshift alteration. She then sat again and made no sound as Abigail set to work with the comb and fought her way through several nasty knotted tangles. Finally the hair flowed straight and smooth and Beatrice stepped in to roll and pin the pale cornsilk into a simple, low bun at the nape of the neck. With her hair up the girl looked less like a frightened child and more like a young woman recently out of the schoolroom. Beatrice judged her to be seventeen or so.

'What's going on here?' said Mrs Turber, stepping into the courtyard with a glowering face. 'Water all over the floor and a fire blazing like it's November.'

'Abigail was helping me bathe our guest, Mrs Turber,' said Beatrice.

'Just because I offered a roof, doesn't mean . . .' The girl turned to look at her, and Mrs Turber stopped as suddenly as she had started. 'Well, bless me, she's quite the angel, isn't she?' she added and then did not seem to know what to say next.

Beatrice translated for the girl that the large, red-faced woman thought she looked like an angel. The girl gave a shy smile and stepped forward.

'*Non, non. Vous êtes un ange, madame,*' she said quietly. 'An angel.' With that she kissed Mrs Turber's rough hand.

'Bless me, she speaks English,' said Mrs Turber and patted the girl's hand, adding, 'You are *très* welcome *dans ma maison, mam'selle.*'

'Thank you, *chère madame,*' said the girl, her English romantically accented. 'I am Celeste, I am daughter of Professor Fontaine.'

'Well, don't just stand there with your mouth open, Abigail,' said Mrs Turber to her dumbfounded maid. 'Take Miss Celeste in and get her some breakfast. Make sure you bring her a bowl of the good cream, and perhaps she'd like some smoked haddock and poached eggs?'

'Your generosity is unbounded, Mrs Turber,' said Beatrice, as Abigail led Celeste into the house. She wondered if she too was to partake of haddock and cream or whether her usual breakfast of porridge and toast, and the occasional overboiled egg, would be served.

'She needs feeding up,' said Mrs Turber, frowning as if Beatrice had failed to see this. 'And she'll be needing better than that rag of a dress, I'm sure. I have some bits put by from when I was younger. I had the waist of a humming-bird, my husband used to say . . .'

'That's my second-best tea dress,' said Beatrice, distracted by trying to picture any bird with an appreciable waist.

'Well, I'm sure it's perfectly adequate,' said Mrs Turber, giving her a doubtful look. 'But Miss Celeste is clearly a girl of great refinement.' She let the thought trail away, and Beatrice had an unworthy urge to drop Aunt Marbely's name in rebuke. The thought made her snappish.

'She is very blonde and lovely,' she said. 'But were fairness the accepted test of rank and refinement, no doubt the royal family would all be albino.'

'I was referring to her respectful manners,' said Mrs Turber. 'Something some of us could no doubt learn from.'

'Touché, Mrs Turber,' said Beatrice. 'You are right, of course, and I am a shrew.'

'The royal family indeed,' said Mrs Turber. 'I've never been so shocked.'

'Then I am doubly sorry, for I know you are a woman who is often shocked, Mrs Turber,' said Beatrice. 'I am stiff and grumpy from sleeping on the floor and waking up too early.'

'I suppose now you'll be wanting the bed back again?' said Mrs Turber. Beatrice could think of nothing worse. No doubt the wormy frame and lumpy mattress had been rendered more wormy, lumpy and damp from being kept in Mrs Turber's cellar and chewed by mice.

'Mrs Kent has promised to send another bed,' said Beatrice. 'But if you do have clothing and linens put by, I'm sure Celeste would be deeply indebted for your trouble.'

Mrs Turber brightened considerably at this suggestion. 'I'll alter them for her with my own hands, bless her,' she said. 'I have a dress or two and some red flannel petticoats that still have years of strength in them. A lady needs good, stout petticoats.'

'In all seasons and climates, Mrs Turber,' said Beatrice. As Mrs Turber bustled into the house, Beatrice grinned. She was surprised to feel a warmth of purpose in being now connected to the great enterprise under way. To provide sanctuary was an ancient tradition, and as long as pride did not become hubris – she must not start talking of 'my refugee', like Mrs Fothergill – she acknowledged that it felt gratifying to have found some small connection to the war.

Mrs Turber was not the only citizen of Rye to be taken with Celeste. Mrs Saunders, who did the washing and mending, was summoned after breakfast to take away the spoiled dress. In the passageway, she shook her head at Beatrice over the impossibility of cleaning such fine ruined silk, but when Beatrice brought her into the parlour to explain the matter to Celeste, not wanting to dispose of even this ruined item without consultation, Mrs Saunders began to weep at the girl's shy shrug of understanding and made tearful promises to do the work of Hercules himself to save the dress.

'Please tell her it does not matter,' said Celeste in a whisper to Beatrice. 'I shall never wear it again.'

'You will if these hands ever 'ad any skill and learning,' said Mrs Saunders. 'And you shall 'ave the lace off it sure as I'm a good Englishwoman, for I will clean that with the blessed Sunday bread and eat potatoes instead.'

Mrs Saunders must have gone to gossip about Celeste at Pike Brothers' haberdashery department, because not an hour later, Arty's mother knocked at the door to drop in a small sewing kit and several lengths of hair ribbon for the 'poor young lady', while just before lunch the Misses Porter brought one of the nuns to visit, in case the girl had need of spiritual counselling, and presented Celeste with a small jar of their own gooseberry preserves. Lunch itself was interrupted by the arrival of Agatha Kent's man with the bed in the farm cart, and Celeste looked to Beatrice as if she would drop in limp exhaustion as Smith and the farm boy laboured loudly up the stairs and bumped about moving the writing desk and knocking the bed together with wooden mallets while the horse snorted at the open window and then put his head in the window box to nibble on Mrs Turber's pelargoniums.

Beatrice had sent Celeste to rest in her newly curtained nook and was contemplating retiring to her own room, now stripped of its dirty linens, when there was a hideous shriek downstairs and Abigail called her down to receive a freshly killed rabbit that had sent Mrs Turber into a fit of the vapours. The three boys she tutored had sneaked in through the back gate to knock at the kitchen door with the gift and to ask if the Belgian princess might be induced to wave at them from the upstairs window. Not to worry, reported Abigail, she had given Snout a box on the ear for his impudence and sent the lot of them packing. Beatrice suggested that for a girl her size, the boxing of boys' ears was not a safe pursuit.

'He's my big brother, miss,' said Abigail. 'He knows I'll give him worse than that if he don't mind his manners.'

Beatrice was horrified. How had she not seen the family resemblance, the same streak of resolve in the thin faces? How close had she come, several times, to making some remark or giving some warning to Abigail about the boy's family?

'The rabbit is quite a prize,' said Beatrice, blushing with confusion. 'Please thank your brother for me.'

'Best not,' said Abigail. 'Likely he poached it. He'll come to no good, if he's not careful.'

'Your brother is quite the scholar,' said Beatrice, looking to make amends, if only to appease her own conscience.

'If only he had his mind fixed on the schooling and not half of it always off in the woods,' the young maid replied. 'I hope you'll be hard on him, miss. Keep him up to his work.'

'Did you like school?' asked Beatrice. If she was as sharp as her brother, it seemed a sorry waste that she should spend her life blacking grates and emptying chamber pots.

'Oh, I loved it, miss,' she said. 'But too much learning's a waste for a girl like me. I'll be married most likely and a few years in service and a bit o' money put by means I'll get to have my pick, rather than have to take pot luck. You know how it is?'

'It can surely never be a waste to feed one's mind,' said Beatrice, shocked but impressed at the girl's practical grasp of her prospects.

'No offence, miss,' she said. 'That's all well and good for a lady like you, but I'm a farrier's daughter. The husband I'll be after likely won't take kindly to a wife with airs of reading books and such.'

'I think you'll find most women in pursuit of a husband share an interest in appearing less educated than they really are,' said Beatrice. 'It is why I have a low opinion of them.'

'Of women, miss?' said Abigail.

'No, of husbands,' said Beatrice.

'Maybe I won't need one if my brother does make something fine of himself with all his schooling,' said Abigail, wistfully. 'At least if I kept house for him, I'd know who was in charge – and it wouldn't be him.'

CHAPTER ELEVEN

Mr Tillingham and the Professor were seated on the lawn, two dark silhouettes at a white iron table, under the spreading sunlit boughs of an ancient mulberry tree. The tea urn had not yet been brought out, but a stand of small cakes and a silver platter of thinly sliced bread and butter suggested its imminent arrival. Only the white cloth on the folding side table flapped to break the green and silent tableau. Hugh wondered whether the scene before him was an illusion or whether the day before, among the suffering refugees on the docks of Folkestone, had been just a dream, for surely the two scenes were from incompatible worlds.

When Mr Tillingham had sent a note that morning inviting Aunt Agatha and her nephews to tea, Hugh had tried gently to suggest that Mr Tillingham's exhausted refugees should be allowed quiet.

'That is precisely why we must go,' said his aunt. 'If we decline, there is no knowing whom Mr Tillingham might invite instead.'

'Gentlemen, welcome,' said Mr Tillingham, waving his cane. 'I do hope the ladies are en route?' He turned to the Professor and added, 'This fine weather does tend to make the bread curl and these days it's a shame to waste good butter.' The Professor stood to greet them, and Hugh, who had not paid much attention to him during the long trip from Folkestone, saw that he was not as old a man as he had appeared. In fresh clothing and clean-shaven, he presented a compact but upright figure. He wore a dark tweed jacket over a high-collared white shirt and dull red tie, some dun-coloured flannels pulled in at the waist and a pair of soft shoes. That his shirt moved independently about the neck showed that it was too big. Hugh assumed from Mr Tillingham's approving glance that he himself had donated the items and was not displeased with the professorial effect.

'You look so much better, Professor,' said Hugh. 'I hope you had a good night's sleep?'

'The home of Monsieur Tillingham has provided sanctuary for the body and balm for the soul,' said the Professor. 'I was just saying that I feel as if returned to civilisation from a long expedition to a darker continent.'

'You will be shocked at the privations the Professor has endured,' said Mr Tillingham. 'I only wonder if they will be too much for the ladies to bear.'

'Aunt Agatha and Miss Nash will have words for you if you dare suggest they are too fragile for such stories,' said Daniel, casually removing a slice of bread from the tea table and settling in a chair to munch on it.

'But perhaps the Professor's daughter will not like to relive such difficulties?' said Hugh. 'How is your daughter, sir?'

'I have not yet seen her. It was better for her to rest,' said the Professor. 'For though I shielded her as much as any father could, my poor child, she has glimpsed *des horreurs*.'

'Heroic,' said Mr Tillingham, stroking his chin. 'The learned man stands against the brutish horde. It is an ancient theme.'

'I visited the hostel today,' said Hugh. 'Some of your compatriots report great difficulties sleeping. Dr Lawton and I had to prescribe sleeping draughts to several.'

'I'm not surprised they are undone.' The Professor sighed. 'To the peasant, the loss of a few possessions, and the eviction from home – I am sure it feels as large to them as it does to persons of real property. Yet even my own not inconsiderable losses must be of no account against the destruction of civilisation to which I was witness.'

'The Germans burned the ancient library at the Professor's university,' said Mr Tillingham. 'If we needed any further proof that civilisation stands in the breach . . .'

'I was able to persuade the commanding officer to save some of the rarest volumes,' said the Professor. 'But even he, an educated gentleman to whom I could beg for reason, he could not keep his troops from putting the buildings to the flame.' He produced a large handkerchief from his pocket and turned aside his face.

Hugh felt some doubt as to whether the burning of books should be counted a greater crime than forcing poor families from their homes at bayonet point. And the suffering he had witnessed on the docks had seemed to make no distinction between rich and poor. But he held his tongue. He did not think the present company would welcome a debate on such questions – for he had no doubt that spirited debate was the first casualty of any war.

For Beatrice the opening of Mr Tillingham's front door was the opening of the temple. Stepping in behind Agatha Kent and Celeste, she could already smell the books, even above the waxy note of wood polish and the hint of recently baked cakes from the unseen kitchen. Leather-bound books, old books with yellowed pages, new books with the sharp scent of printers' ink and the promise of crisp, uncut pages awaiting the paper knife. Pamphlets and chapbooks in boxes, clean paper awaiting the typewriter or pen. She could feel a familiarity, and a tiny, tremulous awakening of a hope that she belonged in this tiled hall, these high-ceilinged parlours. Might Mr Tillingham indeed invite her to use his library? Might not Mr Tillingham's secretary experience a sudden temporary illness and Beatrice be allowed to step in and assist as she had done so often for her father? Might the great man, in his gratitude, not then take an avuncular interest in her writings as he already did for Daniel? For a moment Beatrice allowed her mind to indulge in these happy thoughts and to feel a glow of possibility that she had not felt since losing her father.

Her reverie was interrupted by Celeste, whose grip upon her arm tightened. The girl trembled violently, and her face was once again pale. Beatrice was reminded sharply that the pleasures of at last reaching Mr Tillingham's inner sanctum were purchased on the back of much loss and distress, and that it was foolish of them all to subject the girl to a garden full of strangers.

'*Courage, ma petite*,' said Beatrice, patting Celeste's hand. 'We go to see your papa.'

At tea, the Professor and Mr Tillingham held forth at length about conditions in Belgium. Beatrice gently refused a second cup of tea and was glad when Agatha whispered that she was welcome to slip away from the table to admire the gardens. She had stopped to peer at a blowsy purple clematis flower which spread its velvet petals against the old brick of the garden wall when Daniel, smoking a foul-smelling cigarillo, and Hugh came strolling along the narrow path.

'A more sentimental picture for the artist could hardly be imagined,' said Daniel, nodding his head across the lawn towards the Professor and his daughter. The Professor inhabited his chair like a wicker throne, thought Beatrice, and Celeste, seated on a low wicker stool at his side, her hand on his sleeve, her skirts pooling on the grass, her body twisted slightly to his and her face tilted up, looked like a supplicating princess. The Professor, rendered perhaps more heroic by her air of adoration, was still lecturing, and Agatha Kent and Mr Tillingham were settled in attitudes of the closest attention. 'Perhaps to be titled "Respite from the Storm"? Or "The Grateful Guests"?' he added. 'She does make a compelling case for an immediate call to arms.'

'Must you always be so mocking?' asked Hugh, looking grim. 'They have lost their home, their country – everything.

The desperation we witnessed at the port is beyond anything we have imagined.'

'At least they have each other,' said Beatrice. 'Her father is everything to her.' Her own voice developed an unwanted tremor as she spoke.

'Sombre thoughts for such a lovely afternoon,' said Hugh.

'I do not make light of their suffering,' said Daniel. 'It is just human nature to be more interested in fighting to rescue beautiful young maidens. I am ready to run to the recruiter if only she will drop her handkerchief.'

'If she dropped a handkerchief, no doubt you would be too lazy to even pick it up,' said Hugh.

'You are right,' said Daniel, with a sigh. 'But I may feel a poem coming on.'

'Miss Nash, it does you much credit to have taken in the young lady,' said Hugh. 'I think they ask too much of you.'

'Aunt Agatha could take her,' said Daniel. 'Then we would see her every day at breakfast, Hugh.'

'Forgive my cousin,' said Hugh. 'He is only playing the fool.'

'Really?' asked Beatrice. 'He is so convincing.'

'The balloon of my pride is thus pierced by the steel pin of your wit, Miss Nash,' said Daniel. 'I shall deflate in a suitable chair.' He set off at a fast clip to make a second assault upon the cake stand.

'Not many ladies would be so ready to share their home,' said Hugh as they slowly followed Daniel back to the tea table. 'You are to be admired.' Beatrice felt a small glow of pleasure at such a compliment from the serious Hugh, but when she turned her smile towards him, she saw he was absorbed in studying Celeste and frowning at Daniel, who had pulled up a chair to engage her in conversation. Her pleasure died and she crushed her own injured feelings with a sharp response.

'It was quite selfish on my part,' she said. 'Don't you know that it is deeply fashionable to take in a refugee?'

'No one could ever suspect you of being fashionable,' said Hugh.

'Just what a woman wants to hear,' said Beatrice with a sigh.

Hugh stopped in his tracks to face her, his eyes anxious. 'By which I mean only that no one . . . I mean, I do not mean . . . oh my goodness, Miss Nash . . .'

'I am teasing you, Mr Grange,' said Beatrice, satisfied to have demanded his full attention but sorry to have succumbed to her own vanity. 'I thank you for your faith in my altruism.' She was also painfully aware that she might not have been altogether altruistic in acceding to Mr Tillingham's request for help. However, she was now up to her neck in a responsibility both serious and of an indeterminate length, and therefore she was rather a saint whether she liked it or not.

'Hugh, please,' said Hugh.

'Hugh,' she replied.

'She seems calm,' said Hugh, looking again at Celeste. 'Did she sleep?'

'Not well,' said Beatrice. 'But I assume any nightmares will abate now she is safe?'

'These people have seen things no civilised person expects to see in their country town,' said Hugh. 'I fear neurasthenia in some and ongoing nightmares even in the strongest of them.'

'What can we do?' asked Beatrice.

'Just observe her closely,' said Hugh. 'Treat her as one might a recent invalid. Plenty of hot, sweet tea or beef broth, fresh air, rest – and call on Dr Lawton if you need a sleeping draught for her.'

'Thank you,' said Beatrice. 'And will you come and check on us?' He looked at her for a moment, and she could not read his face. 'Was there some mention of cream tea?' she added, smiling.

'I haven't told my aunt and cousin yet, but I may not be in Sussex for much longer,' said Hugh. He hesitated and then, lowering his voice, he added, 'I am going to London tomorrow to enlist.'

'You can't mean it?' Beatrice sat down abruptly on a small rustic bench under the garden wall. 'I mean . . . I thought soldiering was for the Harry Wheatons of the world. You have so much important work to do.'

'I'll be furthering that work,' said Hugh. 'Just under the auspices of the Royal Army Medical Corps.'

'But what about your surgeon?' she asked. 'Does he not count on you?'

'He is leading the charge,' said Hugh. 'He offered me more patients and more experience to be had on the battle-field, and the chance to do my duty while furthering my own career.' His lip twisted in apparent distaste.

'An irresistible combination, I should think,' said Beatrice slowly.

'And yet every sense revolted against the idea of it,' said Hugh. He sat beside her. 'To go to war for the advancement of one's career seemed wrong somehow.'

'And your surgeon's daughter?' she asked. 'Surely she must have suffered at the idea?' To her surprise, she felt a bitter sorrow that he would be in harm's way, and she chided herself for being such a poor patriot as to wish her own acquaintances exempt from service.

'Miss Lucy has such enthusiasm for recruiting that Lord Kitchener should put her entreating eyes on a poster,' said Hugh. 'Out of loyalty and affection, I suppose I must allow her to claim me as her recruit.' He gazed across the lawn at the Professor and Celeste. 'But in truth, it was going to the docks yesterday that changed my mind; the dozens of refugees, the wounded, the chaos . . .' His voice trailed away, and she could see in his eyes that he was replaying pictures of the scene.

'I imagine it was very difficult,' said Beatrice. But as she spoke, she knew she could not imagine. The exhaustion, dirty clothes and pungent smell of the few refugees crowded into the Town Hall had been overwhelming enough.

'Grandmothers with bleeding feet from walking for days in wooden clogs,' he said, his voice brimming with emotion. 'Babies thrust into the arms of complete strangers just to get them to safety, women desperate for news of detained husbands pinning their information to every fence.' He paused and then shook his head as if to clear the images from his mind. 'All other considerations melted away and I knew I had to go where I can be at least useful.'

'No one who knows you would doubt that duty is uppermost in your mind,' said Beatrice. 'They will all be proud of you.'

'Thank you for your kindness,' he said. He held out his hand, and she gave him hers to clasp. 'I know you always speak your mind, Miss Nash, and therefore I value your kind words all the more. I hope I have not offended you with my descriptions?'

'I appreciate your frankness,' she said. She looked over to the tea table, where Agatha was laughing at some remark of Daniel's. She knew the pain Hugh's news would bring. 'When will you tell your aunt?' she asked.

'No sooner than I have to,' he said.

CHAPTER TWELVE

TWO LETTERS ARRIVED ON Beatrice's breakfast tray, one from Lady Marbely's solicitors and one from her father's publisher, Mr Caraway. She set them aside on the small table while she ate in order to prolong the pleasing sense of anticipation that all her worries, both financial and aspirational, might be laid to rest. A week or so after Celeste's arrival, she had written to Aunt Marbely with a polite request that she be allowed to draw a slightly larger monthly allowance from her trust now that she was participating, in a modest way, in the war relief efforts of the town. With much chewing of her pen over the need to combine modesty with selflessness, she had described the recent taking in of her young refugee, and all the patriotic teas, committees and events that they would be expected to attend, at some considerable increase in her personal expenses. She enlarged shamelessly upon the famous

Mr Tillingham's gratitude, embroidered upon Lady Emily's continuing patronage and made sure to mention in passing that Agatha Kent's husband was intimately connected to the highest echelons of government. Describing a life of almost missionary simplicity, yet one in which an increase in dress allowance was vital to maintaining a suitable reputation, the finished document was so satisfyingly manipulative that she was forced to bargain with her pricking conscience, promising to make up for such amorality at a later date.

As she ate her porridge and sliced green apple, she tried to concentrate her excitement on the envelope from the publisher, which was too thin to contain a returned manuscript and therefore promised an answer to her literary dreams. But she was distracted by the fat one from the solicitors, which might contain a bank draft. Setting aside literature, she spent a pleasant moment choosing between purchasing a straw hat of Agatha Kent quality and buying a three-volume set of the works of Jane Austen, bound in dark blue morocco and hand-tooled gilt, which she coveted at the local bookshop. She was grinning in rueful self-awareness that the books would always win against personal adornment as she ripped open the heavy envelope.

The letter and enclosed agreement were thick with legal terms, and yet even as she struggled to decipher the words with accuracy, she understood enough to feel a flush of rage in her cheeks. It appeared that, upon Lady Marbely's suggestion, the executors felt it necessary to maintain a paternal watch over a woman of such tender years. There was language as to the limited feminine capacity for financial matters and to the loyalty to family honour – the upshot of which seemed to be that, in order to provide an increase in her allowance, they intended to engage a local solicitor to oversee her financial life and that she would be expected to deposit her salary with them as well as submit all accounts and seek advance approval for any expense above usual weekly necessities. To add the last note of humiliation, it seemed that her trust would be responsible for the expenses of maintaining such oversight. The enclosed agreement required her signature – her agreement to pay for her own jailers – and the letter closed with assurance that upon its signing and presentation, the local solicitor would make available an immediate draft of ten pounds.

The suggestion that she might be bought for ten pounds made her eyes water with humiliation. The small parlour, so recently scrubbed and furnished for her independence, blurred and became insubstantial. She blinked hard and, crumpling the letter in her fist, tried to focus on finding it amusing that a woman who had run her father's household accounts on several continents should need supervision of all purchases other than ribbons and teacakes. She bade a silent farewell to the new books as the envelope contained no drafts and the letter indicated that she would have to wait to hear from whatever local solicitor was provisionally engaged.

Turning to the thin envelope, she now wished she had asked for an advance and wondered whether it would have occurred to Mr Caraway to offer one of his own volition. Her father had always complained of the man's tight-fisted ways, so she had little cause to expect it. As she opened the letter, she reminded herself that it was more important to the writer to have work than money.

The letter from her father's publisher was scarcely less disappointing than the missive from her aunt Marbely's solicitor. Mr Caraway was pleased to remember her, and sent warm thoughts and a cheerful anecdote about her father. But on the subject of her volume of her father's letters, he wrote to tell her that her father's archive having been left to the family trust, he had been contracted by the family to find a suitable editor and to publish an official volume.

> . . . I hope you will be pleased to hear that, at the suggestion of your father's family, we are in negotiations with an illustrious writer of the greatest possible reputation to undertake the editing and the introduction to such a volume. You will agree that your father's reputation will be immeasurably enhanced by a work of this scholarly nature and that his legacy demands an editor of international renown. As you seem to have some correspondence not in your father's archive, and your own introduction contains one or two charming insights, we have taken the liberty of forwarding your manuscript as a valuable piece of research. Lady Marbely assures us that the project will meet with your approval and that you will be glad to send us, by return post, any original letters missing from the official archive. I remain yours faithfully . . .

Beatrice's fury buzzed in her temples, and she could feel the vibration of blood in her fingertips. Her work had been her only refuge and consolation during the dark year of mourning, and every fresh insight had been a moment of closeness to her father. The small volume would have been not just a solid first work from which to build a modest reputation as a writer but a direct connection from her father to her own future. Though she could see the undeniable benefit of the larger project to her father's public memory, the publisher's casual dismissal of her work as mere research and his suggestion that she had removed letters from her father's archive made her despair. She buried her face in her hands and allowed herself a single hollow groan, for her lost father and for the impossibility of her own wants.

Recovering her composure by pouring a last cup of tea from the teapot, Beatrice tried to think about her situation in a more objective way. It was a trick her father had taught her as a child when she was sad or angry. To analyse the problem in a larger, more empirical way would, he always said, improve her mood and her intellect at the same time. Though she now thought it possibly a very unsuitable response to a crying child, she often found herself rearranging her problems as if planning to present them in a small treatise.

She had never been concerned with money, its acquisition or its excesses, and yet now that she had very little, and her dreams of remuneration through publication were to be dashed, she could appreciate at last how money had always been comfortably accessible. Her father had been proud of what he considered their modest housekeeping, and their ability to keep well within his annual private income. Yet they had been comfortable enough that when he had a yearning for partridge, or a desire to lay in a few cases of obscure but highly fragrant claret, she had simply arranged the matter and then paid the bill with a swift signature and a smile. She had considered it a virtue to sit down every month and see to the prompt payment of accounts, but she could see now that it had been in fact a matter of pride – and that pride was a sin for which she was now perhaps to be punished.

The solicitor offered ten pounds; she removed a small black account book from the nearest of Agatha Kent's charming Georgian bookcases and opened it to go over her finances one more time. In stark figures she could see that her small stock of accumulated money had mostly been spent in getting herself to Rye and in paying for her first two months of room and board. Her job, when it began, would pay Mrs Turber with only a small amount left over – enough for sundry small daily needs, a modest donation to the Sunday church plate and a few shillings put by for emergencies. She would no longer be able to afford books by subscription and she was not sure how she was to afford new clothing when the time came. If she was to write, she would also have to buy paper and ink, new pens and stamps for the mailing of manuscripts – such things had seemed inconsequential in the past, but now she would be reduced to counting coins at the stationer's and at the Post Office, like the old widows with their fumbling hands and threadbare gloves.

Gloves were of immediate concern. She had offered two pairs to Celeste and now only retained three cotton summer pairs and two pairs of silk evening gloves. She had not remembered that one of her remaining cotton pairs had a sizable ink stain on the cuff. She was not willing to go about in the sort of cheap gloves that shop assistants wore on

Sundays, and yet to buy another pair of quality would take a week's extra money. She smiled to herself as she put away the accounts book. She understood now why some people – housekeepers, governesses, Mrs Turber – might appear conservative and limited in their outlook. She had secretly thought it some character flaw to be disdained but now saw with rueful clarity that it might be the acute need to avoid any exuberance resulting in the spoiling of gloves or the ruining of shoes. For the first time, as her tea grew cold in the cup and her porridge gelled in its bowl, she saw what it meant to be of limited income. It was a noble concept for the church sermon or the pages of an improving novel, but a chilling prospect on a sunny Sussex morning.

Celeste came down to breakfast in an atrocious pink silk dress donated by Mrs Turber. It swamped her small frame and threw a blush into her cheek that looked like paint. Beatrice could not restrain a slight start of shock.

'I am wishing to 'ave a needle and some scissors,' said Celeste, fingering a large ruffle of linen cabbage roses at the waist. 'If it is *d'accord* to make *quelques changements*?'

'I think you might need garden shears, not scissors,' said Beatrice. 'Have some breakfast, and then Abigail and I will help you do some trimming.' She rang a small brass bell, and Abigail, who brought more hot water and some toast, gave an open-mouthed stare at the dress and said that Mrs Saunders should be summoned.

'Oh no, I must not agree,' said Celeste, a blush of her own adding to the glow from her bodice. 'I must make my own repair and I am content.'

'Mrs Saunders will be glad to help,' said Beatrice. 'It makes us all happy to contribute.'

'I have already, how you say, accept too much pity?' said Celeste. She pressed her lips together and her fingers fumbled at the tiny gold crucifix around her neck. 'This kind lady, she washed my lace and I cannot pay. I will not presume to demand her to make fashionable a dress.'

Beatrice perceived a desperate pride, and she felt ashamed that not ten minutes earlier she, Beatrice, had been poring over her accounts with all the pride of a miser. She had regretted a simple gift of gloves to a girl with nothing but the ruined clothes on her back. She had not thought what it must be to have no linen, no shoes, not so much as a bar of soap or a tin of tooth powder to one's name and to have to accept the sort of charity which girls of their background were used to giving out.

'I am sorry,' she said. 'We will manage together and make some small improvements.'

'I would like to fix it this morning,' said Celeste. 'I am expected next door this afternoon.'

'Best chop it in half, miss,' said Abigail. 'Happen we can make a walking skirt and a pair of window curtains from the lower half.'

Beatrice abandoned another morning's writing, and Abigail her morning tasks, so that they might all three cut, gather and sew the dress into something more fitting. Beatrice and Abigail laboured at the long plain seams, while Celeste proved swift and dainty with the needle, stitching some of Beatrice's grey grosgrain ribbon into neat loops down the bodice and in a flat band around the hem. By midday the pink silk was tamed into a slender, quiet,

afternoon dress, and Mrs Turber, who came screeching
about dinner not being made, was so mollified to see how
well her dress looked on Celeste that she only huffed about
it being far too fine to wear for an ordinary afternoon
helping refugees. Celeste merely pressed her hand and told
her, in her most charming broken English, how kind she
was, and Mrs Turber was forced to retreat before the
language barrier.

Beatrice had the sudden thought that perhaps Celeste
understood more English, and spoke it more fluently, than
she professed. If so, she would not blame Celeste for choosing to protect herself behind the mask of foreign
inscrutability. Beatrice had done the same in certain
awkward situations abroad and once, to her shame, at
home, fending off the advances of an incomprehensible
and aged friend of Lady Marbely at a local hunt ball by
looking the poor man in the face and saying quite clearly,
'I'm afraid I do not speak English,' before retiring to the
other end of the ballroom.

After a cold luncheon of bread and cheese, Beatrice left
Celeste next door, where Mr Tillingham had made his
garden studio available as a club for Belgian refugees, and
slipped into Mr Tillingham's library, where she did not
linger, for she hoped to maintain her privileges by being
undetectable to the great man. With a new book in hand,
she turned her steps to the gravelled paths of the churchyard and a sheltered corner of a stone buttress which had
become a favourite place to sit and read under the dappled
shade of ancient trees.

The gravestones were mossy and weathered amid the
cool grass, so that it appeared as if no one had died in at

least a century. Thinking that she might like to write a small observation on the incongruity of immutable gravestones recording the fragile brevity of life, Beatrice reached in her satchel for a pencil and notebook but instead pulled out her letter from Mr Caraway. She was reading it for a second time, as if the act of reading might change the words on the page, when a shadow fell across the paper. She looked up to see a young officer in stiff khaki. It took Beatrice a moment to recognise Hugh Grange, for he was thinner, and altered by the uniform and more severely clipped hair, though pleasantly familiar with his blunt chin and frank smile.

'Miss Beatrice, how do you do,' he said, removing his cap. She was much happier to see him than she could have expected and thought perhaps that the shock of the uniform inspired its own empathy.

'Just Beatrice,' she said firmly. 'Formality, like many things, seems so silly these days.'

'I am honoured,' he said. 'I hope my uniform did not startle you?'

'There are so many men in uniform I did not expect it to feel so strange to see you,' she said. 'Was your aunt very shocked?'

'I fear I have caused her the sort of palpitations she despises in other women,' said Hugh. 'My arrival yesterday was impossible for us both, even though my uncle John had prepared the way. Daniel could not stop making humorous remarks in the worst possible taste, and my aunt said nothing. I found myself wishing you were at dinner just to break the tension.'

'One longs to be invited where one is useful,' she said, but she smiled to soften her teasing because he was clearly too worried to have guarded his words and even now did not realise that he should have perhaps mentioned another young woman instead. She invited him to sit down.

'I have mostly been hiding in my workshop today, and at last I escaped through a hedge, at great risk to the new uniform, to take a walk.' He examined his sleeves as if for possible leaf stains and ran a hand through his hair. A slight strain was visible on his face, and Beatrice imagined Agatha's face pale and lined with worry. 'I've only been in training for a couple of weeks,' he added. 'I suppose the more one wears it the less of an impostor one will feel?'

Beatrice wished she could say something of comfort to him.

'Your aunt is the most sensible woman I know,' she said at last. 'Her distress shows deep affection and conceals great pride. I am sure she will come around more swiftly if you stop hiding away.'

'You are the second most sensible woman I know,' he said. 'May I ask why you are hiding away in the churchyard?'

'I am pretending to read, but really I am here to wallow in self-pity because my father's publisher declines my talents,' she said. 'Such concerns are set in their insignificant place by your arrival.' She handed him the letter, which had remained crumpled in her hand, and added, 'At least my father's letters are to be presented to the world in grand style.'

Hugh read the letter with a serious face.

'This is deplorable,' he said. 'Your aunt has no business betraying your interests in this manner.'

'I'm not sure she has done so deliberately,' said Beatrice. 'But even if she has, I should thank her for doing my father's legacy such a service.'

'It is a betrayal,' he said.

'It is perhaps I who sought to betray my father,' she said. 'My efforts might have limited the project and thereby limited his legacy for the purposes of my own literary start.'

'Anyone can toss off an introduction,' said Hugh. 'No one could match the close insight you would bring.'

'Of course, you don't even know if I can write,' she said, his frown making her somehow much more cheerful. 'After all, I am merely a woman.'

'I take you at your word and assume a basic competence is open to both sexes,' said Hugh.

'Your casual assumption is heresy to most,' said Beatrice. 'As I say, it now seems much less important in the grand scheme of the times. I will of course help as I can, and my father's legacy will no doubt be assured.'

'Who do you think they have asked?' said Hugh, still frowning at the letter.

'I can't imagine,' said Beatrice. 'My aunt only reads sermons. I think the great John Wesley is dead, so I can't think who else they know. When I wrote to Aunt Marbely I had to explain to her who Mr Tillingham was.' Even as she said the words, a great cold feeling of dread crept up her throat. She turned slowly to look at Hugh, and she could feel her eyes grow wide with a consternation she could not disguise.

'You don't think—?' he asked.

'Do you think—?' she replied.

'Surely Tillingham would have consulted you if he had been approached on such a project,' said Hugh.

'Why would he?' asked Beatrice, her voice bitter. 'I am invisible to him, especially when it comes to writing.'

'We are merely being fanciful,' said Hugh. 'It is impossible that Mr Tillingham would agree to such a project when he barely remembered your father.'

'That is true,' said Beatrice. 'How incongruous that a moment of literary invisibility might turn out to be a saving grace.'

'Mr Tillingham is as ambitious as he is proud, and your father is hardly the sort of celebrated literary name with which he might look to gild his reputation. Quite beneath Tillingham's notice, I should think.'

'I believe my father to be quietly respected in the literary and historical communities,' she said, blinking away the sharp sting of a tear and trying to laugh.

Hugh must have noticed, she thought, because he coughed and added, 'I'm not the biggest acolyte of our Mr Tillingham. I speak only of his faults, not of your father's achievements.'

'You speak the truth,' she said. 'But my father was pleased with the modesty of his contributions and content to live the quiet life of a scholar.'

'And such a life and work would have been well served by your own efforts,' said Hugh. 'It makes me angry to see you pushed aside. We must think what is to be done.'

'It makes me happy to have friends who would feel that way,' she said. 'You cannot know what it means to me.' In the kind expression of his grey eyes, she felt as strong a sense of comfort as if he had put an arm around her shoulders.

'One does not like to see injustice,' he said, patting her hand. His palm was warm and heavy on her skin. 'You must not give up.'

'I will not,' said Beatrice. A confusing warmth of feeling caused her to withdraw her hand. She stood up and retrieved her satchel. With some effort she met his eyes again and smiled. 'But right now I must make my fortune tutoring certain boys whose previous tutor seems to have spent more time on science experiments than Latin translation.'

'I trust they are not making your life too difficult?' he said.

'I did not expect young Snout to have such an understanding of Virgil,' she said. 'Of course he would rather die than display his interest in front of the others, so all three sigh through the lesson as if they were saints being martyred.'

'As we discussed, Snout might make something of himself with a scholarship and a better attitude,' said Hugh. 'But I've found that intelligence is often no match for the circumstances of life, Miss Beatrice. It takes an exceptional boy to fulfil such early promise.'

'I hope a determined teacher might make a difference,' said Beatrice. 'I can only follow my father's example and give them the knowledge I have.'

'I would come with you, but I fear I must go home and face my aunt Agatha,' said Hugh. 'I report back for duty on Monday. Let's hope she recovers her usual sensible demeanour next week or I may have to spend all my future days off in London.'

'That would be a great loss to your friends,' she said, and she held his gaze, though a flush in her cheeks threatened to betray her.

It was hot in the kitchen. The back door was propped open with a chair and all the windows secured on the furthest points of their long iron catches, but the breeze could not quite clear the steam from the large copper pans of peaches and plums bubbling on the stove and the glass preserving jars and lids jiggling about nicely in their baths of boiling water. Piles of runner beans as fat as baby eels lay on sacking in the scullery along with small hills of carrots, cauliflowers and small, early beetroots thick with mud about the roots. Agatha, swathed in a voluminous white apron, with her hair tucked under an old mobcap that was a relic of her mother's trousseau, was helping Cook to put up as much preserved fruit and vegetables as they could make against any further food shortages to come. Extra jars had been rescued from Hugh's workroom and from various corners of the stable, amid some grumbling as preserved laboratory specimens and Smith's collections of screws and nails were summarily tipped into less suitable containers.

If Cook wondered at the outsized effort, and Agatha's insistence on working in the kitchen all day, she did not say, and Agatha was grateful for her unusual lack of inquisitiveness. Hard manual labour seemed to Agatha to be just the thing to keep her thoughts from racing and her heart palpitating at Hugh's appearance in uniform. Though John had sent her a note to let her know Hugh's intentions, it had been a shock to see him step off the train with John, all nonchalant in his khaki and brimming with talk of battlefield surgery.

'My ability to serve has removed all my father's and mother's objections to my continued medical studies,' he had said over dinner as he and John discussed the details of the surgeon's plans for specific head-injury facilities.

'I expect you Medical Corps chaps all have a signed doctor's note in your pocket in case you need a quick escape to Blighty,' Daniel had added. 'How will you feel about amputating your own leg if necessary?'

Agatha had sipped her Earl Grey and tried not to feel sick. She had treated the war as another civic duty and had entered willingly into her many new commitments. She truly believed that all must serve to the best of their abilities, but the sight of Hugh in uniform, and the realisation that his talents would send him to the battlefield, was like a physical blow to her enthusiasm.

'We shall have to clean out the cellar properly this year,' said Agatha. 'I fear we have become used to ordering from the high street whenever we wish.'

'You'll be needing us to send boxes up to town as well, then,' said Cook. 'I wouldn't want Mr Kent to go hungry.' Cook had a countrywoman's disdain for the town and was quite sure that there would be starvation in London where there were minor shortages in Sussex.

'I expect Mr Kent can always get dinner at his club,' said Agatha. 'I'm not sure I shall be up in town much with all the work to do here.'

'We'll be using just about all our sugar and salt if we're to fill all these jars,' said Cook.

'When Smith comes back from the mill, we'll send him to the grocer's again and see if there are any new supplies to be had,' said Agatha. Smith had been dispatched in the hopes of purchasing larger bags of flour than were available in the town shops and to pursue any information about rumours of the government buying up future corn crops for the army. It was not Agatha's intention to indulge in hoarding, but to refrain from such practices called for credible information that food would continue to be in adequate supply. She was not above doing her own information-gathering to supplement her husband's assurances.

'We could maybe keep a pig or two if we dug up a bit o' grass,' said Cook. She was not content with Agatha's carefully manicured vegetable garden and had been upset when she got rid of the chicken coop on account of the smell and an obnoxious rooster who woke up houseguests. Cook did not hold with large areas of grass just lying there, mowed, for playing croquet or walking about.

'I think we'll keep patronising the butcher as long as possible,' said Agatha. 'The poor man is so embarrassed at how little he has in stock.'

'Tongue was all he had yesterday,' said Cook. 'So many I had a sudden vision of a whole field of silent cows. Quite a nasty turn it gave me.'

'I had no idea you were so imaginative,' said Agatha. As she looked up from forcing the last half of a fat peach into a jar, she saw that Cook had lost all the ruddy colour from her face. 'Are you all right?' she added.

'I'm sorry, madam,' said Cook, sitting down too fast on a chair, a large carrot forgotten in each hand. 'Only my daughter's husband has up and gone to the army, and her with the little girl to take care of.'

'I believe there are special allowances to wives and children,' said Agatha gently.

'Oh, he says it's more money and a bit of adventure, like,' said Cook. 'But what if he comes home maimed or dead? What if he takes up with some camp follower and doesn't come home at all?' She shook her head and wiped away a tear. 'He's never been happy to have a cripple for a daughter.' Agatha did not know what to say. An unworthy concern flickered through her mind that Cook might now take to being absent without warning, burning gravy because of tiredness, bringing her granddaughter with her to get underfoot in the kitchen. Agatha was forced to consider whether her sympathetic interest in her staff's families might have more to do with appearing generous than with any willingness to be inconvenienced by their actual problems.

'I'm sure everything will be fine,' she said, wincing at her own weakness.

'You're very kind, ma'am,' said Cook. 'I always tell my daughter, not a kinder lady in Rye than my Mrs Kent.'

The telephone could be heard ringing in its little room under the front stairs, and Agatha was grateful when Jenny came in to inform her that she was wanted by Lady Emily.

'Lady Emily on the telephone?' asked Agatha, who was well aware of Lady Emily's opinion of the instrument as impossibly vulgar. She had installed one, but had it placed in her husband's library, hidden in a wooden box so that it often went unanswered because no one could hear it ringing.

'I think it's her daughter, ma'am,' said Jenny. 'But she said Lady Emily for Mrs Kent.'

'Tell her I'm coming right away,' said Agatha, washing peach juice from her hands at the big iron sink.

As she hurried down the hall, she took off the mobcap, which she knew could not be seen on the telephone but which she removed as a nod to the importance of maintaining standards.

'This is Agatha Kent,' she said into the heavy black telephone, trying not to raise her voice as so many did, as if they could thus force their voices down the copper wiring.

'Hello, this is Eleanor Wheaton, here with my mother,' said the caller. There was a muffled conversation in the background. 'My mother apologises for not coming to the telephone herself, but you can't be too careful about the germs.'

'I know she hates the telephone,' said Agatha. 'She usually just sends a message.'

'She has,' said Eleanor. 'But she was becoming anxious before the footman left the house, so I offered to just ring you up and say that my mother simply must have you and Mr Kent for dinner on Saturday. Earl North is coming.'

'Earl Who?'

'Well, it goes without saying,' said the voice.

'I'm sorry?' said Agatha. 'What did you say?'

'Oh, I was just telling my mother it goes without saying that you would come together.'

'I'm not sure I can guarantee my husband's presence, given the situation,' said Agatha. 'You know he's very busy what with the war and such. I can always have one of the boys escort me if that would do?' There was more muffled conversation as Eleanor conveyed this to her mother. A series of clicks on the line reassured Agatha that the telephone operator and the one or two neighbours who had also put in telephones were listening in on the party line. 'Yes, they simply cannot run the war without him,' she added, taking a mischievous delight in the opportunity to flaunt her husband's importance in a way she would never do in person. She heard a muffled cough on the line and swallowed a guilty chuckle. So many people were concerned to announce evidence of their own status, but her husband preferred to keep his work a private matter, and it amused him when people assumed he was some insignificant government clerk. It was not as amusing to Agatha, who sometimes bit her tongue not to mention the Prime Minister, or boast of some national issue in which his work had been of vital importance.

'Sorry, what were you saying?' said Eleanor.

'Nothing,' said Agatha.

'Well, Mother assures me that you will not take it amiss if we say that it is really your husband whom she needs,' said Eleanor. 'Lord North is touring all the local defences, and we need people who can speak to the war. Your husband is vital to my mother's plans.'

'I understand, and I shall do my very best to produce him,' said Agatha.

'My mother says you are simply the only person in Rye who would be so understanding,' said Eleanor. A muffled grunt indicated those on the line did not take the comment well. 'You and Mr Tillingham are the only ones Lord North would possibly want to meet.'

'I am delighted to be passable,' said Agatha.

'I think we have it all worked out now. It was a bit of a sticky question as to whether we invite Mr Tillingham's Belgians. And then of course the girl is staying with Miss Nash, and I adore Miss Nash, but Mother thought she could not be invited, and then Lord North's son is a friend of your Daniel and there were just too many young people.'

'It's never easy to compose the right table,' said Agatha. Eleanor conveyed this message to her mother, and there was an excited murmuring again.

'My mother appreciates your sympathy,' said Eleanor. 'But we solved the problem to everyone's benefit. My brother and I are hosting all the young people to the last day of hopping at Long Meadow Farm, and then we shall enjoy a picnic in the fields and stay for the evening's festival.'

'I'm sure the young people will be happy to be excused from dinner,' said Agatha. She would also have preferred the hop farm expedition and had been meaning to arrange such an outing. Now she would be stuffed into her tightest corset and seated according to rank in the Wheatons' sombre stone dining room while Daniel and Hugh would be helping to cut hops, drinking the local cider from warm stone flagons, and singing the wagons home on a starlit country road without her. Her favourite summer memories were not of events themselves, of picnics, sea bathing, tennis afternoons and cricket matches, but of watching Hugh and Daniel enjoying them and locking into memory the delight in their faces and their open laughter. Hugh would be cutting hops one last time before going away to France, she realised, and the thought made her grip the telephone very hard.

'Let Hugh and Daniel know I am depending on them,' Eleanor said.

'I think your footman is just arriving,' said Agatha, hearing the back doorbell. 'If you don't mind, I won't make him wait while I write an answer.'

'Of course, we heard you were very busy with preserving today,' said Eleanor. 'Mother was just remembering that you make the most delectable peach jam.'

'Thank you,' said Agatha in a dry tone. She never failed to be surprised by the swiftness of gossip between houses. Over short distances, a word to the right housemaid was faster than sending a telegram. 'We also put up some of Cook's mustard pickles yesterday. Shall I send you some of both?'

'Wait – my mother wants to say something,' said Eleanor. There was a murmur and then a voice, shouting as if from across a ravine.

'You are too kind . . . couldn't possibly . . . but much appreciated . . .'

'Did you hear?' asked Eleanor. 'I can't persuade her to come any closer.'

'Please thank your mother,' said Agatha, who was sure it was better to speak quietly on the telephone than to shout at it across a room but knew that social niceties often had an inverse relationship with rational thought. 'I'll send some of both.' She put down the telephone and went to make sure Cook gave Lady Emily's footman two jars large enough to appear gracious but not so large as to suggest an abundant larder able to supply jars every time someone paid a compliment.

CHAPTER THIRTEEN

THE OFFICES OF FOTHERGILL and Son were housed in a brick-fronted Georgian house near the railway station. A suite of severe bottle-green horsehair furniture occupied the dark-panelled front room, and Beatrice tried not to slide about as she waited, perched on the edge of a curli-cued sofa. Heavy curtains disguised the elegance of the large windows and stopped the sun from penetrating. A thick Turkey rug in shades of purple and brown added a note of smug affluence. As she waited, she grew quite sick at the impending intimacy of negotiating financial matters with Mayor Fothergill, of all people. She wished she had the moral strength, or the funds, to decline her trust's assis-tance altogether. At last a door opened in the panelling and the Mayor trod silently across the thick pile towards her.

'So very good of you, Miss Nash, to agree to visit my humble office,' he said. 'I would have been glad to wait upon you at your home, but I thought we might be just a little more comfortable and discreet here.' His note, disclosing his appointment to act in the matter of her trust, had suggested such a convenience, referring to her cottage as 'your rented room'.

'Thank you, Mr Fothergill,' said Beatrice, trying not to feel the subtle sting of his condescension.

'Would you like some tea?'

'No thank you,' she said, thinking of Persephone refusing to take food or drink from Hades. 'I do not wish to take up any more of your time than is necessary. I came merely to hear the full details of my aunt's proposition so that I might reply to her in all points.'

'We are delighted to have been asked to be of assistance,' he said. 'As one of the oldest firms in the town, we may not be surprised at how far our name may travel, but we are always humbled and grateful.' He did not seem at all humble as he put a pair of small round spectacles on his nose and seemed to be appraising her closely from over the top of them. 'You are to be congratulated on your resources and your connections,' he went on. 'It is understandable that you would wish to be modest about such matters. There are many who would seek to take advantage.' He dropped his eyes to a thick stack of papers in his hand and ran a fat finger down the top page.

'I have no intention of allowing anyone to take advantage,' said Beatrice, hoping he understood from her firm tone that she included him in that population.

'A woman whose trust is released, and only released, upon the instance of her marriage must be an attractive target to all manner of adventurers,' he continued in a low, conspiratorial voice. 'Though your trustees indicate that your income would be more in the nature of a competency than any sort of riches, it is understandable that they would seek to retain close rein.'

'I will never marry,' she said. 'I intend to live modestly on my own income, and I have requested only such small funds as the terms of the trust might allow, in order to maintain my person in an appropriately genteel manner.'

Mr Fothergill peered at her closely as if looking for signs of madness.

Beatrice's aunt had looked at her the same way when Beatrice had asked her to cease presenting a certain favourite curate as a suitor. That a rational woman would reject the chance to secure a husband and thereby inherit an annual income of several thousand pounds had been inconceivable to Aunt Marbely. Beatrice had been unable to convince her that the curate's willingness to take her, despite, as he said, her age and excessive education, was an indignity to which she would rather starve than surrender. In her anger, Aunt Marbely had made it painfully clear that Beatrice's father had been persuaded both to the trust and to the curate, and that it was his dying wish to see his daughter safe in the embrace of a suitable husband. Having survived the livid-white face and scalding insults of her thwarted aunt, and sworn to never give her satisfaction, she now faced the frowning Mr Fothergill with equanimity.

'I see no need for supervision or approval of such small amounts?' she added, pressing her advantage.

'I can assure you I have little interest in poring in detail over the expenses of a sober spinster life,' said Mr Fothergill. Still looking slightly confused, he held up an imperious hand and shuffled some papers as he cast about for his next line of attack. 'But within the bounds of the agreement suggested, I hope I may propose a solution that will seem as easy to you as it would be for me.'

'What do you propose?' said Beatrice.

'What if I propose merely that you supply a monthly list of all expenses, along with copies of all tradesmen's bills, and that I ask dear Mrs Fothergill, my wife, to review and approve them? Not only can she advise me but she can be a great help to you, alone as you are and without female guidance.'

'I could not possibly burden your wife with such a task,' said Beatrice, horrified.

'She would welcome the opportunity,' said Mr Fothergill. 'I have already sounded her most discreetly on the prospect, and her noble head bent at once in agreement.'

'My affairs are not to be so discussed,' said Beatrice.

'I assure you my wife is the soul of discretion and that I mentioned neither name nor financial detail – merely spoke of a poor young spinster with no woman's hand to guide her. We have no daughter of our own, you know . . .'

'Mrs Kent and Lady Emily have both been very kind to me,' said Beatrice.

'Well, that is my point exactly,' said the Mayor. 'Very great women in their way, of course, but Lady Emily must not be imposed upon.' He gave her a solemn look as if she had been caught making daily supplications for advice and financial support at Lady Emily's great oak door. 'And as for Mrs Kent' – he went on, leaning forward now as conspiratorially as his ample stomach would allow – 'she and my wife were girls together, you know, and while their long friendship must prevent me from speaking, my fiduciary responsibility must urge me to caution you.' He placed a finger alongside his nose.

'I cannot imagine what you mean,' said Beatrice. 'I believe her husband is an important Whitehall official.'

'Unfortunate to expose one's wife to so many years abroad, where the minor laxities of character might be encouraged,' he said. 'Now, my own dear wife has never left the bounds of southern England and will not set foot in London unless I command. Propriety is everything it should be to her.'

Beatrice got to her feet and collected her sunshade and her composure.

'With the greatest respect, I think we are finished, Mr Fothergill,' she said. 'I am appalled that my trustees would ask a solicitor of your stature to oversee such a tiny matter, and you should write immediately to decline to act.' She drew on her gloves with a calm that hid a furious desire to rage at him. 'I will not say anything to them, of course. They are a firm of the highest order of correctness, and I am afraid they might look askance at your proposal, however well meaning and delightful.'

'They can be stiff, these London chaps,' said Mr Fothergill. He frowned, and she could see she had nicely confused him. 'But then again, I am certain they mean to impose such conditions.' He looked again at the papers, and Beatrice was sure he was regretting the loss of such fees as might be allowed. 'They are offering you an immediate ten pounds,' he added.

'You and I, Mr Fothergill, we scoff at their ten pounds,' she said. 'Our integrity cannot be bought so inexpensively.'

'No, I do usually deal in larger transactions,' he said, but she was already saying, 'Good day,' and sweeping from the room with as much of her aunt's haughty attitude as she could imitate under the duress.

In the street she feared she might weep with frustration. Not sure of privacy in her own cottage, she strode very fast uphill, towards the old tower that overlooked the marsh, hoping to stand at the railing and cool her hot face in a breeze from the sea until she could regain her calm. She was only vaguely aware of the sound of footsteps behind her, but as she gained the garden entrance, she heard a 'hulloo' and was appalled to see Mr Poot, Fothergill's nephew, panting up the street behind her, waving his hat and looking distinctly uncomfortable and hot in his woollen three-piece suit. She had some faint hope that he was waving his crushed hat at someone else, but as he made his way across the lawn, wiping his face with a large handkerchief, it was plain that he had followed her from the Fothergill offices and meant to talk to her.

'Miss Nash,' he said, 'I beg a word with you.'

'Mr Poot, I believe we have only barely been introduced,' she said. 'I do not wish to be rude, but it is not quite nice for you to accost me in the street.'

'I beg your pardon, Miss Nash,' he said. 'But I believe we may be of service to each other, and if you will give me a few moments of private conversation, it might be to your advantage.'

'You are mistaken, Mr Poot,' she said. 'I wish you a good day.' She turned away and moved down the railing, wishing that the garden had one or two other people within its walls, if only a lady artist at an easel to provide a watchful eye.

'How about if I say you owe me a minute of your time?' he said with a barely disguised sneer. 'On account of your friends seeing to it that you took my teaching job.'

'I can't imagine what you mean, Mr Poot,' she said, tightening her grip on her sunshade. She turned to face him, her face carefully blank, as he stuffed away the handkerchief. She would not give him the satisfaction of asking what his employment troubles might have to do with her. 'I must ask you to leave me alone,' she added.

Poot stared back at her a minute and then laughed, a short laugh like the bark of a dog.

'Oh, I suppose you didn't know those nephews of the Kents, and that Wheaton fellow, tricked me into a tipple that morning?' he said. 'Ruined my chances.'

'A man who is drunk must bear responsibility for the drinking,' said Beatrice.

'If a man spills rum on the back of your jacket, it may be enough that you smell of the tavern,' said Poot. 'I ask you, is that fair, Miss Nash?'

'It is not, Mr Poot,' she said, wondering whether he intended to complain and if her job might still be taken from her. Perhaps her face showed her consternation, because he laughed again.

'Oh, don't worry, they did me a favour,' he said. 'My uncle tried to arrange the teaching job so he wouldn't have to take me into his office, but since it didn't work out . . . well, here I am, clerking for him.'

'I assure you, I knew nothing, Mr Poot,' she said. 'I wished nothing but to be hired on my own merits.'

'As you were, Miss Nash,' he said with a slight bow. 'And I wish only that you will hear me out a few minutes and judge me on my merits.'

'I will hear you, but if your uncle sent you, it is a waste of time,' she said. 'I will starve rather than submit to unreasonable conditions from my trustees.' She looked away over the Channel so he might not see a flush of humiliation in her face. It was anathema to her to realise that he too must have been made privy to her trustees' proposals.

'Those of us unfairly restrained by circumstance must often bear more than our share of humiliation,' he said. 'I believe we should find ways to help each other.'

'How do you propose to help me?' she asked. She moved to a small iron table and sat down.

'By asking you to help me,' he said. Now very circumspect, he waited for her to ask him to sit, and she indicated with her hand that he should sit down. He settled himself slowly.

'I believe you and I might be of great assistance to our country and to each other,' he went on. 'Are you interested in work that is perhaps more vital and intellectual than ladies' committees and fundraising?'

'I am always ready to serve, Mr Poot,' she said. 'But the need for paid employment keeps me from some more important opportunities.' It was a sore matter to Beatrice that donating one's service full-time to the cause seemed to have become the social currency of the town.

'In this we are alike,' he said. 'Without the connections and fortune to lubricate the acquisition of a cosy command, I have had to watch the less competent be raised to positions for which I would willingly give my life.'

'We must all help as we can,' she said. 'You know Hugh Grange has just joined the Medical Corps? A competent officer and a worthy endeavour, don't you agree?'

'Indeed,' he said. 'And I have been called, at last, to serve.' He held his hand to his heart. 'I am to join a small cadre of legal minds to do a great service to the people of Belgium and to our country by collecting accounts of the horrors of the German invasion from every Belgian refugee in the area.'

'Mr Poot, I think that is wonderful,' said Beatrice.

'The account, collected and collated, will be published as an official British Government Report, which, it is hoped, will weigh heavy on the scales of justice against the Kaiser.'

'And how may I help you in this endeavour?' asked Beatrice.

'Suffice it to say that in this effort to bear witness, no horror or brutality must go unnamed, no feelings must be spared, no compromise can be made for daintiness,' he said. 'I made this quite clear to each of the Belgians whom I visited at the hostel, and yet I could gain no cooperation, and indeed all seemed to lose their ability to speak English as I pressed them.'

'Perhaps you overwhelmed them, Mr Poot?' asked Beatrice. 'They have been so bullied and tormented by the Germans they may be frightened of your obvious authority.'

'I told the commission that a military uniform would have cowed them in a way a bowler hat cannot,' he said. 'But perhaps you are right, Miss Nash. I do sometimes forget my natural power of authority. It is important to know how to soften one's approach, how to tease out the truth with suggestion and a little sympathetic coddling.'

'I'm sure when you ask them nicely . . .' began Beatrice.

'I believe you have established a rapport which might diffuse any defiance on their part,' he said.

'I have every faith in your powers of gentle persuasion, Mr Poot,' she said.

'Also, the fact is that they don't all speak good English – after all, why would they? – and my French, while serviceable, is not, shall we say, nuanced?' From the ugly red flush on the tips of his ears, it appeared Mr Poot knew full well that his French was rustier than the job required. 'I just thank the good Lord they didn't send us the Flemish ones.'

'I imagine a firm grasp of the language is required,' said Beatrice.

'You would serve your country by assisting me for just a few hours with this vital work,' he said. 'But you see, I throw myself completely at your mercy in the asking and I would be for ever beholden.'

'I desire to make no one beholden to me,' said Beatrice. 'I know too well how it feels.'

'It is of the utmost importance to my aunt and uncle that I perform well in this commission,' he said. 'It has been suggested that those who produce the most compelling findings may be offered a more permanent government position.' His face betrayed a naked eagerness for such advancement.

Beatrice considered him carefully.

'Your uncle's proposal to monitor my funds is unacceptable,' she said. It was an abrupt comment, and she wondered if she had made herself too vulnerable. 'You must understand my position?'

'To be denied access to sufficient funds and treated as a child is demeaning,' he said. 'If I had your proxy to act, I would insist to my uncle that a simple written tally of accounts, submitted once a month, was more than adequate?'

'He wished to make me accountable to Mrs Fothergill,' she said.

'No, no, this is a simple clerk's job, nothing more,' he said. 'I would take on the responsibility myself, and you can imagine I would be most strict about not prying into the detail of any expenses but merely reporting that they are of a reasonable size.'

'Why would he agree, Mr Poot?' she asked.

'My uncle is very flattered to be approached by such august London solicitors,' he said. 'He was quite downcast at your refusal but considers your stubbornness insurmountable. Were I to return with your agreement to our arrangement, I believe he would be amenable.'

'I will help you, Mr Poot,' she said. 'It is only right that we help our country and that our Belgian guests have the opportunity to expose the evils they have endured.'

'Thank you,' he said.

'And I will agree to your oversight of my accounts on a trial basis for one quarter,' she said.

'I will be happy to be of service and you can rely on my absolute discretion,' he said.

'I do not wish our arrangements to be taken as making either of us in the least beholden to the other, Mr Poot,' she said.

'Your bluntness is admirable, Miss Nash,' he said. 'Let me say in return that I hope for no ties but, perhaps, the bonds of friendship.'

'Unfortunately, our legal business must render any friendship moot,' she said. 'But we are not really acquainted, so it will be no loss to either of us to maintain a strictly business relationship.'

'Of course,' he said. He did not look entirely happy, but relief at her acceptance of his plans must have outweighed any desire to protest.

'May I expect your office to deliver the promised draft for ten pounds to my lodgings by close of day tomorrow?' she asked, rising to leave.

'I do believe your trustees will approve our arrangements, but you must understand it will take some time for the final papers to be drawn up, and given the times, our local bank may be slow to release any draft they receive,' he said. 'I think I can get you two pounds?'

'Thank you, Mr Poot,' she said. 'Two pounds will be most satisfactory and I shall preserve myself in all patience for the rest.' Trying to leave the gardens with an appearance of dignity she did not feel, Beatrice felt a brief pang for her old life, in which she and her father would never have lowered their integrity to haggle for coinage. The world seemed a little less black and white than it had been in the sheltering presence of her father. But perhaps, she thought, it had always been grey, and she merely naïve?

She walked along the high street, towards the ancient stone gate at the eastern edge of the town, where the shops gave way to a pleasant stretch of cliff-top promenade high above the town Salts, with the river below and the sweep of marshes beyond. Here, Beatrice was surprised to see Mr Tillingham standing at the black iron railings. He stood so immobile that he seemed to slow the feet of those who passed, and yet his stillness discouraged the usual friendly tipping of hats and nodding pleasantries; he did not so much as move his head as the people of Rye stepped around his bulk and went on their way. Beatrice would not have spoken to him, but his fixed stare, and his hand gripping an iron finial as if for more support than his silver-tipped walking stick could provide, caused her a rush of concern. She stepped forward and placed a hand on his arm.

'Mr Tillingham, are you all right?' she asked. He started and then turned as if from sleep and blinked his hooded eyes at her. 'Are you quite well?' she added.

'They do not know what is to come,' he said in a slow voice, as if committing the words to memory as he spoke. 'The enchantment of this fixed and ancient land, this town, is but a fragile scrim.'

'Do you need to sit down?' There was a wooden bench nearby, sheltered under a large potted tree, and Beatrice gestured. 'May we sit a moment, Mr Tillingham?'

'Do forgive me,' he said, giving his head a slow shake, as a large dog might toss its ears upon waking. He offered her his arm and led her to the bench. 'I was composing a few lines for an essay and I became completely lost in my thoughts. I am quite rude when I'm thinking.' Beatrice bit her lip to keep from smiling and sat down, shading her eyes with her hand to gaze out over the marsh as Mr Tillingham had been doing.

'It is a lovely view,' she said. 'The sea's retreat through time cleanly measured and recorded in the cutting of dykes.'

'Well observed, Miss Nash,' he said. He fumbled his fingers along his watch chain as if counting rosary beads. 'Yet I think there is a danger of complacency under the illusion of our ever-expanding green buffer. Perhaps we are like King Canute watching the tide go out and thinking we have triumphed over nature.'

'You are a pessimist today, Mr Tillingham,' she said.

'I have been remembering the great American conflict of my youth,' he said. 'Not a hundred years from gaining our independence, we tore each other apart – brother against brother, patriot against patriot – the wheat fields dressed in the blood of young farm boys, towns burned to the ground by neighbours.' He took out a large silk handkerchief and pressed it to his forehead. 'Most of all I remember that what begins with drums and fife, flags and bunting, becomes too swiftly a long and grey winter of the spirit.'

'It is hard to imagine war on such a glorious day,' said Beatrice.

'Yet it is ablaze just beyond the rim of the horizon there,' said Mr Tillingham, gesturing with his stick. 'I am asked to compose a rousing essay to urge America to our glorious cause.'

She was cautious in choosing her words, eager not to disturb the rare opportunity to hear the writer's expression of his thoughts. 'What will you tell them?'

'I do not have my thoughts around the words just yet,' said Mr Tillingham. 'I fear my premonition that England, dreaming under summer skies and wrapped in her mantle of marshes and calm Channel waters, is to face a long darkness of the soul, will not be enough to inspire action.' He fiddled with his watch chain and moved his great jaw as if chewing on his own thoughts. 'Some argument must be made as to whether America, if it stands by while all that is fine and ancient in the civilised world is put to the sword, can still hope to build its own shining city.'

'Perhaps a less philosophical approach?' asked Beatrice, fearing that Mr Tillingham's fondness for lengthy sentences and multiple ellipses might not serve a call to war. 'The newspapers are full of stories of bayoneted infants and murdered peasants.'

'We cannot win by meeting the German bloodlust and savagery with cheap propaganda,' he said. 'We must be strong in our convictions and girded about with reason, else we will lose honour even in winning the action. I must make my case for protecting innocent Belgium and ancient England as the crucible of all settled civilisation.'

'A noble vision,' said Beatrice. 'I think it very fine.'

Mr Tillingham peered at her as if she had just offered him a veiled insult. 'Always tricky to be embraced by the ladies,' he said. 'The risk of dismissal by serious minds. The label of romantic chivalry. One strives for a sterner reading.'

'We are not all just flighty readers of English novels,' said Beatrice.

'And on the other hand, it is the ladies who seem able to whip up a frenzy for some idea,' he mused. 'One would prefer to make one's main idea simple enough for the female eye to catch it up and make it the talk of the town.'

'Surely we can all embrace this particular cause?' asked Beatrice.

'And I'm sure all will just as soon as I do some more fleshing out,' said Mr Tillingham. He thought for a moment and added, to himself, 'I must ask young Daniel to dinner and get the younger generation's view.'

Beatrice could only look away over the marsh to hide a flush of disappointment. His thoughtlessness evaporated her previous sense of concern, and she decided to ask him about the matter of her father's letters.

'Work of such importance must take up all your time, Mr Tillingham,' she said. 'Do you regret having to set aside your own writing to serve?'

'We are all called upon to sacrifice,' he said. 'I have one or two small projects, just enough to keep body and soul together, though I have never subscribed to the idea that austerity of the body is good for the soul, or for the muse.'

'I had hoped to publish a small book of my own,' said Beatrice. 'Letters of my father's with my own introduction.'

'Ah,' said Mr Tillingham, and he peered with great concentration at a sailing barge negotiating the river below.

'My father's publisher has asked another writer to undertake the project instead,' she said.

'Have they indeed?' he said. The barge was very low in the waterline under a heavy cargo of coal and seemed to require Mr Tillingham's absolute focus to make the turn under the bridge.

'They have kept my manuscript,' she added. 'But I am expected to make no further contribution.'

'Impossible to share the writing of books, you know,' he said. 'I tried it once or twice with friends, quite popular published writers in their own right, but it was injurious to our friendship.'

They sat in silence for a moment, and then Mr Tillingham gave a big sigh. 'Look here, it may be that I am the writer in question,' he admitted.

'What a strange coincidence,' she said. 'I'm sure you would have mentioned it to me, had you not been so busy?'

'It slipped my mind,' he said. 'I was approached about just such a project, and now I recollect your father's name may have been attached. Yes, I would normally not have considered it, but you had led me to pull out that little book of his, and so I must have been in a sympathetic place when the publisher wrote to me.'

'It should be my book to write, Mr Tillingham,' she said. 'They had no right to ask another writer.'

'Another writer, you say, Miss Nash?' He raised an eyebrow, and she felt the crush of his sarcasm.

'I do not pretend to aspire to the heights you occupy, Mr Tillingham,' she said. 'But I believe I am in a unique position to edit my father's work.'

'I would not wish to squabble over a small book of letters for which the audience will be respectable at best, even with my name on the boards,' he said. 'Against the scale of this international calamity, for which we are all making such sacrifice of blood and tears, I know you will share my distaste for petty argument.' He turned to look at her, lowering his heavy eyelids in an approximation of the self-effacing stare of a saint.

'You are right,' she said. 'In such a tragic time, I should be grateful that my father's name is not just to be considered irrelevant.'

'We must all suffer from such anxiety,' he said in what seemed a moment of unguarded honesty. 'In war, age may be swept aside by vigour and art crushed by mere sensationalism. In our careful stewardship of your father's work, we may strike a blow for both.'

'I assume you mean to invoke an authorial plural pronoun,' said Beatrice. 'People keep saying "we", but I find they rarely mean to include me.'

'Why not give the matter some further thought, Miss Nash?' said Mr Tillingham. 'If you continue to feel strongly, I shall be happy to recuse myself and return your manuscript unread. If, upon further reflection, you think me the man for the job, why then I would be honoured to use your drafted notes to augment my research, and perhaps I could find the time to look over one or two of your other pieces?'

She said nothing. She had to quell a childish thrill that the famous writer might read her work.

'And you would of course come to dinner and give me all your thoughts on the subject,' he added, rising with difficulty from the wooden bench. 'Good day, Miss Nash.' He kissed her hand with his dry lips and went away along the high street with his peculiar shuffling walk, tapping with his silver-headed stick.

As she watched him go, Beatrice knew she had been almost ready to put aside her anger for a seat at the great man's dinner table, and she smiled to think how much closer Mr Tillingham had come to bribing her than poor Mayor Fothergill with his ten pounds. She wondered how many other young writers and artists Mr Tillingham had seduced so easily with his fame and his reputation. As she rose to continue down towards the lower street, she told herself that if she let him edit the book, it would be for the sake of her father's legacy, not for the opportunity to be counted among the great man's young protégés. But as she walked home, her desire was all to be welcomed into such a fortunate circle.

Out on the marshes, the sun was burning Snout's back as he bent low to the burnished steel of the railway tracks.

Heat radiated from the brown timbers that anchored the line to the ground, and sweat matted his hair and trickled down his chest. There was little shade. Only scrubby trees and rough thickets of bramble separated the railway from the fields. Rooks lived in some of the thickets and flapped about him, cawing in their angry language and pecking the ground, all the while holding their black wings aside as if trying to shed a wet mackintosh. Sometimes, when his bucket grew heavy, he would step aside under one of the scrubby trees, hawthorn mostly, with thin, shivering leaves, and rest awhile, smelling where flaming cinders blown from passing trains had burnt circles into the grasses and turned tree limbs to charcoal.

He seemed to be the only one who collected the spilled coal and coke from the trains in the summer. He wondered at the short memories of those who only thought to scrabble along the line when the frost was on the fields and the price of coal went up. His father paid him a penny a bucket to add his foragings to the forge's coal cellar. But Snout saved another third of every bucket for himself and stored it against the winter, when the town ladies who beckoned him from their windows were willing to slip him tuppence to empty his bucket into their scuttles. With the price of coal soaring, he had some hopes of more this year. His storehouse was an old badger hole in a steep bank where the railway crossed a stream. A mat of brambles hid it, and as trains came only a few times a day, it was safe from passing eyes.

Last summer he had employed two younger boys to pick with him, offering them a ha'penny a bucket. But they had proved to be lazy and prone to complaining. One of them, unhappy to be paid a ha'penny for the half bucket he had taken hours to fill, fetched his father, who threatened to box Snout's ears if he didn't hand over more. Snout had been quick to produce a shiny tuppence, but as he expected, the father gave him a hard punch to the side of his head anyway and threatened to fetch the railway officials.

Such were the vagaries of business. Snout did not dwell on his failures but rather on his accumulating wealth, which he kept in a glass jar hidden beneath a loose board under his bed and known only to him and his sister, Abigail, who could keep a secret better than any grown man or woman. He did not play with the jar, or raid it for sweet money, or aspire to turn coins into gold buttons on a waistcoat like his great-grandmother's people. He just regularly lifted up the board and unscrewed the metal lid to drop in more coins against the day when he might leave Rye.

He had no intention of staying to follow his father, who had been taken in at the forge when he married Snout's mother. His father had the best eye for horses in the county, and there was often a nice piebald Gypsy cob, with hairy mane and feathered legs, tucked in the large box stall behind the forge awaiting a sale. He had the knack of talking all horses into sweetness and all buyers into believing they were fine judges of horseflesh, and as he only sold good horses, they were never proved wrong. So they liked him and his reputation spread, but Snout saw how the recommendations sometimes came with a finger laid along the nose and a whisper of his father's Romany pedigree.

He also saw how his great-grandmother never came to their home. He would see her walking with her basket of lucky white heather, knocking on all the doors except the little cottage next to the forge. Not a cup of water or a chair in the shade was she offered by her grandson's family. If Snout passed her in the town, he would step into the road to pass her and they would never look at each other. It was his own shame at this unspoken arrangement, more than the taunts of others, which made him yearn to leave.

He had visions of owning a business in some prosperous town where he would be respected, and had even promised Abigail that she might come to look after him. But now Miss Nash had explained about scholarships, his plans had a new urgency that came from being possible. A train whistle sounded and the clanking black engine came rushing by, spewing steam and cinders, dragging its blue and scarlet wooden carriages, wheels shrieking and banging against the steel rails. When it was gone, he stepped casually across to the far side and picked up a rook, knocked senseless by the train. The rooks never seemed to learn their lesson. The train drivers would sometimes stop and pick them up, but today the train went on and Snout knew his father would not be averse to a rook pie for dinner.

CHAPTER FOURTEEN

AGATHA KENT WAS CURRENTLY engaged in throwing open all the windows of Mr Tillingham's garden studio to air it out before the weekly meeting of the Belgian Relief Committee. As committee secretary, she made a point of coming early to supervise the arrangement of the sandwiches and tea urn. The other committee ladies claimed not to have the patience for such menial work as taking minutes and ordering sandwiches. They could not understand that such a position meant complete control over the committee, whether in the arrangement of the chairs or in their decisions and plans, all of which Agatha was at complete liberty to shade and direct in the small space between note-taking and transcription into the public record.

'That tall-backed teak chair with the carving should be moved to opposite Mr Tillingham's,' she said, directing

Mr Tillingham's man to place the knobby throne, a relic of some previous owner's trip to the Far East and the favourite perch of Mrs Fothergill, as far away as possible. 'Perfect, thank you,' she added, dropping her shawl on a chair to the left of the chairman's seat and a spare pair of cream-coloured gloves on the chair to its right for Lady Emily. Taking an atomiser of lavender water from her bag, she began discreetly to spray the curtains. The room, used every afternoon by the Belgian refugees as a clubroom, was always filled with the acrid smoke of their thick black pipe tobacco.

As she looked out of the window, she could see several small groups of refugees still lingering in the garden. Young Celeste, who seemed to have swiftly taken upon herself the smooth running of the afternoons, was reading a story to some small children under a tree. Agatha admired the quiet grace with which the girl was always ready to read, to write correspondence for those who required a scribe, or to cross the lawn to refill carafes of lemon water and fetch stands of small cakes donated by the ladies of the town. When at rest, she seemed always to gravitate to the same low stool, set in close proximity to her garrulous father. The Professor ignored her presence to a degree that Agatha thought inexcusable, but the girl seemed perfectly content, quietly listening with lowered eyes and knitting hats and jerkins for Belgian children out of the kinked wool unpicked from old, donated woollens.

Under the studio window, Mr Poot and Beatrice Nash were sitting at a table, finishing one of their interviews with an elderly refugee. Mr Poot had been coming most afternoons, looking officious in his black suit and bowler hat, to bully the refugees for stories that would make headlines in the yellow press. Were it not for Beatrice having asked her help, Agatha thought, she might have put a stop to him already. As she watched, the elderly man banged his walking stick on the table and left with a well-rounded string of curses.

'I'm not sure I can translate the last bit accurately,' Agatha heard Beatrice say. She was trying to look demure. 'Did you get the gist?'

'Goats again!' said Mr Poot, lifting his hat momentarily to mop his forehead with a pocket handkerchief. 'I'm trying to collect atrocities here and all they want to do is log the size of their goats for possible reparations.'

'Apparently his was a very large goat with a good stud reputation,' said Beatrice.

'It's not funny,' said Mr Poot.

'No, it's not,' said Beatrice. 'I know it is not an atrocity exactly, but these people have lost everything. To you and me it's just a few goats, but to them it represents all their wealth, all their income.'

'Two nannies, one stud billy, four wooden chairs, three cooking pots, one cotton quilt and a wooden crucifix,' said Mr Poot. 'Did I forget anything?'

'No German hordes, I'm afraid,' said Beatrice, reading back from the notes she had written. They began to pack away their papers, and Agatha turned away to inspect the sandwiches one last time.

As the Belgians departed, the committee began to arrive and Agatha moved to the open doorway to greet the procession of nodding hats coming up the path of Mr Tillingham's garden. A shadow at an upstairs window of the main house suggested that Mr Tillingham was watching. He preferred to make an entrance after all were gathered. It seemed to Agatha that he delighted in making small talk and dispensing greetings when his interlocutors were encumbered by mouths full of cucumber sandwich.

'I do hope you've made sure the tea is a little weaker today,' said Bettina Fothergill, sweeping up the steps under one of her absurd hats and frowning as if the tea were Agatha's fault. 'Last week it was far too strong and hot for the weather and I felt quite faint on the way home.'

'Lovely to see you, Bettina,' said Agatha.

'Strong tea flushes the veins and opens the mind,' said Alice Finch, coming in behind with her friend Minnie Buttles clutching her arm. 'Stronger tea and looser corsets, Mrs Fothergill!'

'I have never heard such nonsense,' said Bettina Fothergill. She stared rudely up and down at Alice's ensemble of narrow flannel skirt suit, striped waistcoat, and mannish straw boater before sweeping off to the tea table murmuring, 'As if we needed looser women.'

'I'm so glad you are both here,' said Agatha, shaking hands with Miss Finch and Miss Buttles. 'I hear you are making great strides with your subscriptions.' Going door-to-door to sign people up to a weekly subscription towards Belgian Relief was a critical task, but one that had sent the other committee ladies scurrying for excuses. Agatha had invited the two ladies onto the committee for the sole purpose of irritating Bettina Fothergill, who sputtered in their presence as if she would like to denounce them for something but could not be sure what, but in taking on the subscriptions they had proved themselves two of Agatha's most useful members.

'People are very generous by the time we're done with them,' said Alice Finch. 'Though there are some who'd feign poverty to Saint Peter if they thought they could get away with it.'

'I'm afraid some people might not be able to afford their own generosity,' said Minnie Buttles, looking worried as she twirled a bodice ribbon on her voluminous sprigged muslin tea dress. 'The Misses Porter are already hosting the nuns, yet they insisted on signing at sixpence a week.'

'I've had a long talk with Minnie's father, so I've pretty much mapped out who has the income,' said Alice. She produced a folded paper from a leather folio and proceeded to open and smooth it out on a convenient side table. 'A good vicar always knows who puts what in the collection plate.'

'You don't mean you have an actual map?' asked Agatha.

'No competent general launches a campaign without scouting the battlefield,' said Alice. The map of the town contained arrows from most residences, with tiny notations in the margin as to the occupants and their circumstances. 'This afternoon we're making a second foray up Rye Hill. Some of your neighbours are very astute about not being home, Mrs Kent, but Minnie has made little pots of damson jam, which we shall employ as Trojan horses.'

'Goodness, better not let this map fall into German hands,' said Agatha. 'In fact, I'd suggest not displaying it to the entire committee. Its brilliance lies in its secrecy, does it not?'

'I think you're right,' said Alice, folding the document again and stuffing it away. 'We shall remain modest about our contribution and silent on our methods. Shall we get a sandwich, Minnie?'

'Yes, please,' said Minnie. 'I shall ask dear Mrs Fothergill to recommend a selection from the many she is now enjoying.'

Lady Emily arrived with two dachshunds running about her ankles. She seemed hot and cross and drank a glass of cold water standing with her gloves on.

'I am exhausted to the point of collapse,' she said to Agatha. 'I came to get away and rest for a few moments.'

'How are the plans for the hospital?' asked Agatha.

'We are ready to receive patients now, but some puffed-up little inspector from Headquarters had the effrontery to tell me that they had a surfeit of officers' hospitals,' she said. 'He asked me to consider housing regular troops or perhaps Indian and other colonial casualties.'

'I suppose we have an equal duty to all who serve King and Empire,' said Agatha.

'Yet I see no reason why I should be unduly imposed upon,' said Lady Emily. 'As I told Major Frank, the director, some of the ancient and draughty estates on the list are much more suited to those used to deprivation. I can only assume approval is coming.' She had taken off her gloves and now began peeling ham sandwiches apart, feeding the ham to her dogs.

'And how is Eleanor?' said Agatha. 'One feels for her.'

'She is worried for Otto, of course, but we have assured her that no one will think this nonsense was the fault of such old German families as his.'

'Quite so,' said Agatha, trying to quell a smile. 'Here is Beatrice with tea. Will you have some?'

'Where is Mr Tillingham?' asked Lady Emily, taking a cup and saucer from Beatrice and dropping two sugar cubes into her tea.

'Perhaps Mr Tillingham is still writing,' said Beatrice. 'I know from my own father that it is often difficult to keep track of time in the midst of the creative flow.'

'We must give the great man the benefit of the doubt,' said Lady Emily. 'Though I fail to see why art should not exist in harmony with good manners.'

Mr Tillingham made his entrance just after his house-keeper arrived with a platter of fresh sandwiches.

'So good of you to come. I have rushed from my labours, as you see.' He wore a loose scarlet-and-blue cravat with his suit, flourished a large linen handkerchief, and displayed his hands as if they were stained with the ink of his profession. Since he dictated all his work to his lady secretary, his hands were clean and pink and the handker-chief was freshly starched and not at all wrung with a poet's agonies. Still, the ladies pressed about him with eager faces as Mr Tillingham graced them with a summary of his work in London in the national cause of Belgian Relief, for which he had received from their limited coffers several large stipends before Agatha had put her foot down and reminded them of their duty to their local refugees. It was with some difficulty that she called the committee to order.

The Belgian Relief Committee's fundraising plans for a Grand Fete and Parade had grown into an undertaking not unlike a small war of its own. The town Salts and cricket ground had been secured for the day's events, which were to feature, in addition to the usual stalls, games, pony rides and food, an entire military encampment. Two squads of Colonel Wheaton's newest recruits were to display their skills at trenching and infantry drills, the Royal Army Medical Corps was sending a model field ambulance under Hugh's command, and the local Boy Scouts were planning a display of camp skills as well as being in charge of the largest group of latrines ever assembled for one event in Rye. Agatha had taken the calculated risk of asking Bettina Fothergill to be in charge of the big parade. As the wife of the Mayor she would already have demanded a prime place in the procession, and putting her in charge had ensured permission from the council for everything from digging holes to serving beer and champagne in the tents.

'And so after the town brass band, the Scouts, and the horse-drawn steam engine, we envision long lines of schoolgirls all in white dresses and bare feet, wearing wreaths of white chrysanthemums in their free-flowing hair,' said Bettina.

'Wouldn't the schoolgirls prefer to march ahead of the horses if they're going to be in bare feet?' asked Alice Finch, grinning.

'Well, if you're not going to take this seriously,' said Bettina.

'Mrs Fothergill can always adjust the order later,' said Agatha. 'Or perhaps add Wellington boots?' Beatrice appeared to choke into a handkerchief, and Agatha gave her a severe look as she added, 'I fear horses are not to be altogether avoided.'

'Then we feature our dignitaries in motorcars, only I'm not sure whether they should play characters or just appear as themselves,' said Bettina. 'Do you see yourself as Shakespeare, Mr Tillingham?'

Mr Tillingham, whose attention had wandered, was completely put out of countenance by the question. 'Well, it would not be fitting . . . I mean it is for others, not the mere writer . . .'

'In the parade, Mr Tillingham,' said Agatha, patting his hand. 'Do you want to wear a ruff and tights in the parade?'

'Good heavens no,' said Tillingham.

'Then we have Boadicea, Queen Elizabeth with Sir Walter Raleigh, and Nelson, all driven in pony traps decorated with laurel,' continued Bettina.

'Perhaps I could wear the ruff and tights as Sir Walter,' said Alice, still grinning at Bettina's earnest presentation. 'Minnie has the hair to play the Faerie Queen.'

'No doubt you would play Sir Walter as usually depicted, with full beard and moustache,' said Bettina sweetly. 'I only fear the Vicar would not wish to see his daughter associated with such strange irregularity.'

'It's a costume parade, is it not?' Alice's eyes narrowed, and Minnie placed a gentle hand on her arm.

'Personally, I think all costumes and theatricals are designed expressly to allow people to cavort in indecent attire without being ostracised,' said Lady Emily. 'I hardly think you need single out Miss Finch's suggestion as odd, dear Bettina.' The room became very quiet.

'No indeed, Lady Emily,' said Bettina. 'But I assure you all our costumes will be most tastefully done and completely respectable.'

'Good. If we can just get to the end of the parade?' said Lady Emily.

With a chastened air, Bettina Fothergill took a large drawing block from behind her chair and displayed an elaborate pen-and-ink sketch.

'Britannia herself, on a golden throne, surrounded by representatives from England, Ireland, Scotland and Wales; and sheltering in her skirts the innocent handmaid of Belgium.'

There was a general pause at the scale of both the idea and the sketch. Bettina grew red at the silence.

'Where will we get a cart that big?' asked Alice slowly. 'Not that I am criticising, not at all.'

'I like the six white horses,' said Lady Emily. 'But I am not aware of any such matched set for hire in the county. The army has already commandeered so many.'

Bettina looked hurt. Her long face seemed to stretch, her eyes assuming a sad slant, like those of a bloodhound. From the corner of her eye, Agatha saw Beatrice's lips begin to twitch.

'Do tell us who shall play your Britannia and handmaidens?' asked Minnie Buttles, cautiously adding her sweet compassion to the discussion. 'Miss Nash would make a lovely red rose of England against the snow white of Miss Celeste's Belgium?'

'Miss Nash will have her hands full with the procession of her Latin scholars,' snapped Bettina. Agatha sighed to see compassion wither again on that stony bosom. 'I will be selecting the maidens on the basis of their utmost respectability and their ability to purchase their own white silk,' she continued. 'We must have only the best to represent our country's finest act of patriotism.'

Agatha admired the way Beatrice Nash refused to flinch at the slight. Several stinging set-downs hovered on her lips, but she did not utter them. She could only hope Beatrice would understand that the strategic advantage lay in encouraging Bettina in her absurdity. The grandiosity of the finale was a perfect opportunity to keep Bettina busy, and if it failed, so much the better for her thorough defeat.

'Well, I think it's a triumph,' said Agatha. There was a satisfying silence around the chairs. 'I have complete faith that Mrs Fothergill will pull off this Herculean task all by herself.'

'Thank you,' said Bettina.

'And we hope, dear Bettina, that you, yourself, will grace us as Britannia?' added Agatha.

Bettina looked so absurdly grateful that Agatha thought it almost unfair.

'Well, I was going to suggest asking Ellen Terry,' said the Mayoress. 'But if you insist?'

'We do!' said Agatha, feeling the thrill of victory as she led them in a small round of applause. Bettina Fothergill blushed like a girl.

As the committee dispersed into the heavy fragrance of evening in the garden and the elongating shadows of the chimney pots, Beatrice paused to stand with Agatha in the doorway of the garden studio and watch until the last hat ducked under the arch of the gate.

'I'm sorry about Mrs Fothergill,' said Agatha. 'She can be so unthinking.' She would have liked to say more, to offer to assist Beatrice in the purchase of a silk dress should she care to be a handmaiden, but instinctively she knew such an offer would be as humiliating to this independent young woman as any of Bettina's blunt insults.

'I try to find her lack of subtlety amusing,' said Beatrice. 'Poor Mrs Fothergill stands such little chance against your powers of diplomacy that one could almost feel sorry for her.' She hesitated before adding, 'But then she does bear you such very particular enmity.'

'I was once engaged to marry a man she admired,' said Agatha. 'And then my fiancé died, and though I went away for quite some time, we have somehow never been able to move beyond our silly girlhood rivalries.'

'I'm so sorry,' said Beatrice, her expression softening in a way that invited further confidences. Agatha chided herself for bringing up old stories she had no intention of repeating.

'Now we are at war I really must try harder to be generous to her,' she said. 'I have no great hope that Bettina will follow my good example, but at least it may confuse her long enough for us to seize advantage.'

CHAPTER FIFTEEN

'THERE IS NOTHING QUITE as satisfying as helping with real work such as this,' said Eleanor Wheaton. Eleanor, Celeste and Beatrice were comfortably seated on chairs in the cool shade of an oak tree, stripping hops from a pile of long vines. 'One feels such a connection to the land.' Eleanor, dressed for the occasion in a pink-and-white cotton lawn dress worthy of a shepherdess in an operetta, seemed cool and serene, as if stripping hops were no different from embroidering with silk thread. Her gloved fingers worked nimbly as hop flowers tumbled in a steady stream down her apron to the large piece of burlap spread at their feet. Celeste was also calmly engaged, though she picked the hops more daintily, as if she were coaxing butterflies from a flower. Beatrice found the task frustrating: the scratching of the woody vines, the bitter green smell of the buds, the wet streaks of sap across her gloves. She ripped and pulled, and bent to pick shredded leaves from the pile of bruised hops at her feet.

'There is nothing quite as satisfying as doing work because one chooses to and not because one is under an obligation,' she said, feeling waspish as she tried to wipe perspiration from her cheek without allowing any itchy sap to touch her skin. 'I doubt farm work is as much fun for those who must scratch a living working the various harvests.'

'Everyone looks forward to hopping,' said Hugh, dumping a fresh armful of vines behind Beatrice's chair. His shirt, stained from carrying armfuls of hops, was open at the neck, and her eye caught a hint of the shadowed hollow of his throat. His sleeves flapped loose over his leather gauntlets as he waved a hand at the field. 'It's a holiday for the London families and a child's winter coat earned for the country women.' A holiday atmosphere did seem to hang over the hop field. Women gossiped along the rows, small children played in the hedges, and cooking fires sent streams of smoke into the air from a group of rough wooden huts along the riverbank. In the full sun of the field, groups of men, women and older children followed the falling rows of vines, singing as they picked. The other young men of the party, Harry Wheaton, Daniel and Daniel's friend Craigmore, were cutting vines with the best of them. As Hugh surveyed the field, Beatrice saw a brief shadow cross his face. 'I can't help but wonder how many of the young men harvesting here today will be here next year,' he added, so quietly that Beatrice doubted he had meant to speak aloud at all. She felt a chill brush the golden afternoon.

'It is true that if we lived by our harvesting talents we would quickly starve,' said Eleanor. 'But it feels good to join in rather than just walk around and look, like a queen with her peasants.'

'The peasants are especially impressed that you brought them an earl's son this year,' said Hugh. It was hard not to admire the broad-shouldered young viscount, thought Beatrice. Craigmore carried himself with an easy politeness, with no trace of hauteur, and his pink cheeks added a touch of boyish humility to a strong chin and a brush of thick blond hair. As they watched him help an old woman to push her huge sack of hops onto a cart, Beatrice was forced to consider that in Craigmore's shining golden youth, the nobility of England might find some argument for pedigree that she had found absent in the withered remnants of the Marbely family.

'And unlike Harry, he doesn't try to compete with all the local boys and pinch all the girls,' said Eleanor, looking to where Harry was hacking at the tall strings of vine with the wildness of a pirate. 'My brother must always try to win,' she added. 'It's so unreasonable of him.'

'All young men try to win,' said Hugh. 'That's why I prefer not to join in at all.' At this, Beatrice could not contain a bubbling chuckle. Hugh looked confused and then frowned as he added, 'I didn't mean to imply any prowess on my part. I merely understand, as a man of science, that I am not immune to the competitive urges of youth.'

Daniel and Craigmore soon left Harry Wheaton to his labours and made their way to the tree, carrying additional piles of vines.

'Cold drinks must be fetched at once,' said Eleanor as they arrived. 'Daniel, do go and find the footman. He will have put the bottles in the river somewhere.'

'Hugh, be a sport and go instead, will you?' asked Daniel, throwing down his gloves and pulling a small notebook from his pocket. 'Only I must get down a few lines that have been dancing around in my head.' He slumped to the ground, rolled away onto his stomach and began to scribble with a chewed stump of pencil.

'Daniel is always inspired to write just when someone suggests real exertion,' said Hugh.

'In Florence, he once seriously considered renting a bath chair to carry him up into the hills just so he could finish a villanelle,' said Craigmore with a broad smile. 'I offered to break his leg to make him look less ridiculous.'

'I'm not listening,' said Daniel.

'The inherent laziness of the creative classes,' said Hugh.

'I assure you it's just the poets,' said Craigmore. 'We artists are always more than ready to put a shoulder to the wheel.'

'You are ruining my concentration worse than that dreadful singing,' said Daniel. 'I shall fetch refreshments just to have some peace.'

'I will come with you in case you swoon into a sonnet between here and the river,' said Craigmore.

The two young men set off down the slope to the meandering green river, laughing, exchanging a few shoves as they leaped over tussocks of rough grass and negotiated patches of hairy thistle. Beatrice was forced to admire the easy way in which they seemed to manage their friendship, as if they were still young boys, with none of the hesitancies and awkwardness that she felt as a woman. She could argue that it came from less perception, less thought as to social negotiation, but she still envied the ease with which they strode down the field, with no thought but the present task and the delight of each other's company.

'I like Craigmore,' said Eleanor. 'Not as stuffy as his father, who is terrorising all the footmen with his long stare.'

'It must be a strain to entertain guests while also getting ready to open the hospital,' said Beatrice. 'Your mother must be quite exhausted.'

'Major Frank, who is in charge of the hospital, keeps suggesting the same,' said Eleanor. 'But Mother assures him that she will continue, indefatigable in her efforts.'

'I'm sure he is quite reassured,' said Hugh, laughing.

'I would feel sorry for him,' said Eleanor. 'But he stutters so whenever I enter the room that I'm reasonably sure he thinks my marriage to Otto makes me a spy.'

'You and the German nanny make quite a nest of terror,' said Hugh.

'Harry likes to egg him on by asking Fräulein to take all our letters to the Post Office,' said Eleanor. 'He sends her right by the Major's office window, and she does have a rather furtive way of clutching the post to her bosom.'

'No one could seriously doubt your loyalties,' said Beatrice. 'The man must be a complete idiot.'

'Of course I would not be foolish enough to have anything of importance sent to or from my mother's house,' said Eleanor. She spoke with no wink or other hint of guile, but as Beatrice caught Hugh's eye she saw reflected her own consternation that perhaps Eleanor was foolish enough to believe the new restrictions on mail did not apply to her.

'Madame is married to a German?' asked Celeste in a small voice. Beatrice was surprised, as she had never heard Celeste make such an abrupt comment. She realised that in all the small talk of their tea visits and sundry gatherings, there had never been an occasion to discuss Eleanor's situation. The Wheaton family had quietly resumed referring to Eleanor as Miss Wheaton, and of course the baby was simply baby George. No one in the county seemed to dare gossip about them, one of the privileges of rank.

'Yes I am,' said Eleanor. 'I am sorry for any pain that might cause you, but I assure you he is completely opposed to the horrid tactics of the Prussian hordes who overran your country.' There was an awkward pause. Celeste picked at a hop flower in her lap, Eleanor looked away to the river, and Beatrice dropped her eyes to the grass.

'I am sorry you and your baby cannot be with your husband,' said Celeste at last. 'There are so many families who have been divided. It is a great suffering.'

'It is indeed,' said Eleanor. 'You put it so gracefully, my dear.' They worked on in silence, save for the sound of hop flowers softly dropping onto the canvas at their feet.

Daniel and Craigmore came back from the river, each loaded down with sodden wicker baskets containing stoppered bottles of lemon cordial and barley water, which had been cooling in a pool under the shady riverbank. They were accompanied by a man and woman dressed in the flowing linens and broad straw hats of farm workers from some entirely different country. Possibly Italy or southern Spain, thought Beatrice, looking at the woman's dark bodice laced loosely across a muslin blouse, the bright overskirt looped on one hip. The woman carried her hat, her thick auburn hair glowing in the sun as it threatened to escape from its tortoiseshell combs. The man, in his shapeless tunic and broad breeches tucked into tall, rough socks, carried a basket in one hand and a stack of cake boxes dangling from a string in the other. His forearms, sticking out from rolled sleeves, were as tightly muscled as a peasant's, but his face, under his broad, fraying hat, was pale and smooth, as if he were seldom outdoors.

'We have found unexpected friends at the riverbank,' called Daniel, placing his baskets in the shade of Eleanor's chair and popping open a bottle of cordial. 'Eleanor, may I present Mr and Mrs Frith? They are great friends of Mr Tillingham's, and Mr Frith has been a friend to many a young poet, including myself.'

'Pleased to meet you,' said Eleanor. 'May I introduce Miss Beatrice Nash, and this is Miss Celeste, our Belgian refugee friend.'

'Mr Frith?' asked Beatrice as she shook hands. 'Are you Algernon Frith?'

'Are you one of my creditors?' asked the wiry man with a serious face.

'No. I mean . . .' Beatrice stumbled. 'Only if you are Algernon Frith, the writer, it might explain your romantic garb.'

'Great powers of observation,' said the man, shaking her hand. 'I am indeed Algernon Frith, writer, newly returned from a long and financially prudent honeymoon in Andalusia. Hence the garments. I haven't had time to ask my tailor for appropriate hopping attire.'

'Don't listen to him,' said the woman. 'He has an insatiable appetite for wearing costumes, and I assist his muse, though it renders me ridiculous in company.'

'On the contrary,' said Eleanor. 'You look most charming and romantic, Mrs Frith.'

'Do call me Amberleigh,' said the woman.

'Mrs Frith is better known as the writer A. A. de Witte,' said Daniel.

'I am a great admirer of your work,' said Beatrice, unsure by which name to address the author of several famous medieval novels so frank and sensational Beatrice had not thought they were written by a woman. Then the newspapers had shown a picture of A. A. de Witte as the cause of Algernon Frith's marital troubles. 'Though I must admit,' she continued, 'it is the only work I have ever read without telling my father.'

'You are very kind,' said Amberleigh, laughing. 'But I wouldn't broadcast it about. It is more fashionable never to have read a word of mine.'

'My wife and I are grateful to hear any kind opinion these days,' said Frith. 'I'm afraid I have not made her life easy these past two years.' The two lovers had fled to Europe, where Frith claimed to have been granted a divorce, and where they had married. Perhaps because of the reputation of her books, Amberleigh de Witte's marriage was the subject of scurrilous whisperings.

'Mr Frith has some twelve books in print and three volumes of poetry,' said Daniel to Eleanor. 'He is one of our great voices.'

'The boy is very kind, but as Miss Nash will agree, my wife, Amberleigh, is the real writer in the family. Old Tillingham would tell you that I am a charming fellow and a complete hack. It's one of Tillingham's great qualities that he tells all his friends they are hacks and yet he manages to keep them.'

'He doesn't tell me I'm a hack,' said Daniel. 'He is being very strict but encouraging.'

'Beauty is his weakness, which is perhaps why he is also kind to my wife,' said Frith. 'But his literary nature will savage you in the end.'

'Will you join us for the festivities this evening, Mrs Frith?' asked Eleanor. 'We have plenty of room at our table.'

'I think we are promised elsewhere,' said Amberleigh, a shade too quickly. 'We are to meet Miss Finch, the photographer, and Miss Buttles.' She turned away as if to scan the field for her friends, and her hat, held as a shade against the sun, obscured her face.

'The more the merrier,' said Eleanor. 'I wonder if Miss Finch might be persuaded to take our photograph.'

'My wife and I live largely in seclusion,' said Frith, dropping his voice to add, 'We do not look for social invitations, given the business about my divorce.'

'It has been suggested that I confine myself to a more secluded life because of my German husband, but I think we have to resist such nonsense, don't you?' asked Eleanor, a note of ringing determination in her voice. 'Besides,' she added. 'It's a picnic and we are dining with everyone from farmers to Gypsies. There can be no drawing-room ceremony here.'

'You must join us, old man,' said Daniel. 'You and Amberleigh will completely enliven the proceedings.' Frith looked to his wife, who lowered her hat and gave the briefest nod of her head.

'If you please, Baroness, we will be happy to accept your kind invitation,' said Frith.

'Good, we will be a thoroughly bohemian party,' she replied with an air of satisfaction. 'And do call me Eleanor. We needn't stand on ceremony.'

Agatha Kent had promised herself that on this particular evening she would keep her opinions to herself. It was important to Colonel Wheaton and Lady Emily that they appear entirely nonchalant about entertaining an earl, and they were consequently wound as tightly as Swiss clocks and would have held their chins at an uncomfortably raised angle even if they had not been both attired in collars of the highest and stiffest appearance. Lady Emily's high-collared dress of thick black lace was decorated with a simple diamond pin. It was the size of a quail's egg but did not sparkle, which indicated that it was the best kind of discreet old family jewel. Colonel Wheaton appeared in the dress uniform of his previous service, to which he had added a small armband with the insignia of his new Sussex Reserves. It appeared tight, but, thought Agatha, Colonel Wheaton would have been just as fidgety in a dressing gown, given the importance of the occasion.

Lord North, who seemed to hold several military commissions as well as Ministry portfolios, strolled into the sitting room in a short dinner jacket and soft shoes. His wife wore plain black silk and a string of pearls long enough to wrap round her throat several times. They were shorter than Agatha had expected and both built square across the shoulders. They might have been a pair of school inspectors or a brewer and his wife as they marched across the carpet to shake hands.

'On the road, you see,' said Lord North, by way of apology as to his dress. 'Just the necessities and not a box more, I say.'

'We try to avoid any affair too formal while we are inspecting,' said his wife. 'In case it sends the wrong message to the people working so hard to prepare the country.'

'I quite agree with you,' said Lady Emily, and Agatha could see her mentally whisking away the menu cards and getting rid of the smoked oyster course and perhaps the second pudding. 'We shall be quite informal tonight. Just a small party. May I introduce Mr Kent from the Foreign Office and his wife?'

She might have pulled off this sudden change in tone, for Agatha and John had both dressed with the proper sense of deference, John in a black tailcoat and Agatha suitably demure in her dark blue, but just then the butler announced the Mayor and his wife, and any sense of nonchalance was destroyed by their magnificence.

The Mayor's fur-trimmed scarlet robes and chain of office were a resplendent backdrop for Mrs Fothergill's dress of gold thread with an overlay of transparent silk crêpe de Chine. Diamonds sparkled at her throat, waist and wrists, while a tall hair ornament of peacock and burnt ostrich feathers threatened to dust the chandelier as she traversed the room.

'So delighted to be invited, dear Emily,' said Bettina, kissing Emily Wheaton on the cheek with her plumes bobbing like swords. 'Agatha, how nice you look. So appropriate.' As she kissed Agatha, she whispered, 'Where is the Earl? Are they making a formal entrance?'

'Lord North, Lady North – may I introduce to you our Mayor, Mr Frederick Fothergill, and his dear wife,' said Colonel Wheaton. 'You had most particularly requested to meet our local officials, and here he is.'

'Good, we've got the Ministry, the army and the local view, so now maybe we can have a frank talk about the need for urgency and the Hun practically at our door,' said Lord North.

'Now do let us have dinner before you start stealing the cruet to make maps of sea defences,' said his wife. 'You will get indigestion again if you start lecturing while you eat.'

'Small price to pay. Must keep moving,' he said, turning to Lady Emily. 'How many more stand between us and the dinner table, dear lady, only it doesn't do to tax the eager stomach with waiting.'

'Just Mr Tillingham and the Professor,' said Lady Emily. 'Here they come.'

'Tillingham? Tillingham?' asked Lord North. 'I know that name. . . .'

'He's that writer chap, American. He agitates for the Belgian refugees,' said his wife, sotto voce. 'Wrote that piece in *The Times* that gave you hiccups.'

'Writers,' he said, loudly. 'Always writing instead of doing. And then they have the most extraordinary opinions.'

'A man of action is always to be preferred,' said Mr Tillingham. 'Of course, all such heroes require a scribe to record their great deeds, and I am your humble servant, Lord North.'

If he was offended by the comment, he did not show it, and his response seemed to soften the Earl, who shook his hand quite vigorously and said, 'I think we met you at the Duchess's fundraising dinner in Belgrave Square?'

'Horrible crush, but some of the best minds in the country sat around the port that night,' said Tillingham. 'I believe you were the heart of that discussion, Lord North?'

'And Mr Tillingham comes with his own darling refugee,' interrupted Bettina. 'The Professor is quite a marvellous addition to the cultural life of our town, and we are all perfectly fond of him.' She took the Professor's hand in both of hers and thrust it towards Lord North.

'How d'you do?' said Lord North. He shook the Professor's hand and raised his voice. 'Do you speak English?'

'I am delighted to meet you and your lovely wife,' said the Professor. '*Enchanté, madame.*' He kissed Lady North's hand.

'Only it's difficult to get any organisation going when these chaps insist on speaking some other language,' said Lord North. 'Hard enough running a war in English.'

'How ever did we defeat the Boers?' said Agatha. The words escaped before she could think, and she tried hard to look serene and hoped John would not step on her foot.

'How, indeed, Mrs Kent, you are quite right to ask,' said Lord North. 'If you ask me, we could have been in Mafeking six months earlier if we hadn't had to translate all the signposts and work with different railway gauges.'

'Our refugees are so simple and so contented when they can have a good dinner and a pipe,' interrupted Bettina. Agatha bit her tongue not to bring up the departure of

Bettina's own refugees, the accountant and his wife, who had removed themselves to a hotel in Bexhill after just a week of her overbearing hospitality. 'They are taking to knitting as if they were simple English peasants,' Bettina added.

Agatha felt her mouth begin to twitch, and she lowered her eyes in an attempt to hide her amusement.

'Mrs Fothergill has such an admirable grasp of the essential nature of our refugee guests,' said John, lofting his brows in an expression of utmost innocence. 'If you had to sum them up for Lord North in a word or two, Mrs Fothergill?' He let the question trail off as Bettina blushed for pleasure.

'Why, I would call them simple, Mr Kent,' she answered, and Agatha was forced to press her gloved hand to her lips and pretend to cough.

'I am sure the lady does not mean to call us simpletons?' said the Professor.

'Of course not, Professor,' said Bettina, her feathers quivering. 'I only meant—' She broke off in confusion as to what she might say next.

'Well, I hope the desire for a simple life around one's own hearth, with a good dinner and a good wife, might just as easily describe us English,' said Colonel Wheaton.

'And I can only hope we would be half as grateful were we driven from our land,' said Agatha.

'The English spirit will not stand to be driven out of its land,' said Mr Tillingham, in the rapturous way he spoke when trying on a phrase for possible posterity. 'But will surely stand to its defences to the last man and boy.'

'First we need the defences to which we can stand,' said Lord North. 'So far I've seen more Boy Scouts on patrol than soldiers, and we are weeks behind in gathering sand-bags and building defensive positions.'

'As the Rye Voluntary Aid Detachment President, I can assure you my ladies are quite ready to be called into action,' said Bettina. 'We are ready to serve at a moment's notice.'

'I'm happy to hear it,' said Lady North, looking with some scepticism at Bettina's attire.

'Maggots, lice, suppurating sores,' said her husband with relish. 'It's going to be bloody work and quite a shock for your average volunteer bandage-roller.'

Bettina gave a muffled groan and turned her head aside.

'We are to be a convalescent hospital,' said Lady Emily faintly. She sat down rather abruptly on a chaise longue. 'We plan to make our own beef tea and to offer plenty of board games in the conservatory.'

'I'm sure Lord North merely seeks to brace us up with his bluntness,' said John. 'But we should be careful not to indulge in any scaremongering.'

'Scaremongering?' said Lord North. 'You Whitehall chaps can peddle your propaganda of Berlin by Christmas, but I'm planning to fight back a full invasion, the Hun pillaging up the London Road, bayoneting our children and violating our women.' He banged his fist on a small table, and Bettina Fothergill gave out a slight shriek.

'I feel quite faint at the thought,' she said. 'What must you feel, dear Lady Emily, to have your own daughter married to one of . . . one of them?' There was an uncomfortable stiffening of faces around the room, and Agatha saw Emily Wheaton press her lips together until they were bloodless.

'It's the damned Prussians,' said Colonel Wheaton. 'My daughter's husband is from Saxony, landowning aristocracy going back to the Crusades. Not the same thing at all.'

'We mean no disrespect to the poor young man,' said the Mayor. 'My wife has only been most concerned for you and for your daughter, Lady Emily.'

'My daughter is happily hopping with Mrs Kent's nephews and a whole group of young people,' said Lady Wheaton, her voice icy. 'I believe your son has also gone with them, Lord North?' she added.

'Yes, he was happy to be spared another official dinner party,' he replied.

'The last day of the hops is always quite the festival,' said Agatha, trying not to sigh. 'Country dancing, games, performances, dinner by the river – they will be having such fun.'

'A large festival, is it?' said Lord North.

'Impossibly so,' said Bettina. 'All kinds of rough types allowed. I never attend.'

'The farm in question is leased from us, and my son and daughter always give their patronage to the farmer on the last day of hopping' said Lady Wheaton. 'We regard it as a duty to participate, and I hope my children are not afraid to offer thanks to those below them.'

'What better representation of the nation for which we fight than town and country, rich and poor, young and old, coming together in the timeless gathering in of the crops of the field?' said Lord North. 'I believe Lady North and I would like to take a look at these festivities.'

'Are you sure?' said Colonel Wheaton. 'Our Lady Mayoress is correct that it can become quite colourful and raucous.'

'What is this "raucous"?' said the Professor. 'My child has been at this entertainment, *n'est-ce pas?*'

'Oh, it's just country dancing and local entertainment,' said Agatha.

'All perfectly proper,' said Colonel Wheaton. 'Only I wasn't sure our lovely wives would care to sit on a plank over two barrels just to watch a lot of people gallop about the grass.'

'Quite pastoral,' added Mr Tillingham. 'Though as with all good pastorals, one delights in spotting the storm on the horizon and the wolf hidden in the thicket.'

'There are wolves?' asked the Professor.

'Figure of speech, dear sir,' said Mr Tillingham. 'Some years they have quite a good Gypsy band. I took a young Italian artist once and he was quite struck.'

'Well, I would love to go,' said Lady North, folding her fan with finality. 'To serve the people we must go to the people.'

'Perhaps the poor hop pickers should to be left in peace to enjoy their holiday,' said Agatha. 'They have worked very hard, and they may not feel able to celebrate as freely with such eminent visitors.'

'Nonsense, it's only us,' said Lady Emily. She signalled to the butler. 'Would you telephone the farm and let them know we're coming after dinner? Please mention we intend to be very informal so everyone should proceed as if we were not there at all.'

'The farms of Sussex have the telephone?' said Lord North.

'Mine do,' said Colonel Wheaton. 'Put one in every farm kitchen, and now all my farmers know I may telephone at any hour. Keeps them up to the mark, I can tell you.'

'Terrible thing, the telephone,' said Lady Emily. 'I refuse to be a slave to it.'

'All our embassies are now connected, of course,' said John. 'But it's not much use for diplomacy, what with all the party lines and operators listening in.'

'You might get a funny skit for one of your plays out of that, Mr Tillingham,' said the Mayor. 'The Kaiser's got a crossed line and the Russians keep calling for vodka. That sort of thing.'

'I don't do "skits", Mr Fothergill,' said Tillingham, his lips pinched to the point of disappearing. 'You have me confused with the music halls.'

'Nothing like a bit of humour to liven up a play,' said the Mayor. 'Why, your next play might be as popular as Gilbert and Sullivan.'

Mr Tillingham looked as if he might succumb to apoplexy.

'I'm afraid we are not dressed for the fields,' Bettina pointed out, smoothing her golden gown.

'Indeed, on no account should you risk the ruin of so stunning a dress,' said Lady Emily. 'We will release you and your dear husband from all obligations, dear Bettina. Our chauffeur shall run you home while the rest of us disperse to find our boots.'

'Well, I'm sure we don't care to break up your party, Lady Emily,' said the Mayor, looking at his wife, whose face was quivering.

'Oh, you do us a service, dear Mayor Fothergill,' said Lady Emily. 'There would not be room for you in the cars.'

She smiled in a way that brooked no further discussion and added, 'Shall we go in to dinner?'

The light was all but drained from the sky and, in the orange glare of a large bonfire, boisterous country dancing was well under way as Agatha and John led the Professor and Mr Tillingham across the cleared hop field. The Wheatons were a few minutes behind, Emily Wheaton having whispered to Agatha her hope that all would be found in order for the appropriate reception of Lord and Lady North.

'I'm not sure how Emily expects such an event to be anything other than it is,' said Agatha to John as the bonfire made the long shadows dance. Around the field, rough trestles were crammed with hoppers, the Londoners and the locals keeping to their own tables but mingling happily in the dancing. In addition to their own foods, platters of sausages were being heaped hot from coal braziers and baked potatoes plucked from the fire with long iron tongs.

'A pagan revel to its core,' agreed John, sniffing appreciatively after a passing platter. 'But it will do Lord North good to be reminded that this is England the ancient and that we fight for her as much as for the prim town and the glittering city.'

'I'm not sure he will appreciate your historical view,' said Agatha as a man slipped to the ground at a table where revellers were making very free with the farmer's jugs of cider.

In a prime spot, the farmer and his family occupied a long trestle decorated with hay bales and bunting, and to one side Agatha spied Eleanor's party of young people.

'I see that the attempt to mingle with the people has its limits,' said John as they approached Eleanor's table, which was distinguished by a linen cloth, silver candlesticks and a footman hovering with several wine bottles.

'I doubt any of us would enjoy sitting on a rough plank and eating with our fingers,' said Mr Tillingham. 'I for one would appreciate a cold glass of champagne.'

Agatha caught Hugh's eye, and as she waved her handkerchief at him, a look of consternation crossed his face.

'What are you doing here, Aunt?' he asked, hurrying forward to greet them.

'Didn't you get the message we were coming?' she asked. 'Lady Emily gave explicit instructions to telephone the farmhouse.'

'I don't think anyone remains indoors to answer,' said Hugh.

'Is my mother coming too?' asked Eleanor as they approached. 'I would have set another table.'

'Quite another table, I imagine,' said Mr Tillingham. Agatha followed the direction of his eyeglass to see with horror that Algernon Frith and Amberleigh de Witte were seated at the table with Minnie Buttles. Tillingham gave them a short bow but did not introduce the Professor. Agatha pressed John on the arm, a small alarm signal.

'Papa, you are here!' said Celeste, running from the table with rosy cheeks and a giddy laugh to envelop her father in a hug from which he visibly flinched. The girl was flushed from more than the mere excitement of dancing, and Agatha's grip on her husband tightened.

'Evening, Tillingham, old boy,' said Algernon Frith. 'You find us all quite rustic and comfortable this evening.'

'I hope there is adequate champagne,' said Daniel. 'The cider is as rough as salt water and quite without poetry.'

'Are you well, my child?' said the Professor, holding his daughter away from him and peering at the bright spots of her cheeks. 'Your colour is quite high.'

'Mr and Mrs Kent, how lovely to see you,' said Amberleigh de Witte. She smiled, but Agatha could see fear flit across her eyes. 'Miss Wheaton was kind enough to include our party at her table.' Minnie was also rising from the table and looking anxiously around the field for Alice Finch.

'Baroness, you are always most gracious,' said Agatha to Eleanor. 'But it appears you were not informed that your mother and father will be arriving any moment with Lord North and his wife.'

'Shall I find the footman and arrange more chairs?' asked Hugh.

'I fear what we need is fewer chairs,' said Agatha. 'Were Lord North not of the party, we could of course be perfectly comfortable . . .' She trailed off, smiling at Algernon and trying not to look at Amberleigh's pressed lips.

'Perhaps my wife and I may steal some of your guests away to join us at another table, Baroness?' said John. He gave the footman a discreet signal, and the footman began to look around for a table from which the occupants might be dislodged. Agatha could have kissed him in public for his smoothing of such an awkward moment. And since Bettina was not coming, Agatha felt she had no objection to sacrificing herself and being free to country-dance without the stultifying effect of being part of an earl's retinue.

'No, no, we will not break up your arriving party, my dear Mr Kent,' said Algernon. 'My wife and I were about to make our excuses anyway.' He gestured to indicate both all of those gathered and no one in particular. 'You must excuse us. We are promised to visit neighbours at other tables.'

'I will come with you and find Alice,' said Minnie. 'She insisted on my sitting, but I should help her with her equipment.' Across the field Alice Finch could be seen setting down her heavy camera and directing two young Gypsy dancers to pose against the painted wheel of a caravan.

'I would join you,' said Mr Tillingham. 'But Lord North has asked my particular opinion on one or two matters of national importance, and I must look after the Professor.'

'Yes, it does not do to abandon one's friends,' said Amberleigh, collecting her shawl and directing a cool look at Agatha. 'I completely understand.'

'I believe I would like to come with you,' said Beatrice, rising from the table. Agatha forgave her the angry look in her eyes. She did not expect Beatrice to understand, in the same way Amberleigh did, that she meant to save them all humiliation.

'No, no,' said Daniel. 'We must get ready to perform our tableau. We are to perform right after Harry and Craigmore's hornpipe.'

'It was lovely to meet you, Miss Nash,' said Amberleigh. 'You must come and see me and bring me some of your work to read.' As she took her husband's arm to leave, she added, 'We women must stick together, must we not?'

'Daniel has written an ode to the King of the Hops,' explained Hugh as Agatha watched the Friths departing. 'Craigmore is to be king, and Miss Beatrice and Miss Celeste are handmaidens to the farmer's daughter, who is to be queen.'

'Are you sure that's a good idea?' asked Agatha. 'Lady Emily is not a fan of amateur theatricals.'

'My dear aunt, poetry is not some low amateur folly,' said Daniel. 'I have adapted my "Ode to the *David*" just for the occasion.' He waved a sheaf of papers as he herded Beatrice and Celeste from the table. 'Never fear, we will elevate the evening to new heights, which may be just in time.' As he spoke, a pennywhistle struck up a lively jig and two men in rolled-up trousers, with buckets on their heads and pitchforks in hand, strode to the stage.

'Oh, I like the boy's ode,' said Tillingham. 'Quite visceral and raw.'

'What do you mean, "visceral"?' asked Agatha, but she was already distracted as she realised the two men clowning a hornpipe, to much laughter and some thrown sausages, were Harry Wheaton and young Craigmore. Lord and Lady North and Colonel Wheaton and Lady Emily, now advancing over the grass towards the table, did not appear amused to see their sons making fools of themselves for the delight of bumpkins.

'I need to sit down,' said Agatha. Hugh caught her arm and helped her to a chair. 'And I think I need a large glass of that champagne.'

'Why is it funny?' the Professor asked, as Craigmore and Harry swung pitchforks in dangerous proximity to limbs and minced over crossed rakes in an improvised sword dance.

'They appreciate that the Colonel's son makes himself ridiculous for them,' said John. 'And this year he brings an earl's son too.'

'I fear Lady North is not laughing,' said Agatha. The visit already seemed a terrible mistake. But she could only continue to smile while Hugh and the footman attempted to arrange a forest of excess chairs.

Hugh was glad to see the hornpipe conclude as the cheering and whistles from the crowd did not seem to improve the slightly grim faces of Lord North and his wife. As the country dance caller stepped forward to announce the poetic recitation, Hugh felt a sudden hollowing of his breath.

'I do hope Daniel hasn't overreached in what the audience is expecting,' he heard his aunt Agatha whisper to Uncle John, his own anxiety reflected in her voice.

'Let's pray for brevity,' said Uncle John. 'But resign ourselves to an epic.' As the crowd clapped, Hugh whispered to the footman to make sure the champagne glasses were refilled at every opportunity.

Two boys with flaming torches marched to stand at either side of the stage, and a single fiddler began a slow version of an old minuet as the players processed from behind the stage and around the grass in a circle. Everyone but Daniel wore a spreading crown of hops, and on the ladies, long bud-filled vines, caught in ribbons and pinned over one shoulder, trailed on the ground like the trains of ballgowns. Craigmore, moving at a king's slow pace, carried willow sticks lashed together in the manner of an ancient Roman sceptre and led the farmer's daughter, who cradled an armful of wildflowers as pink as her flushed cheeks. Beatrice held apples in a basket at her waist and Celeste a jug of cider on one shoulder, in the manner of a nymph on a Greek vase. Wearing a scarlet scarf tied in dashing style around his neck and carrying a large leather portfolio, Daniel brought up the rear.

'It's not a tableau if they're moving,' said Mr Tillingham, his voice made louder than he imagined by a tankard of cider.

'No, but what a lovely effect,' said Aunt Agatha. Hugh had to admit that in the waning, horizontal light of evening, with the flicker of the torches and bonfire, trees darkening all around and the colourful crowd pressing forward from their tables to see, the procession held a strange power.

As the music paused, the players moved into a square formation, ready to dance. There was some clapping from the crowd, and small children wriggled forward under their mothers' skirts to better see the show.

'"The Crowning of the Hop King",' announced Daniel, reading from a paper plucked from his opened portfolio and then allowing it to flutter to the ground.

'Being a special adaptation of the poem "Ode to the *David* of Florence" by Daniel Bookham, reimagined as homage to the last day of our harvest . . .'

'Perhaps the last harvest?' he added and dropped the second page as the fiddler scrambled through a brief musical fanfare.

'I do hope it rhymes,' said Lady Emily. 'It's not proper poetry if it isn't in iambic pentameter.'

> 'Your marble thigh so sinewed, whitely,
> Would that my hand might press to warm
> Life to the veins, set sap to running—
> And harvest the shepherd home to the farm.'

As Daniel paused, the fiddle, joined by a pennywhistle, began the same minuet again, in a minor key, and Beatrice and Celeste laid their gifts at the farm girl's feet and entwined their arms for the first figure of the dance.

> 'King of your own flesh, Prince of your own eyes,
> None has dominion higher than the pure.
> I touch like a priest but the rope of your sandal,
> Pledge you all honour, and faith that endures.'

Craigmore and the farmer's daughter took their turn at the figure. Hugh could not be sure at such a distance, but he thought Beatrice's shoulders might be shuddering with suppressed laughter. All four dancers began a stately circle, hands aloft.

> 'Boy, man and king, thy reign o'erpowers me,
> Renders my lyre faint like unto death.
> King of the hop fields, kiss but my forehead,
> Wake me, your giant, and let flower all the earth.'

The last pages fluttered from Daniel's grasp as he lowered himself to one knee. The dancers came to a stop, the Hop

King bowing to his Queen, the handmaidens in low curtsies, arms raised to the sky. As the players stilled in final tableau, three small girls ran from behind the stage with baskets and began to pelt the dancers with flowers. Agatha saw Beatrice take a large dahlia to the cheek but remain still, albeit blinking. The music finished with a long last note.

The crowd erupted in applause and laughter and loud discussions up and down the tables.

'Bravo, bravo,' said Mr Tillingham, clapping from his chair. 'Poet, poet!'

Daniel rose slowly, removing the red scarf from his neck and using it to lead the players in a sweeping bow. As he stepped back into the line, Craigmore dropped the hand of the farmer's daughter and caught Daniel round the neck in a friendly hold. Daniel squirmed and grinned but made no effort to free himself until Craigmore let go to offer him a slap on the back and to grab his hand as all the players linked arms for another set of bows. The applause was louder and more sustained than Hugh thought warranted as Craigmore led the farmer's daughter to her father and the others returned to their table. Hugh leaned towards his aunt to say, 'Daniel will be impossibly smug in the morning.'

'It was well done, though,' said his aunt.

'You young ladies performed beautifully,' said Lady Emily. 'Bettina Fothergill must secure all three of you at once for her grand float in the parade. So far she has suggested only girls so homely I fear she means to be sure Britannia is not outshone by her handmaidens.'

Hugh noticed Lord North, who was not clapping but stood with his hands clasped behind him, whisper something to his wife. He then pursed his lips and frowned. To

Colonel Wheaton's asking him how he enjoyed the performance, he responded with a nod. 'I enjoyed the musical
background. Partial to the violin.'

'Your son is a good sport to jump in and help with our
amateur entertainments,' said Agatha to the Countess. 'It's
nice to bring the people more wholesome fare than music-
hall numbers and dancing girls.'

'Though there may be hidden decadence in poetry dedi-
cated to spirits and such,' said Lady North. 'We must be
always on our guard against the slippery attractions of
false idols.'

'That we must,' said Lord North.

'Of course we must,' said Agatha and then turned to roll
her eyes at Hugh and Beatrice.

'I think we've seen enough,' said Lord North, turning to
Colonel Wheaton. 'We are expected early at Dover for the
review at the castle, and I know my wife tires easily.'

'Will you not be dancing?' asked Agatha. 'The band will
play for hours.'

'I regret our duties must come first,' said Lord North. 'It
has been a pleasure to meet you and your husband, Mrs
Kent.'

'Are you leaving too, Aunt?' asked Hugh in a low voice
as Colonel Wheaton and Lady Emily gathered themselves
to leave.

'I certainly am not,' said Agatha. 'Why, they are just call-
ing for the Gay Gordons, and I may possibly dance the Sir
Roger de Coverley if the digestion of my dinner allows.'
She leaned closer to Hugh and Beatrice to whisper, 'If Mr
Tillingham wants to leave, he can commandeer a farm
cart.'

'Good for you, Mrs Kent,' said Beatrice as Agatha allowed her husband to lead her away to the forming dance sets.

'Do you dance, Mademoiselle Celeste?' asked Daniel. Upon her assent, he begged the privilege, and she gave him her hand with the sort of trusting smile that only Daniel could draw from young ladies. Hugh felt a sharp envy at his cousin's easy, open manner and found it harder than usual to compose both his face and his thoughts to make his own awkward overture.

'Will you dance, Miss Nash?' he asked. 'Only I must warn you my country dancing experience is largely theoretical.'

'I would be happy to, Mr Grange,' said Beatrice. 'Fortunately for you, in my schoolgirl dancing class, I was always one of the tallest and so I am used to leading.' He would have bantered again, finding some self-deprecation with which to puncture the awkwardness of conversation. But her hand was warm from her exertions, and she seemed to glow under her crown of hops. In the flicker from the bonfire and the swell of the music, Hugh found her transformed, and he did not want to speak but only to lead her whirling and laughing into the dance.

CHAPTER SIXTEEN

THE FOLLOWING MORNING, HUGH was settled in a wing chair in his workroom, nominally enthralled by a new book on the composition of monkey brains, an advance copy sent by a leading German researcher to Hugh's surgeon just before war was declared. But in reality, after the weeks of sleepless nights cramming for examinations while drilling all day, and shivering through the finals in a chilly mess hall that seemed to breathe failure, he was enjoying dozing in a slab of sunlight, feeling the pleasant after-effects of a good breakfast. He did wonder idly whether the German scientist would be able to keep his monkeys through the war, whether monkeys learned German commands as easily as English, and whether human language had a hierarchy and where English should be considered on such a hierarchy against, say, French or Latin.

This naturally led to his considering what Miss Beatrice Nash, who was coming to luncheon with Celeste and the younger set from the Wheaton house, would have to say on the poetry of competing languages. As his mind wandered into this thought, he was aware of the scent of a late-blooming climbing rose coming in the stable window on a puff of air and he noted that the scent might have prompted the thought and he wondered if monkeys associated smells with people in the same way as humans did; whether Smith would still be Smith if he smelled of bay rum instead of diesel and boot polish, and whether Miss Nash, who smelled of roses and lime blossom to him, was even now putting on her bonnet to come for an alfresco afternoon on the terrace . . .

A swift clatter of boots on the stairs heralded his cousin Daniel's arrival, and he closed the book, not without relief, for it was a dense tome, printed in close-set type, as if the printer had struggled to squeeze its impossible length into some manageable slab of pages.

'Craigmore's gone,' said Daniel. His face was constricted into a mask of distress, and his tone threatened to compromise his preferred demeanour of bored indifference.

'Gone where?' asked Hugh.

'Urgent family business, they say,' said Daniel. He tugged at his crumpled shirt collar, and Hugh could see he was warm with sweat about the neck, as if he had run all the way home. 'The Wheatons' butler said he couldn't say where, just that Craigmore left with his mother on the early train.'

'What did Harry and Eleanor say?'

'Didn't see them. Eleanor sent word she is not feeling well, and Harry was apparently out riding and not expected back until nightfall.' Daniel slumped in the other wing chair and covered his face with one arm.

'Well, that's certainly a blow to Aunt Agatha's plans,' said Hugh, keeping his tone light in the hope that his cousin would follow his lead and calm down. 'I do hope it's not anything serious with Craigmore's family.'

'Don't be an idiot, Hugh, it's nothing to do with family business,' said Daniel from under his sleeve. 'It's Lord North.' He groaned and added, 'My life is over.'

'Do try and string together rational sentences, Daniel,' said Hugh.

'Don't you see?' said Daniel. 'Craigmore must have told his father about the journal, about our plans. He's been sent away.'

'You're being a bit dramatic,' said Hugh. 'You can't know that.' Even as Hugh spoke he felt the hypocrisy of offering comfort instead of truth. But what truth would he speak to his cousin? Remembering the whispered conversation between Lord North and his wife after Daniel's recitation, Hugh knew, with a sinking feeling, that it was not the journal to which he objected.

'Craigmore would never have left without leaving me a note,' said Daniel. 'I always thought his father might try to make things sticky.'

'Well, it's unfortunate that our luncheon party has been substantially reduced,' said Hugh. 'We had better inform Cook.'

'How can you talk of luncheons?' groaned Daniel, hanging his head so that his face was hidden beneath the fall of his hair. 'You have no idea what it is to lose such a friendship as that which Craigmore and I share.'

'Pull yourself together, Cousin,' said Hugh. He stood and tugged the edges of his jacket down as if to reinforce his words. 'It will not serve to allow the entire household to hear such agitation. Craigmore would not wish a conspicuous fuss, I'm sure.' There was a pause, and Hugh gazed out of the window to allow his cousin time to compose himself. While he envied his cousin's free and easy, passionate nature, and his capacity for intense friendships, he felt squeamish in the face of Daniel's occasional displays of emotion.

'You are right, of course,' said Daniel at last. He pulled a large silk handkerchief from a pocket and blew his nose with abandon. 'You are lucky to be made of more rational stuff, Hugh. You will never be carried away by your emotions.'

'Thank you,' said Hugh, fully aware that Daniel did not altogether mean it as a compliment. It was hardly fair that Daniel should provoke him into a purse-lipped rigidity and then insult him for it, but Hugh's first concern was to protect his cousin from his own self-indulgence. 'Now why don't we make a suitable plan?' he added. 'Beginning with some appearance of indifference to their sudden departure.'

'I will write to Craigmore at his father's in London,' said Daniel.

'I think not,' said Hugh. 'Aunt Agatha will surely be writing a note of thanks to Lady Emily this morning. We'll ask her to make casual enquiries.'

'What if Lady Emily knows nothing?' said Daniel. 'I can still catch the noon post.'

'If matters stand as you fear, your letter may be intercepted,' said Hugh. 'I will write to Craigmore myself – but by late-afternoon post at the earliest.'

'Why the delay?' asked Daniel.

'Craigmore seemed very interested in our hospital laboratories,' said Hugh. 'As I'm expected in London on Tuesday, it will probably occur to me, by mid-afternoon at the earliest, to send him a casual invitation to tour. All very indifferent, you see?'

Daniel groaned. 'I can't wait until Tuesday.'

'I hope it will prompt him to send me a reply that might shed light on the situation,' said Hugh. 'But meanwhile, Daniel, you simply must recover your composure. No good can come from physical or emotional dishevelment.'

A sound of voices in the stable below was followed by a light knocking on the stairwell wall and Beatrice Nash's voice saying, 'Hello, is anyone at home?'

'I'm not sure I can face anyone,' said Daniel urgently. Hugh noticed that he did have a strange, pale look about the gills, but perhaps, he thought, this was the properly deserved effect of too much rough cider and champagne.

'For goodness' sake, it's only Beatrice and Celeste,' he said. 'You and Miss Celeste can look pale and interesting together. Of course, she's come from a war zone. Perhaps her situation will help your sense of perspective.'

'Your sarcasm lacks the delicacy that would render it amusing,' said Daniel. He caught Hugh by the sleeve. 'But I thank you for your help. What would I do without you to bail me out of scrapes?'

'One day you'll have to take care of yourself,' said Hugh. 'Now smile for our guests.'

'You sound just like Uncle John sometimes,' said Daniel. 'Hello, ladies, do come up. It's mercifully clear of blood and guts today.'

Beatrice and Celeste came up the stairs, and Hugh was glad to note that he was not mistaken; Beatrice did smell of roses and lime blossom. Celeste carried the faintest perfume of soap and talcum powder, and neither lady seemed to wear any hint of the previous night's festivities.

'Welcome,' he said. 'How did you find us?'

'I asked Jenny not to stand on ceremony but to direct us to where you were,' said Beatrice. 'We are a trifle early, and I hoped you would be up here so I might show Celeste your lair.'

'Welcome, Miss Celeste,' said Hugh. 'My humble work-room is at your disposal.'

'It is a privilege,' said Celeste. 'I want to see the dead chickens.' Daniel laughed, and Hugh hoped the presence of the ladies might make him sensible. But Daniel could not keep such anguish contained.

'Craigmore has gone,' he blurted out. 'My friend vanished before breakfast.'

'Well, that is sad for our lunch party,' said Beatrice. 'But I do hope it was not bad news in the family?'

'I am sure everything is fine,' said Hugh, pleased at how exactly her response mirrored his own. 'I'm going to ask my aunt Agatha to enquire as much of Lady Emily, just to reassure us.'

'But this is terrible,' said Celeste to Daniel. 'How could your friend leave without a word?'

'My thought exactly,' said Daniel. 'I am in an agony of uncertainty. *L'angoisse du doute.*'

'It is not right to leave no word in these days,' said Celeste. 'Anything could have happened, *n'est-ce pas*?'

'At last someone understands,' said Daniel, shooting Hugh a look. Hugh could only roll his eyes as Daniel and

Celeste drifted to the two wing chairs, where they sat and continued, for some minutes, to turn over the circumstances of Craigmore's departure in a low and urgent mix of English and French.

'I'm sure there is a simple explanation,' said Beatrice to Hugh. 'Perhaps we had better excuse ourselves and relieve your aunt of the need to entertain us?'

'Do not leave me to lunch alone with Daniel in his current agonies,' said Hugh. 'I shall get indigestion.'

Beatrice laughed, and Hugh heard an echo of the night's music and had to quell an urge to sweep her into another spinning dance.

'Just as well,' she said. 'I told Mrs Turber we would be out, and there is no producing spontaneous nourishment in the Turber kitchen.'

Aunt Agatha was in her small upstairs porch, where she spent most mornings at her desk, in a loose wrapper and slippers, writing letters and reading magazines. Uncle John was smoking his pipe in the window seat and looking over last week's racing papers. Hugh knocked at the open door and went in.

'Am I late?' asked Aunt Agatha. 'I was just trying to finish a couple of notes before they arrive.'

'Celeste and Beatrice are here,' said Hugh. 'But Celeste is deep in conversation with Daniel, and Beatrice was keen to tour the kitchen garden.'

'We had best be getting dressed, then,' said his uncle.

'Did you write a note of thanks to Lady Emily yet?' Hugh asked, affecting an air of nonchalance. From the sharp look on his aunt's face, he knew he had overplayed his hand.

'I am writing it now,' she said, one eyebrow raised.

'Only it seems that the Countess left in a hurry for London this morning,' said Hugh. 'Took Craigmore with her without so much as a word to anyone.'

'Seems a little abrupt?' said Uncle John.

'How upsetting for Daniel,' said Agatha. 'He was so glad to have his friend here.'

Hugh did his best to meet her gaze with an expression of frankness. 'Not really,' he said. 'We were just hoping that it is not some family emergency. Perhaps Lady Emily might reassure us on that point?'

'It seems quite rude after all the trouble Lady Emily took to entertain them – but of course I shall be discreet and merely note our concern for Lady North's family,' said Agatha.

'Harry and Eleanor are also apparently unavailable for luncheon,' said Hugh. 'I've already spoken to Cook.'

When Hugh had left, Agatha took up her pen and, after some hesitation, composed a brief line offering an expression of concern for the Countess and sympathy for the disarrangement such a hasty departure must bring to any hostess.

While she was reading it over, John folded up his paper and took his pipe from his mouth. 'To be expected, you know,' he said.

'What is?' asked Agatha.

'Son of an earl,' said John. 'Not likely to be allowed to dabble in the arts when there is a war on.'

'I quite agree,' said Agatha. 'Yet I hardly see the need to order the boy away.'

'Some things are best nipped in the bud,' said John. 'Time for Daniel to see some sense too.'

'I am as concerned as you about Daniel's future,' said Agatha. 'Yet he does have more than a usual talent, John. Tillingham has said so.'

'Tillingham is an old sybarite with particular interests.'

'John!' said Agatha. 'You are quite mistaken. I have had to comfort several ladies I know after Mr Tillingham has been most rude about the talents of their sons. Some who are even more handsome than Daniel.'

'Ah, then you do admit to that possibility?' asked her husband.

'You are quite awful this morning,' said Agatha. 'Do be serious for a moment, John. Do you not think Daniel should pursue his art? He could be the next Coleridge.'

'I think Mr Kipling is more the fashion now,' said John. 'Besides, Coleridge lived a life of poverty and had to be sustained by charitable friends.'

'Perhaps you think he should be a postman like Trollope?' said Agatha.

'You forget that it is not up to us,' said John, mildly, folding away the paper and tucking it in the back of a basket. He was quite pleased to read old copies over again and rotated them carefully so that while he might feel a familiarity in the stories, he would be sure to have forgotten the specifics. Though it pained Agatha that he might appear frugal to the staff, he did it not to save money but because to read stories of races already won and horses long put out to stud was, he said, a welcome relaxation after the constant influx of new crises that dominated his working life. Since he had few other vices about which a reasonable wife could complain, she was obliged to find this habit endearing. She was not similarly inclined and spent too much of her household allowance on weekly copies of the *Gentlewoman* and *Country Life*, and, more recently, had begun to pick up the less vulgar of the illustrated papers.

'I believe Daniel will go his own way despite his father,' said Agatha. 'Or even to spite him outright. I would like to think we might be a mediating influence.'

'You are to stay out of their business, Agatha,' said John. 'We have been over this before. We agreed long ago on our proper roles as aunt and uncle to both Hugh and Daniel.'

'Yes but—'

'No "buts", my dear,' he said. His voice was still as mild as before, but she knew he would not be countermanded. 'I have made Daniel's father aware of the assistance I can provide, and not provide, in securing Daniel a spot in the civil or diplomatic service. I have no particular assistance to offer in the way of a literary career, so even if I did not know it to be against his father's intentions, I could offer no help there.'

'He wants to start a poetry magazine.'

'If he wanted a military commission, I might be able to pull a few strings,' said John. 'At least, many people seem to think I can, judging by the dozens of requests I am getting.'

'No, don't mention such a thing,' said Agatha. 'Isn't it bad enough that Hugh has enlisted?'

'Many of our finest young aristocrats are falling over themselves to get in on the action,' said her husband. 'Careers and fortunes may be made in these next few months. I think Hugh was wise to follow his surgeon's advice.'

'You are not to speak of it to Daniel,' said Agatha. 'I should worry all the time.'

'Then I will not bring it up,' said her husband. 'And you in turn will leave the boy and his father to discuss his future.'

'I must get this note over to Emily Wheaton,' said Agatha. 'I'll not wait for the post. I'll send Smith instead.'

After the fresh sea air and green lawns of Sussex, all of London seemed breathless under the accumulated dust of a long summer. Having received only an elliptical note from Craigmore, saying he would be at home Tuesday morning but unable to visit Hugh's hospital, the two cousins had decided to consider themselves invited to visit and had gained entrance through the formidable gates and courtyard of Lord North's London mansion, in part because Hugh was in uniform and a uniform seemed to create respect and open doors these days. They had been shown to a small antechamber, panelled in heavy oak. It contained only small, stiff settees, an empty fireplace with cast-iron mantel, and, between two large windows, an imposing, green malachite bust of Cromwell on a matching plinth so floridly carved with vines and flowers that Cromwell himself would surely have had it destroyed. Hugh was not familiar with any connection of the Earl North family to Cromwell. Perhaps, he thought, there was none and that was why the ugly heirloom had been consigned to oaken purgatory to intimidate unwanted guests. Daniel was pacing the four corners of the room as if to measure it for carpet. His hands clasped behind his back and his shoulders hunched, he looked as miserable as Cromwell and almost as green. Hugh hoped that his cousin would be able to preserve his dignity.

'It will not do to seem anxious,' he said quietly. 'And remember, any mention of the journal on your part might seem to be about money rather than friendship.'

'I don't give a damn about the journal or about money,' said Daniel.

'I know that,' said Hugh. 'Just be silent and let Craigmore tell us what is happening.'

Daniel came over and clasped Hugh's hand. 'Thank you, Cousin,' he said. 'Your permanent frown always brings me to my senses.'

'I do not have a permanent frown,' said Hugh. He took a brief look into the pier glass over the mantel and consciously adjusted his features to a half smile, smoothing out the deep lines between his eyes. He adjusted his cap a little higher under his arm. 'Or at least I would not have such a frown were you to cause me less concern.'

'I can manage my own affairs, you know,' said Daniel, a note of schoolboy petulance in his tone.

'You came to the railway station this morning with no money,' said Hugh.

'Very good of you to advance me the ticket,' said Daniel. 'I don't think we would have gained seats at all if you were not on orders.'

'Let's hope you are allowed to travel home,' said Hugh. 'Troop priority seems to have overwhelmed the railways.'

'I remember now I was using some notes as bookmarks. Think I rushed out and left all my money tucked into my

Longfellow.' Daniel's humour seemed to improve in consideration of his own foolishness. 'All poets should be assigned a Hugh to watch over them.'

'Thank you,' said Hugh, turning his head to the sound of footsteps in the hall. 'I've always wanted to be a valet.'

The door to the room swung open, pushed by a footman, and Craigmore advanced with an air of stiff dignity, an ambassador asked to receive a party of minor colonial dignitaries. With chin high and lips pursed, his stiff demeanour was accented by the thick wool of a dull blue uniform so new even the elbows had not creased. He wore polished boots, walking slowly as if they pinched in several places, and carried a blue cap with shiny black brim under his arm. In only two days, his upper lip had acquired the solid underpinnings of a blunt moustache, and only his golden hair, trimmed short but still insistent on its curl, disturbed his military air.

'Oh my God, are you playing in *HMS Pinafore*?' Daniel asked with a laugh. His face was wreathed in smiles, and his anxiety seemed to have evaporated now his friend was in the room. 'What have they done to you?'

'Hugh, Daniel, good of you both to come,' said Craigmore. 'I'm afraid I don't have much time. My mother is giving a luncheon.' He shook hands with Hugh and then with Daniel, who grasped his hand with two hands.

'I am beyond measure glad to see you,' said Daniel.

Craigmore withdrew his hand gently and placed it behind his back. His cheeks reddened and he rocked slightly on his heels, as if considering his next words with care. As he spoke, he waved to the settees, and Hugh followed his lead and sat down. Daniel remained standing.

'I wanted to apologise for the hurried nature of our departure from Sussex,' said Craigmore. 'It was unpardonably rude, and yet we had not a moment to write. We had an early morning telegram, and my mother and I simply dashed for the train.'

'We were glad to hear from Lady Emily that no tragedy had occurred,' said Hugh, offering it somewhere between a statement and a question.

'No, rather an opportunity to be seized,' said Craigmore slowly. 'An old friend of my father's offered to provide me an advantage, but he was only in London briefly so we were forced to hurry to town.'

'Not a word to your friends?' asked Daniel. He stood behind Hugh, and Hugh could sense that he was gripping the wooden frame of the settee.

'I confess,' said Craigmore, 'that even had I a moment I would not have known what to write.' He took a slow breath and looked Daniel directly in the face. 'My good fortune was to overturn all our deepest held ambitions, my friend, and I could not, in all honour, convey such news in a letter.'

'It appears you have secured a military commission?' said Hugh, moving cautiously to the obvious and hoping his tone would prevent any violent outburst from Daniel, who let go the settee and came to slump beside him. He did not want to look at his cousin's face. He and Craigmore talked as if Daniel were not in the room.

'I knew you had joined the Medical Corps, of course,' said Craigmore to Hugh. 'Are you already on orders?'

'Six weeks or so of training,' said Hugh. 'Mostly the military aspects. They've rushed us through our final exams already.'

'Royal Flying Corps,' said Craigmore. 'Uniform is still a bit up in the air – if you'll excuse the pun. Of course we'll have more suitable flying gear for daily use. Leathers and so forth. I'm off to Burberry's later today to get a great-coat, and they do a very good aviator helmet with goggles, the best hand-ground lenses.'

'I didn't know you flew,' said Hugh.

'Yes, been doing a bit this last year. Took Daniel up a couple of times over Florence this summer,' said Craigmore. 'Damned good fun. Dozens of chaps looking for commissions, of course, so when my father arranged for me to meet the Commodore – well, I can tell you I had no interest in enlisting in an ordinary war, but the Flying Corps – this is the newest thing.' He reddened some more and added, 'Damned good fun!'

'What about art?' asked Daniel, his voice low and miserable.

'I was never as good a painter as Daniel thought,' said Craigmore, still talking to Hugh. 'I knew it even if he didn't.' He fidgeted up from the settee and went to put his boot on the fireplace fender, one arm on the mantel. 'I was always going to be the one tolerated for his money and connections.'

'I never thought of you that way,' said Daniel quietly.

'I know that, I know,' said Craigmore hurriedly, risking a quick glance in his direction. 'I accuse you only of being perhaps blinded by – by friendship.'

'And what of such a friendship?' asked Daniel. 'Is it to be tossed aside as a casual convenience?'

'My father says the time calls for men, not for sensitive boys,' said Craigmore. 'Many friendships will be changed by the events of the coming days.'

'Since when have we listened to our fathers?' asked Daniel. 'Do we not share the deepest aversion to their calculated hypocrisies?'

'Café chatter and schoolboy manifestos,' said Craigmore. 'It is time we grew up, Daniel.'

'I grew up this summer,' said Daniel. 'I found my life's true compass. Unfortunately, it seems it is broken. I must spin in place.'

'Always with a simile or a metaphor in the face of hard truths,' said Craigmore. 'We have no claim upon each other, Daniel. I made no contract. I breach no promise that would stand in the light of public gaze.'

'We needed no promises,' said Daniel.

'I have committed to serve my country in its time of need,' said Craigmore. 'One cannot argue with patriotism.'

'What rot,' said Daniel, his voice bitter. 'Your father has purchased you the opportunity to fly expensive aeroplanes and drink good wine in the mess with other men of breeding, and be admired in parades with your silver braid and your polished boots. It is theatre of the most amateur kind. No doubt you will be in all the cheapest illustrated papers.'

'I think there is no more to be said.' Craigmore drew himself up into as stiff a column as he could, and Hugh saw him clamp his teeth down on a small quiver of the jaw. 'I hope to remain friends. If you can recover from today's emotion and be civil, I would be glad to receive your correspondence.'

'Where shall we find you?' asked Hugh, rising. He felt a protective need to remove Daniel before his cousin destroyed his friendship entirely.

'As soon as I have a military address I will forward it to you.' There was the sound of voices in the hall and a woman's laugh. 'If you will excuse me, our luncheon guests are arriving.'

Before he could take his leave, the door was opened by the same footman, and a young woman entered. She wore a fashionable narrow-skirted blue dress with black braiding and brass toggles on the bodice and an ethereal hat of large dimension. She smiled with the relaxed certainty of the privileged, and though she was not pretty, her demeanour gave her an air of attractive polish.

'The footman said you had friends, and I am so impatient to meet any of Craigmore's friends that I just thought I would be entirely outrageous and barge in.' She gave Craigmore a kiss on the cheek and took his arm. 'Do introduce me, darling.' Craigmore looked somewhat helpless, like a kitchen boy caught red-handed with a stolen chicken. An involuntary smile came to Hugh's lips, which may have added to Craigmore's discomfort. The young man adopted a stiff frown.

'Miss Charter, may I present Mr Hugh Grange and Mr Daniel Bookham. Mr Grange, Mr Bookham . . .' He took in a large gulp of air before finishing. 'May I present Miss Joy Charter, my fiancée.'

They left the mansion in silence and did not speak until they parted ways outside a small public house where Daniel and other writers were fond of gathering. Hugh was anxious about leaving him alone, but Daniel insisted that he was fine and that Craigmore's sudden production of a fiancée was not a blow.

'Well, not beyond the obvious disappointment that she is, in fact, a complete horse,' said Daniel. For Daniel to be rude in so blunt a manner was telling of his anger and misery, but Hugh could only send him inside the smoke-filled pub to his friends and his whisky, because Hugh was already late for his own appointment.

'I'll come and find you when I'm done,' he said. 'Try to be restrained.'

'I'll be communing with my fiancée, the goddess of the far Scottish isles,' said Daniel. 'But I will attempt to remain upright, at least in my chair.'

In Sir Alex Ramsey's red-brick house, the gilded wallpaper smelled of dry glue and the thick Turkey carpet gave off an odour of old wool. No windows were open, and the still air seemed to have been already breathed by other people. The butler showed Hugh upstairs to his surgeon's private study. The inner sanctum was thick with pictures and antique bronzes. It held several comfortable club chairs and smelled of leather from a desk exposed to the afternoon sun in the bay window. 'Come in, my boy,' said the surgeon, busy selecting a decanter from a loaded tray. 'I've been waiting to give you the good news.' Without asking, he poured two glasses, adding the thick amber smell of brandy to the room.

'Please tell me they are dropping all drilling exercises as superfluous to our training,' said Hugh, perching on a stiff upholstered chair and trying not to fidget with his uniform. 'I can't tell you how it would hearten our foes to see a hundred doctors stepping on each other's feet and waving their wooden guns in all the wrong directions.'

'I have heard we are not giving a good impression,' said the surgeon, passing him a glass. 'That so much intelligence is somehow a barrier to simple rote manoeuvres . . . does it suggest a withering of those brain parts not used for study, I wonder?'

'I think it might be more a correlation between lack of athleticism and choosing such a career,' said Hugh. 'Or perhaps we just think too much about what it means to face left.'

'Stick with it, my boy, and in another six weeks or so you'll be in France,' said Sir Alex. 'It is my great privilege to tell you that you have passed your final examinations. Congratulations, you'll go to the front as a full surgeon.' He raised his glass and drank it in a swallow.

'I am astonished,' said Hugh. 'I didn't dare to hope I had done enough.'

'Top of the class, dear boy,' said his surgeon. 'I detect more leniency than usual in the marks, since the examinations were brought forward by so many months, but you can be reassured that you would have passed in any year, as I expected.'

'Thank you, sir,' said Hugh. 'That means a lot.'

'In the immediate future, while we plan for our hospital, we are being asked to distribute our surgeons so we have broad capabilities across the front, but I'm assured our group will be able to pick and choose their own patients, so do not let the administrators push you into the general cases. And watch out for the orthopaedic chaps. Making quite a push for themselves; bit of an upstart bunch.'

'Yes, sir,' said Hugh.

'Pick the most useful cases and make sure you keep your own copy of all case notes,' he added. 'Each case is only as useful to the future of the science as the notes we amass.'

'I understand,' said Hugh. 'Meticulous notes.'

'An extra set is always a good idea,' said his surgeon. 'The record that goes with the patient is always subject to getting lost in transit, especially if he dies.'

'I won't let you down, sir,' said Hugh as he stood to shake hands.

Sir Alex gave him a careful look and then cleared his throat in a way that signalled he had more to add.

'These are very trying times for all, my boy, but especially for the ladies we leave behind,' he said. For a moment Hugh entertained the horrible notion that Aunt Agatha had written to Sir Alex. 'It is very hard for my daughter, who is much distressed at the imminent departure of so many young friends,' he added.

'I had no idea,' said Hugh. He had seen her briefly at the surgeon's first lecture, but she had been too busy with her flags and her feathers to do more than give him her most dazzling smile at his new uniform.

'She hides her feelings admirably behind such youthful effervescence,' said Sir Alex, sighing. 'So like her late mother.' He picked up a heavy silver photograph frame from his desk and showed Hugh his late wife, who peered unsmiling in black dress and pearls, a Bible in one hand and a peacock somewhat improbably walking along the stone balustrade on which she leaned. While the photograph did not suggest a family history of effervescence, Hugh was touched by the showing of it. Sir Alex had never offered much in the way of personal anecdote.

'One sees the similar beauty,' said Hugh and was rewarded with a glimpse of some strong emotion smothered in a cough.

'Fact is, these are such extraordinary times,' said Sir Alex. 'I just wanted to say that I will not stand in your way, my boy. We must not falter; we must not hesitate into the breach, as it were.' He subsided into an awkward silence, pulling at his moustache and turning away to the window so as to resolutely not look at Hugh. It occurred to Hugh that Sir Alex was talking about Lucy, that Sir Alex was giving his permission where none had yet been asked. That the great man would anticipate what was in Hugh's mind was not a surprise, but that he should offer support seemed an honour too great to be believed.

'Miss Ramsey's happiness must be the first concern of her friends,' offered Hugh.

'I told her as much,' said the surgeon. 'I told her I will stand by her choice, regardless of rank or excellence, but to be frank, I have my concerns, Grange.'

'About me?' asked Hugh, surprised into bluntness.

'No, no, you'll do absolutely,' said Sir Alex. 'One or two of the other chaps, let's just say, no good having a coronet if you've no head to put it on.'

'Am I to understand, sir, that you wish Miss Ramsey to marry as she pleases?' asked Hugh. His tone was drier than he intended, perhaps because he was less than happy to be told he might 'do' given the difficulty of the times.

'It's not exactly a carte blanche,' said the surgeon. 'But I will suggest prompt action on the part of any suitor so interested. Fact is, she won't go to Wales without an engagement notice sent out. She fears she'll be isolated and

left on the shelf out in the country. Frankly, I'm at my wits'
end to get her out of London.'

'There is surely no imminent threat to London,' said
Hugh. He had a sudden image of Lucy, in her frothiest of
frocks, sitting in a darkened Welsh parlour with an old
aunt asleep over some knitting, her youth and freshness
entombed and the rain beating at the windows. 'It would
be a hardship for her to be exiled.'

'There may not be Zeppelins coming up the Thames
yet,' said the surgeon. 'But London, in wartime, is a place
of licentiousness and chaos. My dear wife refused to so
much as sit on a public bench in the park, but yesterday my
daughter rode on an omnibus and brought home to tea
three young men she had coaxed to a recruiting office.'

'With your permission, it would be my honour to talk to
her,' said Hugh. 'And regardless of how she looks upon me,
I give you my word that I will urge her to consider her
safety.'

'Thank you,' said Sir Alex. 'Her aunt lives in the heart of
Cardiff, not some lonely crag on Snowdon. She will have
plenty of suitable social life, and I can devote myself to our
cause with a clear conscience.'

In the garden, Hugh found Lucy tucked into a chair in the
small summerhouse. The chairs were covered in quilts, as
if against the sort of autumnal chill that the calendar would
suggest. But the weather was hot, and only the strong,
peppery scent of asters signalled the changing season. As
he approached, Lucy greeted him with both hands
outstretched.

'You look very . . . smart,' he said as he bent to kiss each hand. She wore a blue serge skirt and jacket, trimmed with scarlet epaulettes and a red-and-white sash over her shoulder. Her hair was tucked under a jaunty cap sporting a flag of St George pin. It was a fetching little uniform.

'I'm so glad you've come to see me at last,' she said. 'Every inch the soldier and now a fully fledged surgeon too.'

'Your father told you,' he said.

'I wormed it out of him,' said Lucy. 'I have learned to be very persistent these days.'

'Indeed,' he said.

'Do you like my uniform?' she asked, standing up and smoothing her narrow skirt. 'My friends and I have started our own organisation, the St George Recruitment Brigade.'

'Do you need committees and by-laws to hand out feathers?' he asked.

'The newspaper took our photograph yesterday and published it under the headline "George's Girls!" Look, Hugh.' She presented him with a page cut from an illustrated paper which featured a large photograph of a dozen girls all hanging from the back of an omnibus and waving wildly at the camera.

'You're going to be famous,' said Hugh. Such a photograph required several minutes of keeping still, so the waving was somewhat artificial. 'That poor girl in the back has no arms,' he added.

'Maisie forgot to keep still, and so she actually waved and her arms got all blurry,' said Lucy, peering at the photograph over his shoulder.

'And is it possible you're all wearing paint?'

'Don't be stuffy, Hugh. Everyone knows you need a little theatrical paint for a professional photograph,' she said. 'The important thing is that with such attention we can make a real contribution to the war effort.'

'Still, I can't imagine your father is too happy,' said Hugh.

'I haven't shown him,' she admitted. She folded up the newspaper page and tucked it in her pocket. 'Now that we have helped him recruit his hundred medical men, he can't expect me to just stop,' she continued. 'The country needs all available men, and we are just the girls to get the job done.'

'Just because we're at war doesn't mean we should disregard propriety,' said Hugh. 'I'm sure your father is only concerned about your reputation.'

'Why do you chaps insist on keeping the war all to yourselves?' asked Lucy. 'We girls are not just going to sit home and knit while you go off on your adventures.'

'War is hardly an adventure,' said Hugh.

As he spoke, she glared. 'Exactly my point,' she said. 'In a time of national peril, all must be allowed to chip in.'

'I'm sorry,' he added. 'Your father and I share the urge to protect you.'

'Sounding like one's father is not the most attractive trait in a young man,' she said.

'I am an idiot,' he said, beating his forehead with a fist in mock despair as she laughed at him. 'Tell me your adventures?' he added, hoping with all his heart to hear nothing but the most banal of activities.

Touring London in a hired and decorated omnibus seemed to be the group's main activity. They had been invited to appear at the Albert Hall and gone to a recruiting dinner in Whitehall, but the omnibus seemed to thrill Lucy the most.

'And next month there is to be a garden party at the Palace, and we will provide an honour guard at the door and then join the party, each carrying a spray of tea roses.' She sighed.

'It sounds very exciting,' he said, resisting the urge to ask where they would find tea roses in October.

'You can't imagine how much more exciting it is to actually do something in the world that matters,' she said, looking quite serious and clasping her hands together for emphasis. 'So much more gratifying than the endless copying of case files, answering correspondence like some paid girl, or having to dust my father's consulting room because he doesn't trust the housemaid.' She looked so sad that Hugh was moved to clasp her hands in his. A ray of late-afternoon sun, dipping between rooftops, tipped her hair in rosy gold, and her breath escaped from plump lips pink with health and youth. Hugh could feel her hands tremble under his and see her little jacket fill with her sharp intake of breath.

'I had no idea you were unhappy,' he said.

'Until I marry, I must do my duty to my father,' she said. 'But I trust you, Hugh, and I confess that I long to escape the very smell of the consulting room.'

'You deserve your adventures,' he said. 'You deserve everything.' She lowered her thick lashes to her cheeks and blushed, and they sat in what Hugh hoped was an understanding silence as he tried to find words for a formal declaration.

'You know I have promised my father that were I to become engaged to be married, I would be content to go to Wales and stay with my aunt,' she said, her voice soft.

'It would be a relief to both of us to know you are safe in the bosom of family,' said Hugh.

'But next month is the royal garden party,' she said. She made a small pout with her distracting lips. 'You will understand my difficulty?' she added.

'As a bride-to-be, surely you would have other concerns to attend to,' said Hugh, smiling. 'I wish to ask you . . .' he began.

'No, no, do not ask me, Hugh,' she said, withdrawing her hands to wave them at him as if she were shooing away a small dog. 'I do not wish to say no, and yet were I betrayed into saying yes, I would have to go away. Let us have an understanding without words, without promises.'

'What kind of understanding?' he asked. 'And what will I tell your father?'

'I ask only for a few months, Hugh,' she said. 'Then you will have everything you wanted. One day all this can be yours.' She waved her hand at the house to which she had just expressed a decided aversion.

'I ask only for you,' he said, wondering if she was really willing to join him in a serviced flat in the Old Brompton Road, or a small villa in the sort of distant suburb within the means of a young surgeon.

'Your integrity is one of your most endearing qualities, Hugh,' she said. 'Not all men have it.' She frowned so seriously that he could not help but laugh at her.

'I can only hope you did not discover this truth on an omnibus?' he asked.

'Oh, Hugh!' she said, slapping him playfully. 'This is why I adore you.'

He was surprised to find that instead of being devastated by her wish to delay everything a few more months, he felt strangely contented, if not slightly relieved, to continue just as they were. It was probably the war, he thought, inspiring people to hold on to the lives they already had. A brief image of laughing and dancing in a Sussex hop field flitted unbidden across his mind. He pushed it away and, for the next half an hour, was very earnest in paying attention as Lucy regaled him with stories of her much transformed London life.

After the bright of the sunny day outside, the gloom and fug of the small, black-beamed pub was almost impenetrable, the smell of frying liver and stale beer, the acrid catch in the throat from so many pipes and cigars. Students, law clerks and tradesmen stood four deep at the copper bar, and Hugh pushed through with some difficulty to where his cousin and two friends were grouped close around a barrel table, eating pies with all the grace of dockworkers. Daniel was in his shirtsleeves, tie stuffed in his pocket, a dark stain of spilled liquor over his heart. A pint of beer and a glass of sticky whisky sat by his plate, and in the midst of loud debate, one of the men rose to his feet and refilled the whisky glasses to the brim.

'To poetry and to death!' he said, raising his glass and drinking it in one swallow.

'To poetry that transcends death!' said the other, downing his glass and slumping away from his plate.

'Above all to poetry!' said Daniel and would have drunk but Hugh reached to stay his arm.

'Hello, Cousin,' he said.

'Hu-Hugh,' said Daniel, having some difficulty with the *h* sound of his name. 'You are just in time to toast the King. We are all going in the army!'

'The King!' said the friend with the bottle, raising the bottle itself and drinking from its neck.

'To King and Country!' squeaked the other, unable to rise again from his seat.

'The King!' The pub erupted in cheers, and Hugh could not make himself heard amid a rousing chorus of 'Land of Hope and Glory', made mercifully short by the inability of all to remember more than four lines of the chorus. As the noise died away, Hugh perched on a low stool and asked a passing barmaid to bring him a steak and kidney pie.

'Anything for an officer, love,' she said, giving him a suggestive wink.

'Just the pie, no peas or gravy,' he added.

'Hugh, you will be very proud of me,' said Daniel. 'My father will be proud. My friends, those that are left to me in this cruel world' – (with this he pulled out his tie and wiped his eyes with it) – 'will be proud. We are off to war, Hugh. We are off – *all in the valley of death rode the five hundred.*'

'Six hundred,' said the friend trapped in his own chair.

'What, Tubby? This is my friend Tubby Archer, Hugh.'

'Six hundred – Light Brigade . . . six hundred,' said Tubby.

'Six hundred? Shit, that's a lot of horses,' said the other. He was now cradling the bottle as if it were a small child.

'Longshanks, my friend – it is indeed – that's a, tha's a . . .' Daniel could not speak for laughing, his mouth hanging open, his eyes streaming with tears.

'Landlord says keep it down a bit, will you, gents?' said the barmaid, squeezing through with a steaming pie for Hugh.

'Sorry,' said Hugh. 'Perhaps you could bring a pot of coffee.'

'No, no, no!' said Daniel, waving a stern finger at Hugh. 'We're off to enlist in His Majesty's army and we won't go sober.'

'No, we won't go sober, if we go at all,' sang the three friends.

'Sorry,' said Hugh again.

'Not to worry,' said the barmaid. 'You let 'em holler all they want, poor dears. They'll be a lot more quiet when they wake up under the sergeant major.'

She gave Hugh another wink and squeezed away while Daniel moaned, 'Come back, Peg o' my heart. I love you!'

The three friends subsided into a low, harmonic rendition of 'Peg o' My Heart' with only a passing adherence to any particular key. At least they were quiet enough for Hugh to be able to take a few bites of his pie and a draught of strong beer. When they were finished, all three seemed maudlin and close to tears, a marginal improvement on drunk and loud.

'What's all this about enlisting?' said Hugh. 'I thought you were rather the pacifist.'

'No, not a pacifist, just a poet,' said Daniel. 'But the time has come, Cousin, the time has come to show the likes of some that real men, real bravery lies in the trenches.'

'Heading for the infantry, are you?' asked Hugh. He could not hide a smile at the thought of fastidious Daniel in a muddy trench.

'Longshanks here – this is Bill Longshanks from the Poet's Circle of Greater Pimlico – Longshanks has an uncle can get us in the Artists Rifles. Officer training. All poets and artists and so forth. No rich dilettantes, but only true artists on a mission to limn new forms of bravery and construct, with sonnet and brush, a new brotherhood of artist-soldiers.' He paused to peer in his beer tankard, and, finding it still half filled, he raised it high as if to toast. 'We are away this very afternoon, my boys.'

'You should probably sober up. Things may seem different with a clear head.'

'No, no, I will hurl myself into the valley with the horses,' proclaimed Daniel. 'No time to lose.'

'No horses,' said Longshanks. 'Just rifles and so on. Probably go by train. Four o'clock from Kings Cross.'

'They need me, Hugh,' said Daniel. 'They need an editor for the regimental journal.'

'I said Daniel Bookham is the man to write our history in epic verse,' said Longshanks.

'Even under the barrage I shall toil in my dugout by a single candle,' said Daniel. 'And when the bugle sounds the end of day, and they pull our battered bodies from the carnage, they shall find me clutching to my breast the final issue . . .' He wiped a tear from his eye, and his friends, too, nodded their heads low and seemed to mourn already the destruction of the regiment.

'I think you're putting the cart before the horse, non-existent as the horses may be,' said Hugh. 'This is not a decision to be made in your cups.'

'It is the biggest adventure our age shall see,' said Longshanks, who did not seem quite as drunk as Hugh had first thought. 'It is the ultimate canvas, and no second-raters invited!'

'Hear, hear,' chorused Daniel and Tubby Archer. Hugh understood, with a sinking feeling, that the whispering recruiters would resort to no end of stratagems; that flattery and insult, career prospects, and love, family honour and the shining gold of opportunity would all serve equally well for the purpose of recruiting men to wear the khaki.

'I signed up, so I am the last to dissuade you,' said Hugh. 'But I asked my father's permission and my mother's blessing before I did, and you, Cousin Daniel, will do the same, and best to warn Uncle John and Aunt Agatha as well, I think.'

'We could go tomorrow,' said Tubby. 'Earlier train, you know – time to pack a hearty lunch and settle our affairs.'

'Tomorrow would do as well,' said Longshanks. 'But I will telegraph my uncle today of our intent, and you will not, I know, make me a liar by any shirking?'

'But might Tubby's landlady not discover his purpose in the delay?' asked Daniel. 'I thought he meant to leave via the back window.'

'I shall pack my brushes and leave via the front door,' said Tubby. 'I shall inform the lady of my purpose in the gravest tone and promise her a pound of my flesh from the King's own pay.'

'Best we plan to have a hansom cab standing by,' said Daniel. 'We might have to make a quick getaway.'

'I have time to take you to your father's house,' said Hugh to Daniel. 'Or perhaps we can find him at his club?'

'No need of that,' said Daniel. 'A note by the last post will do. My father will be nothing but ecstra-extar-ecstatic at the news.'

'Then I think we had better go and see Uncle John at the Ministry,' said Hugh. 'I have a feeling you will need his help to tell Aunt Agatha that her favourite nephew is going to war.'

'I am not the favourite, you are the favourite,' said Daniel. He turned to his friends. 'They think he is ever so clever with his science and his medicine, and I am just a poor penniless poet . . .'

'And I bet you can't say "poor penniless poet" three times without spitting beer at everyone,' said Hugh. 'Let's be getting along now, Daniel.' Tucking a hand under his cousin's arm, and with much protestation from the friends and shouted arrangements that made no sense to anyone, Hugh pulled Daniel bodily from the public house and marched him at a half-run in the direction of a bus to Whitehall.

CHAPTER SEVENTEEN

THE COTTAGE OF ALGERNON Frith and Amberleigh de Witte was a low, thatched building standing amid the fields in a tangle of untended garden. Paint flaked on the green-painted windows, and the eaves and the plastered walls were greyish with mildew. The front gate hung open, green and rotten on its posts, and a bicycle lay carelessly toppled against the porch, where two large glazed pots, of the most intense blue, foamed with flowers in hues of Mediterranean red, pink and orange. The cottage should have inspired only disdain for its tumbledown air, but instead Beatrice, approaching with Celeste along the narrow, grassy lane, found it strangely romantic. A girl appeared at the doorway and curtsied as they approached. 'Come in, misses, if you please,' she said, a little breathless and wide-eyed, as if she were unused to guests. 'Mistress is in the back garden.'

From the rough stones of a back hall, they emerged into a garden thick with shade from trees bent under the weight of ancient vines. Beneath a smothered pergola by the edge of a pond, Amberleigh de Witte reclined in a sagging wicker chaise, dressed in a loose green tea dress with her hair down over her left shoulder, tamed only by a narrow ribbon. She was writing in a large leather book and did not get up as Beatrice and Celeste approached but merely waved a long, thin hand and called out to them.

'Do come and have some tea. I've asked for champagne, but it's still chilling in the icehouse.' On a wooden table at her elbow, a tea urn hissed above its small burner, and a stack of old blue-and-white china teacups waited to be filled. A cake stand held an assortment of the usual small sandwiches and the plain rock cakes that were popular now that sugar was scarce. But a stoneware plate nearby held a glistening pork pie. And a bowl of what looked to be confit duck legs, furred with yellow fat, was propped on an old barrel and attended with rapt attention by a panting spaniel, whose nose came almost to the rim. Champagne glasses and a dark bottle of some unknown liquor completed the lavish, unconventional tea setting.

'It was very kind of you to invite us,' said Beatrice. The note, on pale blue stationery suffused with the smell of iris, had reiterated Amberleigh de Witte's hope that Beatrice might bring some of her writings. Such an overture from the prominent authoress was balm to Beatrice's bruised hopes, and she had spent much effort in picking over her meagre stock of original poems and written sketches. Any whisper of hesitation, any thought that Agatha Kent might fault her for visiting a woman now as notorious as she was renowned, could not stand against the thrill of being asked to share her work.

'And I see you have brought some pages for me to read?' asked Amberleigh, setting aside her own book and pen and indicating the cardboard portfolio Beatrice clutched under one arm.

'I hardly dare to ask you,' said Beatrice, blushing at presenting the usual self-deprecations of the eager student to Amberleigh's all-piercing hazel eyes.

'I would much rather read your work than pen my own on such a lovely afternoon,' she replied, turning her head towards the lake to call out, 'Johnny, Minnie, we have visitors.' With some surprise, Beatrice looked for an unexpected man, but across the pond she saw only Miss Finch, the photographer, crouched in a large bank of rushes. She wore a long linen coat and knee–length cycling bags tucked into boots. A large trilby hat shaded her head and her camera.

'Coming,' called Miss Finch, waving at them. 'Just one more shot, Minnie. This time half a turn towards me.' Minnie Buttles now emerged from what Beatrice had assumed was a clump of weed and rose naked to her waist from the water. She draped herself partially in one end of a wet linen sheet that spread itself on the green surface. Her hair hung wet and loose down her back, and the crown of weedy fronds and blowsy roses tilted over her eyes.

'This is the last one, Johnny,' she called back. 'This nymph of the spring is about to become a victim of pneumonia.'

'You know Miss Finch and Miss Buttles,' said Amberleigh, as casually as to suggest it was perfectly normal to have one's guests swim naked in one's pond in the middle of the afternoon. 'Oh, do tip the cat off that chair and sit down,' she added, waving towards a collection of rather down-at-heel lawn chairs. 'He knows he has to make way for guests.'

'I – we have worked together for Belgian Relief,' said Beatrice. As she tried to gently tip the thin grey cat onto the grass, she wondered at how little you really know the people you meet in the committee room. She could hardly believe that demure Minnie Buttles was in the pond before her, but she dared not look again to confirm. She concentrated on the cat, which spat and hissed as it ripped a claw free of the wicker and slunk away.

'And Mademoiselle Celeste, the princess from Belgium, as the gossip says,' said Amberleigh, holding out a hand to Celeste. 'How nice to see you again.'

'Thank you, *madame*. I am happy to be in your home.'

'You are quite exquisite. Miss Finch may want to take your picture too.'

'No, no I cannot. My father, he does not approve the photography,' said Celeste. 'He thinks the photography, it destroy the art.'

'And what do you think?' asked Amberleigh.

'I do not have the – how you say? – opinions,' said Celeste. She sat down in a light blue chair, the arm of which had been repaired with a tight bandage of red knitting wool.

'A woman must always have an opinion,' said Amberleigh. 'Perhaps no one will ask it, but we cannot be prevented from forming one.' Celeste seemed to take a moment to translate and digest before she replied in her careful English.

'Well, I was sad to leave behind the picture – *la peinture* – of my mother,' she said at last. 'If I had a small photograph, perhaps I could have carried it in my heart.'

'Very well said, Miss Celeste,' said Amberleigh. 'You have all the makings of a true bohemian.'

'I am not sure Celeste's father would approve of such an idea,' said Beatrice.

'Have we shocked you before the tea is poured, Miss Nash?' asked Amberleigh. 'I should have warned you that we would be a garden of women.'

'The gardens of Sussex seem to hold an unexpected number of women *en déshabillé*,' said Beatrice, not to mention, she thought, those that preferred the occasional use of a man's name and trousers.

'*C'est en toute innocence, je vous assure*,' said Amberleigh, smiling at Celeste. 'My afternoons are merely a gathering place where women can rest, discuss, create – with no strictures of fashion or of society. We kick off our shoes and our corsets and enjoy the freedom of our private space.'

'Sort of like the Rational Dress Society?' asked Beatrice.

'Dear God, I hope none of us would be seen wearing such dull attire as they propose,' said Amberleigh. 'Exchanging the limits of the corset for the invisibility of a hemp shift is hardly freedom.'

'I would like to take off my shoes,' said Celeste timidly. 'My feet are hurting a little from walking through the lanes.'

'I'm so sorry, Celeste,' said Beatrice. It was a good three or four miles to Amberleigh's cottage, and Beatrice had tramped at her usual pace, making no allowance for Celeste walking in ill-fitting, donated shoes. As usual, she had been uncomplaining.

'Off with the shoes and stockings,' said Amberleigh. 'You will find the mud in my pond as soothing to tired feet as any treatment imagined. It's the chalk, you know. Makes a wonderful poultice.'

'I'm not sure . . .' began Beatrice, but Celeste had already hitched her skirts into a froth around her thighs and was rolling the thick, dark stockings from her pale legs.

'By claiming a small space for ourselves, we can perhaps return to the innocence of our childhood,' said Amberleigh. 'And through the lens of innocence we can begin to glimpse something true. You must recognise the creative possibilities, Miss Nash?'

'I suppose so,' said Beatrice, but the doubt in her voice forced her to be truthful. 'My father taught me to imagine the arts as the highest form of human endeavour, a distillation beyond mere education and erudition. Not some primal product of muddy toes or . . .' She stopped before she might say something to offend.

Amberleigh let out a peal of laughter. 'Or of drinking in the afternoon,' she said as the serving girl approached with a wooden bucket from which peeked several bottles and a large lump of ice. 'I assure you, dear Miss Nash, that champagne is quite the muse if approached with the proper air of worship.'

'Do pour me some tea before I catch my death of cold,' said Minnie, who had left her pond kingdom and now appeared dressed in a loose wrapper and swathed toga-style in a thick blanket. She was smoking a cigarette in a short ivory holder. 'I sometimes think it would be quicker for Johnny to paint me than to wait for the photograph.'

'Have some champagne?' asked Amberleigh.

'No, no,' said Minnie. 'It makes me sleepy and – I say, Miss Celeste would make a fine subject for Johnny just now, wouldn't she?'

Celeste was tiptoeing on the edge of the pond, squishing the moss and mud between her toes, all her skirts clutched in a ball around her knees. She bent to peer at a large water bug, suspended on the surface by its wide feet, and her reflection in the water arced towards her.

'No photographs, please,' said Beatrice sharply. 'I am bound to look out for Celeste's respectability.' As she finished, Minnie's cheeks began to turn red.

'I'm sorry,' said Beatrice. 'I just meant she is very young and her father is very old-fashioned.'

'So is Minnie's father, the Vicar,' said Alice Finch, setting down her camera and wooden tripod carefully behind Amberleigh's chaise. 'And yet, as I told him, art must be made. And should it be made on the back of some poor girl willing to trade her reputation for bread, or should we be our own models and be willing to appear in the art we will hang above our mantels?'

'But you do not appear,' said Beatrice.

'Believe me, we have tried,' said Miss Finch, as Minnie smiled. 'It turns out I do not have a face the camera can love. My Diana the Huntress – well, I could have been the frontispiece for a builder's catalogue. So in all our constructions of beauty, I stay behind the lens and Minnie shines in front.'

'We are very careful as to which art might be published,' said Minnie. 'I am a vicar's daughter, not some shade of the demi-monde.'

'I'm sorry I implied disapproval,' said Beatrice. 'I am more used to writers than to artists. Please forgive me.'

'Drink some champagne and we'll forgive you,' said Amberleigh.

'Just tea for Celeste and me, thank you,' said Beatrice.

'You writers are just as quick as artists to exploit your characters in ways you would never behave yourselves,' said Miss Finch. 'Then you judge them harshly and cast them into the pit, to the delight of your oh-so-respectable readers.'

'I think I am in about as dire a strait as any I have inflicted upon my characters,' said Amberleigh.

'It will blow over in time,' said Minnie. 'And meanwhile, your friends are glad to have you to ourselves in the country.'

'It appears we do not have as many friends as I thought, dear Minnie,' said Amberleigh, producing a note from her pocket and looking it over. 'Agatha Kent writes to excuse herself from our afternoon tea. She is so busy with relieving the Belgians, she says, that she must deny herself the pleasure and also suffer the shame of being unable to reciprocate in the foreseeable future.'

'I had thought better of her,' said Minnie. Beatrice said nothing, but as she looked at Celeste, drinking tea in her bare feet, a small flicker of concern licked at the edges of her happiness. She would have come to tea at all costs, but now she wished she had made some excuse not to bring Celeste.

'It was Tillingham and Mrs Kent who arranged for us to rent this house,' said Amberleigh. 'I had hoped that meant I would find a welcome in their small town, but it appears the gates are barred.'

'It seems we are all refugees of one sort or another,' sighed Alice Finch, slumping into a chair and stretching out her legs in their thick boots. 'Let's drink to that.'

Beatrice opened her mouth to demur but upon further reflection decided to remain quiet. As the hot tea hit the back of her throat she wondered – if she was to be considered a refugee, then where was the home to which she might hope to be repatriated in due time? She coughed and hoped this would explain the sudden tears in her eyes.

'In honour of the creative friendships that matter,' said Amberleigh, scanning some pages from Beatrice's small portfolio, 'I will beg Miss Nash's permission to read from her work.' Beatrice could not pretend to protest, and for the first time she enjoyed the thrill of hearing her own words spoken aloud for others to hear. To be advised on her story, to be asked to give her creative opinion on some of Alice's photographs, and to have both Alice and Minnie listen carefully to her stumbling thoughts, made her as dizzy as the champagne the older women drank. Amberleigh said she must come and write in the garden whenever she pleased, and so the afternoon drifted on, in a haze of sunlight dazzling on the water, and warm conversation under the trees. It was only when Celeste, who had been busy making chains of daisies for the hissing cat, expressed a firm desire to walk home barefoot that Beatrice noticed the late hour. Horrified, she demanded that Celeste don her shoes like a respectable girl, and with the briefest of goodbyes, she hurried her home to cold plates of supper and more than a few pointed remarks from a highly suspicious Mrs Turber.

CHAPTER EIGHTEEN

MR FOTHERGILL SENT ROUND a note asking Beatrice to
visit his clerk at her convenience, and so she found herself
once again in the thickly carpeted front parlour of his
office, looking at the windows and wondering whether
they were ever opened. There seemed more dust than
oxygen in the room, and she longed to be released into the
sunshine. After a few minutes, Mr Poot emerged from
the warren of back rooms, an eager smile of welcome on
his face as if they were friends. A boy brought in a tray of
tea, and Beatrice, who had always chafed at being chap-
eroned as a younger woman, rather wished she had
brought someone with her now, so lingeringly did he
shake her gloved hand, so close did he pull his chair to
hers.

'It's just a matter of some odd letters,' he said, when she
had declined to have a cup of tea, refused a dish of sugared

almonds and been brief in reply to his comments upon the pleasantness of the weather.

'Excuse me?' she said, in as icy a tone as she could muster.

'I understand your trustees are waiting for you to return some rather valuable letters to the estate?' he asked.

'I assure you they are entitled to no such letters,' said Beatrice. 'I have made it quite clear to my father's publisher, and to my aunt's family, that any letters in my possession are my own copies of correspondence and not part of my father's archive.'

'Well, can't you just make another copy?' asked Mr Poot. 'It seems a silly squabble.' It seemed impossible to explain to Mr Poot the insult of her manuscript being given to Mr Tillingham and her hard work being at once both dismissed and appropriated by others. She could only sigh.

'I see no reason to discuss it,' she said.

'They are threatening to halt your monthly allowance and the rest of the ten pounds,' he said, a frown of what appeared to be genuine worry appearing between his eyes. 'I would hate to see you cut off, Miss Nash.'

'But the two things are not at all connected,' she said.

'And yet when the draft fails to come in, how will you pay your bills?' he asked. 'It has already come to my uncle's attention that just yesterday you ordered not one but two dresses from Pike Brothers' fabric counter.'

'How would it come to his attention?' said Beatrice. She could not help but feel a blush rise into her cheeks. Not that Mr Poot had mentioned the underclothes and stockings she had also purchased, but she had an idea both he and Mr Fothergill had counted every ribbon and seam. 'Is someone spying on me?'

Even as she asked, she remembered Mr Poot had appeared, entering the shop as she was leaving. He had removed his hat and held the door, but his obsequious smile and his greeting – too familiar and projected, for all the customers to hear – had made her flinch. She remembered she had offered only a curt nod and passed on as swiftly as possible. His face now betrayed no smirk of revenge, but his very impassiveness made her angry.

'My dear Miss Nash, it is not important how the information was acquired. I can assure you I was not aware,' he said. 'But since he is now aware of this rather large order, coming so soon after our agreement as to your modest financial intentions, he thought it incumbent that you and I have a talk, just between us, to resolve this letter business to your trustees' satisfaction . . .' He let the comment trail off and appeared to be waiting for an explanation, a coy smile inviting her confidence. She had the strongest sensation that a lowering of her lashes and a blushing appeal might move him to agree with any explanation she cared to fabricate. Instead she looked him full in the face.

'Mr Poot, we agreed that your firm will receive a copy of my monthly accounts and that you would personally refrain from unwarranted parsing of individual expenses,' she said. 'I see no reason for this intrusion.'

'I told him just the very same,' said Mr Poot. 'I told him I had all faith in your sensible nature. But he feels it incumbent on us to seek some assurance that you can pay your debts.'

'I can,' she said.

'I assure you I am your most humble ally,' he said, placing a hand on his chest as if to take a vow. 'But let us not be coy with each other,' he added. 'Such a large order might be considered profligate, and since the rest of your ten pounds has not come in, what is your source of funds?'

'You seek to insult me,' she said. 'Do you accuse me of going to moneylenders?'

'I would not even think to suspect you of such a disrespectable option,' he said, looking down the length of his nose at her as if shocked at her knowledge of their existence. 'Perhaps Mrs Kent has loaned you money?'

'She has not,' said Beatrice. He shook his head with a slow and disappointed air. It occurred to Beatrice that she would like to rap the crown of his oiled head with the ebony handle of her sunshade. She seized it and stood up. 'I will not be spied upon, Mr Poot.'

'I assure you I am your friend in this matter,' he said. 'I am only trying to deter my uncle from writing to your trustees over a matter which, I am certain, will only add to their stubbornness.'

She paused, desperate to leave the room, which seemed to shrink as they consumed its stale air, but wishing to prevent any such communication with her trustees. She sat down again, but kept a hand on her sunshade.

'If you must know, I sold some books,' she said. 'Mr Evans in the high street had a buyer for a rare edition of Boswell's *Life of Johnson*, and as I have always disliked Dr Johnson, for his personal habits and his arrogance, and Mr Boswell, for his uncritical worship, I decided it would serve them both right to be sold off to buy ladies' dresses.'

'I confess myself somewhat shocked,' said Mr Poot.

'You think it unladylike to sell one's possessions for money?' she asked.

'I'm shocked that you can get two dresses and half-a-dozen ladies' unmentionables for the price of a book!'

And yet you must mention them, she thought.

'They were morocco bound with gilding in three volumes,' she said. 'They were a gift to my father from a lady, and he could never part with them, but I always thought both the books and the lady rather vulgar.'

'I am satisfied as to the source of funds,' he said. 'Though I would counsel you, from bitter personal experience, that the disposition of one's belongings is not a long-term solution to one's expenses.' He sighed and polished his spectacles. For a moment he was honest, and she could feel again some sympathy for a young man of straitened circumstance. She was in no position to judge a cheap shirtfront so harshly.

'Ahem . . . I worry also that white silk is not the most serviceable purchase for a woman in your situation,' he added, ruining any flicker of compassion.

'Your aunt was persuaded to ask me, at this late date, to appear on her parade float, but she specifies white silk for all who ride with Britannia,' said Beatrice. 'I feel I must bear my own expenses to further the cause of Belgian Relief and to ensure Mrs Fothergill's triumph in the parade.' What she had felt was a fierce humiliation during the weekly committee meeting when Mrs Fothergill made her offer at the prompting of Lady Emily, but let her obvious reluctance show through her smile. Agatha Kent was not at the meeting to deflect or smooth the awkwardness as Mrs Fothergill had indicated, with a simper, that Beatrice might decline should she be unable to defray the cost of a silk dress. Beatrice had rashly accepted, not just to restore comfort to the rest of the committee, who had lowered their eyes to their agendas in sympathetic avoidance, but to see Mrs Fothergill's smug expression collapse into chagrin. She could only hope the shop assistant was right that the silk could later be dyed a serviceable navy blue.

'Well, I . . . well that is all right then,' said Mr Poot, working his lips to find a graceful compliment.

'These are my first purchases since I have come out of mourning,' she said. 'My only good dress is black, and I feared it a bad omen to wear it.'

'Your sensibility does you much credit,' said Mr Poot. 'Any man would be happy to know a woman with such a level head.' He seemed inclined to pat her hand, and she moved it quickly to rearrange an invisible strand of hair.

'Thank you, Mr Poot,' she said. She stood up, straightening her gloves and inching from behind the low table towards the door.

'And, level-headed as you are,' he continued, 'I should urge you to accommodate your trustees with their demands,' he said.

'I will write to them at once,' she said, though she knew her letter would be quite different in content than he imagined. 'May I count on your support?'

'You may,' he said. 'I will settle my uncle's mind, and I hope you and I will grow to understand each other better. I would welcome your trust, Miss Nash.'

'Of course, Mr Poot,' she said, and she offered him as coy a smile as she could manage and did not flinch when he raised her hand to his lips. In the street, she released her anger by decapitating several dandelions growing in the cracks of the pavements. Each ruined golden head, exploded by the steel tip of her sunshade, was a tiny head of Mr Poot or a tiny Aunt Marbely, to be ground discreetly beneath her heel.

The walk up the hill to Agatha Kent's home did much to restore Beatrice to good humour. Mrs Kent had not been seen about town much the past few days and it was rumoured she was under the weather, which was of great surprise and interest to the town, where she was declared to be usually 'stout as a horse' and 'strong as a dread-nought' and other such phrases, filled with goodwill if not flowering with femininity. Beatrice had volunteered to take the minutes at the Belgian Relief Committee in Agatha's absence, and now that she had transcribed and edited them into a neat report, she planned to deliver it to Agatha's home. With the start of a new term looming next week, she hoped that Agatha would ask her to stay to tea so she might acquire some last-minute advice and reassurance on navigating the treacherous waters of school life.

The maid, Jenny, opened the door and looked relieved to see Beatrice. It was not the look usually offered an unannounced visitor and led her to ask: 'Is everything all right, Jenny?'

'I'm glad you've come, miss,' said the girl, stepping back to welcome her into the front hall. 'Mrs Kent hasn't been home to any visitors at all these past few days. But she likes you.'

'I don't want to intrude,' said Beatrice. 'I just needed to deliver some papers.'

'No, no, come in, come in,' said Jenny. 'Cook and I are at our wits' end how to cheer her up. Cook will tell you herself.' She beckoned, and Mrs Kent's cook slipped from behind the door to the back kitchen and came hurrying up the hall, wiping her hands on her apron.

'Glad to see you, miss,' said the cook.

'I heard Mrs Kent is sick?' asked Beatrice.

'Not so as you'd call the doctor, I don't think,' said Jenny. 'But she keeps to her room and such. Doesn't really get dressed.'

'Yesterday she had all her meals on a tray and hardly touched the steak pudding,' whispered Cook. 'Imagine that! Mrs Kent turning up her nose at my steak pudding? You know she's not herself.'

'I wondered if we should telephone to Mr Kent,' said Jenny. 'But we didn't like to call him, seeing as how he's so busy.'

'What with the war and everything,' added Cook.

'And the young gentlemen are both away,' said Jenny.

'You show Miss Nash up to her study, direct like, and I'll bring the tea tray right on up behind you,' said Cook to Jenny. 'That way she can't say no to the visit.'

'I don't like to intrude,' said Beatrice again.

'Nonsense,' said Cook. 'You'll be a sight for sore eyes. Now just make sure you make her take a sandwich or two, miss.'

Upstairs at the study door, Jenny and Cook gave their mistress no chance to demur. After the briefest of knocks, Jenny announced Beatrice in a cheerful tone, as if she were expected, and Cook almost pushed Beatrice into the small windowed sun porch off Agatha's bedroom, elbowing her from behind with the heavy tea tray.

'I'll just put the tea right here, madam,' said Cook, not phrasing it as a question. She dumped the loaded tray with a clatter on a low table without regard for the papers and magazines strewn across the surface. 'Now you be sure and try the blackberry tarts, miss, they just come out of the oven.' With that, both servants bustled loudly from the room and Beatrice was left alone to face her reluctant hostess.

Agatha was tucked among pillows on the window seat of her porch, wearing the wrapper she had once loaned to Beatrice. Her hair was casually pulled into a loose braid and her legs were bare, her feet tucked into a pair of soft, embroidered slippers. Periodicals and newspapers lay on the seat and had slipped or been tossed onto the floor. A pair of stockings on a chair back and a comb left on the table suggested an incongruous air of carelessness. Agatha raised a quizzical eyebrow, but her face stayed slack and she could not seem to find the energy to speak.

'I'm so sorry to intrude,' said Beatrice. 'I came to bring you the committee minutes and your staff seemed to think you might be in need of cheerful company?'

'Cheerful company is as welcome to melancholy as lemon juice on a burn,' said Agatha. 'But if you promise not to smile and prattle at me, you may stay and pour the tea. I fear I have not even the energy to lift the teapot this afternoon.'

'Are you unwell?' asked Beatrice, pouring tea. 'You seem' – she looked around the room again – 'not quite yourself?'

'You'll forgive my appearance, I hope,' said Agatha, smoothing her hair. 'I was not aware I was entertaining.'

She accepted a cup of tea and leaned to close her eyes and inhale the fragrant steam of the cup. 'I am indeed not myself these days. But who can be in these dreadful times?'

'We missed you at the committee meeting,' said Beatrice. 'Lady Emily cannot control her disdain for Mrs Fothergill in your absence.'

'I had the vague sort of hope that if I curled up in here, it all might stop,' said Agatha, 'as if it were a bad dream.'

'Did you mean to will Mrs Fothergill out of existence?' asked Beatrice. 'I would have enjoyed seeing her disappear from the committee room in a puff of smoke.'

'I mean the war, of course,' said Agatha. 'It is a bad dream, is it not? We are all so caught up in the work of it and the excitement and the urge to do important things, and we have not stopped to see the true nature of it.'

'Celeste and I enjoyed a lovely tea at Amberleigh de Witte's cottage,' said Beatrice, hoping to shock Agatha Kent into some rebuke. Agatha was a compass by which Beatrice had set her course, and this pale, lethargic creature with the strange ideas seemed to have stolen her mind.

'I have been reading over my periodicals,' said Agatha, not appearing to hear her. She balanced her saucer on the bench beside her and picked up a copy of the weekly *Gentlewoman*. 'I had not noticed, you see, how the war has slipped into our lives.' She began to turn the pages slowly in her lap. 'I always liked the social column, the engagements and marriages, such cheerful news of our brightest young things starting their lives . . .'

'At my aunt's house I always read the Positions Available for governesses and parlour maids,' said Beatrice, offering Agatha the small plate of finger sandwiches. 'Not that I planned a career as a parlour maid, but it was reassuring to see that one might manage in a pinch.'

'At first it was just the King cancelling the visit to Cowes,' said Agatha, referring to the August sailing regatta. She waved away the sandwiches. 'Then it was the military commissions added to the names in the notices . . . "Second Lieutenant Viscount Lindsey, of the King's Own, is happy to report his engagement to . . ." and so on.' She paused, and as she sighed she seemed to slowly deflate into the cushions that supported her. 'Then the cancellations . . . "The Viscount and his fiancée were to have been married at St George's Parish Church . . ." First just one or two amid the weddings, then more cancelled than announced. And now the lists run with the names of all the finest young men of Britain, their deaths announced in place of their marriages, their lives ended before they can begin.'

'It is awful,' said Beatrice. 'I expect some very ancient families will lose their heirs and their family lines be cut off on both sides of the conflict.'

'If the scions of the greatest families are not protected, it makes it very clear to me that mothers everywhere are to lose their sons.' She turned her head away and raised a hand to pinch her nose as if to keep tears from coming. Beatrice was silent. Outside, the trees tossed their heads and tapped their branches on the windows, the sun danced on the lawns below, and in the distance the sea glittered; nature seemed for a moment to mock man's frailty with its permanence.

'You must be worried about your nephew, Hugh?' said Beatrice. As she said it, she felt a moment of pain, as if Agatha's worries were contagious. She remembered Mr

Tillingham's grave premonitions and felt a rising concern that Hugh was as likely to be in danger as anyone. 'But won't the doctors be far behind the lines?' she asked and was surprised to find a catch in her throat.

'With Hugh's skills, we expect him to be in a base hospital or no closer than a clearing station,' said Agatha. 'It's still very dangerous, but he's so sensible and we are very proud of him.' She was weeping now, even as she spoke in a measured tone. Tears trickled down the folds beside her cheeks and dripped from her chin. She did not seem to feel them.

'What can I do for you?' said Beatrice. She went to sink on her knees at Agatha's side and put her arms around her. She was bewildered to see the strength gone from a woman on whom she now depended. Self-interest and concern vied equally as she cried, 'Please, please help me understand what is wrong.'

Agatha wiped the tears from her face with the backs of her hands, and then looked at them for a moment before seeming to remember that she had a handkerchief in her wrapper. She took it out and wiped her face. Finally she took a deep breath, as if to help in squeezing out her words.

'Daniel has enlisted too,' she said, her voice faint. 'And he will not be a doctor but is training to be an officer, and all I can see in these pages is his name in all the announcements of the dead.' She looked Beatrice full in the face, and her tears welled again and fell unheeded.

Beatrice could not think of a reassuring reply. Unwanted tears came to her own eyes, and she blinked hard so that she might retain her composure in this moment of need for Agatha. 'I'm sure training must take a long time, and perhaps the war will end sooner than we think?' she managed. She did not believe it, for Agatha's own husband had said otherwise. As Agatha nodded and clutched her hand, Beatrice knew they were both foolish to take comfort in the easy lie.

'I was so quick to push my own work and call others to rally, and so full of my own importance,' said Agatha. 'It's only now I realise how easy it was to do so on the backs of other women's sons.'

'For Daniel's and Hugh's sake you must not fall apart,' said Beatrice. 'Now that you see so clearly what is at stake, your work is all the more important. You must continue to lead this town, Mrs Kent. If you retreat, I fear for our efforts.'

'That is exactly what my husband said,' said Agatha. 'But he at least got to see Daniel before he went away to enlist. They did not tell me until Daniel was gone. Why do men presume to know what is best for us?'

'Your husband is a good man,' was all Beatrice could say, though she was thinking of how her own father had put her money in trust and neglected even to tell her, and how he had allowed her to believe in her own independence, but at the end had treated her as a helpless woman. Such instincts, she realised now, might be ingrained in even the best of men.

'No doubt he feared that I would become impossibly self-indulgent and make a scene,' said Agatha. She sighed again, but some colour came back into her cheeks and she sat up. 'As I believe I have been doing these last few days, foolishly thinking I could just withdraw from the world and make it go away.'

'I'm sure it would be a relief to Mr Kent to know you were up and about again,' said Beatrice. 'You are our centre.'

'I'm not sure where to start,' said Agatha. She looked around her little room and grimaced, as if seeing the disarray for the first time. Beatrice thought a bath and a good hair brushing might be in order, but she settled for holding out a plate of cakes.

'First, have a blackberry tart,' she said. 'Cook's orders.'

'Thank you for coming to pull me from my slough of despond,' said Agatha. 'Now, while I eat, perhaps you can try to explain to me why our respected Latin mistress would be so careless of her reputation and mine as to visit the de Witte woman.'

CHAPTER NINETEEN

THE FIRST DAY OF school was a relief to Beatrice. The schoolroom called to her as if it were the sweet voice of civilisation itself, summoning her to the white marble halls where poetry and mathematics, painting and song all echoed together in peaceful harmony. As she descended the hill, skirted the busy railway yard and approached the neat school with its red-tiled gables and bright window boxes, a hope swelled within her that the innocence of schoolchildren might sweep the war from her eyes on this bright September day, and from the earth tomorrow.

A large clod of grass hit her skirt as she entered the school gates, and she had a brief vision of boys throwing clods and stones and even an old shoe at one another from two sides of a hedge before a voice split the air with a high-pitched shout.

'Teacher! Leg it!' And a scrum of figures ran away towards the side of the school, keeping their faces averted and their identities undistinguishable in matching boaters and brown blazers.

'Are you all right, miss?' asked a girl in a similar brown jacket, her hair scraped back tight enough to pull the skin from her face. She held a stack of books and a hat in her hands. 'I can give you all their names, miss, if you like?'

'Not at this time, but if it happens again, I may be forced to ask,' said Beatrice, frowning to discourage such easy telling of tales. The girl looked crestfallen, so Beatrice softened her gaze, brushed the dirt from her skirt with a glove, and asked, 'What is your name?'

'Jane, miss,' said the girl, with enthusiasm. 'Those boys are always playing war, throwing things at each other. Then if they hit someone, they call out, "Got the Hun," and they run away like they're all on one side again. Who would want to play such a stupid game, anyway?' From this comment Beatrice understood that the girl would dearly love to be invited.

Two boys carrying long sticks across their bodies came running around the front of the building, pointing and making the sound of rifle shots at each other. Other boys, cantering on imaginary horses with wooden swords aloft, charged them from behind with bloodcurdling screams and oaths.

'Oi! No running in the front court,' said a man's voice, and Mr Dimbly, the gymnastics master, came hurrying from the front door.

'Sorry, sir,' called one of the boys, but neither they nor the horsemen slackened their pace one bit as they all disappeared towards the tennis courts.

'Miss Nash, welcome to the second Western Front,' said Mr Dimbly, his academic gown flying from his shoulders as he strode out to greet her. 'Run along, Miss Jane. No pupils through the front door, as you know.'

'Yes, sir,' said Jane, and she hurried off to find the girls' side entrance, shoulders hunched as if under expectation of further humiliations to come.

'Hard to keep the girls in their own area before and after school,' said Mr Dimbly. 'Wouldn't do to have some girl pushed down but can't keep these boys from their war games, these days. All the excitement in the air – makes them more boisterous than usual.'

'You sound as if you almost approve, Mr Dimbly?' said Beatrice.

'Boys who think they're soldiers try that much harder in the gymnasium,' he said. 'Of course it makes it dashed hard for 'em to keep quiet in the Latin classroom, but that's not my problem any more, is it?' He smiled in a way that took any suggestion of malice from his words.

'I shall have to hope Latin comes before gymnastics in the school day,' said Beatrice.

'Come in and I'll show you to the staffroom,' he said. 'We have our own stove and kettle, and sometimes the ladies among us are kind enough to bring in homemade biscuits or rock cakes, though with the war on I'm not sure we shall be as comfortably situated this term.' He had about as much guile as a puppy in his importuning of baked goods, and Beatrice could not be angry at him.

'I am sorry to report that I lack any baking skills at all, Mr Dimbly,' she said. 'However shall I hold up my head in the staffroom?'

'Not to worry,' he said. 'Not as if it's required – and that Miss Devon makes a rock cake that's a bit of a rock if you ask me.' He opened the heavy oak and leaded-glass front door for her, and as she passed he winked at her. 'If the cupboard is bare, I'm always happy to boil an egg over a Bunsen burner, Miss Nash,' he said. 'So if you get peckish, come and find me in the science room.'

'I'm sure I can wait for my dinner, Mr Dimbly,' she said, hoping her tone was severe enough to quell any further desire on his part for flirtation.

'An army marches on its stomach, Miss Nash,' he said. 'You'll soon see.'

The noise of the classroom filling with boys was not unlike the roar of a crowded theatre, only at a higher pitch. How swiftly the freshly whitewashed room, with its scrubbed oak desks and clean blackboard, filled with the stench of damp wool, leather boots and the odour of feet and armpits, steaming from the exertions of the playing fields and streets. Beatrice stood with her knuckles white from gripping the edge of her desk and tried not to recoil from the assault. After a summer of tutoring Agatha Kent's three scholarship boys, she had not expected some quiet room of pale scholars, tow-headed youths bent diligently to the tutelage of Virgil, but she felt ill-prepared to meet the large group of sweating, pimply faces before her. Some were as scrawny and young as Snout, who slumped in a desk at the rear and quietly shot several boys in the neck with balls of chewed paper spat from a straw. Others seemed almost men, sporting strange tufted outcroppings of facial hair and shouting in husky voices. She had not even noticed that the girl from the front courtyard and another girl had also slipped into the room and taken desks together in the furthest back corner.

Beatrice had already cleared her throat several times and rapped her ruler against the desk for quiet, but chaos reigned until the door opened once more and a loud voice, the Headmaster's voice, shouted for quiet.

'All right, gentlemen – and ladies – anyone still talking will feel the sting of my cane and receive an hour of detention. Who's still working his mouth?' There was a collective stiffening, arms by sides, chins up and immediate silence in the room. Beatrice, ears ringing from the chaos, could only nod her head in gratitude.

'Sit down!' said the Headmaster. There was a general slump into chairs, with some scraping of hobnails on the oak floors and a lowering of heads. The Headmaster, growling at the rows of pupils as if his eyes might bore right through any remaining recalcitrant skull, strode to the front of the room and stood between Beatrice and her pupils. 'All right then,' he said. 'Miss Nash is your new Latin mistress, and I expect you will show her respect. If I hear any more nonsense from Miss Nash's room, I shall be in to administer consequences. Is that clear?'

'Yes, Headmaster, sir,' came the chorused reply.

'*Nanos gigantium humeris insidentes*,' he declaimed, hand on heart. 'Never forget your duty to those giants on whose shoulders you ride, whose words are passed down the millennia even to your unwashed and undeserving heads.'

'Yes, Headmaster, sir,' said the class in dull unison.

'Right you are then, Miss Nash,' he said in a normal, bright tone. 'Welcome to Upper Form Latin. Keep their noses to the grindstone and don't be afraid to switch a few knuckles as you go. *Oderint dum metuant*, as they say.' And he swept away again, shutting the door behind him, leaving only mute cooperation in the ranks. Beatrice did not want her students to hate her, but she was grateful for the brief interlude of fear, one that even now was waning from their faces as they began to peek at her and shuffle in their seats.

'Jack, please mark the attendance,' she said in a stern voice, happy to pick on a face she knew. 'Then we shall begin with a brief review of all that you learned last year.'

It sometimes seemed as if the first two weeks were a thousand days long. Beatrice could not remember the first day, nor did the Saturday half-day or Sunday seem to provide any real rest. She lived in a half-light of exhaustion from the din of unruly feet kicking desk legs, the smell of boys infusing the very whitewash of the walls and the parade of blank faces that met her whenever she turned from the blackboard with a question for a class. She did her best not to single out her tutees more than necessary, but from their stony expressions, she knew she had caused them unwanted attention. Her most egregious mistake was to call on Snout to recite what was, as she informed the whole class, his favourite passage from Virgil, Aeneas rescuing his father from the flames of Troy. Snout had given her a look of utter betrayal and resorted to spilling his inkpot over the entire book to distract from his humiliation. Coming to her senses, Beatrice ordered him to the Headmaster's office, and he went, winking at the laughter and cheers of his classmates.

In the evenings, she ate her supper in a profound silence, trying not to fall asleep in her plate, and apologised nightly to poor Celeste, who would reply in a concerned whisper. Each day Beatrice hoped to wake refreshed and hardened to her new position, but she felt she was slowly sinking under the onslaught of children, who were silent only when asked to share in the delights of Latin.

'You look terrible,' said Mr Dimbly on the second Saturday morning, handing her a cup of strong tea as she struggled into the staff's small room during the mid-morning break.

'Just what a lady wants to hear, thank you,' she snapped, gulping the tea in the hope a burning throat would force her to wake up.

'I have something for you,' he said, and produced from the pocket of his voluminous gown a slightly warm brown egg. 'Hard-boiled this morning.'

'It's awfully kind of you,' she began, waving it away.

'You need to keep up your strength,' said Miss Clauvert, who was seated by the stove with her friend Miss Devon. Both had set aside their knitting and were nibbling on similar boiled eggs with some gusto. 'My first month, I fainted on a regular basis until Mr Dimbly here gave me his advice.' She simpered at Mr Dimbly, who coloured.

'Plenty of eggs, apples, strong tea and a spoonful of cod-liver oil twice a week,' he said gruffly. 'Keeps up the strength and wards off all the pestilence and disease carried by a roomful of unwashed urchins.'

'Thank you, Mr Dimbly,' said Beatrice. 'Upon Miss Clauvert's recommendation I will take you up on your kindness.' She accepted the warm egg, cracked the shell on a chair back, and peeled the egg into the open top of the staffroom's small black stove.

'I always tell him, he is a kind man and a gentleman, our Mr Dimbly,' said Miss Clauvert, and she matched him blush for blush so that Miss Devon forgot her age and giggled at them.

'I swear by strong camphor and a small sliver of chalk once a week,' said Mr Dobbins, the mathematics teacher, who wore a gown so old it had become a nasty grey colour. Beatrice imagined him standing at his blackboard taking his time with a complex formula and absently chewing on his chalk for health purposes. 'I can't eat eggs. They give me flatulence,' he added.

'Mr Dobbins, really!' said Miss Devon.

'Sorry,' he replied, shrinking into his armchair. He put up his newspaper as a screen, and Beatrice heard him mutter, 'Used to be able to speak freely in the staffroom. Ought to have their own room if they don't like it.'

'When will I stop feeling utterly tired?' asked Beatrice. 'I have made expeditions, I have hiked mountains . . .'

'These pupils, they are very tiresome or tiring – how do you say it, Miss Devon?' said Miss Clauvert.

'I think you mean both,' said Miss Devon. 'They'll try to wear you down, Miss Nash.'

'You 'ave to fight them with your wits,' said Miss Clauvert. 'Set them the exercises impossible and watch how they will be silent.'

'Just lay about you with the ruler on a more regular basis,' said Mr Dimbly. 'Swish swat . . . it's good exercise for you and keeps them right up to the mark.'

'I don't believe indiscriminate corporal punishment is a valid teaching method,' said Beatrice. 'I intend to reach them through rational thought and a shared thirst for knowledge.' This caused peals of laughter from all gathered in the snug staffroom.

'When you stop talking like that is when you'll stop feeling so dead,' said Miss Devon. 'Won't she, Mr Dimbly?' There was more laughter, and Beatrice could only munch on her egg in miserable silence. Later that morning she found occasion to rap her ruler smartly on the edge of two desks. And when Snout appeared to deliberately break wind right in the middle of her explanation of how the next day's test would determine those who might be scholarship examination material, she made sure to whistle the ruler past his ear. The class seemed to sit up and become less like blank mutes, and, as Snout gave her the slightest nod of acknowledgement, Beatrice felt the pressure to sleep slip from her brow like the pulling off of a heavy wool cap.

With only half an hour to go before the class was released into the Saturday afternoon, the Headmaster stuck his head around the classroom door and asked to speak to her a moment in the library about the plans for the upcoming town fete. Her Upper Form Latin class's participation in the afternoon was to consist of parading through the streets dressed as Roman warriors and then a handful of rousing war speeches selected from the *Aeneid*, to be recited from the stage in both Latin and the pupils' own English translations. Her three summer pupils had taken a leadership role, Arty and Jack with a certain swaggering air of expertise and Snout with continued protestations of complete indifference. But the whole class had shown an unusual diligence in the project, though their excitement seemed largely to do with the promised costumes and swords.

It seemed the Headmaster wished to suggest that a particular pupil, the captain of the rugby team, should take over Snout's role as Aeneas in the Latin class's performance.

'Headmaster, I should be allowed to put together my Latin recitation based on what will best represent the school,' said Beatrice. 'The boy I have chosen to play the Trojan hero has a particular passion for the piece and fluent recitation. He is my best student and I believe one of our strongest candidates to win a scholarship in the Latin examinations. The boy you suggest is more at home on the rugby pitch than in Latin class and recites like a wooden post.'

'We have a great sense of camaraderie here,' said the Headmaster. 'You will find I employ only the lightest touch on the tiller to keep our little ship moving to the wind.'

'That is wonderful to hear, Headmaster,' she said.

'Only in recognition that you are new here, it does behove me to just hint to you when there are matters which may have a bearing on the situation,' he continued. 'I think only of guiding you to the greatest understanding and success.'

'Is there something I should know?' she asked.

'The young man in question has received much from us. He has been granted a fuller education than most boys of his background enjoy and I believe he has reason to be appreciative of all we have done for him.'

'He is very bright,' said Beatrice.

'One must wonder, of course, whether too much education at some point may make a young person frustrated with his or her life,' he mused. 'It can be very upsetting to find that one cannot go further but has gone so far that one no longer fits comfortably into the life to which one is born.'

'Most people welcome the opportunity for advancement,' said Beatrice. 'I think young Master Sidley has a great chance of bringing honour to the school with a scholarship, and of going on to achieve much.'

'I regret that, despite Mrs Kent's desire for change, we must face the fact that the boy must not sit for the scholarship,' said the Headmaster, shaking his head with an air of gentle sorrow. 'It is a question of leadership, you see,' he continued. 'The natural leaders among our pupils do the greatest credit to the school, and I think you'll find, Miss Nash – when you've been here a little longer – that the pupils themselves accept and admire such leadership; they expect and desire to see themselves so represented.'

'Surely the best and brightest . . .' she began. 'I really must protest, Headmaster.'

'Such a boy could never adequately represent our school, Miss Nash,' he said. His tone was so gentle she was almost lulled into agreement. 'So he can parrot a little Latin – little more than a parlour trick really – but he would never manage in the company of boys of real learning, of real families. Why, he would find it unbearable and be a laughing stock.'

'The rugby captain, is he such a leader?' asked Beatrice. But she knew the answer and, to her shame, that further protestation would only damage her own position.

'You see it too!' said the Headmaster. 'I am so glad you understand. I had no desire to step in and usurp your authority.' He rubbed his hands in delight. 'Only think how well our young athlete will fill out the Trojan general's breastplate and with what authority he will hoist his sword.'

'If only he could recite Latin with any feeling,' said Beatrice, defeated.

'As long as he is loud, Miss Nash, as long as he is loud,' said the Headmaster.

Snout had sneaked away from the gymnasium, where the smell of India-rubber mats and hot feet overwhelmed him, and Mr Dimbly, cheering on some feat of strength by one or two of the strongest athletes, left the other boys to bump and jostle him up the rough ropes and over the leather vaulting horses. Escaping into the fresh air of the afternoon, he slipped into the bare dirt patch behind an overgrown yew bush near the library windows, to roll and smoke his last few strands of tobacco.

Miss Nash's voice came blunt and urgent through the open window. The slower, old-man voice of the Headmaster, with his longer sentences and digressions into this and that, was unmistakable. Eavesdroppers, as his great-grandmother would tell him, will have their ears burned off with a hot coal. His eyes watched the curl of smoke from the tip of his cigarette paper as he scratched at the itchy wool of his school uniform. He felt the tightness of the hatband around his head, smelled the dry dirt and the green cemetery waxiness of the yew. His neck grew hot and his teeth clenched.

It was hard to endure the steady stream of petty humiliations from the other boys. It was hard to do his homework by smoky oil lamp under the small, dark eaves of the cottage. He wished he had a father who understood the geometry of triangles, or could discuss which word might bring the heat of ancient battles to life from the dry simplicity of Latin. But his father worked with bellows and hammer, and kept his accounts in his head. It was lonely writing reports on places he could barely imagine, poring over the atlas, the pictures of native princes from around the Empire, or the treasures brought back to British museums by various scientific expeditions. He found geography to be no less fantastical than history, so that he found it no harder to imagine ancient Troy or Rome than modern Bombay, and found Latin more alive and exciting than living French.

The hardest lesson of all, heard once more from the library window today, was that Miss Nash's promises had come to nothing and he could never escape who he was. In this he was no different from any other lad in the county. By face, by name and by accent, everyone knew who everyone else was, going back a hundred years. It was like a big brown label tied to his jacket with his family history printed in big letters. Or like being one of Mr Hugh's specimens, floating in a jar of foul-smelling preservative with a sticky label on the lid. It was not possible to change places with another boy, even for a day. It was not possible to be different.

'Oh, that's only the Sidley boy – his father's a Gypsy . . .'

'Aye, blood will out in the end, they say . . .'

And now the Headmaster's voice rang again in his ear, 'Such a boy could never adequately represent our school . . .'

He had dared to hope that sticking with the school-room, though the constraints chafed at him like chains, might be his escape. But it was clear now that he would never be allowed to leave the prison of who he was. They would smile, but their eyes would say 'dirty Gypsy'. He was destined to live and die within a few miles of his father's sooty forge, and all his fancy schooling would likely suggest only that he was wilier and less trustworthy than his father, who had never learned to read.

He pinched the butt of his cigarette between his fingers, feeling the sting of hot ash. The burn was like an offering to seal his vow. He would prove them all wrong about Richard Sidley. He would turn soldier, and like the wander-ing Trojan warriors of the *Aeneid*, he would seek his destiny on a grand adventure in foreign parts. He scram-bled from the bushes and set off at a lope across the playing field towards the railway line. If he could sneak onto the next train as it slowed for the crossing, he might make it to Colonel Wheaton's camp before tea.

Part Three

Over the railway line, across the grass,

While up above the golden wings are spread,

Flying, ever flying overhead,

Here still I see your khaki figure pass,

And when I leave the meadow, almost wait,

That you should open first the wooden gate.

MARIAN ALLEN, 'The Wind on the Downs'

CHAPTER TWENTY

THE MORNING OF THE fete dawned clear, the bite of early
October air quickly succumbing to the warmth of another
Indian summer day. Beatrice opened her stiff casement and
leaned her head from the cold room into a shaft of morning sun. A scattering of birds from the cobbles signalled a
lone figure climbing the steep street, and Beatrice recognised the slow steps and bent back of the fishmonger's
wife, whose son had been among those lost in the first
battles of the Expeditionary Force. How proud she and her
husband had been of their young soldier, already a veteran
of some years, and how much excited interest and respect
the town had showered upon them in the earliest weeks,
as the thirst for information and for the chance to feel close
to the action had made the fishmonger's a hive of activity
and gossip. Now the woman seemed to have aged
many years, and business was slower in the shop as many

townspeople gave in to the callow instinct to avoid the grieving parents.

Beatrice had seen the same in her aunt's village. For every person who stopped to smile in sympathy and speak a word about her father, there were others who turned aside into shop doorways or whisked across the street, lowering their umbrellas to obscure their faces. When forced to meet later, they would be so surprised not to have seen more of her.

On such a day as today, the widows and the grieving mothers were expected to keep their black weeds and pale faces in their shuttered homes. In history, and in the great art hanging in the museums, those who had borne the sacrifice of husbands and sons seemed always missing from pageant and feast, thought Beatrice. No parade of victory or peace ever included the biers of the dead. Held at the window by a consciousness of her own desire to hide, Beatrice made sure to catch the fishmonger's wife's eye and give a quick smile and a wave before retreating inside.

Hugh took one last look in the mirror and adjusted his stiff cap to an angle that might make him look less like a bus driver. The cap made his ears look large, he thought, and its shiny peak made a permanent frowning shadow over his eyes. He would have been happier and more dashing, he thought, in a surgical coat, but an officer must appear on public occasions in dress uniform, no matter how stiff and uncomfortable. Daniel, who was lacing his boots in a chair across the day nursery, managed to make his dress uniform look relaxed almost to the point of informality and seemed not to be suffering from constriction through the shoulders or the itch of new wool against any exposed skin. His hair had been cut and oiled flat but still curled across his forehead, and his face was cheerful as he poked lace through brass rivet and puffed on an illicit early cigarette.

'Your jacket will smell of tobacco all day,' said Hugh. 'Aunt Agatha will lecture you.'

'All soldiers smell of tobacco,' said Daniel. 'The Tommy of tobacco, sweat and cabbage; the officer of tobacco, shoe blacking and bay rum. It is an extraordinary universality.'

'My chaps smell of iodine,' said Hugh. 'I've had two baths this morning, and a splash of Uncle John's cologne, just so I don't have to be sick of myself.'

'I just hope the Hun smell different,' said Daniel. 'Hard to bayonet something that smells like your bunkmate.'

'According to the papers, the Germans will stink of the blood of innocents,' said Hugh.

'Words cast at the world like stones,' said Daniel. 'These journalists risk turning a moral obligation to act into a blind crusade of revenge.'

'Who's on a blind crusade?' asked Uncle John, knocking on the door and coming in.

'The press,' said Daniel. 'They are inflaming the common man beyond all reason.'

'Is that the common view in your outfit?'

'We have a wide range of views,' said Daniel. 'We enjoy some spirited debates in the mess.'

'And that is why it was always a bad idea to put all the writers and artists in one brigade,' said Uncle John, shaking his head but smiling. 'If you can cease the sedition for half an hour, your aunt is telling me we must eat breakfast now if we are to be on time.'

'If you don't mind, I'm going to run down and see my chaps at their lodgings,' said Hugh. 'Give the turnout one last look before the parade. I expect they'll have rustled up some grub.'

'My comrades will have to wait,' said Daniel. 'Cook told me she's been keeping back a nice piece of bacon just for today. I refuse to let duty come between me and fresh rashers.'

Downstairs in the front hall, as Hugh paused to adjust his cap one futile last time in the mirror, he caught the scent of bacon and saw, through the open door, a corner of the set breakfast table, the blue of hydrangeas on the sideboard, the white linen curtains stirred by a small breeze. Muffled sounds of pots and pans came from the kitchen, a shimmer of sun spilled across the dark oak floor, and the scents of wood polish and clean paint added to the more insistent smells of the breakfast table. Hugh felt a sudden sense of the importance of the usual breakfast table rituals, the value of the ordinary front hall with its umbrella stand and the sun through the panes of the front door. A desire to join Daniel and the family at breakfast after all delayed his hand on the doorknob, but a stronger voice told him he was being sentimental, if not maudlin. His departure from the house would not tear it apart like some fragile theatre scenery, and he would not allow the war to freight every entrance and exit with the weight of tragedy. His departure would mean nothing except extra bacon for Daniel. In service of such a brisk resolution, Hugh immediately detoured into the dining room and wrapped several slices of bacon in a napkin so that he might eat them on his way down the hill.

The brass band, on its small platform, was on its third rendition of 'Daisy, Daisy, give me your answer, do'. The trombone was flat, but all in all Agatha Kent was extremely happy with the parade so far. The day was brilliant with sun but refreshed by a breeze strong enough to ensure the proper fluttering of pennants, the stir of petticoats and the occasional hand grabbing for a hat brim on the street corners. The parade, squeezed between the narrow houses and the thick clumps of people pressing into the street from the pavement, seemed to foam like a slow waterfall out into the wider street in front of the reviewing stand, a glorious succession of floats, decorated cars and processions of local clubs and institutions. In her large notebook, Agatha ticked off participants as they passed. Mr Tillingham rode by in an open car, accompanied by a girl dressed as Literature, holding a large parchment and a golden quill. Miss Buttles and Miss Finch received much applause and laughter as Queen Elizabeth I and Sir Walter Raleigh, with Sir Walter driving her new Triumph motorcycle and the Faerie Queen stuffed, ruff and all, into the sidecar like a prize chicken. The Mayor in his regalia waved from high up on a large horse-drawn omnibus, surrounded by representations of all of Rye's trades, including a fisherman who dangled a large dead cod on a short pole. The baying, snapping hounds of the Working Dog Association paraded in doggie coats featuring the St George's Cross and the county coat of arms, except for a border terrier that appeared to have ripped off his coat and was carrying its crumpled remains in his jaws. And all along the parade, girls in pretty summer dresses and red, white and blue sashes squeezed through the crowds with trays of small paper lapel flags and decorated buckets, flirting and cajoling the audience to buy a flag for the cause.

The reviewing stands were full, and Colonel Wheaton and Lady Emily, whose car had led the parade, had been hard-pressed to clamber up into their centre chairs. Colonel Wheaton, in a dress uniform of his own design with several loops of braid to the right shoulder and an antique Indian sword dangling from an ornately decorated leather belt, was saluting now as his newly official troops marched by, his son, Harry, in the first rank and sporting the pips of a lieutenant's rank. The men straggled somewhat, some limping in boots that looked hastily gathered. They carried wooden models of rifles, as official ones had yet to arrive.

'Don't Daddy's men look marvellous?' asked Eleanor Wheaton. 'Quite the real soldiers.'

'The khaki is not as striking as a dress uniform,' said Agatha.

'But it's harder to get shot at on the battlefield,' said her husband, John, dressed in a blazer and flannels. For a moment, Agatha experienced a pang. He would have looked so handsome in uniform, she thought, and he was not a year older than Colonel Wheaton, who seemed intent on being allowed into combat. 'Best leave the braid and colours to the ladies,' added John, nodding at Eleanor. She was wearing a navy blue jacket of military design, much frogged across the bodice and pinched at the waist with a belt of scarlet wool.

'Between Father and me, we have rather cornered the market in braid,' she said, not seeming at all offended. 'After the incident with the dogs, I may have been trying too hard to demonstrate my patriotism.' John raised an eyebrow in enquiry and Agatha found herself in the awkward position of having neglected to communicate a story that was of great consequence to one party and of little importance to the other. In such a situation, John's feelings would have to be sacrificed.

'You remember, dear,' she said. 'I told you how some boys threw stones at Lady Emily's dachshunds while Eleanor was walking them and made the most appalling comments to both her and the poor doggies about being German.'

'Of course you did,' said John, demonstrating his diplomatic skills with only the slightest raising of an eyebrow. 'Appalling! No one of intelligence would ever doubt the patriotism of such an English rose.'

'Thank you, Mr Kent,' said Eleanor. 'But I think Mother is more concerned about the accusations against the dogs.'

'How anyone could doubt the patriotism of my dachshunds is just shocking,' said Lady Emily. 'It's an outrage.'

'The Breeders' Association is changing the breed name from dachshund to Freedom Hound,' said Eleanor. 'They will be running newspaper advertisements and hopefully that will help.'

'Such vulgar pandering to the masses,' said Lady Emily. 'But if it saves even a single little dog's life, it must be endured, I suppose.'

'Speaking of saving lives, here comes Hugh's ambulance,' said Agatha. 'Doesn't he look handsome?' Hugh walked ahead of his ambulance, his face stern. The ambulance, polished to a fault, had its back doors open, and two of Hugh's men waved their caps at the crowd from their perches inside. They were followed by another, who proudly carried a box labelled PORTABLE X-RAY. The box was a fraud, a portable X-ray being much too large and too valuable to send out to a country parade, but the Medical Corps was proud enough of its newest medical advance to have allowed Hugh to construct a crude model for the occasion.

Behind Hugh came Daniel's group of eight officers, marching two abreast, all in new khaki and caps, with the officer's Sam Browne leather belt and a pistol holster on the left hip. Boots were polished, and the lack of limping suggested to Agatha that the boots and the officers who wore them were properly broken in.

'So thrilling Daniel's outfit came to join in,' said Eleanor. 'But I had hoped the Artists Rifles might be wearing linen shirts and daggers in their belts.'

'They are not pirates,' said Agatha. 'It's an Officer Training Corps, and they take it very seriously, as you can tell by their demeanour.'

'I can't wait to tour the model trench,' said Eleanor. 'Beatrice Nash tells me they have bookshelves and willow furniture, and that they read poetry every night before taps.'

'The parade seems to be progressing with complete efficiency,' said John. 'You ladies are generals in your own right.'

'Let us not count our chickens,' said Agatha. She had noticed one or two of the bucket girls seemed a little forward in their soliciting of men in the crowd, and she had also spotted that Snout, in Roman toga and sandals, seemed to have ditched his classmates and was also wielding a collection bucket. One of the fire-station horses had gone lame, and some of the schoolchildren seemed congenitally unable to walk in a straight line; their marching formation resembled a flock of worried sheep and the teachers had spent the parade herding rather than waving. The parade was going well, but it could not be assumed to be a success until the last float, containing the Britannia tableau, had stopped at the reviewing stand for the playing of the national anthems of Belgium and Great Britain and then moved on to the parade grounds to a rousing rendition of 'Land of Hope and Glory'. It was hoped the entire crowd would be singing and would be motivated to spend their money on the afternoon's attractions. Then and only then, thought Agatha, would she breathe freely.

Beatrice could not deny that she was enjoying herself. Her new dress fell in becoming folds about her golden sandals; her hair had cooperated and was pinned up in soft rolls under a circlet of laurel. She felt an unusual happiness and understood that it came from feeling young and pretty, or at least remembering what it had felt like to feel young and pretty, before the more recent years of her father's decline had rendered such feelings pointless. Seated on a carpet-covered box at the right hand of Britannia's flower-covered throne, she carried a shield decorated with the St George's Cross. As she waved to the crowd, she reserved her friendliest smiles for the delighted children, who sat openmouthed on their fathers' shoulders, clutching little flags and sticky lollipops and wondering at the pageant unfolding before them. She knew the children thought it was all real and did not recognise even Mrs Fothergill, whose painted face had acquired a regal air under her laurel crown and who waved with all the restraint of a true monarch. Celeste, as Belgium, sat on a lower box at Britannia's feet, wearing her own white dress, its lace hastily attached all down the front of the skirt, a simple white cotton cap with strings and a small shawl knitted in the colours of the Belgian flag. She carried a posy of wildflowers in a basket. On boxes of different heights, all covered in green baize to suggest the land's undulating landscape, the young ladies of Scotland, Wales and Ireland stood to the rear of the throne. Ahead, a small section of a military band from Kent played patriotic songs and hymns, and the crowd sang snatches of the words and waved their hats as the float passed so that even Beatrice felt her eyes grow wet with sentimental tears. It was impossible that the hardest of hearts not be moved by the sunny day and the fervour of the country crowd's simple patriotism.

As the float approached the viewing stand, Beatrice felt a flutter of nerves that had little to do with being reviewed by Colonel Wheaton, Lady Emily, and the other dignitaries, and more to do with whether Hugh and Daniel would keep their promise to double back to see her and Celeste's triumphal arrival. Even Celeste put a hand to a stray tendril of hair, and Beatrice understood that she too was not immune to such flattery. Beatrice sat a little taller on her box but refused to pat her own hair and tried not to look around for familiar faces. As the float slowed to a stop,

Mrs Fothergill rose to her feet to the rousing applause of the reviewing stands and, after a dignified nod of acknowledgement, unsheathed the sword that hung so decoratively from a tapestry girdle around her waist.

'Women of Britain, prepare to defend Belgium,' she said in ringing tones.

'What are we doing?' whispered Beatrice. 'I thought this was a silent tableau.'

'The element of surprise, dear,' said Mrs Fothergill. 'Be ready!' Before she could say more, a roar went up from behind both stands and a pack of men, dressed in blue uniform jackets and sporting the distinctive spiked brass helmet preferred by Germanic regiments, burst forth waving swords, shotguns and farm implements, and rushed the float with bloodcurdling oaths. The band struck up a rousing march as Mrs Fothergill began to swing her sword left and right over her head and shriek like a banshee. Scotland and Ireland levelled their javelins and began to poke away at the men below, giggling all the time, while Wales crouched behind her shield and called for them to stop.

'You come one step near me and my father will have you up to the magistrate, Ernic Phillips,' she could be heard to say. 'And you, Arthur Day, can stop waving that pitchfork like a lunatic.'

'We shall defend Belgium to our last breath,' shouted Mrs Fothergill as Beatrice stood and parried a rather too enthusiastic poke from a bayonet that, close up, could be seen to be of the blunt-ended, theatrical type.

'Really, Mrs Fothergill,' said Beatrice. 'You arranged German hordes?' But her words were drowned out as

Celeste, who had become frozen still on her box, began to scream, a slowly rising scream that suggested she had been dealt a mortal wound or was being stretched on a medieval rack. It went on and on, so that the band stopped their instruments one by one and the German hordes froze in their spots.

'Celeste, are you hurt?' Beatrice flung away her shield and knelt to cradle Celeste in her arms. The girl struggled and thrashed as if Beatrice were the enemy, and Beatrice looked around wildly for help. She saw a commotion in the street, and then Hugh was pushing his way through to vault onto the float.

'She's beside herself,' said Beatrice. Celeste's keening scream went suddenly quiet, the silence almost as deafening, and small flecks of spittle frothed around her mouth as her eyes rolled back in her head.

'She's in a dead faint,' said Hugh. 'Some sort of seizure, I fear.'

'I am trained for first aid,' said Mrs Fothergill. 'Perhaps I should assist?'

'I think you've done enough,' said Beatrice, without thinking. 'Perhaps you can all clear the area and give her some air.' The crowd, which had pressed forward to view the distress, began to step back, and Beatrice tried to move her own body to shield Celeste as Hugh picked her up and carried her down from the float.

'Well, I do not think I deserve to be spoken to in such a manner,' she heard Bettina Fothergill say, but Beatrice was prevented from making some further hasty answer by the reasonable tones of Agatha Kent.

'Mrs Fothergill, the Mayor needs you to open the flower tent. I think all is covered here and my nephew is a doctor.'

'May I help you down, Mrs Fothergill?' added John. 'Here is a step for you.'

'I cannot imagine what distressed the poor child,' Mrs Fothergill said, her voice carrying even as she allowed herself to be led away. 'In Bexhill, they staged just such a small skirmish and doubled their donations.'

'Did Bexhill stage their attack on a real Belgian?' asked John.

'Well no, that's precisely where we were to have improved upon their efforts,' came the faint reply as he led Mrs Fothergill away.

'Do you want smelling salts?' asked Agatha.

'Best to get her home,' said Hugh, holding Celeste in his arms while Beatrice waved the tiny brown bottle under her nose. Celeste groaned and turned her head away to curl into Hugh's shoulder like a child.

'I'll send for her father,' said Agatha. 'And the Headmaster will have to manage your Latin performers.'

Beatrice thanked her and then, gathering up the many folds of her gown in her hands, she hurried to follow Hugh up the steps towards the high street. She remembered being a child in her own father's arms, the sensation of flying above the ground, the safety of strong arms, the warm, familiar smell of him against the new smells of street or woods. She had to quell a sudden wish that she, not Celeste, had fainted. It was a stupid thought, not worthy of the current crisis, and, as she rebuked herself silently, she was much larger and heavier than Celeste and would no doubt have been unceremoniously dumped into a wheelbarrow.

Reaching the cottage, Hugh carried Celeste up to her little alcove, which now contained Agatha's second spare wooden bed, a small dresser and a floor-length tapestry curtain to screen the nook from the stair. Laying her on the bed, he took her pulse with his pocket watch in his hand. His face showed frowning concern.

'Her pulse is steady,' he said. 'Did she eat breakfast?'

'Not much,' said Beatrice. 'We were both a little anxious about the parade.' Truth be told, she now thought that Celeste might have had nothing but a cup of tea. Meanwhile she, Beatrice, had breakfasted in a manner that now seemed unattractively hearty. It had seemed a shame to leave Celeste's toast and gooseberry jam to go to waste, and her own nerves about the day had made her hungrier than usual.

'I'm sure it's probably just a bit of a shock and lack of food,' said Hugh. 'But just to be certain, someone should remain with her. Lukewarm tea with plenty of sugar and a light diet for the rest of the day. Boiled egg or that sort of thing.'

He went to wait downstairs while Beatrice struggled to help Celeste out of her dress and stays and under the covers. Celeste felt feverish and shivered at her touch, reduced again to the dishevelled and exhausted refugee of the first night.

'You are safe now,' said Beatrice, smoothing the golden hair across the pillow. 'You are going to be all right.' Celeste merely turned her head away and closed her eyes. Beatrice sat on the bed and looked with sorrow at the little winged sandals spilled on the floor.

When Beatrice came down to the parlour a few moments later, the Professor had arrived. He stood by the window shuffling his feet and fussing with his watch chain.

'How is my daughter?' he asked. His face seemed tensed for bad news.

'As I said, I'm sure it is nothing to worry about,' said Hugh. 'Just a bit of a shock on top of a morning of nerves and no breakfast, I expect. Unless she has any medical condition of which I am unaware?'

'But this is all my fault,' said the Professor, shaking his head. 'A child should not be exposed to such roughness. I should not have given my permission for her to participate.'

'She will be fine after a day's rest,' said Hugh. 'I can ask Dr Lawton to call tomorrow if you prefer?'

'No, that will not be necessary,' said the Professor. 'I came at a great pace from the festival, where Mr Tillingham had desired me to judge with him the marrows. I am much relieved to know my daughter is well.'

'Would you like to go up and see her?' said Beatrice, cheerfully. She was already thinking about donning an apron over her new dress to make Celeste some tea and a lightly poached egg.

'No, no, best she not be disarranged,' he said. 'You will tell her I was here, and with your permission, I will call on you later for a further report. I fear I must return to my duties at the fete.'

'Are you sure, Professor?' asked Beatrice, whose duties to her own Latin scholars had been set aside the moment Celeste fainted. She looked to the stairs and thought of the trembling young girl and how much a father's hand on her arm might soothe.

'You have my thanks for your kind care of my child,' he said, as if she had suggested otherwise. 'Your young doctor says she will be quite well, and so there is nothing more to be said.' With that he put his hat on his head and almost knocked it off again getting out under the low door lintel.

'It hardly seems fair to leave you to look after Celeste and be deprived of the afternoon's festivities,' said Hugh as they watched the Professor hurry away up the street. Faint sounds of a carnival organ and the competing cacophony of a brass band hinted at the fete on the marsh below.

'I will be sorry to miss the pig racing,' she said in a dry tone. He laughed. 'It serves no purpose to diminish anyone else's enjoyment of the day,' she added. 'You should get back to the fete.'

For a moment, he wavered, as if he wanted to stay. 'I trust Abigail will return in time for you to attend the gala dance at the inn?' he asked at last.

'I don't think Celeste will be well enough, so I will probably stay here,' she replied. While she would have denied any need of a chaperone, no woman could relish attending a public ball alone.

'Nonsense,' said Hugh. 'Daniel and I simply can't abide having to ask strange women to dance. I will come and fetch you myself, and you must keep some of your dance card open for us.'

'But you will have your card full,' she said.

'I am prepared to do my social duty in all corners of the room,' he said. 'If you prefer my aunt Agatha to call for you, I will arrange it.'

'That won't be necessary,' she said. 'I am not a child.'

'About seven then,' said Hugh. 'Meanwhile, keep the patient very quiet and I will assume you know how to boil her an egg?'

The fete was in full swing, and Agatha, standing in the shade afforded by a flap of the tea tent, set her notebook down on a convenient upturned barrel and looked around with the cautious optimism of one who has prepared well and whose efforts are bearing the expected fruit, but for whom any display of gratification or relaxation of effort would be premature.

'Everything seems to be going marvellously well,' said her husband, coming out of the tent bearing two glasses of cold lemonade and a plate of finger sandwiches. 'You have pulled it off, old girl.'

'I am not superstitious,' said Agatha. 'But I must refuse to agree with you lest Bettina Fothergill unleash some further outrage on the afternoon.'

'People who say they are not superstitious are fooling no one but themselves,' said John, handing her a glass and setting down the plate. 'May I offer you a lucky cheese sandwich?'

'What makes it lucky?' asked Agatha.

'It is not egg salad,' said her husband. 'Therefore it is less likely to cause gastric distress after spending much of the day on an open platter under a hot tent.'

'You make my mouth water in anticipation,' she said, peering with great suspicion at the dry edges of the bread. 'However, I am completely famished, thank you.'

'That boy Snout, the one with the suspicious donation bucket?' said John. 'He was inside treating several pals to iced buns.'

'I'll box his ears,' said Agatha. 'After all we've done for him . . .'

'I gave him a very stern eye, to which he responded by paying for your lemonade,' said John. 'He was very charming about it too, so if you make a fuss you should know you may be an accessory.'

'You are incorrigible, John,' she said. 'Just because it's amusing to you does not mean you should allow him to get away with his mischief.'

'One wishes to allow room for the flourishing of personal conscience,' said John. 'The dread hand of authority can instil fear, but it cannot build character. I'm sure by the wee hours young Snout will be racked by guilt. But besides, I am on holiday today. I'm going to revel in being an authority over absolutely nothing.'

'You should have warned me,' said Agatha. 'I put you down for judging beautiful babies at two o'clock and staffing the cashbox from four to five.' Her husband groaned into his cheese sandwich, but he did not refuse his help. Other husbands happily took credit for the work of their wives and accepted honours in exchange for their financial donations, but they were often noticeably absent from any of the actual work of philanthropy. Agatha held it to be the greatest of all John's many qualities as a husband that he always stood shoulder to shoulder with her, or rather, did exactly as he was told.

'I want to tour Daniel's model trench first, and take a look at Hugh's ambulance,' said John, consulting his pocket watch. 'Will you come with me?'

'I really should perambulate around all the stalls and then check the entertainment programme,' said Agatha.

'Don't you want to see your nephews besieged by adoring young women with a passionate interest in trenching shovels and medical splints?' said John, swallowing the last bite of his sandwich. 'I'm sure both boys are completely confounded by all the attention.'

'Oh, very well,' said Agatha. 'But if the entire afternoon falls apart, it will be your fault for distracting me.'

Having nibbled at the less stale centre of her sandwich and drunk her lemonade, Agatha accompanied John to the far edge of the field, where the municipal grass had been torn up and the dark smell of fresh earth drew them to the model trenches. There was only room to walk single file on freshly cut duckboards and Agatha had to be content to watch her nephew's blushes above the heads of three talkative flag girls, who giggled behind him as he tried to explain the construction advancements his trench displayed.

'And you can see that by placing each sandbag perpendicular, as in the Flemish brick pattern, we get a stronger wall,' said Daniel, patting the eight-foot-high stack of bags that made the trench cool and muted the sounds of the fete outside.

Agatha took her turn peeping in at the snug dugout with its folding cot and table, oil lamp and a willow shelf containing three poetry books. Two or three poems had been pinned to the walls, where they fluttered like moths. The doorway to the dugout could be closed with a hanging blanket, now tied back with a long plaited straw, and in a small window in the sandbags, framed and divided with whittled alder branches, sat a small earthenware vase containing a handful of corn and wild poppies. Further down the trench itself, a small alcove contained a rustic bench woven from willow, and on this bench a fellow officer of the Rifles sat smoking a large pipe and painting on a small handheld watercolour pad.

'It's like the darlingest little cottage, isn't it?' said one of the girls.

'A cottage made for two,' said another, and they giggled some more as they wandered away.

'I'm not sure what we were thinking, asking girls to hawk flags like pedlars,' said Agatha. 'We have created monsters of forwardness, it seems.'

'Very well built, Second Lieutenant,' said John to Daniel.

'The trench or the girls, sir?' asked Daniel.

'Daniel!' said Agatha.

'Aunt Agatha, may I introduce my friend, Worthington? He's a painter from Norfolk. Had a piece accepted to the Academy last year.'

'Your work is lovely,' said Agatha, looking at the seascape brushed quickly but with confidence on the thick paper.

'Watercolour is not really my thing, madam,' said the officer, rising from his bench and giving an awkward sort of salute, encumbered as he was in both hands by his tools. 'But we wanted to give a little artists' atmosphere, you know, and oil paint is awfully smelly in confined spaces.'

'The entire effect is very well done,' said Agatha. 'Will it be very hard to keep clean in all the action?'

'We've made a whisk broom of local straw,' said Daniel, 'but I expect it will get pretty muddy underfoot with twelve of us in an area this big.'

'What, will you sleep one at a time?' asked Agatha.

'Dugout is for the ranking officer and maybe signals,' said Worthington. 'Rest of the men won't get any sleep until they get back behind the lines.'

'That's why we need poetry, singing, daubing pictures on the walls with clay,' said Daniel. 'Keeps up the spirits in battle.'

'Perhaps the vase is a little much,' said Agatha. 'I'm not sure flower arranging will keep up the martial spirit.'

'Quite right,' said Daniel. 'We were a little competitive and eager to show off in front of Colonel Wheaton's lot. Their trench is no more than a big ditch.'

'But they have beer in it,' said Worthington. 'Quite against regulations, but they are getting more visitors than we are.'

Agatha was slowly becoming aware of a buzzing mechanical sound growing louder above the excited voices outside. 'What on earth is that sound?' she said.

'That is my big surprise for you, dearest Aunt Agatha,' said Daniel, planting a hearty kiss on her cheek. 'A big surprise for your fete, for which you shall have all the credit.'

'Sounds like a broken steam engine,' said Agatha. 'Whatever have you done now, Daniel?'

'Just come and see,' said Daniel, catching up her hand. While she was alarmed at what he might be up to, Agatha was absurdly happy as he pulled her along. Not since he was a small boy had Daniel wanted to be hugged or lavished with affection, and for her, a clasp of the hand was surprise enough.

They left the trench and, with the flowing crowd, climbed up the dyke to the open path that ran between the town Salts and the river. Hugh and two of his men waved as they pushed through the crowd to join them. The splutter and buzz of multiple engines grew even more raucous coming from the west, and then a line of four biplanes, each cabled like a box kite with a bulbous engine in the front like the head of a fly, came into focus, flying single file towards them across the marshes from the west.

'How can this be happening?' asked Agatha.

'It's Craigmore and his platoon,' said Daniel, kissing her cheek. 'They are on their way to Folkestone, and I asked him to come and buzz the fete for you.'

'I can't believe it,' said Agatha. 'They are so beautiful.'

'What brings them to Folkestone?' asked Hugh, shading his eyes as the small craft came closer to the gathering crowd and each pilot rolled his craft upside down and back again, sending herds of sheep scattering in the fields.

'They are embarking for France, and Craigmore wrote to say he could not go without saying goodbye,' said Daniel. 'He is catching a train here just as soon as they land.'

'What a surprise,' said Hugh. 'I am so happy for you.'

'Bettina Fothergill will be beside herself with envy,' said Agatha. 'Let's wave.' John Kent stood watching intently, his eyes shaded, while Agatha joined Daniel, Hugh and the rest of the crowd clapping and cheering like the children among them. They waved handkerchiefs and fans and hats, and gasped and ducked as the planes buzzed lower over their very heads. The band struck up a jolly march as high over the church spire they soared, round and down again, dipping towards the river like a flock of geese. Then up and over the crowd once more. After several such loops in the sky, the band segued into its fifteenth rendition of 'Land of Hope and Glory' as the planes flew off across the marsh. The last pilot peeled away from the disappearing line to execute his own finale, a long, slow pass, parallel to river and fete, the plane so low and close that they could see the pilot push back his helmet and goggles to wave wildly at the crowd. It was young Craigmore with his golden hair streaming and a big grin on his face. Agatha could see his face etched as clearly as if he were standing on the other riverbank.

'Craigmore!' screamed Daniel, waving. 'I'm here, I'm here!' Craigmore waved once more and gave a brief salute, but Agatha doubted he had seen any of them individually, not with the air rushing into his eyes.

'Three cheers for the Royal Flying Corps,' shouted John, and the crowd took up the loudest of hoorays as Craigmore's craft sped away to catch up to his flock. Daniel watched until the last tail of smoke disappeared against the blue sky, and they waited with him, even as the crowd flowed away, back to the fete's other amusements.

'However did you keep such a secret?' asked Agatha, when Daniel finally stopped looking and turned around. She took advantage of his obvious happiness to kiss both his cheeks and squeeze his hand one more time. 'It was superb, my darling boy.'

'Young Craigmore is off to the front already?' asked John. 'I'm sorry to hear it.'

'He assures me he begged for the opportunity,' said Daniel. His face grew wistful. 'I would argue the case, but he asked to see me before he leaves, and I must not risk our fragile reunion by urging him to stay. His father must win that argument for now.'

'Your aunt and I are proud of you,' said John, putting a hand on his shoulder. 'Your maturity is showing, my boy.'

'Youth's lost companion may be the measured friend of old age, I hope,' said Daniel. 'I may write a poem on the subject.'

'Dear God, it sounds more like a cross-stitched pillow than a poem,' said Hugh.

'Says the old man of my youth,' said Daniel. 'He of the ancient wisdom and sour face.'

'Well, I for one am ready for a ride on the roundabout,' said Agatha. 'Let's make sure we see Bettina on the way so she can congratulate me on the day's complete triumph.'

CHAPTER TWENTY-ONE

When Hugh knocked at Mrs Turber's front door promptly at seven o'clock, he found himself more anxious than expected. Offering to escort a lady neighbour to a dance was hardly a cause for jitters, but his cousin Daniel, who was at his side, was in such an irrepressible good humour that he had not been able to restrain himself from teasing Hugh all the way down the hill to town and up the hill to Mrs Turber's house.

'You really should have obtained a hansom cab, don't you think?' he whispered into Hugh's ear. 'So gauche to make a lady walk.'

'The ball is a few hundred yards away at the inn,' said Hugh. 'All the people in carriages will be waiting in a jam while we are already at supper.'

'I'm just saying you might look frugal,' said Daniel.

'I'll punch you if you don't behave,' said Hugh. 'I'm merely doing a good turn here. Poor Miss Nash didn't get to enjoy any of the afternoon, so I thought the least we could do is to offer her an arm down to the party.'

'Spinsters aren't supposed to enjoy themselves,' said Daniel. 'I think they live to be useful.'

The door opened, and Abigail the maid grinned at them in a most familiar way. 'You do know we can hear everything you're saying through the window?' she asked.

'One day I'll die of shame because of you, Daniel,' said Hugh, hurrying into the cottage after his cousin.

In the front parlour, Beatrice stood at the fireplace, wearing a white silk dress. Hugh supposed it to be the same dress as she had worn in the parade, but some Grecian draperies must have been removed, and the sweep of a low neckline and the snug neatness of the waist were revealed. Her dark hair was piled up, bound with a single dahlia of a deep pink colour, and around her neck an old cameo hung from a dark crimson velvet ribbon. She wore no other jewellery, and though she attempted a frown of mock severity, Hugh thought her beautiful.

'Miss Nash, you look wonderful,' said Daniel. 'You are a high priestess of the temple.'

'That is just another word for spinster, is it?' said Beatrice, pulling on long gloves.

'Beatrice, you must excuse my cousin,' said Hugh. 'He would insist on coming when he is obviously not in his right mind.' Hugh would have liked to add his own compliment, but he could not be sure his cousin would not ridicule his efforts.

'I am a little giddy, Miss Nash,' said Daniel. 'My dear friend Craigmore is coming to see me and we shall all dance until dawn.'

'I am happy for you,' said Beatrice. 'I hope all the young ladies of Rye have brought their stoutest dancing slippers.'

'How is Celeste?' asked Hugh.

'She ate an egg and drank several cups of lukewarm tea,' said Beatrice. 'She is still a little feverish, but she is resting calmly and Abigail will stay with her.'

'Then let us away to our merry masque,' said Daniel. 'I am as dizzy as if the champagne was already flowing.'

Hugh opened the diminutive front door and handed Beatrice out into the street while Daniel fell in behind them. Hugh was very aware of the curve of her neck, the smell of the flower in her hair and her slim figure as she slipped past him. Her hair seemed made for unpinning, and on the back of her dress, tightly laced with ribbon, a single knotted bow made him suddenly dazed with the desire to tug on it. He took in a sharp breath of evening air and reminded himself that he was promised to another woman, and that to overstep in his friendship with Beatrice might render life in Rye very complicated. He offered her his arm with a stiff bow.

'Miss Nash?'

'Mr Grange.'

She took his arm, and as they walked to the coaching inn, the pressure of her hand on his sleeve made him flush so hard, he did not dare to look at her.

The inn was ablaze with light and thick with banks of peppery-scented dahlias and chrysanthemums. Beatrice had not seen such a party since her return to England, and she had forgotten how just the anticipation could fill one with pleasure. The orchestra was playing on the small stage in the ballroom, and three adjoining lounges had been thrown open for supper and for sitting. The rooms were already full with laughter. In the foyer, Alice Finch beckoned them to a flowered arbour, where she set the three of them about a mossy tree trunk draped in a velvet shawl and photographed them with a burst of her upraised flash.

In the ballroom itself the chandeliers were newly electrified.

'My God, the light is so good all the women risk looking their age,' said Daniel.

'You are horrible,' said Beatrice.

'Be careful,' he said. 'Schoolgirls are not allowed out this late.' She laughed and slapped at him with her dance card.

'May I ask for one of your dances?' said Hugh. He looked rather serious, and Beatrice was about to tease him when she decided instead that she would like to dance and so she handed over the little book with its silver pencil.

'Oh, do allow me some too,' said Daniel. 'So much better than some marriageable girl with a pushing mother.'

'Daniel!' said Hugh.

'Miss Nash knows I'm only teasing her like a sister,' said Daniel. 'No need to look all pugnacious, Hugh.' Hugh realised he was frowning as he hesitated between pencilling in his name for the waltz or the less visible commitment of the following mazurka.

'I may give you one of the country dances, Mr Bookham,' said Beatrice equably. 'But I shall be sure to trip you up.' Hugh laughed aloud at her swift put-down of his cousin and decided to match her boldness by demanding the waltz.

Agatha was waltzing with her husband, and though her feet ached after such a long day, she rested in the shelter of his arms and allowed herself to enjoy the ball in a simple way. The day had been a success, the funds raised had exceeded all their expectations, and even the minor fiasco with Bettina's Germans seemed to have done no lasting harm.

'Are you happy, my dear?' said John, swinging her with aplomb past two very lumbering couples in one corner. 'You look a little preoccupied for one whose day was such a triumph.'

'I am happy,' she said, giving him the smile he wanted. 'I am dancing with you, both our nephews are here with us, and I'm not going to think about committees or about war for the rest of the evening.'

'I think Hugh looks very happy to be dancing with Miss Nash,' said John. Agatha, who always had to look at a fixed point in order not to get dizzy with the spinning about, risked a peek at Hugh and lost her footing.

'You are just being provocative,' she said, doing an awkward skip and shuffle to catch up. 'You know he is as good as engaged to Lucy Ramsey.'

'Well, she is not here and he does not seem to be pining,' said her husband. 'And Miss Nash is such an intelligent woman.'

'Compounding lack of funds with intelligence, she makes herself unmarriageable,' said Agatha. 'I adore Beatrice, but she would not advance Hugh's prospects, and he is too sensible to throw away a surgeon's practice for a penniless teacher.'

'My parents told me to marry for money,' said her husband. 'But I chose the love of a strong woman.'

'And look what trouble I turned out to be,' she said.

Beatrice found it hard to concentrate on her steps with Hugh holding her waist. Hugh remained silent, though he seemed at times to want to speak and many expressions chased across his face. When the dance ended, he handed her to an empty chair at his aunt's table and offered to fetch her some lemonade.

'I would be pleased to drink some lemonade,' she said graciously. 'But I hope we are friends enough that you will not feel any obligation to hover about when you should be mingling.'

'I shall try not to take that as a dismissal,' said Hugh. 'I shall return with lemonade.'

Beatrice was happily watching the swirl of the crowded dance floor and admiring the way the townsfolk looked in their unusual finery when she caught the sound of ladies whispering behind a large fern.

'I'm not saying it's true,' said Mrs Turber's voice. 'But did you see the way she fainted? Something is fishy, I tell you.'

'Not normal at all,' said another, 'but they're all highly emotional, aren't they?'

Beatrice did not wish to hear more. Her cheeks blazed as she rose without speaking and moved away swiftly towards the salon into which Hugh had vanished. There were mostly gentlemen in the room, gathered at the large bar or fetching drinks to other rooms. Beatrice was turning to leave when she heard another familiar voice, that of

Mr Poot, saying, 'Well, of course it's all strictly confidential, but let me say – well, it would make your hair curl to hear what some of these young girls have suffered.'

'If it were my sister or daughter, I'd rather she died,' said another.

'Some of them beg to die,' said Poot. 'Of course, I tell them it is the nature of war and they must bravely bear it.' He wandered away, and Beatrice found herself drifting to the dance floor. As she looked around the room, she seemed to see whispering everywhere, heads bent towards each other, eyes swivelling about the room.

'Smile,' said Eleanor Wheaton, appearing at her shoulder. 'It makes them crazy when you appear to be happy.'

'Who?' asked Beatrice.

'All the gossips,' said Eleanor. 'Look at them. Always whispering.' As she spoke, she frowned and touched her fingers to a small, diamond-studded gold locket suspended around her neck.

'Are they talking about you?' asked Beatrice.

'Well, it's often about me, the German Baroness,' said Eleanor. 'And of course they're whispering about Amberleigh de Witte . . .'

'I haven't seen Amberleigh or Mr Frith,' said Beatrice.

'That's because they were refused tickets,' said Eleanor. 'Too disreputable for the polite society of Rye.'

'It's just a public-subscription dance,' said Beatrice.

'And let's see, well, they like to chatter about Alice Finch, because she's from London and so, obviously, odd. They gossip even as they take the photographs she's donating.' Eleanor waved to several people in the room and seemed happy to see several more groups of people turn to stare at her.

'It's horrible,' said Beatrice.

'And they should gossip about my brother, who deserves more criticism than he gets, but he's a handsome young man, so they don't berate him too badly.'

'What else do you hear?' asked Beatrice.

'My point, dear girl, is that it is pointless to ask,' said Eleanor. 'Gossip is only corrosive to the spirit if one entertains it. Do as I do and let it roll off you like water off a duck's back.'

'What did you hear, Eleanor?' said Beatrice.

'Oh, well, there may be some whispers about Celeste's little fainting spell,' she said reluctantly. 'Then there are rumours that you have your hooks into both of Agatha Kent's nephews and Bettina Fothergill's to boot.'

'Mr Poot?' asked Beatrice. 'Are they mad?'

'Exactly my point,' said Eleanor. 'Quite mad. Possibly from the boredom of living here. Not to be taken any notice of. Oh good, here comes Hugh with champagne.' Hugh arrived bearing two lemonade cups.

'Ladies, your lemonade, as Eleanor requested,' he said. Beatrice took a deep draught and found it was indeed champagne in the glass cup.

'I intercepted Hugh,' said Eleanor. 'No reasonable man expects a lady to drink that awful sticky lemonade stuff.'

'You are a bad influence, Eleanor,' he said.

'And you, dear Hugh, are in dire need of a bit of bad influence,' she said. 'I hope Miss Nash will see to it.' So saying, she waved and floated off into the thick of the crowd, sipping champagne and kissing cheeks as she went, the gossiping heads bending like stalks of reed in her wake.

'She lives in her own world,' said Hugh. 'But she's a kind girl.'

'We were talking about gossip,' said Beatrice.

'Let's not talk,' said Hugh. 'Let's drink our champagne. And then may I have the honour of the entire next set?' Perhaps it was the champagne, but Beatrice felt herself blush like a girl in her first season as she fumbled for her dance card. Hugh had just taken the little silver pencil when a voice called to them from across the room and Beatrice saw a gloved hand waving a dance card and a white ostrich feather fan.

'Hello, Hugh, surprise, surprise!' said the owner of the fan. A girl of no more than nineteen, decked in a teal blue ballgown and silver shoes, was smiling at him with complete confidence that her surprise was a joyous one. 'I've come to surprise you.'

'Miss Nash,' said Hugh, looking distinctly flustered. 'May I present Miss Lucy Ramsey, daughter of Sir Alex Ramsey, my surgeon?'

'How do you do,' said Beatrice, but the girl was busy hanging on Hugh's arm and gazing up into his face.

'Oh, Hugh, isn't it the most delightful surprise?' she asked. 'I had no idea that the Hartleys' weekend house was so near to Rye. We are in Bexhill, and my friend Jemima Hartley and I have been all day on the promenade selling flag pins, and we had to give the white feather to no fewer than three insolent fellows who insisted on proposing to us even though they were not in uniform.'

'Good grief,' said Hugh, eyeing her fan as if for holes. 'I hope you don't plan to start handing them out here.'

'Don't worry, these are ostrich and much too valuable,' she said. 'Anyway, as soon as I saw a handbill for your festivities, I just insisted that we drive over this evening to see you.'

'I am shocked,' said Hugh. 'And delighted, of course. I must introduce you to my aunt and uncle.'

'I'm only sorry we did not arrive earlier,' said Lucy. 'I do hope you haven't committed yourself to every country damsel in the room?'

'I believe Mr Grange is free of any obligations,' said Beatrice, smiling as wide as she could manage while she quelled an unexpected surge of disappointment. 'I wish you both a very pleasant evening, Miss Ramsey.'

As she walked away, she heard Lucy Ramsey say, 'Oh, Hugh, were you unwilling to dance in my absence? How romantic of you!'

Refusing to give in to an unhappiness to which she was not in any way entitled, Beatrice scratched Hugh's name from her dance card and made sure to smilingly accept other partners. But when Mr Dimbly took her out for the quadrille, she found herself scanning the room for Hugh's face, and when Mr Kent asked her to polka, she spent the entire dance asking him about Hugh and Daniel as small boys and remembering only the bits about Hugh. She found it difficult to make conversation while looking over her shoulder to see Hugh and Lucy whirling their way through a suite of country dances. The girl was pretty and flirtatious, and had a tinkling laugh that travelled, despite the loud orchestra and the roar of conversation. Beatrice could fault her for appearing less than intellectually gifted but, as she waspishly told herself, even men as educated as Hugh seemed to prefer their women that way.

Beatrice became so distracted that when Mr Poot appeared at her side to request her company in a Scottish reel, she could not come up with a suitable excuse and so had to gallop up and down the room with both her hands grasped tight in his sweating palms.

'Dancing is such good exercise, don't you think?' he said. 'While I would not go so far as to endorse such excesses as the tango, I do think it a most pleasant excuse for men and women to join hands in vigorous activity.'

'You make it sound quite excessive enough,' said Beatrice. 'I am glad we are all wearing gloves.'

'Your sense of humour is as sharp as an arrow, Miss Nash,' said Mr Poot as they made an arch for the procession of the other laughing dancers. 'I myself am quite struck through the heart.'

'Perhaps you need to sit down then, Mr Poot,' she said as they parted again to skip around the edge of the group.

'Indeed, let us slip aside a moment,' he said as they joined hands, and he pulled her swiftly behind a potted palm and the heavy swag of curtains onto a small balcony. That the balcony overlooked the rather smelly stable yard of the inn, and that Beatrice was quick to withdraw her hand and to shrink back towards the ballroom, did not seem to offer any impediment to Mr Poot.

'I must beg the indulgence of a few moments of conversation with you,' he said. 'Won't you sit down?' He indicated a small wrought-iron chair in the window, and she eyed it with suspicion.

'Thank you, Mr Poot,' she said. 'But just for a moment. I am promised to Mr Kent for the next waltz.'

'I think they are offering a violin interlude,' said Mr Poot, peering beyond the curtain. 'We shall not be interrupted.'

'Perhaps some lemonade?' she asked, hoping to send him away so she might make her escape from his company.

'I will gladly provide you lemonade, or anything your heart may desire,' said Mr Poot. 'Only give me one moment to speak what I can no longer hide.' So saying, he dropped to one knee and placed a hand on his heart.

'Good heavens, no, Mr Poot,' she said, her voice coming as an anxious squeak of horror. 'I beg you.'

'It is I who must beg you, Miss Nash,' he said. 'I had prepared to make the most rational of cases for the joining of two people in mutual advantage, but in the face of your beauty today, both as stately England and tonight, as a figure of grace in the ballroom, I find I am swept away.'

'It cannot be, Mr Poot,' she said, doing her best to rise and make a polite withdrawal. But he grabbed her hand in both of his and she sat down abruptly. 'I do not look for a declaration,' she added.

'I know it may come as a surprise, as you have long given up your dreams of matrimony for a lonely spinsterhood,' he said. 'But you have captured my attention and my heart, Miss Nash. I ask you to become mine and make our fortunes one in the world.'

'Whose fortune exactly?' she said, and could not keep a sharp note from her voice as she recovered her composure.

'Your trusts, while I do not yet know their full extent, are no more than an agreeable boost to our common cause,' he said. 'A gentleman's independence will allow me to pursue the law and thereby provide you with the comfortable life and, dare I say, enviable social position of being a solicitor's wife.' He looked to the ceiling in contemplation and added, 'Perhaps in time, a judge's wife, perhaps a mayoress, like my aunt?'

'Ah, to be just like your aunt,' said Beatrice. 'That is quite the temptation.'

'You make a gentle jest, I know,' he said. 'But only think how marriage to me will render you free of your trustees.'

'You would control my portion instead,' she said.

'Have I not already proved myself your friend and advocate?' he said. 'Did I not approve this very dress and pay you two pounds from my own pocket?'

'You made me an advance from your own funds?' she asked, horrified. He made a gesture of airy dismissal.

'I do not regard it as a debt,' he said. 'Though your trustees have yet to reimburse me, I did not mean you to hear of it, I assure you. It was a pleasure to carry the obligation privately next to my heart.' For a moment they both contemplated the enormity of his actions. Beatrice felt anger rise in her with an intensity of feeling she had not experienced since the awful moment of her father's death. Such strong emotion was likely to produce tears, and she was determined not to give Mr Poot the satisfaction. She yanked away her hand from his and rose from the chair, paying no attention to his proximity. Mr Poot was forced to scuttle backwards lest his face be buried in her skirts as she towered over him.

'I decline your offer and ask you never to repeat it,' she said, allowing a hint of her fury into her clipped tone. 'Please get out of my way.'

'There is no need to be so rude,' he said, scrambling to his feet, his face ugly with disappointment. 'I think I have made you the most respectable offer you are likely to receive and you could at least provide some explanation of why a woman like you should be so quick to turn it down.'

'Mr Poot—' she began. She was planning to lecture him on exactly why he was owed no explanation, but a rousing mazurka had begun in the ballroom and she caught a glimpse of Lucy Ramsey, skipping by and twirling under Hugh's arm, her ostrich fan sweeping in an elaborate circle. Her previous disappointment and her current rage seemed to die away in a long sigh. How foolish, she thought, to waste her anger on either the impossible or the absurd. When she turned back to him, it was with a resigned smile on her face. 'I will give you an explanation, Mr Poot,' she continued, drawing on a corner of her dance card and tearing off the piece to hand to him. 'I must follow the fashionable lead of Sir Alex Ramsey's daughter, Miss Lucy Ramsey.'

'What are you giving me?' he asked, looking puzzled at her scribbled drawing.

'Oh, I'm sorry, Mr Poot, I am such a bad artist,' she said, visibly engaged in looking for friends in the ballroom. 'That is my pitiful representation of a feather. Please be assured that I would never accuse you of cowardice, sir, but I understand the white feather is the only suitable response to give to any suitor not wearing the uniform. Now if you'll excuse me, I see Miss Devon is looking for me.'

'It is so nice to sit and watch the young people dance, is it not?' said Miss Devon, when Beatrice had sat down. The

Misses Porter, who had brought their knitting, nodded in agreement. 'I am too old for it myself, and I would not put myself forward when there are so many young ladies, but it is a pleasure to see all the amusement and to have a little supper, no?' she added. Having so lately both inflicted and suffered romantic rejection, Beatrice did not quite know how to respond. A sudden glimpse of her future, sitting by the wall with a dowdy posy of feathers on her head, nodding along to the music while others danced, made her blanch. She had long maintained no interest in marriage, but perhaps she had not properly considered the full implications of the spinster life.

When an extra waltz was announced and Lucy went onto the dance floor on the arm of a captain with a large moustache, Beatrice kept her eyes on the floor and hoped that by winding a ball of wool for the Misses Porter she might discourage any gentlemen from importuning her. But Hugh's shoes arrived on the polished boards, and when she looked up, he smiled and offered his hand.

As she surrendered to the delight of sweeping around the room, her dress swinging about her like a bell, she turned her face to his and both of them were soon laughing as she gave him a brief and comic version of Mr Poot's declaration.

'Daniel will insist we challenge him to a duel,' said Hugh. 'But I think I can get Harry Wheaton to thrash the bounder instead.'

'No, no, you are sworn to secrecy,' she said. 'I do not wish to humiliate the man; I only thought I would die if I could not tell someone.'

'Why does everyone burden me with their secrets?' asked Hugh. 'It's an unfair slur on my character to always be considered dependable.'

The dance floor could barely contain the crush of so many waltzing couples, and the crowd squeezed them out to dance on a quiet colonnade. When they realised they were dancing alone, it seemed only respectable to sit out the rest of the dance on a small sofa in a flowered alcove. Unlike being penned into a window nook with Mr Poot, it was entirely satisfying, thought Beatrice, to sit together quietly with Hugh and to feel the comfort of mutual friendship. It could not be more, and yet something seemed to hang between them, and she tried not to feel giddy.

'I would like to say that I think you are very brave,' said Hugh. 'To have set up house and to work all alone and to live from the fruits of your own labour – I admire your perseverance, especially in the face of obstacles such as Mr Poot.'

'I do only what is needed to keep body and soul together,' she said. 'I have done so little for any cause beyond my own.'

'You have taken in another girl in distress,' he said.

'Her beauty and youth have made me much more popular,' Beatrice said with a laugh. 'A dozen ladies would kill to take her off my hands.'

'You will deflect all praise, so I shall merely admire you in silence,' said Hugh.

As they sat together, the world seemed far away, and so she was confused and not quite sure who called for Hugh, or how Agatha was by her side, gripping her hand. Somehow they were no longer in the colonnade but in the inn's lobby, and a young man in a Royal Flying Corps uniform was speaking to Daniel, and Daniel slumped to his knees and Hugh grabbed to support him with both arms. When Daniel gave a howl of pain, Beatrice finally snapped out of her reverie.

'We just saw you all,' said John Kent. 'How did it happen?'

'The landing was windy, sir. Hard gusts off the sea and he just clipped a tree on the way in and spiralled right onto the field.'

'Did he suffer?' asked John.

'Died on impact, sir,' said the young officer. 'Aeroplane went up like a bomb. We're all pretty cut up about it.' He wiped his eyes, and John signalled to someone from the inn and asked for brandy.

Daniel was rocking in Hugh's arms and moaning like a mortally wounded animal. Hugh spoke to him quietly, but his cousin only seemed to sink lower to the ground, as if he would lean over and whisper his grief to the rough carpet. Hugh looked to his uncle, and John Kent and the young officer went to help him drag Daniel to a bench. The brandy came, and they forced some between his lips. The young officer took a glass too and sat quietly on a chair, his cap on his knees.

'It was good of you to come,' said John. 'I am sure you wanted to be with your men.'

'He was so keen to come up this evening,' said the officer. 'He wanted to see his friend before we pushed off tomorrow.'

'Will you still go on?' asked John.

'Yes, sir. At first light, sir.' He looked at Daniel, who could not lift his head from his knees. 'In fact, I have to go, sir. Catch the last train back.'

'Of course,' said John. He looked around and signalled to Harry Wheaton, who was standing with Eleanor in the doorway to the ballroom. All around them the nodding heads of the crowd made Beatrice feel sick. 'I say, Wheaton, would you walk Craigmore's friend to the train?'

'Yes, sir,' said Wheaton, and there was no trace of his usual laconic smile in his grave face. 'My honour.'

'Our car is outside,' said Eleanor, stepping forward. 'Would you like to take Daniel home, Mr Kent?' As John Kent accepted, he looked around for his wife, and Beatrice realised that Agatha was still gripping her hand. A helpful manager hurried forward with Agatha's wrap, and Eleanor came to assist Agatha out to the car. John and Hugh followed, Daniel stumbling between them, silent now.

Following them to the inn's door, Beatrice felt a presence at her elbow. It was the surgeon's daughter.

'It's a reminder of how fragile life is these days,' sighed Lucy Ramsey. 'Did you know him?'

'I did,' said Beatrice. 'He was Lord North's son and a close friend of Hugh's cousin.'

'Every day is precious, isn't it?' said Lucy. 'Poor Hugh. I see now that it was wrong of me to make him wait.'

'Excuse me?' said Beatrice.

'I was content for our connection to remain secret, but now I think I must let him send the engagement notice right away.' She tucked a piece of fair hair behind her ear and smiled with just her lips. 'How childlike of me to dwell on the form and ceremony of marriage and not the value of it to a man bound for the front lines,' she added. 'We women must do our duty too.' She looked around and waved towards some unseen figure in the ballroom.

'I hope you'll be very happy,' said Beatrice. But the taste in her mouth was of ashes, and she struggled to keep her voice even. She told herself it was the shock of Craigmore's death, but the ache vibrating through her was of a more selfish nature.

'We've always known we would be,' said Lucy. She looked Beatrice square in the face, and there was nothing but steel in her blue eyes. 'Lovely to meet you,' she murmured as she walked away.

The orchestra was still playing in the hot, festive ball-room; the shadows of dancing couples played against the windows and walls of the façades opposite and in the puddles from a light rain in the streets. No doubt the gossip still flowed with the wine and champagne. But as Beatrice stepped from the warm inn to the cold street outside, the night was already a faded dream.

Hugh was standing by the car, speaking to his uncle, and she shrank into the dark embrace of the doorway, for she did not know how to speak to him now. As she watched, a dark figure ran up and plucked his sleeve.

'Oh, Mr Grange, you must come,' said a voice, and Beatrice recognised Abigail. The pinched face of the maid turned as she stepped from her hiding place. 'You and Miss Beatrice must come. Miss Celeste is dying and I don't know what to do for her.' As Hugh hesitated, looking at Beatrice and then at the car, his uncle took him by the arm.

'Don't worry, I'll take care of them, Hugh,' he said. 'You must see to your patient.'

It was hard for Beatrice to remain conscious, and she fought to slow her breathing and remain upright and of assistance. Her lungs hurt from running so wildly through the dark streets, and a stitch in her side required her to press a hand to her ribs. But it was the sight of Celeste writhing in pain, and the blood-smeared sheets, that threatened to make her faint. Celeste hardly saw them enter her little room; she was busy murmuring her final prayers and begging *le bon Dieu* to take her.

'It just keeps getting worse,' said Abigail, crying. 'She's dying.'

'Bring some clean towelling, clean rags, whatever you have,' said Hugh. 'And a basin of hot water.'

'Celeste, we are here,' said Beatrice. She knelt at the bedside to take Celeste's small white hand, and tried not to recoil from the smell of sweat and the streaks of blood.

'Leave me alone,' whispered Celeste. 'God is punishing me.' She whimpered and drew up her knees in pain.

'I don't think you're dying,' said Hugh, his face slightly averted from the patient. 'Not really my area of expertise, of course. I'll need to examine her.'

'No, no,' said Celeste. She shrank away and clutched at Beatrice's hand. 'Make him go away and let me die.'

'It's just Hugh,' said Beatrice, urgently. 'He is a good man and he is the only doctor we have right now. You must let him help.'

'No, I will die of the shame,' she said. 'Please, please make him go away.'

'What shall we do?' asked Beatrice, looking at Hugh, who seemed rather relieved to be ordered away. Abigail came running up the stairs with an armful of linen and a jug of warm water. Hugh hesitated for a moment, thinking.

'I can't call my aunt . . .' he began. Then his face lit up. 'I say, Abigail, Mrs Stokes was camped on the Salts telling fortunes all day. Is she still there?'

'I couldn't say,' said Abigail, her face wearing a frown that said she was ready neither to acknowledge her great-grandmother nor to be responsible for her whereabouts.

'We need her,' said Hugh. 'I know Dr Lawton sometimes calls on her to help with – with some of the women.'

'Happen she might be there,' said Abigail.

'Then run and fetch her fast as you can,' said Hugh. 'I believe she will know exactly what to do.'

At Hugh's direction, from where he stood as far away as possible from the bed, Beatrice tucked a clean old sheet around Celeste and used some warm water and soap to at least wipe the sweat from her brow. As Beatrice pushed back her matted hair, Celeste seemed to quiet under her touch. Her breath became more regular even as she continued to grimace through stabs of pain.

'What is happening to her?' whispered Beatrice as she took the jug to fetch more warm water from the kitchen stove.

'I'd rather not speculate until Mrs Stokes gets here,' said Hugh. 'Complicated matter to get wrong.'

'We should fetch her father,' said Beatrice.

'Why don't we wait for Mrs Stokes?' Hugh said. 'Some things are best left until we know for sure.'

After many interminable minutes, in which Hugh frowned over the patient's pulse several times and Beatrice stroked her hair and tried not to faint from the iron smell of the blood, Mrs Stokes stumped up the stairs, bringing the welcome scents of bonfire smoke and hair oil. She wore a thick, much-embroidered dress and a velvet sash adorned with several rows of gold coins. Her hair was braided and coiled under a bright red kerchief, and she had jingling gold bracelets on her arms. Before approaching the bed, she removed the bracelets and tucked them in a large canvas bag, which she carried on her shoulder.

'Celeste, Mrs Stokes is here to help you,' said Beatrice. Celeste opened her eyes, and they grew very round at the sight of the old woman. 'Don't be frightened.'

'No reason to be frightened o' me,' said Mrs Stokes. 'I birthed six children o' my own and no counting the others,' she said. 'I seen every woman's problem from gout to the stuff a husband gives 'em from consorting with the Lord knows who, and then he tells her it's just her imagination.' She pulled a clean rag from the pile Abigail had brought and tied it around her waist as an apron.

'I'm here with you,' said Beatrice, smoothing Celeste's hair.

'You'll be leaving us now, miss,' said Mrs Stokes. 'Abigail and me'll see to her.'

'But . . .'

'Last thing she wants is you seeing all that ails her,' said Mrs Stokes. 'Out, out. Let me do what you'll be paying me to do.'

'We'll be right downstairs, Mrs Stokes,' said Hugh. 'Do call on me if you need me.'

'Put some water on to boil,' she said. 'We'll all be wanting tea.'

For twenty minutes, Hugh and Beatrice sat in silence on the parlour settee, listening to the creak of floors, the stamping of feet and the muffled commands of Mrs Stokes. Beatrice trimmed the lamp once, and Hugh got up several times to poke the fire into leaping flames or to rattle the tongs around in the scuttle for extra coals. Abigail hurried down twice to fetch more water, and the second time she carried down a handful of dried plants and made a foul-smelling tea for the patient. Beatrice trembled with a deep anxiety for Celeste that was rapidly becoming a physical headache. She was conscious of some satisfaction that Hugh and she were bound together in this emergency and that it had brought them here in the low lamplight. But while she took comfort in his steadying presence next to her, she was aware of a new sense of loss that came from the news of his pending engagement. With some surprise she realised that a small flame of jealousy burned in her that Lucy Ramsey was to take him away and that his marriage must change what had become an easy friendship.

At last Mrs Stokes came slowly, one heavy step at a time, down the stairs. She carried a bundle of knotted-up linen, which she set by the door.

'It's late for these old bones to be running up hills and climbing stairs,' she said. 'If you have any cake, or maybe a meat sandwich, I'd be grateful for a mouthful of sustenance.'

'Abigail, will you see to it?' asked Beatrice.

'How is the patient, Mrs Stokes?' said Hugh. 'I am anxious to hear your diagnosis.'

'The patient wasn't too happy to hear it, believe me,' said Mrs Stokes. 'Always a surprise and a bluster with them young girls.'

'Would you both please tell me what is happening?' said Beatrice. 'I must tell her father.'

'He's the doctor,' said Mrs Stokes, nodding at Hugh. 'He knows.' Abigail brought a hunk of meat between two thick slabs of bread. Mrs Stokes sniffed at the plate and then wrapped the sandwich in a clean handkerchief and put it in her bag.

'Heavy cramping and some bleeding?' said Hugh, who had grown red about the face. 'Did she lose it?'

'No, not as far as I can make out,' said the old woman. 'I gave her some of my viburnum tea and she'll be needing to stay in bed awhile; that is, assuming you wish to keep away the cramps?' She spoke in the matter-of-fact way of one medical expert to another. Hugh did not respond but only grew redder, and opened and closed his mouth several times. 'Abigail knows what to do for her,' Mrs Stokes added, accepting a cup of tea.

'Yes, Gran,' said Abigail.

'There is a child,' said Beatrice, sitting down slowly. The breath seemed to leave her body. 'Surely it's not possible.'

'She is with child, missy,' said Mrs Stokes. 'Pregnant, and by a man unless the angel Gabriel has come among us again.'

'How?' asked Beatrice. 'She's a sheltered girl.'

'I'm an old woman now,' said Mrs Stokes. She sighed. 'Time was I thought all girls went unknowing and pure to their marriage beds. Now I know better. There's a thousand stories how and none of them any the wiser as to what happened.'

'I believe she is a casualty of war,' said Hugh. 'As such she must be held blameless.'

'Do you mean to imply a violation?' Beatrice felt the nausea rising and covered her face with her hands. 'Oh, please, please, God, let it not be.'

'Else she had some shepherd boy playing his pipe in her fields.' Mrs Stokes chuckled. 'Will ye be paying my fee now or will I be asking her father for it?'

'We thank you for coming,' said Hugh, his face stern. He rifled his pockets for coins and held out a palm to Mrs Stokes. 'Please take what you will, and Dr Lawton assures me we can rely on your discretion?'

Mrs Stokes squinted at the coins in his hand and swept all into her own palm. 'If she was forced, don't think the town will hold her innocent,' she said. She picked up the linen bundle, and Abigail ran to open the little door for her. 'I'll burn the linen for free to get rid of the bad luck.'

Just outside the door, Mrs Turber jumped back as if startled by its opening and gave a little shriek.

'Who's that?' said Mrs Stokes, jingling her bangles as she waved a hand in Mrs Turber's face. 'Who shrieks in the street and smells of liquor?'

'Gypsies!' shrieked Mrs Turber. 'Gypsies in my house and stealing from me? Help, someone help!'

'Mrs Turber, don't scream so,' said Beatrice, pushing past Abigail into the street. 'It's just Mrs Stokes come to help us. Miss Celeste was taken gravely ill.'

'She's stealing from me,' said Mrs Turber. 'I know my own linen, thank you.' She pointed a bony finger at the bundle and tried to grab for it.

'The linen must be burned unless you want the seven years of bad fortune to visit your house,' said Mrs Stokes.

'And I'll thank 'ee to remember there's a special curse for those who thwart a traveller in the doing of a blessing.'

'How dare you invite a Gypsy into my house?' said Mrs Turber to Beatrice. 'I'll wager there's half my silver in that bundle.'

'I'll guarantee there is not, Mrs Turber,' said Hugh, coming out behind Beatrice and stepping between the two older ladies. 'I asked Mrs Stokes to help in Dr Lawton's absence, and I'll guarantee her good faith or replace your silver myself.'

'A dirty old Gypsy?' said Mrs Turber. 'She's a party to some shame, I'll be bound.'

'Perhaps you heard all about it at the window?' asked Beatrice, barely controlling a spitting rage in her voice. Mrs Turber tried to hide a flush by screwing her eyes into a scowl.

'Turber?' said Mrs Stokes, and Beatrice saw a crafty look come into her eye. 'Would that be the widow of old Captain Turber as had the schooner *Toreador* and shipped the sherry from Spain twice a year?'

'I'll thank you not to sully my husband's name by speaking it,' said Mrs Turber. 'A poor widow and to be insulted in the streets!'

'I will beg your pardon, madam,' said Mrs Stokes. 'I would never wish to insult the widow of the late Captain Turber, nor offer her any words but blessings.'

'He was a much-respected man,' said Mrs Turber. She seemed somewhat mollified to hear her husband spoken of in such a respectful manner.

'I know my old age, and probably yours, Mrs Turber, is protected thanks to certain barrels that might have come in by the beach and not under the excise man's nose,' said Mrs Stokes. 'A very good man, the late Captain.'

'I don't have any idea to what you are referring,' said Mrs Turber. She seemed close to tears. She put a hand to her eyes as if dizzy, and Hugh reached his hand under her elbow.

'I think perhaps the air was warm in the ballroom and you are exhausted, Mrs Turber,' he said. 'May I assist you to your door?'

'Thank you, Mr Grange, I am quite tired, I think,' she said. She seemed almost asleep, slurring her words as the effects of her long evening at the ball took their toll. Hugh assisted the three steps to her larger front door, and Abigail dodged through the passage to open it.

'Here you are, Mrs Turber, safe and sound,' he said.

'Such a shame about that angelic girl,' she said to Hugh as Abigail helped her in at the door. Inside she could be heard speaking loudly to Abigail. 'The Captain never went to sea but he bade me again to mind the pistol he gave me. One bullet to save me, he said, and I still sleep with it under my pillow.'

'Give her the tea twice a day and we're off at the apple picking if you need me again,' said Mrs Stokes to Hugh. She extended her hand to Beatrice, and when Beatrice reached to shake it, she found her palm turned upright and Mrs Stokes squinting at it in the moonlight. 'Children in your future, I see,' she said. 'Best get yourself married off before they come, dearie.' She chuckled with laughter all the way down the hill. Beatrice rubbed her palm as if to wipe away an ink stain, and Hugh looked as embarrassed as at any time in the evening.

'She makes it all up,' he said. 'She's a good healer but a terrible fortune teller.'

'I will not be superstitious,' said Beatrice. She put her hands at her sides and looked at Hugh.

'I need to go home and see to my cousin and my poor aunt,' he said. 'I am so sorry to leave you.'

'Of course you must go to them,' said Beatrice. 'I hope you will let me know how they are, and I will watch over Celeste.'

'She is so very lucky to have you.' He pressed her hand in both of his. 'You are exceptional, Beatrice.'

'But what can I do for her, Hugh?' asked Beatrice, and they both knew it was not just the current illness to which she referred. 'What is to be done?'

'I will speak to my aunt,' said Hugh. 'But let's wait a few days.'

As he turned to leave, Beatrice could not help but speak. 'Will you see Miss Ramsey on your way home?' she asked.

'Miss Ramsey?' said Hugh, his face confused at first and then looking quite shocked. 'Good God, I had completely forgotten!'

CHAPTER TWENTY-TWO

THERE HAD BEEN NO word for Beatrice from Hugh after
the ball, and none of the Kent family attended church
service on Sunday. While she understood the busy nature
of grief, she felt very alone. Celeste did not awaken until
after lunch and kept to her bed, staring at the window
with a glazed and listless air. There was no question of
discussing the previous evening's events, though they
hung over the little cottage like an invisible cloud. Beatrice
knew it was cowardly to avoid the little nook above the
stairs, but she let Abigail give up her Sunday afternoon to
come in and nurse Celeste while she spent the day reading
in her parlour and looking up at every noise outside her
window.

In the early hours of Monday morning, a quiet knock
disturbed her breakfast, and she went quickly to the door,
hoping Mrs Turber would not hear.

'I can't come in,' said Hugh. 'I'm leaving for London by train with my cousin. He wants to go to Craigmore's family.'

'How is he?' she asked.

'Holding up quite well after a day of rest,' said Hugh. He seemed to redden as he spoke, as if he knew as well as she that by such rote conversational rituals they would stave off any real and painful conversation. 'How is our patient?' he added with excess cheeriness.

'She rested all day,' said Beatrice. Unable to speak of the bleeding, she added, 'Her symptoms seem to have subsided.'

'Not that one knows what to wish for in such circumstances,' said Hugh. He shuffled his feet and looked down the hill as if he might see the steam of the train arriving. 'I've left a detailed message for Dr Lawton,' he added. 'And I have confided in my aunt, who asks that you let her know, by note, how things progress.'

Beatrice felt a stab of disappointment. She realised how much she had hoped Agatha Kent would come running up to the cottage, with a basket of beef tea and her matronly cheer, to relieve Beatrice of such a heavy duty.

'I do hope Miss Ramsey was not inconvenienced by events?' asked Beatrice, trying to keep any hint of bitterness from her voice.

'She was all concern,' said Hugh. 'Of course I said nothing of our patient.'

'One would want to protect her from such coarseness,' said Beatrice.

'Nothing to do with delicacy,' he said, stumbling over his words. 'I looked to protect Celeste, and you. Miss Ramsey is a wonderful girl but not burdened with discretion.'

'Please forgive me,' said Beatrice. 'The times are dark, but that is no excuse for me to give offence to you or Miss Ramsey.'

'I wish I did not have to hurry away and leave you with this burden.' He took her hand and pressed it. 'If I did not have to run for my train I would tell you, at greater length, the many ways in which you are to be admired, Miss Nash.'

'Then you might be the one to offend Miss Ramsey,' she said, and though she smiled she found it difficult to look at his face without betraying her pain.

'She is a wonderful girl,' he said again, in the firm tone of a man who hopes repetition will reinforce truth. Perhaps she betrayed her surprise, for he flushed and looked as if he might have more to say to her. But the train's whistle could be heard, out on the marsh, announcing its imminent arrival at the level crossing, and the moment was lost.

'Please know I will be thinking of you and Daniel,' she said. Her heart was a tumult of confusion, and it was a sharp satisfaction not to include Miss Ramsey. But no sooner had Hugh left than she regretted her pettiness. It was not becoming, she thought, and promised that her thoughts in the days ahead would be all for the two cousins and the terrible loss of their friend.

Still thinking of Hugh Grange on Monday, and trying not to dwell on what might have been spoken had the tyranny of the railway schedules not interfered, Beatrice arrived at school to find all in chaos and excitement. Mr Dimbly had enlisted. With no notice to the school, he had followed the call from Colonel Wheaton and signed up right at the fete. He now appeared in his uniform to let the Headmaster know that he would not be conducting classes today but was reporting to the camp on the next train. Miss Clauvert had collapsed in paroxysms of grief in the staffroom, and while Miss Devon vainly attempted to minister to her by dabbing eau de cologne on her temples, children ran amok in the hallways and shrieked in the classrooms. The Headmaster tried to restore order by bellowing in various directions, making menacing moves with his stick as children skipped past the staffroom door.

'Miss Nash, thank goodness you have arrived,' said the Headmaster. 'Please help Mr Dobbins to gather the pupils for an immediate assembly to bid farewell to our erstwhile colleague. Such an unnecessary disruption.' He disappeared in the direction of the library, and Beatrice looked from the distraught Miss Clauvert to the shamefaced Mr Dimbly and took charge.

'Mr Dimbly, since you are here, let us assemble the children so they may give you a proper send-off,' she said. 'If you'll take your form and Miss Devon's, I'll bring Miss Clauvert's room and my own.'

'Of course, Miss Nash. Good idea,' he said, relieved to move beyond the awkward announcement and female tears. He held the door open for her, and as they passed into the hallway, which was, for one moment, free of grubby schoolchildren, he added, 'I was wondering, Miss Nash, if I might ask you to write to me?'

'To write, Mr Dimbly?' she asked.

'At the front,' he said. 'In the midst of all the danger, it would be a comfort, you see, to have letters to keep close to my heart.' He gazed at her in what she could only assume was a meaningful manner. He seemed very red about the ears and almost cross-eyed in his earnest stare.

'You might do better to keep them dry and secure in your barracks, Mr Dimbly,' she said. 'I imagine conditions may become very wet and muddy.'

'I could wrap them in oilcloth,' he said. He seemed confused, as if the conversation were not going as he had hoped. 'I'm not sure what one is supposed to do.'

'If you let me know where to send correspondence, I would be honoured to write you a line now and then,' she said, taking pity on him. 'I am sure I can find a few amusing stories about our little school to pass on to you, if you would find such stories welcome?'

'Thank you, Miss Nash,' he said. He grabbed her hand and kissed it. 'It stiffens the resolve of any soldier to know he has loving thoughts coming to him from home.' He hurried off down the hallway before she could object to such a characterisation. Shaking her head, she dismissed Mr Dimbly from her mind and went to her classroom to begin the herding of her flock.

Mr Dimbly was sent off to war with several loud hymns and a little speech from the Headmaster that managed to telegraph his disapproval to the staff while prompting rousing cheers from the pupils. It was only after all the excitement, when Beatrice finally managed to quell the chatter in her class, that she realised there was another absence.

'Where is Snout – I mean Master Sidley?' she asked Upper Latin. There was an awkward silence and some nudging among the desks, and then Jack got to his feet with great reluctance.

'He went and enlisted,' he said. 'Didn't want us to say nothing until it was all set, miss.'

'Enlisted? Fifteen is not old enough to enlist,' said Beatrice. Her knuckles whitened as she gripped her desk and struggled to keep her voice even.

'Happen his dad signed for him as giving his permission,' said Jack.

'Jack's dad wouldn't give his permission,' said Arty. 'On account of Jack having to do the important war work of managing sheep.' A chorus of baa sounds and laughter echoed around the classroom as Jack turned very red.

'At least I tried,' he said, his voice a hard sneer. 'Some people are too much the coward to even try.'

'Are you calling me a coward?' asked Arty, jumping to his feet. 'I'll have you know I'm in the Scouts, patrolling every night while you sleep safe in your bed like a little girl.'

'Who you calling a girl?' asked Jack, balling up his fists.

'Sit down before I knock both of your heads together,' said Beatrice, her voice fierce. She strode to Arty's desk and stood over him. 'Is this a joke to you, this war?'

'No, miss,' said Arty, sullen as he sat down.

'Both of you, all of you – do you think it makes you some kind of patriot to goad and bully others about enlisting?'

'No, miss,' chorused the class.

'Is this how you honour those like Mr Dimbly who are even now preparing for the front?'

'No, miss,' came the chorus, quieter and more sullen. One of the girls, Jane, started to cry.

'What we must do to support our soldiers is to do the work set before us and to help each other as best we can,' she said. 'It is time to put aside your childish name-calling and your silly games.' There were more than a few sniffles now. Beatrice went to the tall windows and looked out onto the sunny day without seeing it.

'I'm really sorry, miss,' came a voice. It was Arty.

'Me too, miss,' said Jack. 'Me and Arty didn't mean nothing, miss.'

'Did Snout really enlist, Jack?' she asked quietly.

'Yes, miss. Off to big adventures in France and three square meals a day, he said, miss.'

'He's never been beyond Hastings, miss,' said Arty. 'Not as how many of us have.'

'War is a very hard duty, and people die doing it,' said Beatrice. 'I hope you will all listen when I say it is not some schoolboy adventure story.' She went to the blackboard to write the day's quotation with squeaking chalk: *Nulla dies umquam memori vos eximet aevo*.

But today she could not see the glory in the quote's famous promise to dead warriors that time would remember them. All she could see were two young Trojan boys, filled with bravado and youthful foolishness, going together to their slaughter. She remained at the blackboard a moment as she struggled to compose her face, and when she looked around, all the heads were lowered, the sniffling quiet. The excitement of the day had dribbled from the room.

'Who wants to begin translating our Virgil this morning?' she said in as gentle a voice as possible.

After school, Beatrice made her way to the western edge of the town, where businesses and workmen's cottages crowded towards the riverside wharf. The forge was a low, ramshackle building fronted by open stable doors. It was loud with hammering and the smell of horses, and the glow of the fire made the rest of the inside inky black. The small cottage home of the Sidleys was attached to one side, with a low door, painted the kind of brown that suggests left-over paint, and a single polished window with a worn curtain on the narrow ground floor. In a window box some marigolds struggled for existence. Beatrice knocked with the iron door knocker and noted that the step was freshly washed and limed.

'Who is it?' asked a thin voice, and the sound of cough-ing came slowly to the door.

'Beatrice Nash, from the grammar school,' said Beatrice. There was some hesitation behind the door and then a slow turning of the lock, as if it were a stiff and heavy task. The door opened a little, and a woman, Snout's mother, clung to the frame, breathing hard.

'Sorry,' she said. 'I can't catch my breath too well these days. Won't you come in?' She did not wait for an answer but turned back into the house, and Beatrice followed her into the narrow parlour. It was smaller than her cottage, one room deep with a narrow scullery across the back. It was dark, and though the hearth was newly blackened and laid, and the rag rug on the boards clean, the room smelled faintly of soot. There were no settees, just a few wooden chairs set around the edge and a wicker chaise by the fire, to which Mrs Sidley returned.

'I came to ask you about your son,' said Beatrice, perch-ing on a chair. 'They said at school that he enlisted, but he's far too young, isn't he?'

There was silence for a few moments. Mrs Sidley gazed into the unlit pile of paper and coal as if looking at a puzzle.

'Could you put a match to the fire?' she asked, at last. 'Abigail is working and my husband when he gets into the shoeing, he forgets to come and light it for me.'

'Of course,' said Beatrice. She took a long match from a brass cup on the mantel and knelt to strike it against the fender.

'They don't mean to forget me, you know,' she said. 'It's hard to remember an invalid all the time. I don't want to be a drag on their hopes.' She coughed blood into a lace handkerchief. Beatrice averted her eyes to give the woman some privacy.

'Where is your son?' asked Beatrice.

'I don't want to be a drag on his hopes neither,' said his mother. 'But it was awful hard to let him go. Thought I was like to up and die from the pain in my heart right then when he left.'

'Did he really enlist?' asked Beatrice.

'Begged his father for a week to sign the paper,' said Mrs Sidley. 'Said he'd run off and enlist anyways if he said no.'

'But he needs his schooling,' said Beatrice. 'He can do very well.'

'Said he heard it himself the school had no more use for him,' said the invalid, gazing drowsily at the now licking flame. 'Not allowed to sit the Latin Scholarship on account of they still hold his father's family against him.' She looked at Beatrice and gave her a small smile. 'Soon as I saw my husband, I forgot it mattered,' she added. 'All that nonsense – I could see nothing in his eyes but how he worshipped me.'

'Not everyone can – there are many requirements beyond the academic,' said Beatrice, but she blushed to say it and the words stuck in her throat. She hung her head and added, 'There are people who do not want to see your son give up on his studies.'

'Very practical, my children,' said Mrs Sidley. 'Abigail up and tells me blunt like that she don't want to be stuck home after I'm dead, doing for her father and having no life and no children of her own.' She paused to put the handkerchief to her lips again and take several laboured breaths before going on. 'Still, she comes home every night and starts in on the cleaning here,' she said. 'Never says anything about it – just gets on with it like a good girl.'

'I live at Mrs Turber's house,' said Beatrice.

'Oh, I know who you are,' said Mrs Sidley. 'My Dickie thinks the world of you, Miss Nash. Says you would've stuck up for him more, only they don't have so much use for you either there, so you have to be careful, Dickie says.'

'Your children are old souls, Mrs Sidley,' said Beatrice. She felt faint with shame that the boy would make excuses for her own weakness.

'They come from old blood,' said the invalid. 'My father's family has been farriers and smiths about these parts for generations. And my husband's family has been coming through this county same time every year for over five hundred years.'

'That is astonishing, Mrs Sidley,' said Beatrice, ashamed that she had not thought of Maria Stokes's people as anything but ephemeral.

'They got all the stories,' she said. 'Course they don't tell 'em to nobody outside the family.' She paused and then added, 'My husband's grandmother, Mrs Stokes, has a Bible three feet tall with all the records pencilled in it.'

'I know Mrs Stokes,' said Beatrice. Then she hurriedly added, 'Mrs Kent took me to visit her.'

'Good woman, that Mrs Kent,' she said. 'Often comes by with some of her beef tea for me.'

'Seeing as you are so sick, I wonder that you let your son go away,' said Beatrice. 'Won't you miss him?' Snout's mother did not cry, but she seemed to turn a little greyer and worked her dry, wrinkled hands together as if she were weeping. 'I didn't mean to upset you,' added Beatrice. 'I just hate to see him leave school.'

'He is too tender an age to be a soldier,' said his mother.

'But he made his case, didn't he?' said a voice, and Beatrice jumped to see the farrier, a man with a face black from the soot of the fire and shoulders thick from a life of hammering and lifting iron, coming in from the scullery with his arm around his son. Snout blushed as he twisted a new army cap in his hand. His uniform was big for his frame and seemed to be tied to him by its belt like a laundry bundle tied with string. 'Who's to naysay his goin'?' said Mr Sidley.

'I'm Beatrice Nash,' said Beatrice, standing up to show she was not afraid. 'I teach your son Latin.'

'And ye taught him in the summer,' said Mr Sidley. His Sussex brogue was much thicker than those of most of the townspeople and pegged him as a countryman. His eyes wrinkled in the same manner as Mrs Stokes's, and his sharp chin was the image of his son's. 'And he were grateful for it, weren't you, Son? Though like enough he didn't say nothing.'

'He brought me a rabbit once,' said Beatrice. 'It made Mrs Turber scream, but she enjoyed the rabbit stew.'

'It weren't nothing,' said Snout, shrugging.

'You're a good lad,' said his mother.

'He's a lad knows his own business,' said Mr Sidley. 'He came and told me how it is in that school and how much better off he'd be seeing a bit o' the Continent and learning soldiering.'

'He's very bright,' said Beatrice. 'He belongs in school.'

'I was working at eleven, as was my father, and beholden to no man,' said Snout's father. 'So when he come and asked me, I gave him my blessing, my best bone-handled knife and two gold sovereigns, and I told him to go show the buggers that the Sidleys are as patriotic as any other Englishmen and better than most.' He gave Snout a slap on the back that seemed liable to knock the boy over. Snout's mother turned her head away, her crumpled handkerchief pressed to her mouth. 'Plenty boys his age working and married an' all,' added the farrier.

'I thought maybe you had run off without permission, Snout,' said Beatrice. 'I see I was wrong, so I'll not trouble you or your family any further.'

'If you please, miss, I'm grateful for everything you did for me,' said Snout. 'No one ever talked to me like you did, like I was a real person.'

'I wish you would reconsider,' said Beatrice, her voice urgent. 'If you come back, I promise I will fight harder.'

'I'll always remember what you did for me, but I'm glad to be a soldier now, not a schoolboy,' said Snout, squaring his shoulders.

There seemed nothing more to say. She fumbled in her satchel and produced at last her father's copy of Virgil's *Aeneid*.

'Something of comfort on your long quest,' she said. He bit his lip hard to keep from any display of weakness, but as he took it from her, his voice trembled.

'*Audentis fortuna iuvat*, miss.'

'I pray that fortune does indeed favour you, Snout,' she said. How hard it was to hear the famous quote, spoken by a warrior destined to die, dropped from the lips of this boy in an ill-fitting man's uniform.

'We'll be off to the train, miss,' said the farrier. 'He's due back in camp by supper.'

As Snout left, his father's arm again about his shoulders, Beatrice stayed in the doorway to offer her arm to his gently weeping mother.

'He would've run off if we'd said no,' said Mrs Sidley. She sank against the doorframe, and it was all Beatrice could do to keep her on her feet. 'Our hearts are plenty heavy, miss, but at least this way his poor sister and I will get a postcard now and then.'

CHAPTER TWENTY-THREE

THE DEATH OF LIEUTENANT Lancelot Chalfont North, Viscount Craigmore, First Battalion, Royal Flying Corps, only son of Earl North, was announced with solemnity in all the newspapers. Since there seemed no reason to single out his titled family amid a steady trickle of aristocratic deaths, and as the death was not part of a major battle or act of heroism, Hugh was left to conclude that the interest lay more in their ability to accompany the news with a dashing photograph of Craigmore in full flying gear and white scarf, waving from the cockpit of his Farman trainer.

The service in London was to be private and there was a rush to obtain invitations. The saddest of occasions became a social prize and, with the whisper that a member of the royal family might attend, the manoeuvrings among London hostesses were fierce. Colonel Wheaton and Lady Emily had received an invitation, and Aunt Agatha reported that Mr Tillingham had written a letter of condolence running to three pages of praise for the youth – in whose company he had spent such a delightful evening as could never fade from the mind – and had been rewarded with a black-edged envelope.

When Hugh went to tea with Lucy, prepared to apologise again for abandoning her at the dance in Rye, she had been more eager to ask about whether he planned to attend the funeral of his cousin's good friend and whether she might support him with her presence. He tried to answer in a vague manner. He would have been glad to support his cousin, Daniel, if asked, but he could not tell Lucy that Daniel had not received an invitation.

'If we need to be officially engaged . . .' she said, looking demure. From this Hugh understood she would trade much for an invitation.

'I do not expect to be invited,' he said curtly and begged her pardon for leaving early to look after his grieving cousin.

Daniel had obtained leave and come to London, but having sent a note of condolence in which he begged to be called upon to do whatever service the family might need, he had received no communication, not at his father's house, where he went each day to check the post, or at Hugh's lodgings. When he was not keeping busy at the offices of *The Poetry Review*, which had agreed to publish his *David* poem in honour of the young son of Lord North, Daniel lay for hours in a grieving stupor on the cot in Hugh's dressing room and caused Hugh's landlady to weep for 'the poor young man' and his dead friend.

On the evening before the funeral, Hugh came home from a day of field medicine training and drilling exercises to find Daniel sitting on the doorstep of his building, counting pigeons on an opposite rooftop.

'I am shut out,' said Daniel, in response to Hugh's greeting.

Hugh sighed. After a long day, it was sometimes hard to be patient with Daniel, who was as fragile as a pierced and blown eggshell. 'Isn't the landlady home? Must you sit on the step like a vagrant?' he asked.

'I went to Craigmore's home, only to find I am barred,' said Daniel.

'What did they say?' asked Hugh. With some concern for his uniform, Hugh squeezed in alongside his cousin, hitching his trousers at the knees and splaying his feet out from the low step. It was an undignified but, he hoped, supportive gesture.

'I was refused entry by the footman, but I stood fast at the door of the gatehouse, even when they threatened to call the constable,' said Daniel. 'Finally, Craigmore's sister beckoned me from a side door in the long wall and came out into the street to talk to me.'

'You thought her a bland miss, I seem to remember,' said Hugh.

'Only she had the courage to face me,' said Daniel, 'to let me know that I am blamed for Craigmore's death.'

'That's ridiculous,' said Hugh.

'They settled on the Flying Corps to get him away from my bad influence,' said Daniel. 'He had refused all urging to join his father's old regiment, but he could not resist the lure of flying, and his father offered him a commission to give me up.'

'Preposterous!' said Hugh, knowing in his heart it was true. 'Even so, you cannot be held responsible for what happened.'

'A father's loss, a mother's grief,' said Daniel. 'I am to be the sacrificial goat that is to carry all our sins into the desert.'

'And the funeral?'

'I am not wanted,' said Daniel. 'Twenty-four college friends and professors will follow the coffin in cap and gown, but I am asked to stay away.'

'It is cruel,' said Hugh.

'She offered me a ticket for a balcony seat reserved for former tutors, retired retainers and so on,' said Daniel. He did not look offended, but more astonished. 'She risked the wrath of her parents and injury to her reputation, and apologised because it was all she could do for me.'

'At least you can attend then,' said Hugh.

'I refused, of course,' said Daniel.

'Why?' asked Hugh. 'At least you would be in the church!'

'What's a funeral but pageantry and sentimental hymns, and ladies fanning themselves through the prayers while comparing hats?' To Hugh's relief, he stood up and rubbed a hand across his forehead as if to wake his brain. 'I have made my eulogy in the form of a poem. I shall stand in the street in the rain and watch my friend pass one last time.'

'How do you know it will rain?' asked Hugh, making a mental note to make sure he had two umbrellas at his lodgings.

'God would not be so cruel as to taunt us with sunshine,' said Daniel. 'Grief begs for dark skies.'

It rained as Daniel wished, a chill, persistent rain that wilted ladies' hats and lingered in wool coats to chill the watchers in the street and the funeral guests in the cold stone of the church. A large crowd gathered on the roadside to watch the cortège pass. Some came to salute the dead: old soldiers in their medals and a few Chelsea pensioners in their scarlet coats. Many more, whipped into a frenzy of maudlin fascination by the illustrated papers, had come to point and exclaim over the parade of notables and to scan the carriages for any royal guests.

The yellow press had continued to fill their pages with photographic arrays: Craigmore as a child, Craigmore in a rowing blue with an oar over the shoulder, a misty panorama of his family's estate. A newly commissioned photograph showed his sister and his fiancée, weeping around an elaborate fountain in flowing black crêpe and drooping feathers, the one holding a Bible and the other a sword in its scabbard. Even *The Times* had published the funeral programme this morning and featured an excerpt from a eulogising poem. To Hugh's slow-dawning astonishment, as he read lines that seemed strangely familiar, the excerpt was from Daniel's 'Ode to the *David* of florence', reprinted from *The Poetry Review*.

In a street near the church, Hugh and Daniel took up a position in a doorway where they could see the procession from an elevated step and keep off some of the rain. Daniel, who had expressed no elation at being in *The Times*, and who had objected to Hugh running out to buy extra copies, was shivering in his wool coat, with the collar turned up, a copy of the *The Poetry Review* stuffed in one pocket. He insisted on being bareheaded, and his hair was already plastered to his face. Hugh thought this a ritualistic affectation liable to bring on bronchitis or worse.

The sound of bagpipes and drums signalled the coming of the glass-sided hearse, drawn by four black horses. Their feet were muffled in canvas bags, and they wore heavy purple plumes and large black blinkers to shield their eyes from their sombre task. Two footmen rode on the back step and six outriders to either side. The oak coffin, much set with bronze ornaments and heavy bronze rails, was topped with a flag of the family crest and a blanket of red roses.

As the coffin passed, Hugh gripped Daniel's elbow but said nothing. His cousin only shivered and followed the hearse with his eyes, reaching out a hand as it passed down the street. He stared after it for a long time, as if he could see the hearse now turning in to the street in front of the church, now see the long procession of clergy and acolytes with their swinging thuribles of incense and shining brass crucifix, now see Craigmore's coffin placed, with gentle finality, at the foot of the altar.

'We should get out of this rain,' said Hugh. The carriages had long passed and the street was empty now.

'Give me a moment,' said Daniel. Waiting for a lone omnibus to pass, he walked into the road to retrieve a single purple ostrich feather fallen from one of the horses. It was muddy and bedraggled, but he shook it briefly and pressed it inside his jacket to dry against his shirtfront. Then he allowed Hugh to take his arm and together they walked home in the rain.

CHAPTER TWENTY-FOUR

It was a long three days before Agatha Kent made a loud and public arrival at the cottage at teatime, bearing an assortment of foods for the invalid and a gift for Mrs Turber.

'It is so hard to have influenza in the house, Mrs Turber,' she said, on the doorstep, where the neighbours might hear her. She presented the landlady with a large, beribboned box of dainty marzipan confections. 'My husband sent these especially for you from London.' Mrs Turber could only open her mouth silently, like a carp, for surely in accepting the box, she must in all politeness swallow the grand lie with which it was offered.

'Dr Lawton says she is doing much better,' said Beatrice as Agatha swept in at the door. 'She usually sleeps in the afternoon, but I can go and wake her?'

'Lady Emily says they all miss Celeste's piano playing at the hospital, but of course she is to concentrate on getting better,' said Agatha, still pursuing Mrs Turber's complete domination. 'Don't disturb the patient on my account,' she added. 'I just need a word with Miss Nash on one or two matters.'

Shutting the parlour door on Mrs Turber, Agatha moved to the window and stood, slowly stripping off her driving gloves. Her broad driving hat with its thick veil was cast aside on the window seat. She seemed gloomy.

'I began to doubt you would come,' said Beatrice. 'I'm sorry, but so many ladies would wash their hands of the matter, and then I didn't hear from you . . .'

'I hope I never pretended to be somehow above the other ladies of this town,' said Agatha. 'That would be the height of hubris on my part.' She settled on the window seat and tossed the gloves aside onto the hat. 'I fear I am as small-minded as the next woman. The trick is to know it,' she added.

'I am also shocked,' Beatrice admitted slowly. For the last few days she had found it hard to stay in the cottage with Celeste. The long hours in her room scribbling, with little faith and fewer ideas; her desire to breakfast and be off to school so early that the groundskeeper had to let her in at the side door – excuses so that she would not have to smell Celeste's fresh-soaped skin, or look at her body blooming under her dressing gown, or watch her face lit by the dying embers of the fire and witness the loneliness of her melancholy. She had shrunk from Celeste as if her misfortune was sin burned on her flesh. Agatha was silent and picked at a loose thread on her gloves. 'But in my heart I know it is my duty as a woman to fight my own weakness and stand against injustice,' added Beatrice.

'Women will always bear the shame of Eve, it seems,' said Agatha. 'It was the same in my youth, and I fear it will be the same long after we are gone.' She stared out of the window for a long moment, as if seeing down the years. 'War only makes it worse,' she added. 'A soldier dies, and a girl who considered herself promised is left with shattered dreams and a child. This time, the Vicar tells me, he is twisting every rule to get young couples married off in the space between orders and embarkation.'

'What are we to do?' asked Beatrice.

'I have just come from Amberleigh de Witte's house,' said Agatha. 'I went to her to seek sanctuary for our poor refugee. A few months of rest after her "influenza" and the child placed with an accommodating farmer's wife – sometimes such arrangements are made locally.'

'I knew you had not forsaken us,' said Beatrice. 'Miss de Witte is the perfect solution. She does not go about in society and Celeste already knows her cottage. Why did I not think of her?'

'It does us no good,' said Agatha. 'Amberleigh declines to help.'

'But why?' asked Beatrice. 'Surely she knows what it is to be shunned?'

'Exactly,' said Agatha. 'Miss de Witte told me quite cogently what I could do with my request for her help. As she pointed out, with several mortifying examples, I have made no effort to open my doors to her.'

'You have not?' asked Beatrice.

'Miss Nash, I hope I am a sensible woman, but I am not a revolutionary,' she said. 'Their marriage cannot stand scrutiny, and Miss de Witte must bear the stigma of it. I may not invite her to tea.'

'I thought they preferred their solitude,' said Beatrice. 'They have each other.'

'Few marriages can survive such solitude,' said Agatha. 'The woman will pine for company and she will surely push her husband from her arms by a surfeit of domestic attention.'

'They have their work, their writing,' said Beatrice. 'Surely it sustains them?'

'Have you met many writers, Miss Nash?' asked Agatha. 'I find them to be the greediest for social attention. I fear Mr Tillingham may never publish again, given that he is always gallivanting and so rarely confined to his desk.'

'Will you decline to ask Celeste to tea?' asked Beatrice, hearing Abigail's footsteps and the rattle of the tea tray in the hall. Agatha did not reply immediately but waited in silence for Abigail to place the large tray and set out the cups.

'Thank you, Abigail. That will be all,' Beatrice said. 'I can pour for us.' When the maid was gone, she waited for an answer.

'You cannot know how much compassion I feel for Celeste,' said Agatha. 'But while I might continue to ask her to tea as a charitable act, I would not ask her if other guests were expected and I could never invite her to dinner.' Beatrice's hand shook as she poured the tea and some of the Earl Grey slopped into the saucer. 'I tell you a truth so unflattering to me because we should understand our limits, my dear.'

'What should we do?' asked Beatrice.

'I have also written to my late sister's midwife in Gloucestershire,' said Agatha. 'She was always a woman of great discretion. But if all fails, we must look to preserve your reputation.'

'I don't care about me,' said Beatrice.

'It is also unflattering not to be truthful,' said Agatha. 'We are all social creatures, my dear. I do not think you wish to lose your home or your position, do you?'

Beatrice shook her head. 'But I had thought you more progressive, Mrs Kent,' she said stiffly. 'Celeste is, after all, an innocent in the matter.'

'You think me unenlightened, but now it is you who are being blind,' said Agatha, interrupting. 'There is a reason they call it a fate worse than death. Should such rumour spread, then even if there were no child, I fear no man would consider her for a wife or even a mistress, and no women would receive her.' She drank her tea and gathered her gloves. 'I believe this particular taint will endure long after your suffragettes have achieved every dream of emancipation, my dear.'

'It is horrible,' said Beatrice, but she flushed at the truth of Agatha's words.

'You must be wary of contagion,' said Agatha. 'Sometime soon Celeste's condition will become obvious, and then she cannot stay here with you.'

'I fear Celeste is exhausted with despair,' said Beatrice. 'We must take pity on her.'

'Bettina Fothergill will smell pity a mile away and will take delight in burying all of us,' said Agatha. 'Please, understand that cultivating a convincing level of disinterest is the only way to help.'

Beatrice did her best to carry on as usual, but some rumour, perhaps whispered first by Mrs Turber, exerted an influence as slow and subtle as a change in the barometer before an oncoming bank of rain clouds. Mrs Turber's friends continued to come for tea. But where they once came to catch an eager glimpse of beauty, they now seemed more inclined to stare, chewing sandwiches in silence and whispering to Mrs Turber in the passage afterwards. The Belgians in the garden studio seemed to amuse their own children a little more, leaving Celeste to her silent embroidery, while her father borrowed thicker and thicker books from Mr Tillingham's library and read by himself in the window.

At school Miss Devon and Miss Clauvert were noticeably cool towards Beatrice. Whenever she came to take her regular cup of tea in the staffroom, they seemed to pull their chairs closer together in a corner and turn their shoulders against her. But Beatrice put this down to Miss Clauvert's recent discovery of Beatrice writing a letter to Mr Dimbly before lessons began. As she was informed by a severe Miss Devon, after the weeping Miss Clauvert had to go home with a headache, Mr Dimbly had asked Miss Clauvert to write to him and this had been taken as a promise of some kind, against which Beatrice's letter had the appearance of flagrant interloping. Beatrice had little use for such silliness and was glad to be left alone to her morning tea.

Even Eleanor Wheaton had ceased to drop by unannounced or send invitations, but the absence of Eleanor's cheerful excess and generosity, while it contributed to the air of melancholy in the small cottage, did not raise an alarm. Beatrice's failure to notice was perhaps wilfully blind.

It was the ladies of the Relief Committee who finally gave shape and sound to the intensity of excited feeling collected under the huddled roofs of Rye. At an emergency lunchtime meeting, Mrs Fothergill suggested that Beatrice be excused from the discussions.

'I'm sorry,' said Beatrice. 'What is to be discussed to which I am not allowed to be privy?'

'A delicate matter, my dear,' said Lady Emily. 'We think only of your sensibilities and of your position.'

'I have made it clear that I think this is not the place to discuss such a matter at all,' said Agatha Kent, feigning to be distracted with searching for a handkerchief in one of her pockets.

'And you may make such a note in the minutes, dear Agatha,' said Mrs Fothergill. 'But it is my opinion that we have a responsibility to those who donate to the cause and a moral obligation to supervise our guests.'

'I assure you I am not the most sensitive woman in this room,' said Beatrice. 'You need have no fear of shocking me.'

'As a guardian of young minds, you should perhaps be more protective of your reputation,' said Mrs Fothergill.

'I think this concerns her directly,' said Agatha, ceasing to fiddle about her person and looking Bettina Fothergill in the eye. 'If you are bent on bringing the matter forward, Bettina, let the girl know what she is facing.' Beatrice detected a strain under her neutral tone, and her heart constricted.

'I have no objection to her staying,' said Lady Emily. 'We may need her cooperation.'

'I would like to remind everyone that what we discuss here is to be kept strictly confidential,' said Agatha, glaring at Bettina Fothergill. 'Let's for goodness' sake get it over with before Mr Tillingham comes in.'

Mrs Fothergill, given the floor, seemed suddenly hard-pressed to begin. She gave several little coughs and worked her lips as if practising different opening phrases.

'It is completely regrettable, of course, that the girl has suffered an outrage,' she said. 'Mrs Turber is the most Christian and charitable of ladies, and she is in tears at the impossible nature of the situation.'

'Mrs Turber has an unfortunate taste for gossip and all the compassion of a coal scuttle,' said Agatha Kent. 'I find it hard to imagine her weeping.'

'It is hardly gossip, dear Agatha,' said Mrs Fothergill. 'Mrs Turber assures me she would have confirmed nothing had that de Witte woman not already mentioned it to me.'

'What are they talking about?' Beatrice asked Agatha, though she knew at once and she held her breath in shame at the bald way they proposed to dissect and examine Celeste's private pain as if it were just another problem with subscription tallies or the price of soap for the hostel in the lower road.

Agatha looked at her own shoes and grew flushed about the neck, all attempt at disinterest in tatters. Beatrice had never before seen her at a loss for words.

'It has become common knowledge that your boarder has suffered an unmentionable indignity,' said Alice Finch, to some audible gasps around the table. 'Well, ladies, if we are going to discuss it, we should be plain about it,' she added.

'That poor, poor girl,' said Minnie Buttles.

'So regrettable. Such a lovely girl,' said Mrs Fothergill. 'But this is a respectable town, and something must be done, ladies. Mrs Turber has expressed to me, with the utmost discretion, that she would like her out of the house in a week.'

'I will not have her thrown in the street,' said Beatrice.

'You don't have a choice, my dear,' said Mrs Fothergill. 'The school governors are looking askance at the continuation of your arrangement. Your employment is to be discussed at the very next meeting.' She fanned her face with her handkerchief and added, 'I can only imagine what Lady Marbely might say on the matter.'

'It was not her fault,' said Minnie.

'Is this not the cause for which our armies entered Belgium?' asked Alice Finch. 'To avenge such outrages?'

'We do not shrink from our larger duty,' said Mrs Fothergill. 'But it is impossible that in her condition the girl should continue to be received in our drawing rooms.'

'Will you not speak for me, Mrs Kent?' asked Beatrice. She could not manage a voice above a hoarse whisper. Her horror at the crudeness of the conversation was compounded by the shame of being afraid for her own position.

'I could not imagine until now that England might fall,' said Alice Finch, leaping to her feet. 'But what is England if you will not stand and protect one innocent girl from the wounds of tyranny?'

'Some people's social eccentricities have received more protection in this town than they have any right to expect, Miss Finch,' said Mrs Fothergill, her face gleaming with triumph at Agatha's silent acquiescence. 'Perhaps you would care to take her in?'

'It would put my father, the Vicar, in a very strange posi-tion,' said Minnie as Alice sat down again abruptly and glared. 'But we will try if no other home can be found. Perhaps Mrs Kent can take her?'

Agatha shook her head.

'Were she one of our peasant refugees, we might certainly overlook the situation,' said Lady Emily. 'But she and her father dine in our homes and she mixes with our own daughters. I must agree with Mrs Fothergill that to simply move her to another home will not solve the problem.'

'Mrs Kent has attempted to hide this disgraceful situa-tion from us for days,' said Bettina Fothergill, her eyes glittering with pleasure. 'We could not count on her to confine the girl in an appropriate manner.'

'Where is she to go?' asked Beatrice, her sick feeling of shame challenged by a small flame of anger. 'She has already been driven from her home. She is among strangers here. Having suffered so much, is she really to suffer again at our hands?'

'In a new place no one would know her history,' said Agatha, speaking at last. 'It might be for the best for both Celeste and her father to make a fresh start.'

'It would have to be sufficiently far and secret,' said Lady Emily.

'Beyond the reach of less scrupulous persons who might be tempted to forward their gossip,' said Alice Finch, glar-ing at Bettina Fothergill, who only nodded vigorously in agreement.

'Mr Tillingham is well connected to the national refugee committee,' said Lady Emily. 'I am sure he can help arrange for our guests to be accommodated through some other committee.'

'A shame for the poor, dear Professor,' added Mrs Fothergill. 'Such a learned man does not deserve such troubles.'

'Who is to talk to Mr Tillingham?' asked Minnie. 'I should die of embarrassment to speak of it.'

'Mrs Kent is our finest diplomatic voice,' said Alice Finch.

'I believe Mrs Kent may prefer to do the honourable thing and resign from our little committee,' said Bettina Fothergill, and now she adopted a casual tone as if it were all one to her. 'If so, she would not speak for us.'

There was silence around the table. As Lady Emily contemplated her own gloved hands, Mrs Fothergill smirked. Beatrice thought she looked like a house cat whose mouth is stuffed with a child's pet parakeet. At last Agatha spoke, addressing Lady Emily directly.

'You will have my letter of resignation tomorrow,' she said. 'Mrs Fothergill may speak for you instead of me.'

Lady Emily nodded but did not speak.

'It would be bad for the image of our town should it become known in certain circles that the Mayor and I have any hand in such a removal,' said Mrs Fothergill, flustered. 'If Bexhill got hold of it . . .'

'I'll talk to Tillingham,' said Alice Finch. 'I'll tell him what you propose, but I shan't pretend to agree with it.'

'I see Mr Tillingham coming down the garden,' said Lady Emily. 'Let us adjourn now and leave Miss Finch to her unpleasant duty.'

'Just advise him of the urgency and the need for complete discretion,' said Mrs Fothergill. 'They must be quietly gone in a week.'

As the meeting dispersed, Agatha hurried away without speaking to anyone. To see such a formidable force in defeat left Beatrice weak and nauseous, and for a moment she felt as if the rock on which the town was built, rising so immutable from the sandy soil of the marshes, might itself crack and shift beneath her feet.

Two days later, Beatrice came home from school to find her little parlour full of nuns. Abigail was bringing them more hot water for their tea, and Mrs Turber, hovering in the passage, drew Beatrice aside to say, 'They've had two plates of bread and butter and an entire seed cake. So much for a life of poverty and contemplation.'

'What are they doing here?' asked Beatrice. She and Celeste had visited the three nuns at their lodgings to bring them small supplies and to offer translations for their hostesses, the Misses Porter. But Beatrice had not thought to ask them to tea, and they had never called. Celeste was behind the tea tray, offering cups, but she was so pale and unhappy that it seemed no spiritual cheering up was being accomplished by the visit.

'Her father brought them, and then, quick as you like, he went away,' said Mrs Turber. 'Such a wonderful man; I feel so bad for him.'

'If only his daughter was not ordered from her home,' said Beatrice, 'he would be much less to be pitied.'

'It's a terrible shame,' said Mrs Turber. 'Of course, if it was just my reputation, I would keep her . . .' This was such an outrageous untruth that Beatrice was forced to pause and admire Mrs Turber as one might admire an artist's brushstroke while despising the picture.

'I shall go in and join them,' said Beatrice. 'Please ask Abigail to bring me a cup.'

After some talk it became clear that the nuns were to travel north in a few days to join a group of their order who had been invited to take over part of a large convent. They were as excited as schoolgirls to resume their normal cloistered life and were thrilled that out of the ashes of their flight they were to bring to their order such a wonderful new acolyte. With the slight delay that comes with even the best understanding of another language, it took Beatrice an extra breath to realise that they were talking about Celeste.

'Celeste, it isn't true,' said Beatrice.

Celeste gave her a look of pain and defeat. 'It is my papa's decision that I should take my vows,' she said. 'He says I will bring great joy to him and I will have the innocence of an angel in God's eyes.'

'Do you want to take vows?' asked Beatrice.

'They are not a silent order,' said Celeste slowly. 'I can sing and I can learn to play the organ.' The oldest nun spoke in French to tell Beatrice that Celeste's father had made his decision and that she was to have new shoes and a thick wool cloak for the journey, and that the people of Rye had pledged twenty pounds to the order.

'And what of— of the child?' asked Beatrice, stumbling to speak the word to Celeste for the first time.

'Their order takes in unwed mothers and finds homes for such babies,' said Celeste, her hand moving unconsciously to lie on her stomach. 'They do not ask why.'

'You do not have to do this, Celeste,' said Beatrice. 'We will find another way.'

'If I do this, my father can stay here with Mr Tillingham,' said Celeste. 'Otherwise they say we must both make a long journey, and his health, it is not so good.'

'Of course, it's a brilliant solution for him,' said Beatrice. 'But what about what you want?'

'Did you not serve your father faithfully until his death?' asked Celeste. 'Is it not the daughter's place to bring the father ease?'

'My father never asked me to sacrifice the rest of my life and . . .' As she spoke the words, Beatrice remembered her father telling her they were going home to his family, half-way through her last year at their California university. She had pleaded gently, but he had already booked the tickets, a job usually hers, and told the landlord where to send their furniture. In his knowledge that death was coming for him, he had turned to his childhood home as if it were a talisman. She was not sure of all he had bargained to be taken back into the family fold. She knew only that he had been persuaded to put her inheritance in trust and that he had signed papers. She did not care about money, but it had pierced her to the heart to know that after all the years of being his helpmate, he had not given her freedom. He had traded her future for a few months of nostalgia. She looked at Celeste, sitting amid the rough linen robes and starched wimples, and she could only be honest. 'I think it is a father's task to protect us, but if he fails, if he betrays us, we must protect ourselves.'

The nuns, not understanding any English, munched on the last of their cakes with the satisfaction of those who ask only simple pleasures in life and began to rustle their robes and collect their small belongings for departure. As they left, Celeste bowed her head to receive a kiss from each of them. Beatrice nodded but did not offer to take their hands in farewell. They were amiable old women, for whom the sudden interruption of a contemplative life had surely been as traumatic as for any refugee, and she bore them no ill will. But they represented a prison for Celeste.

'There must be another way,' she told Celeste. 'I will not forsake you.' Even as she said the words, she knew it was not a promise she could keep. If she was to lose her job, and with her allowance stopped, she would have no recourse but to return to Marbely Hall.

'I wonder if even the walls of the convent are high enough to hide my shame,' said Celeste in a whisper. 'Even if God forgives, I must always remember.'

CHAPTER TWENTY-FIVE

DANIEL'S POEM IN *The Times* was of great satisfaction to Agatha, as proof, finally, of his true calling as a poet. It was also much remarked upon around the town of Rye as the newspaper was passed from hand to hand, and this was some compensation for the indignity of being eased from her committee by Bettina Fothergill.

In London, the poem was quoted and reprinted in other papers, to accompany the funeral photographs, and when John came down from town he reported that he had heard it set to a popular tune and sung at one of the music halls to great applause. It was not popular, however, with Lord North, and a stiff letter to *The Times* from the great man objected to the crass vulgarity of reporting his son's death with photographs displayed without permission and with florid verses of a disgraceful nature. He did not bother to write to the lesser press, but perhaps his solicitors did, because several of the illustrated papers printed small apologetic retractions. The objections of the family seemed only to add life to the poem, and Agatha found herself congratulated all the more by neighbours whose interest in the literary form was piqued by the spicy hint of scandal. Even Emily Wheaton paused after church to congratulate her, and while Agatha was alarmed to see the effects of popular attention breaching even the reserve of the gentry, she was pleased that all heard their exchange and that it signalled to a scowling Bettina Fothergill that Agatha was perhaps no longer in disgrace.

Agatha had written to Daniel at his barracks, congratulating him on the poem's publication in a muted way, so as not to sound too delighted about a success that had been contingent on a young man's death. She was surprised to receive in return a telegram saying he was transferring from the Artists Rifles and would be coming home on the Friday evening train with Uncle John.

She was waiting at the station when the evening train from Ashford came in. Usually she would have just sent Smith with the car, or even left Daniel to walk up the hill on his own, but on receipt of his telegram that he was homebound, she had given Jenny and Cook a flurry of orders and told Smith that she would accompany him on the station run.

It had felt good to order the sheets aired, fires laid in the bedrooms and hot water bottles filled. The large mutton joint she had been saving for Sunday was ordered to be dressed for the oven, and she and Cook had stood in the larder and debated between opening tins of salmon or smoked oysters and whether the occasion warranted a jar of white asparagus. Cook was of the opinion that the master of the house, and the young man, would both feel more fussed over if provided a steamed pudding, and Agatha agreed to the use of some of their dwindling reserves of sugar and a pot of cherry jam. Devilled eggs and some late lettuce would fill out the menu, and Cook promised custard for the pudding.

Such domestic logistics seemed a preferable response to the paralysis and fear that had overwhelmed her at the news of young Craigmore's death. As if to prove the truth behind an old cliché, the blood had run cold in her veins; Agatha had felt it pumping through her extremities, as if it would escape, and her hands had gone numb. She was not sure how she had arrived home, but she seemed to remember Beatrice Nash supporting her arm to the inn door and John pressing her hand all the way home in the car. If the coldness and the fear were an excessive response for a young friend of Daniel's whose pleasant face she had seen all too briefly, laughing in a hop field, she was not keen to probe further. But in the last few days, she kept thinking of him, and his loss reminded her of the day in early summer when she had seen a fat honeybee staggering in awkward patterns across the stones of the terrace. She had been bold and compassionate enough to scoop it up on a big blue, quilted hosta leaf and carry it to the lawn, but the bee had continued to struggle and buzz in the grass, like an angrily pressed doorbell, until its tiny threadlike legs crumpled and it died. Later the gardener told her that the hive had collapsed, all the bees dead inside their combs, and that there would be no more honey for the year.

The train arrived, comforting in its ordinary timetable and its progress along straight rails, the regularity of its taking in and disgorging of passengers at uniform brick stations, the hiss of the steam and the acrid smell of cinders. John and Daniel appeared, Daniel carrying his kit bag and still wearing his uniform. She waited as the stationmaster saluted, and Daniel and John shook hands with him and exchanged some pleasantries. Then they saw her waiting, and their smiles broke some reserve in her. She hurried down the platform like a schoolgirl and did her best to envelop both of them in a crushing embrace, crying and laughing all at once.

'Steady on,' said John, gently extricating himself in order to pick up the hat she had knocked to the ground. 'Where's my wife and her famous diplomatic reserve?'

'Life is too precious to waste it any more with etiquette,' she said. 'I shall now kiss you in public, John Kent.' As she did so she waited for Daniel to make some outrageous quip, but he was silent, and when she withdrew from her husband's embrace she saw that her nephew's smile could not hide a grim exhaustion. She kissed his cheek and tucked one hand under his arm, taking John's hand with the other. 'Shall we go home?' she asked.

'If you could drop me at Colonel Wheaton's house first, I'm to report in right away,' said Daniel. 'But don't worry, I should be home in time for dinner.'

'Colonel Wheaton's?' asked Agatha. Neither Daniel nor John seemed to want to meet her eye. She stopped with her hands on her hips. 'What exactly does this mean?'

'I've requested a transfer to Colonel Wheaton's outfit, effective immediately,' said Daniel. 'Aunt Agatha, congratulate me. I'm going to France.'

After dinner, Agatha sat on the terrace in the gathering dark, wrapped in a coat against the late October chill, and contemplated how painful the last rays of a sunset could be to a sorrowing heart. John sat on a nearby bench, drinking his brandy as if nothing were happening. She did not speak to him. She could not speak to him. He had done only what he thought necessary to help Daniel, and yet she felt it as a deep and cutting wound, a betrayal. At the far edge of the lawn, Daniel was almost a shadow, a flat silhouette against the sunset sky, smoking a cigar and thinking his own thoughts.

'If there had been some better option, I would have steered him away,' said John. She could feel him looking at her. No doubt with the honest, open expression he used to such effect in the diplomatic world. She did not reply but only drank her tea and stared out at Daniel and the sky beyond. 'I promise you it was for the best,' he added.

'He is going to France,' said Agatha, the words cold in her mouth. 'You promised me he would never see France.'

'I promised to do my best to find him a safe berth,' said John. 'But the circumstances changed, Agatha. He was to be discharged.'

'An honourable discharge,' said Agatha.

'Well, yes, of course they said so,' said John. 'No one suggested there was any case to answer, but there would always have been a question hanging over the whole thing. Lord North's interference made that clear.'

'He would have been safe,' said Agatha.

'At what price, my dear?' said John. 'A life without honour is no life. And I guarantee you a discharge, however honourable, would have been taken as evidence that there was some truth to the wild complaints of Craigmore's father.'

'To suggest that Daniel is a corrupting influence is ridiculous,' said Agatha. 'To defame him simply because he is a poet?'

'Lord North is distraught to the point of madness, and to him I'm sure all bohemians are suspect,' said John. 'A discreet assignment to Colonel Wheaton's regiment was much the best option, and Wheaton was happy to oblige me, believing as he does that I had some hand in getting him and his territorials commissioned as regulars.'

'Did you?'

'I shall not say, so that you may preserve your faith in my powers of influence.'

'Your influence has failed to protect Daniel, so I shall have no more faith in it,' said Agatha. 'I will not let him go to France, John.'

'Agatha, we've talked about this before,' said John.

'Yes, yes, my boundaries as an aunt,' she said. 'I held my tongue at Hugh's enlistment because he is a doctor and will be well behind the lines. Daniel, however, is different. For God's sake, John, Wheaton's men are bound for the front line.'

'One step at a time,' said John. 'They are still in training. No embarkation orders have been issued.'

'Young Craigmore is dead. The fishmonger's boy is dead. I counted five funerals to every wedding in this week's social columns.' She could feel her voice crack as she spoke. She dropped her chin to hide the trembling of her mouth. She did not want to play the weak and weeping female, and yet when she thought of Daniel waving from the window of a troop train, she felt a lifetime of strength and resilience evaporate, leaving her as hollow as a dry straw.

'You must bear up, my dear,' said John. 'I will do what I can, but we must be subtle. Daniel is no less patriotic than the next young man and would be pained to find us against his going.'

'I would sooner go myself,' said Agatha.

'That would surely put the Germans to flight,' said John. 'Unfortunately, they won't have you.'

'Because I am a woman,' said Agatha.

'Because you are too stubborn and opinionated,' said her husband. 'Imagine an army of Agatha Kents – all refusing to do as they are told.'

'You exaggerate,' she said. But though she knew her husband was deliberately diffusing her misery, she was comforted. It was their way. It had been so when he plucked her from the misery of her life after the death of her fiancé.

It was the uniforms that reminded her now. They had been in a hurry to marry because her fiancé's regiment was posted unexpectedly to Suez, and she had been sitting in her wedding dress, waiting in the quiet afternoon for her father to come for her. There was a small munitions explosion at the railway station. A man in a captain's uniform came to tell them. And then the long months in Gloucestershire, where they hoped her sister's help would wake her from her dangerous lassitude. She could still smell the wilting jasmine in her bouquet. And she hated Gloucestershire, to which she had returned only once, for her sister's funeral.

John had loved her in spite of her best efforts to rebuff him. He took her away to exotic foreign postings, where she became a stronger woman. Even when they knew they would have no children of their own, and she tore her hair and blamed herself, he held her sanity together with his small jokes and his kind words. She was always free to beat her fists on his chest and rail against the world, and he would calmly prevent her from her own undoing. She was ashamed to have been as surly tonight as if he had already failed her. She sighed. 'I suppose I should leave all to you and just take pleasure, as I have always done, from each day that Daniel and Hugh can be with us.'

'In so doing I believe you have collected more maternal happiness than a mother of ten,' said John. 'While I enjoy all the benefits of being an uncle without having to pay any of the expenses that accompany fatherhood. I believe we are both blessed.'

'Now who's exaggerating?' said Agatha, who pretended to be unaware that John made modest contributions to the nephews' educational expenses and slipped them substantial drafts at Christmas and on birthdays. While he enjoyed promoting frugality and hard work, he would, she knew, move heaven and earth for either boy. So she smiled and kissed his hand and did not show that she feared this time, with the earth shifting all over Europe, he might fail her.

In the days that followed, such rumours flew about impending embarkation orders for Colonel Wheaton's troops that Agatha grew horribly anxious. While she had every confidence in her husband, he had sent no word, and what if his help came too late? Determined to set in motion a little scheme of her own to rescue Daniel from his foolish stubbornness, she arrived at the Wheaton residence one afternoon with her biggest smile, and a large basket of sausage rolls and cheese straws.

'A gift for the convalescents' tea,' she said to Major Frank, who met her in the front hall. The hall was bare of paintings, and its statues had been draped with tarpaulins, whether to protect them from damage or to protect the soldiers from their bronze and marble nudity, Agatha could not be sure. A desk was staffed by a young corporal, and a large corkboard for messages was wired to the staircase banister. A drugget runner covered the marble floors.

'Thank you, Mrs Kent,' said the Major. 'They appreciate a bit of the homemade at tea.'

'How are things running?' she asked.

'I'm having some trouble accommodating all the ladies willing to play the piano and sing in the afternoons,' he said. 'Between those who can't hold a note, those who keep weeping over the "poor dear men", and those in search of a lightly wounded future husband, many of our patients are asking to take tea in their wards.'

'And my dear friend Lady Emily?' asked Agatha. 'Are you and she getting along?'

'We have our arrangement,' he said. 'Confidentially, my staff and I agree to all her plans and send to headquarters for immediate approval. Approval takes an appropriate amount of time, and so we go on nicely.'

'You sound just like my husband, Major,' she said. 'Confidentially, there are one or two Cabinet ministers with whom a similar arrangement keeps the work running smoothly.'

'Would you care for a tour of the place?' he asked. 'It's almost teatime and I can offer you a strong cup of tea in the ballroom.'

'Actually, I was hoping to see Colonel Wheaton, if he is home,' said Agatha. 'I didn't want to go out to the camp and bother him on duty.'

'The family has retreated to the east wing,' said the Major. 'But the Colonel usually strolls through at teatime to cheer up the patients. May I take you to him?'

The Colonel finished his round of the ballroom and came to sit with Agatha and the Major. The ever-discreet Major Frank made some excuse to leave, and Agatha thought the low hum of conversation and the rather clumsy but enthusiastic piano playing of Minnie Buttles provided enough privacy for her to make her plea.

'Not the most refined tea in the world. I think the army buys what they deem strong enough to take the fur from one's tongue,' said the Colonel, drinking from his substantial green cup and saucer.

'I'm sure it does your officers no harm,' said Agatha. As she looked around the room, her heart sank at the sight of so many cheerful army officers, drinking tea, reading the newspaper, pretending to ignore a bandaged head, missing limb or hard, racking cough. At the next table, a young captain with no visible injury tried to manage a tremble in his hands that clattered his teacup against its saucer and slopped tea on the tablecloth. As Agatha looked away, a nurse brought him a mug from the kitchen.

'They are terribly brave, aren't they?' added Agatha.

'They are the lucky ones,' said Colonel Wheaton. 'Alive and in Blighty – but likely not fit to serve again. For most of these men, their war is over.'

'I wish it were over for all of us,' said Agatha.

'Give me a chance to get in the thing first!' said the Colonel. 'My lot is expecting orders any day now, you know. We want our crack at the Hun.'

'I know you do, Colonel, and I know it is very important to you and to your son to serve,' she said.

'More important to him than to me,' said the Colonel. 'I'm an old dog brought out of the home. I'm happy to have another crack in the field, but Harry – he's got a bright future. This war will be the making of many a young man's career, and Harry has a real chance to advance if he can just get in the thick of things.'

'My nephew Daniel is not a career soldier,' said Agatha. 'He's a very fine poet. Perhaps you saw his poem in *The Times*?'

'We won't hold that against him,' said the Colonel. 'He's doing very well drilling the men. Very promising officer, I'd say.'

'He is a very sensitive soul,' said Agatha.

'You are not to worry,' said the Colonel. He leaned in and patted her hand. 'I know how to measure a man's character and, believe me, we have one or two about whom I am very doubtful. But your nephew is not one of them. He is passionate to get in the fight. This poetry thing is not to keep a man from serving his country, and I will be writing to Brigadier Lord North to say exactly that.'

'Lord North?'

'Yes, the old duffer wrote me some obscure note suggesting I should turn your Daniel out. Something to do with that poem of his. But as I said to Lady Emily, after the man's rudeness in leaving our home without so much as a thank you, I think him quite soft in the head and I shall pay him no attention. Who does he think he is? He might be a brigadier now, but he is not in charge of me.' The Colonel banged his fist on the table for emphasis, which rattled all the cups and made the pianist stumble. Agatha lowered her voice as heads turned.

'Do you mean he sought my nephew's discharge?' she asked.

'Yes. Quite absurd. Seemed to think the poetry was some appalling decadence.'

'He is ridiculous,' said Agatha. 'But I must admit I do fear for a young poet in the heat of battle. You and your son are bred to arms, dear Colonel. Anyone can see you are forged from England's warrior class and never happier than deep in the fray . . .'

'I thank you for your faith, dear lady,' said the Colonel, looking inordinately pleased.

'But I feel my Daniel would serve his country so much the better were he assigned perhaps to an information post. My husband is looking for just such a posting, where Daniel can use his artistic skills to as great an effect as your martial ones, my dear Colonel.'

'I understand your feeling, Mrs Kent,' said the Colonel. 'But your nephew came to me with an impassioned plea to join the first contingent going out. He seemed adamant that he must go and fight.'

'He is a passionate boy,' she said. She could feel her breath coming faster as anxiety closed, like an iron band, around her chest. 'He is not the best judge of his own actions.'

'I tell you he will not accept such a transfer, Mrs Kent,' he said. 'If you and your husband would talk him into a different frame of mind, I would not stand in his way. I have the greatest respect for Mr Kent, and I would send the boy wherever he wishes. But I tell you he won't go.'

'Then you must discharge him, Colonel Wheaton,' said Agatha. 'Not on Lord North's order, but for my sake. I beg you.'

'Mrs Kent, I think you had better reconsider your words,' said the Colonel. He was looking around now, as if he hoped his wife, or Major Frank, might interrupt the conversation. 'He was already threatened with discharge once. Mr Kent asked me, as a special favour, to take the boy on.'

'I didn't mean you should actually discharge him,' said Agatha. 'The threat alone will be enough. Tell him you are put in an impossible position with Lord North.'

'Madam, Lord North insinuates a pattern of moral decadence,' said the Colonel. 'Your husband cannot wish me to threaten him with such vile information.'

'Sometimes we must guide our young people to the right path,' said Agatha. 'I hope I was helpful to your daughter at the fete ball when I advised her to put away her new locket? Some busybody might have enquired how she came to receive it, with the photograph of her husband in his new uniform inside, when all communication with Germany is banned.' There was a long silence between them. Agatha stood up from the tea table and collected her gloves and bag. The Colonel seemed to have developed a small tic in his moustache. 'Now I merely ask you to help my nephew to see reason, Colonel,' she said in parting. 'We have been friends for such a long time that I know we can trust each other.'

CHAPTER TWENTY-SIX

Receiving his embarkation orders, and three days' leave to put his affairs in order, Hugh decided to begin his war by playing the coward; he would take his three days in the country and then join his troop in Folkestone for the crossing to France. In so doing, he told himself, he hoped to avoid marching with all the conspicuous fuss of brass band and bunting to the train. Such elaborate and ritual departures seemed ripe occasions for irrevocable promises, and the truth he avoided was that while his commitment to Sir Alex was clear, he had developed a mild disinclination to resolve anything with Lucy Ramsey.

After her appearance at the dance in Rye, Lucy had become open about a desire to be officially engaged. But every advance she made towards him caused him to retreat. He seemed to stand these days always on his back foot, tipping away from the conversation, excusing himself from the room, leaving Lucy's pretty face puzzled and hurt. His ambivalence was not resolved by the appearance of his orders, and so he had said goodbye casually, at the end of a tea with her father, and left them both with a hearty hand-shake and without any opportunity for tearful embraces.

The train from London was crowded with troops, and Hugh squeezed into the corner of a carriage filled with Scotsmen, who had already made their goodbyes to family in Aberdeen and were now engaged in a raucous and lewd critique of the farewells taking place on the platform below.

'Aye, he's grabbing a handful there. Go to it, laddie!'

'Look a' the poor bugger there with the wife and three babbies hanging off him. The Hun'll be a bit of a holiday for him.'

'That one's so ugly she'd drive a Quaker to sign up. Could he nae have kissed her at home and saved our eyeballs the searing?'

'Don't be disrespecting the poor London lasses,' said another. 'They're no' as ugly as your own wife.'

'He doesn't have a wife; that were his mother!'

The squashing together of so many kilted backsides above thick, veiny legs, and the good-hearted pushing and shoving as the men jostled to thrust their broad shoulders out of the window made Hugh feel awkward. He would have liked them to be less rowdy, and yet he did not wish to be the sort of stiff and ridiculous officer who would ask.

'Second Lieutenant Grange, Hugh Grange?' said a porter, sticking his head in the compartment.

'I'm Hugh Grange.' He tried to speak quietly, but as he looked at the porter, he knew his companions were already rolling their eyes, and he could hear muttering in their thick, unintelligible brogue.

'Someone come to see you off,' said the porter. ''Scuse me, gents.' He pushed roughly through the Scotsmen and stuck his own head from the window to call out, 'Over here, miss.' Then he and the rest of the compartment made a conspicuous effort to push another aside to allow Hugh to the window. Hugh approached with reluctance and a dreadful sense of being watched by rolling eyes and acerbic tongues.

'Hugh, Hugh, I'm here,' said Lucy Ramsey. She was dressed in a sombre grey coat, purple boots and a black feather boa, looking for all the world as if she were in mourning. She was accompanied by two other young ladies, who were already sniffing into their handkerchiefs at the promise of a touching scene.

'You shouldn't have come,' said Hugh. 'It's such a crush on the platforms.'

'I couldn't let you leave without saying a proper goodbye,' she said.

'Go on down to her, sir,' said one of the Scotsmen, and another must have unlatched the lock because Hugh was half propelled from the carriage by the swinging of the door. He stumbled down the step to the platform and into Lucy's open embrace.

'I don't think I can bear to let you leave,' she said, pulling back to tip up her face and to gaze at him with deep yearning.

'But if I stayed you would hand me a feather,' said Hugh, trying to remain jocular. He smiled at the other young ladies and tried to ignore the urge to wriggle from Lucy's arms. The soldiers leaned from the carriage and watched with much interest.

'Of course I expect you to go, Hugh,' said Lucy. 'But what am I to do while you are gone? Every day will be an agony of not knowing if you live or die.' A tear trickled down her pretty cheek, and she bravely let it fall unchecked. Hugh knew he should feel for her distress, but instead the thought came to him that Beatrice Nash would not dream of subjecting him to such a ridiculous scene.

'I assure you I shall be quite safe,' he said, gently disengaging her arms. He immediately felt guilty at his churlishness; she was young, and her distress was not to be so lightly cast aside. He took her hands in his and added, 'The clearing stations and hospitals are some way behind the lines.'

'If only we had some definite hope to which we might cling,' said Lucy. 'I know I made you wait in the most horrible manner, Hugh, but won't you please let me send a notice to *The Times*? It would warm our darkest moments of fear.'

'Give 'er something to hold on to,' said a rough voice, and several of the men laughed and sniggered in a way Hugh might have rebuked had he not wished to avoid enlarging the scene.

'In good conscience I cannot bind you to any promise in these dangerous times,' he said, in what he hoped was a kind but firm tone. 'I would not want you to waste your youth and beauty in mourning.'

'I think I would make a most interesting widow,' said Lucy. She smoothed a wayward ringlet of hair behind her ear and smiled. 'Not that one would wish such a state on anyone, but a sensible woman might use the gravity of the position to great authority in these times.'

Hugh was not sure of the correct conversational response to such an offer – if she had indeed just offered to be his widow. He was searching about for an answer when the train whistle blew and the porter leaned from the carriage behind him to call out, 'All aboard!'

'I must go,' said Hugh. Lucy gave a sob and leaned on his shirtfront in an attitude that would allow him to take the liberty of a passionate kiss. Hugh hesitated above her porcelain face but moved her gently back and took her hand instead. He kissed it, and then kissed the hands of her friends, who seemed gratified to be thus brought into the small drama. As the engine let out a great cloud of steam, Hugh sprang into the carriage and closed the door. He waved from the window at the three weeping ladies and then was gratefully forced inside by a rush of soldiers all wanting to hang from the window and blow kisses and call out compliments and insults as a military band played out the departing train.

The atmosphere at dinner was so tense that every scrape of a fork on a plate sounded like a shot. Jenny the maid sensed the tension, and in trying to tiptoe through it, she became clumsy, clanking the water jug and spilling Hugh's pea soup from the ladle onto the tablecloth. He covered the spreading pool of green with his napkin, and she threw him a grateful glance.

'How was the trip down?' asked Uncle John.

'Crowded,' said Hugh. Another vibrating silence pressed on his ears.

'When do you have to leave?' his uncle asked.

'Monday morning,' said Hugh. 'First train out.' It was not a successful conversational direction because Aunt Agatha smothered a choked sob in her napkin, pushed back her chair with enough force to crack a leg, and fled the room.

'I don't mean to upset her,' said Hugh. 'I'm sure I'll be quite safe.'

'It's Daniel,' said his uncle.

'Of course it is,' said Hugh, sorry for the unavoidable tiny creep of annoyance in his tone. Even his own departure to the front was to be overshadowed. 'He'll be in the thick of things, I know, but does he have any orders yet?'

'I fear Lord North's vendetta may have raised its ugly head again.'

'That's grossly unfair,' said Hugh.

'Colonel Wheaton was not going to entertain Lord North's ranting, but someone persuaded him to pressure Daniel into resigning.'

'Who pressured him? Who would do such a thing?' said Hugh. If the Colonel had planned to ignore the powerful Lord North, Hugh could not imagine who would have changed his mind.

'There's the rub,' said John. 'The Colonel let slip to Daniel that your aunt Agatha forced his hand.'

'Aunt Agatha?' said Hugh. 'That's impossible.'

'Of course she had no idea what she was really doing. She had no concept of how dangerous Lord North's accusations might be. She has no clear picture of the landscape of moral failings his petitions imply, and I confess I am too much the coward to draw a map and show her of what her nephew might be accused.'

'But it's all rubbish anyway,' said Hugh, blushing. 'I know my own cousin, and he would never . . . it's just outrageous.'

'She thinks she knows best, but she has overstepped this time,' said John. 'Daniel left, and we don't know where he went. All we know is that he does not wish any further contact with us.'

'What is he going to do?'

'Your aunt hoped he would resign and accept a commission with the propaganda office in London,' said John. 'Instead Daniel plans to fight it and has demanded a hearing.'

'Good for him,' said Hugh.

'It's a terrible idea,' said John. 'Mud will stick, regardless of the findings, and they may discharge him anyway.' Uncle John sighed. For the first time, Hugh saw an old man's face before him. His vibrant uncle with the smooth diplomatic air was tired.

'It's sometimes easier to manage a war than a wife,' John continued. 'She knows she did something very wrong, and of course this makes her all the more adamant that she was right. She's heartbroken.'

'It will blow over,' said Hugh, but he felt a cold sinking in his stomach at the unimaginable idea of a breach in the family. Aunt Agatha was like a fixed point in the universe, around which they might find another at all times. It was inconceivable that Daniel might cease to lounge around with his feet on the living room sofas, or bother Cook for cake at breakfast.

'Some terrible words were exchanged,' said his uncle.

'I'm sure Daniel regrets his part already,' said Hugh. 'If you have any idea where he might be, let me go and talk to him.'

'I fear talk is too late,' said his uncle. 'There's a hearing set for Sunday.'

Daniel was in Mr Tillingham's study, seated by the fire with his head in his hands. Hugh had been shown up to see them after waiting an anxious few minutes in the hall below, from where he had a good view of the Professor, enjoying a solitary go at the port and some aromatic cheese in the dining room.

'Come in, my boy,' said Mr Tillingham, who looked relieved to see him. 'I fear my meagre capabilities in the realm of advice-giving are all but depleted, and we could use some reinforcements.'

'Hugh does not need to burden himself with my sordid problems,' said Daniel. 'He is leaving for the front, Mr Tillingham, and is not to be distracted by the petty indignities I must suffer.'

'Stop sipping the proverbial hemlock, Daniel,' said Hugh. 'This is no time for exaggerated gestures.'

'What gestures befit my aunt's betrayal?' asked Daniel. 'Is she done washing my blood from her hands?'

'She meant to save you from going to the front,' said Hugh. 'While it is shameful to try to keep someone you love at home while others go in his place, you must see she operated out of love, not malice.'

'She meddled once too often,' said Daniel. 'She has no idea what I am facing.'

'It's not too late to resign,' said Hugh. 'Uncle John is pretty sure he can get you in at the propaganda office.'

Daniel stood up and went to stand by the fire, hands in his pockets, boot on the fender. He turned his face to the light of the flames and was silent a moment.

'Going to France was important to Craigmore,' he said. 'I didn't hear him when he talked about serving his country. I was too busy talking myself.' He turned and gave a small, strained smile. 'I am going to the front to honour Craigmore, to finish what he started and to serve as he so much wanted to do.'

'Craigmore is dead,' said Hugh. 'What you do in the war won't change that. No amount of vengeance will bring him back.'

'It's not vengeance,' said Daniel. 'It's duty. Craigmore believed in doing his duty, and I will not shirk mine sitting in some London office, writing recruiting posters.'

'If the hearing goes badly, you could be drummed out,' said Hugh. 'I don't think you realise just how much trouble you are in, Daniel.'

'I fear your cousin is right, my young friend,' said Mr Tillingham. 'Some twenty years ago, I remember another young man who chose to make such a stand. His stubbornness led to the greatest scandal of the day.'

'You cannot seek to compare Daniel to that playwright,' said Hugh, horrified. He felt sick as the full implications of the comparison sank in. He found he could not look directly at his cousin. 'Why the man was a— He was a flagrant degenerate.'

Daniel looked at his shoes, and Mr Tillingham considered the silver top of his walking stick and rubbed at a spot of tarnish.

'Hubris or nobility – whatever his motives, the fool earned himself jail and a pauper's death,' said Tillingham in a mild tone of reproof, whether for the playwright or for Hugh, Hugh could not say. His eyes looked more tired and hooded than usual as he gazed into the fire. 'The scandal and fear sent many an artist and writer scurrying for the Continent or a house in the country.'

'Not that he wasn't a good writer,' said Hugh, hurrying to soften his high-handed dismissal. He did not wish to play the moral absolutist in the face of Daniel's brooding silence. 'I mean, it was before my time,' he finished.

'Craigmore's father is doing his best to smear our friendship with such shame, and that is precisely why I cannot just slink away and let his insinuations stand,' said Daniel slowly. 'But it is not at all the same, I assure you. They have nothing with which to impeach me.'

'A few letters, a couple of poems – nothing but the effusive exaggerations of the poet in youthful flood,' said Mr Tillingham. 'I have written more effusive and more outrageous letters in my time. They don't mean anything.'

'Would you come and say that at my hearing?' asked Daniel.

'My dear boy, you know there is nothing I would not do for you,' said Mr Tillingham. Hugh saw an expression of horror quickly suppressed. 'But to expose myself to such a topic would surely put at risk my important national war work?' When Daniel did not immediately reply, he continued, as if he might build up excuses like a legal brief and so be excused. 'I am an old bohemian myself,' he wheedled. 'The respectability I have earned is a thin and crusty garment with which I shield my nakedness from public humiliation and scorn.'

'I understand,' said Daniel. 'I would never put you in such an awkward spot.'

'Besides, a couple of my letters meant exactly what they said, and I can't absolutely rely on the recipients not to produce them should my name become mentioned in such a scandal,' added Tillingham, looking frightened.

'I beg you to resign, Daniel, and not endanger your reputation,' said Hugh. 'But if you insist on going forward, I will be a character witness.' He went to clasp him by the hand. 'I've known you since childhood, Cousin, and I will swear on a Bible that your conduct and morals are both unimpeachable.'

'That is very sweet, Hugh,' said Daniel.

'It's not perjury if he believes it,' said Mr Tillingham.

'Mr Tillingham!' Hugh felt himself spluttering, but Daniel and Tillingham only smiled at each other in the manner of people who understand more than they say.

A knock on the door interrupted them, and the housekeeper came in to say that Miss Nash was downstairs with the Professor and that she understood there was an emergency. In the dining room, Beatrice Nash looked alarmed and the Professor looked as anxious as a man can manage after a large dinner, pudding, cheese and half a bottle of vintage port.

Hugh had much he wished to say to Beatrice and wished that he might smile at her. But her demeanour demanded as serious a face as the discussion in the study.

'Celeste is missing,' said Beatrice. 'She said she was coming here to visit her father and when she did not return I came to find her, but the Professor tells me he has not seen her.'

'I have not,' said the Professor. 'Mr Tillingham and I have been here all evening, having dinner.'

'As this is her last night before she leaves, I thought nothing of her visiting you, Professor,' said Beatrice, her tone sharp.

The Professor looked away and polished his spectacles. 'I thought it best to be quiet,' he said. 'To say our farewell in the morning is enough, no?'

'Perhaps not, Professor,' said Beatrice. 'She is very unhappy, and now she has run away or worse.'

'Did she take anything with her?' asked Hugh.

'I don't know,' said Beatrice. 'I'll go at once and look.'

'I'll come with you,' said Hugh. 'Meanwhile, perhaps, Mr Tillingham, you can telephone to my uncle to start searching the roads by car.'

'Daniel, would you operate the telephone for me?' said Mr Tillingham. 'I live in abject fear of the woman at the exchange.'

'Please be careful what you say,' said Beatrice.

'Yes, we don't need to add any more scandals,' said Hugh. 'For once let's hope all the neighbours are not listening in on the party line.'

At the cottage, Beatrice ran upstairs to search among Celeste's clothes and check under her bed.

'They'll have to dredge the river,' said Mrs Turber, calling up from the bottom of the stairs with her arms folded.

'The only thing missing is her white dress with the lace,' said Beatrice coming back down to the parlour. 'I didn't think she was wearing it, but I can't be sure.'

'Is anything else gone?' asked Hugh. 'I hate to ask, but was there money in the house she might have taken?'

'Good heavens, my money box!' said Mrs Turber, hurrying off. A few moments later a shriek went up, and soon Abigail came running to the parlour.

'Please, miss, the money is there, but Mrs Turber's little pistol is missing. The one the Captain give her.'

'Oh no,' said Beatrice. She felt sick and helpless. How could she not have noticed? What kind of friend was she that she let Celeste slip from the house carrying a pistol in her bundle? Did she hear no tremor in the girl's farewell? Did she notice no fear, no set jaw of determination?

'Beatrice, pay attention,' said Hugh. She felt him shake her by the arm, and her head cleared. 'Let us not speculate, let us look for her in a logical way,' he added.

'They'll find her in the river,' repeated Mrs Turber.

'If they do, may it be on your conscience, Mrs Turber.' Beatrice would have liked to scratch at the smug face of her landlady.

'Well I never,' said Mrs Turber.

'You stay here,' said Hugh. 'Daniel and I will search the riverbank while Mr Tillingham and the Professor walk the upper town. My uncle John and his chauffeur are searching all the main roads for ten miles around.'

'I'm coming with you,' said Beatrice. 'I can't stay here and do nothing.'

'The reserves and the Boy Scouts patrol the canal at night,' said Abigail. 'I can run down to the scoutmaster and see if they can keep an eye out for her?'

'I don't think we can,' said Beatrice. She felt the agony of indecision between having more eyes to search and the knowledge that further scandal might be impossible to overcome. She looked at Hugh and saw that he immediately understood.

'I'm sure it won't be necessary,' he said. 'We should not alarm more people than we need. I'm sure we will find her ourselves, in short order.'

'You'll all be shot walking the marshes at night,' said Mrs Turber. 'Mark my words.'

Hurrying to the dark wharf, Hugh, Daniel and Beatrice began to search among the fishing boats and the sailing barges. A night watchman had seen no woman passing, but a cabin boy thought he might have seen a figure slip by on the opposite bank of the river. For a few coins he shimmied up a tall mast to look out across the dark marsh, and he reported a flicker of white that might be a woman's dress, far downriver along the raised dyke.

'Could be nowt but an old sail dryin' on a fence,' said the night watchman. 'A man sees what he's paid to see.'

They took no notice and hurried across the bridge to take the grassy path towards the sea. The houses gave way immediately to scrubby trees and then fields of low, salty grass tussocks, fit only for sheep and goats.

'If she has a pistol, why would she need to go to the river?' asked Hugh, ever practical.

'Because she has a pistol, the river is more likely than the train,' said Daniel. 'The train – you wouldn't need a pistol, but it's messy.'

'You seem pretty sure,' said Hugh.

'Every poet imagines death,' said Daniel. 'The river is the romantic choice. I imagine the pistol is just for insurance.'

'To apply a logical explanation to an irrational act is madness itself,' said Beatrice. 'Do stop talking and hurry.'

The riverbank passed a small hamlet of fishing cottages, and then the river turned one last time and ran straight to the sea. The land was pebbled scrub now, harder to run across, and the riverbank was higher from the water, edged with thick walls of wooden piles and boards. A single hut, black with tar and roofed in old tin, crouched in the darkness. From the shadow of the hut, a lone figure, a woman, stepped to the edge of the river, and as they watched, she flung a white bundle into the water.

'Celeste!' screamed Beatrice. It was hard to shout, all her breath used for running, and she could feel her heart pounding in her chest. As Celeste turned towards them and the moonlight gleamed on a small pistol in her hand, Beatrice's foot slipped on a clump of weeds amid the pebbles and she fell heavily. She rammed her knees and then her wrists on the pebbles as she tried to break her fall. She bit her lip and tasted blood.

'I've got her,' she heard Hugh say, and then his arms were around her, helping her to her knees. 'You go on, Daniel.'

'I have to get to her,' she said, struggling to rise. 'Help me up, help me, Hugh.'

'Slowly now, let's make sure you are not hurt,' said Hugh. 'Probably best we don't all run at her at once.' It was difficult to stand; her knees were on fire and her breath was hard to catch. The taste of blood in her mouth made her gag.

'I can stand,' she said. Her hands and wrists hurt, and she held them against her chest gingerly.

'Let me help you,' said Hugh. 'With your permission?' He put an arm around her, and with his help, Beatrice began to walk a few stiff steps towards where Daniel stood talking to Celeste.

'Faster,' she said. 'I have to save her.'

'Daniel seems to be doing a good job,' said Hugh. As she looked, Celeste moved away from the very edge of the river to sit down on a low post used for mooring the larger ships that docked in the river mouth. Daniel took a similar perch, at a respectable distance. 'Young girls like Daniel.'

'What if he fails?' Beatrice asked. 'I must get to her.'

'My aunt is in grave trouble today because she thought only she could manage the world,' said Hugh. 'Do you think perhaps you might let others help you sometimes?' His face was kind as he looked down at her. She breathed more deeply and leaned against him, thinking that she would like to drop her head to his shoulder and rest there. They stood together a long time and watched Daniel speaking, and Celeste making shy answers, but they could make out no words.

And then Celeste laughed. The sound carried, and it was as sweet to Beatrice's ear as the larks flying over summer marshes. People who laughed did not shoot themselves with pistols or tumble into a cold river, she thought. People who laughed were surely saved.

'If she throws herself in the river now, my cousin will have some explaining to do,' said Hugh. 'Shall we intervene before he inflicts more of his humour on her?'

They sought shelter in the tiny hut. In silence Hugh lit the potbellied stove, which the fisherman owner had left primed with kindling and coal. In minutes Beatrice was warm, and she sat with her arms around Celeste until she too stopped shivering and became rosy in the face from the stove's heat.

A reconnoitering of the tar-smelling hut produced a bottle of rum, sealed with a waxed cork. Daniel wasted no time in breaking the seal and urging Celeste to drink a tot against the chill. They each drank, and with the heat from the stove and the heat from the rum burning its way into her belly, Beatrice felt that she might happily sit in this poor hut for ever. Hugh took a handkerchief doused in rum and gently cleaned her hands of blood and grit. She was sleepy from the late hour and the relief; she leaned against Hugh's shoulder and her eyelids dropped in a pleasant drowse.

'I suppose we should make our way home?' asked Hugh. 'Many people are out in the dark searching for— for us.'

'I am ready to go home,' said Celeste. 'I have to tell my father I am so sorry.'

'We were so worried,' said Beatrice. 'Please tell me you will let us help you, Celeste. I could not bear it if you tried again to end your life.'

Celeste blushed like a penitent child and spoke very quietly. 'I am so sorry to cause you pain,' she said. 'But I could never take my life. It is a sin.'

'But the river?' said Beatrice. 'And the pistol?'

'Our Miss Celeste had planned to be fiendishly clever,' said Daniel.

'I throw my dress in the river so perhaps for a little while I am thought dead,' she said. 'And I leave to another town to take a train to London. In the big city, I can be a differ-ent refugee perhaps?'

'And the pistol?' asked Beatrice.

Celeste's blush was one of pain and humiliation. 'It is not a sin, Mrs Turber says, to shoot yourself to protect from men,' she said. 'Never again would I endure it.'

'Oh, Celeste, how could you imagine such a plan?' said Beatrice. She enveloped the younger girl in a fierce embrace. 'If you must leave, I will leave with you,' she said. 'I will not let you down again.'

'No need to be uprooting yourself, Miss Nash,' said Daniel. He took Celeste's hand and kissed it. 'Celeste and I are two friends, similarly besieged by scandal and difficulty. We will have no more of it and are firmly decided to rout our enemies with a single stroke of brilliance that is, I must confess, all of my own devising.'

'Whatever can you mean?' said Hugh. 'The position is grave, and this is not the time for levity.'

'Hugh, Beatrice, congratulate us,' said Daniel. 'Celeste has agreed to become my wife.'

'Your wife?' asked Hugh. 'Are you quite mad?'

'On the contrary. We are both very clearheaded,' said Daniel. 'There is nothing like contemplating death and exile, as two completely suitable options, to clear the mind.'

'Will Celeste be saved?' asked Beatrice. She felt only the beginnings of comprehension, but she hoped that Celeste, married to Daniel Bookham, would not be a person to be shunned but a woman to be congratulated.

'She saves me,' said Daniel. 'I will walk into my hearing a newly married man with a beautiful young wife. All innuendo and slander will be conquered by the ancient institution of matrimony.'

'But you will be shackled to each other for life,' said Hugh. 'And there is a child.'

'God willing, we may have a child next year,' said Daniel. 'A little early, we imagine, but welcomed.'

'I thought I was the one against marriage,' said Beatrice. 'For goodness' sake, Hugh Grange, it fixes everything.'

'I want Daniel to be happy,' said Hugh.

'I want Celeste to be happy,' said Beatrice.

'Happiness may have a new and more urgent definition in these dark times,' said Daniel. 'I can assure you I have been very frank in my language. I have offered her all the worldly advantage of marriage and all the protection of a brother. She will suffer no harm from me, and we will both live free from scrutiny.'

'It is an unconventional arrangement,' said Hugh, but his face began to brighten with a cautious relief.

'I believe we can forge a comfortable life together from the ashes in which the small-minded have buried us.'

'Do you want to do this, Celeste?' asked Beatrice. She did not know, from the worshipful smile on Celeste's face, whether she understood exactly what Daniel proposed. Beatrice herself was not quite sure, but could find no suitable language in which to press for particulars.

'I am very happy,' said Celeste.

'Be assured, good Beatrice, I shall not fail my wife in any duty she asks of me, nor embarrass her by my actions in the world,' said Daniel. 'Honour and discretion shall see us to our dotage.'

'She is to be married,' said Beatrice to Hugh. Against her will, and due to the rum and consternation, she burst into tears and buried her head in Hugh's coat to cry.

CHAPTER TWENTY-SEVEN

DIFFICULTIES MIGHT HAVE BEEN expected from the tortuous bureaucratic preferences of both Town Hall and church, but as Beatrice and Celeste waited the next morning in the parlour, Daniel and Hugh arrived waving all necessary papers.

'It's the war,' said Hugh. 'The Vicar said better a marriage with no banns than a rash of unwed girls left behind.'

'As Celeste has been coming to services with you and Mrs Turber, he put us both down as members of the parish and sent me to the Town Hall for a licence,' said Daniel. 'With two witnesses and a contribution in the plate, he will marry us at three.'

'And home for tea,' added Hugh.

'Now all that remains is for me to ask your father's blessing,' said Daniel.

'What if he will not give his permission?' asked Celeste. 'The nuns, they come for me at noon.' She grasped Beatrice's hand, her face fearful. 'What if I have shamed him too much?'

'Be sensible, dear friend,' said Beatrice. 'It is an excellent match. He must be pleased.'

'Come with me,' said Celeste. 'Please come with me?'

'We will all go to Mr Tillingham's,' said Daniel. 'That way, when I'm finished getting your father's blessing, I will announce our happiness and we can all watch Mr Tillingham's face when he realises he must break out his best champagne to toast such a happy occasion.'

'If I were a gambler, I would wager against you,' said Hugh, grinning.

It was a happy foursome that walked next door to Mr Tillingham's, where three of them waited anxiously in the front parlour as Daniel and the Professor spoke in Mr Tillingham's dining room. Only the base rumble of voices came through the thick walls, and Beatrice tried not to listen. Instead she tried to distract Celeste with a thank-you letter to Mr Tillingham from the King, for his war work with refugees, which Mr Tillingham had framed in heavy ebony and displayed between a lamp and a small globe on a side table.

'Oh, is that where the housekeeper put that old thing?' said Mr Tillingham, sauntering in to join them. 'I told her to tuck it away out of sight.' Hugh explained, in brief, their mission, and Mr Tillingham did indeed seem to wrestle a moment with a suitable response. To Beatrice's surprise, he excused himself to go and ask the housekeeper to bring some cold champagne.

'You lose your wager,' she said to Hugh.

'I should know better than to bet against my cousin,' said Hugh.

At last the door to the dining room opened and footsteps approached the parlour door. It was Daniel, and his face was set in anger.

'He refuses,' said Daniel. 'He claims Celeste is promised to the Catholic Church and that, despite the welcome they have received at St Mary's, he could never consider a marriage outside the Catholic faith.'

'All is lost,' said Celeste quietly.

'Now wait a minute, there must be some compromise,' said Hugh.

There were more steps in the hall, and the Professor appeared in the doorway. He gave a short bow and spoke to his daughter. 'You must gather yourself,' he said. 'The sisters will be here soon. I trust you know your duty and are ready to do as I ask?'

'I say, this is all rather high-handed,' said Hugh. 'After all the kindness that has been extended, Professor, I think my cousin deserves better from you.'

'Our gratitude knows no bounds,' said the Professor. 'But my daughter is already promised, and I must be free to make the best choice for her life.'

'But this marriage wipes her reputation clean,' said Beatrice. 'It seals all lips and means she can stay here, with you.'

'I cannot convey to you the importance and mysteries of our Catholic faith, dear lady,' said the Professor. 'But please believe a father knows what is best for his daughter.' All the sunlight seemed to bleed from the room, whether from a passing cloud or from sheer despair, Beatrice could not say.

'My marriage may stop the gossip, but he will still know the truth,' said Celeste at last. 'He sends me away because he cannot bear to look at me.'

'It is not true,' said the Professor, but his face said otherwise.

'This is why I went away to the river, Father,' said Celeste. 'So you would not have to look at me and see my shame become more visible every day.'

'There is nothing more to discuss,' said the Professor. 'I have made my decision.'

'If I am to leave for the cloister,' said Celeste, 'then I will make my confession before I go. I will ask Beatrice to fetch Mr Poot, and I will give him my public testimony.'

'You will do no such thing,' said the Professor, growing very red. 'You will be quiet.'

'I will tell him how the Germans came,' she said. 'How you had me put on my newest dress, heavy with the finest lace, and had the maid put up my hair. And how you pinched my cheeks to make them flush and gave me my mother's gold crucifix to hang on my bosom.'

'You will stop now,' said the Professor. 'You all should leave, please.'

'I do think you might allow me the privilege of dismissing my own guests from my house, Professor,' said Mr Tillingham, who had come up unnoticed behind him. 'Personally, I am riveted by the young lady's narrative.'

'You picked sweet-smelling white roses from the garden, and the maid put one over my ear,' said Celeste. 'And tucked one in the very front lace of my bodice . . .' She stood up from her chair and faced her father squarely. He could not hold her gaze and dropped his eyes, shuffling his feet on the carpet.

'You ordered the best china and a bottle of champagne you were keeping for a celebration. Was it champagne for my wedding, Father? You had champagne and brandy served with tea, and I sat in the parlour and waited while the maid urged me to flee. All the servants fled, but you went out to the front door and asked the officer in to tea.'

'I had an obligation to the library,' said the Professor. He looked around the room, appealing for support. 'We had nothing to fear from the Germans. They are civilised people, and we were not some frightened peasants. We stayed to protect the books.'

'And so we drank tea and he made me many compliments and you did not send me from the room but rather you agreed with him and talked of my mother's beauty and of how my sheltered life had made me so fresh and simple.'

'He had sisters at home,' said the Professor. 'He understood the value of my vigilance.'

'I will testify you spoke of your vigilance,' said Celeste. 'But, Papa, why were you not vigilant that day? When we smelled the smoke, when the library was burning, you told me to stay and then you left me.'

'It was to save the books,' said her father. 'The officer gave me men to help carry them to safety.' He paused and added, 'We had a Gutenberg and a book of hours reputed to belong to Eleanor of Aquitaine. We had many priceless rare manuscripts that I saved that day. We carried them to the chapel and stored them in a dry crypt.'

'He gave you men to save your books, but when I rose to go with you, he asked me for more tea and you told me to stay with the officer and entertain him,' she said. 'He put his lips on my ear, Father, and he whispered things so vile I could not breathe.'

Her voice grew dreamy now, as if she were moving away from what she saw in her mind. '*Il m'a enfoncé sur le canapé, et arraché à mes jupons et à mon corsage. Il m'a fait si mal . . .*' She looked at her father and seemed to collect herself, speaking again in English. 'I cried out for you, but you didn't come for me, Father. I watched the hands on the china clock creep so slowly around the dial; and *Maman*, she watched me from her painted frame, and her face was so sad. And still you did not come.'

'I did not know,' said her father. 'I could never have imagined . . .'

'What is the point of sheltering a daughter if you cannot imagine the monsters from which you should protect her?' asked Beatrice.

'I think he knew,' said Mr Tillingham. 'From a purely literary point of view that is the way I would write about it.'

'It is the greater tragedy,' agreed Daniel. 'The larger betrayal: treasure over honour, the value of a daughter weighed and found wanting.'

'What are you talking about?' said the Professor. 'This is not some topic for your interminable literary dinner conversations.'

'Oh, but it is, my dear Professor,' said Mr Tillingham. 'With your daughter safely cloistered away, we shall be free to explore this theme in our work without risking her further embarrassment.'

'Of course one would change the names,' said Beatrice. 'I would change the names.'

'But that veil of mystery may only serve to inflame speculation,' said Mr Tillingham. 'One can't control the public's fever for salacious information.'

'You would not dare to write such slander,' said the Professor. He shuffled to a chair and slumped down, defeated. 'No decent man would seek to bring such shame on another man's name, on the name of a great university.'

'I would never trespass on the good name of my wife's father,' said Daniel. 'I would protect their reputation, and the reputation of my heirs, at all cost.' Daniel was looking at Mr Tillingham as he spoke, and Mr Tillingham frowned; no doubt, thought Beatrice, he was reluctant to forswear such a story.

'Oh, very well,' said Tillingham. 'But it always hurts to come across a rich vein and not be allowed to mine it. I shall grow dyspeptic.'

'Perhaps you need some champagne,' said Hugh.

'Will you give me your daughter, Professor?' said Daniel. 'I vow she shall never be hurt by my hand. I will acknowledge the child as my own, and our doors will always be open to you.'

'Very well,' said the Professor. He made an effort and raised his eyes to look his daughter in the face. 'I will withdraw my objection to the marriage, and if she wishes, for the sake of decorum, I will walk her down the aisle.' He continued to look severe, but his beard trembled as he spoke.

'I would be very happy,' said Celeste. She stretched a hand towards her father but then seemed to think better of it and covered her mouth as she turned away to look out the window.

'Time for champagne,' said Mr Tillingham, masking the awkward pause by taking a bottle from his housekeeper and discreetly shooing her away with a second. 'I think one bottle should be ample.'

As he passed around glasses of champagne, he took Beatrice's arm and drew her aside to a corner of the room.

'Thank you, Mr Tillingham,' she said. 'You have tipped the balance here today and changed lives for the better.'

'Oh, none of my doing, I assure you,' he replied. 'I am much too selfish to spend my time on other people. You should be warned, my dear, that selfishness is a hazard of living alone.'

'I shall be sure to watch for such an affliction,' she said.

'It is only an affliction if one becomes cruel,' he added. He peered at the Professor as he spoke, and Beatrice saw in his eyes some flash of the piercing judgement that suffused his writings. 'Bettina Fothergill saw fit to approach me regarding your position on our committee and, in complete confidence, your position at the school.'

Perhaps it was exhaustion from a sleepless night, or an accumulation of the recent days of anxiety, but Beatrice felt all the fight leave her. She sank slowly onto a hard chair and set her glass on the neighbouring side table.

'I believe I will be asked to leave at the end of the term,' she said. She could not look at him, and so she looked at a white marble bust on the table and noted, with some residual flicker of humour, that it was of Mr Tillingham himself.

'No, no, your leaving is out of the question,' he said. 'I see now I must visit dear Bettina today and impress upon her how much it would inconvenience me were you to leave the town just as you and I are in the absolute thick of things with our book on your father.'

'I don't understand,' she said.

'It's quite simple, my dear,' said Mr Tillingham. 'I have decided I am much too lazy to begin the project again all by myself. It is much more efficient to use your excellent introduction as a basis for one of my own. You will provide a small afterword – purely personal reflections from a loving daughter; nothing of the academic – and we will put our heads together and discuss one or two changes to the letters we include?'

'You don't mean it, Mr Tillingham?' she said, and she peered at him to see if perhaps he was feeling unwell, or overcome by his own champagne. His stern face revealed nothing, but he was slightly red with the effort of appearing so nonchalant.

'On the contrary,' he said. 'It will give me a not insignificant moment of joy to see that woman's smug face crumple like a ball of paper in a freshly lit fireplace. It will quite outweigh the pain of having to compromise one's time or, say, a fifth of one's fee?'

Beatrice smiled and refrained from a strong desire to seize his hand and kiss it. 'People should know that you conceal a soul of deep generosity.'

'I am sure it is merely a temporary spasm,' said Mr Tillingham, looking horrified. 'Pray do not mention that which would only incite further demands on my time and purse.'

'Then perhaps we can agree that twenty-five per cent of the fee would suitably secure my full cooperation and my silence?' she said, laughing.

Daniel and Celeste were married quietly in St Mary's at three o'clock in the afternoon. Her father supported her down the aisle, and Beatrice and Hugh were witnesses. Mr Tillingham was the only guest, his role being to look severely at the Professor from time to time. Hugh had urged that their aunt and uncle be present, but Daniel had been adamant that they not be told. Beatrice could see the dismay on Hugh's face, and her heart ached at his distress. Daniel sent a telegram to his father, expecting a row, but was surprised to receive curt congratulations and notice of a substantial bank draft by return. As Beatrice heard Mr Tillingham whisper to Hugh, while they filed into the church, his father's relief must have overcome any scruple about such a sudden marriage.

Standing in the lofty old church, resplendent with polished brass and the scent of late chrysanthemums in tall vases, Beatrice was filled with a rare sense of peace, with a feeling that the world did come right sometimes. She looked at Hugh, with his serious face, standing so upright and listening hard so as to be ready when called to sign the register. She thought him like her father, but then was forced to acknowledge that her father had been less dependable, less upright. Her father had often been spontaneous to the point of damage. He had given up positions, changed apartments, and fired valets, all at the most inconvenient of moments. His final journey home had been no better considered than so many of his schemes.

She could not imagine Hugh Grange having any sudden schemes – and that seemed like a perfect quality in a man. As they each threw a small handful of rice at the bride and groom in the churchyard, she wondered if she would see more of him before he went away. She had seen no engagement notice in the papers yet, and this gave her a strange comfort, unearthing some warmth of feeling she had long ago decided to lock away. She would be resolute in damping any such longing as might disturb the life she had made. But as she threw rice at the bride, she allowed herself the hope that he might ask her to take a walk with him.

'I hope all goes well at Daniel's hearing tomorrow,' she said as the bride and groom left in a hansom cab for the train to Hastings and the hotel suite that Daniel had arranged. He would bring his bride and his hotel bill direct to the morning's hearing.

'So do I,' said Hugh. 'If all is resolved, we will leave for France together on Monday morning.'

'France?' asked Beatrice, her heart constricting in her chest.

'We're both bound for the front,' said Hugh. Beatrice felt ill. The front was no longer a grand adventure. Britain's Expeditionary Force was being slowly decimated at Ypres as the opposing armies entrenched in a grim line across Flanders. The outcome of the war was no longer the rousing certainty so touted in the papers.

'I wish you Godspeed,' she said, as all her small hopes shrivelled away in the enormity of his departure.

The hearing was over before it could start. In the rough hut used as the Colonel's headquarters, Celeste's beauty, in a sober dress and a new pair of white gloves from Beatrice, dazzled the Colonel and his small group of assembled officers. Daniel asked the Colonel's blessing on his marriage, and the Colonel looked as relieved as a man reprieved at the scaffold. It would have been almost comical, thought Hugh, to have seen the Colonel try to conduct the hearing. It was surely a topic for which he would have had great difficulty uttering any of the words.

The young couple said their goodbyes on the parade ground, and many a soldier peering from the tents or passing by in formation wiped away a tear to see young lovers parted too soon by the regiment's impending embarkation. Hugh was to accompany Celeste home, and Daniel asked him to convey the news of his marriage and his departure to their aunt and uncle.

'Ask them not to come to the station,' said Daniel. 'I would not like to be discourteous to them in such a public arena.'

'What about me?' said Hugh. 'I'm leaving on the same train. Am I to have no one to wave me off?'

'You must do as you please,' said Daniel. 'I would not deny you that comfort. I can get the sergeant major to hide me under a seat, if I must.'

'I will say my goodbyes at home,' said Hugh. He had a horror of what a scene might ensue at the train station. 'What arrangements have you made for your wife?'

'I'm afraid I have made none at all,' said Daniel. 'I suppose there is an allowance due her? I assumed she would continue to live where she is. Beatrice will take care of her.'

'I don't think it will do,' said Hugh. 'She should go to your father.'

'Good God, no,' said Daniel. 'Better the nunnery after all. What should I do, Hugh?'

'I will talk to Uncle John,' said Hugh. 'Perhaps they will take her in.' He tried to keep his tone neutral, but he was desperate for Daniel to agree. Such an arrangement might be the key to restoring Daniel to the family in due course.

'It won't change my mind,' said Daniel. 'But I would be grateful to you, Hugh, if you could speak to them tonight.' He grinned and shook Hugh's hand. 'See you on the train tomorrow. Let the real war begin.'

The Colonel arranged for Hugh and Celeste to travel back to Rye on a heavy dray loaded with supplies bound for the station, and Hugh walked Celeste home to Beatrice's cottage, where she was welcomed with an effusion of exclamations and good wishes by Mrs Turber, on whom Celeste's marriage had exactly the desired effect. It was to be hoped she would spread the good news as effectively as she had whispered the bad.

'I must go home,' Hugh said to Beatrice, lingering on the doorstep. 'I must try to repair the breach between Daniel and our aunt and uncle.' He looked worried, and Beatrice longed to help him.

'Will they be very angry about the marriage?' she asked. The enormity of what they had done, conspiring to bind Agatha's nephew to Celeste for life without her knowledge, weighed heavily on Beatrice.

'These are difficult times, and what is done is done.' He paused. 'Daniel and I leave in the morning, and I wanted to ask – would you write to me?'

'I got into a spot of trouble for agreeing to write to Mr Dimbly,' she said. 'I was not aware that letter-writing implied some other sort of attachment.' As she said it, she knew she was being coy and the words spilled awkwardly from her tongue. She hesitated and added, 'I would not like to offend Miss Ramsey.'

'There is no obligation or attachment implied,' he said. He hesitated and then added, 'It is always pleasant to get correspondence when one is far from home.'

'Then I will be happy to write?' she said, with a question in her voice.

He seemed to be struggling with some emotion. He caught up her hand and pressed it. 'I cannot truthfully tell you I am entirely free of obligation to Miss Ramsey,' he said. 'I am ashamed to say I may not have behaved in the most forthright manner.' He hesitated again and went on. 'But I can tell you that she and I have no formal claims on each other.'

Her heart leaped as she waited for him to say more. He looked at her so intently that for one bright moment, she thought he might embrace her. 'Hugh?' she asked, his name carrying a new intimacy.

'I fear the time is never right,' he said. 'I leave for France and I would not for the world ask anything of you while I am not free.'

'Then your friendship must be enough, Hugh,' she said, and though her eyes grew blurry, she would not shed tears to spoil his going. 'And we will write to each other as friends.'

'You are the best of women, Beatrice Nash,' he said, and raised her palm to kiss it.

'Shall I come and see you off tomorrow?' she asked, though she wondered how she would endure it. She felt the same yawning loss she had felt at her father's going. She fought away the image of the cold river and the dreadful ferryman. Unlike her father, she prayed, Hugh would return.

'Please do not,' he said. 'I would not expose you to the vulgarity of a railway-station departure.'

'I will think of you often,' she said, blinking back tears.

'If all goes well with my aunt and uncle, I think they will come for Celeste,' he said. 'Will you be all right by yourself, Beatrice?'

'I am used to my independence, Hugh,' she said. But as he walked away down the steep cobbled street, she had to hug her arms about her to keep from calling him back. Never before had she understood so clearly what independence might cost. She had never felt so alone.

Part Four

Now, God be thanked Who has matched us with His hour,

And caught our youth, and wakened us from sleeping,

With hand made sure, clear eye, and sharpened power,

To turn, as swimmers into cleanness leaping,

Glad from a world grown old and cold and weary,

Leave the sick hearts that honour could not move,

And half-men, and their dirty songs and dreary,

And all the little emptiness of love!

RUPERT BROOKE, 'War Sonnets 1: Peace'

CHAPTER TWENTY-EIGHT

THE CIGARETTE DID NOT seem to help the shaking in his hands, but Hugh persisted in trying to force the acrid smoke into his lungs in the hope that it would at least clear out the stink of dried blood and iodine from his nose, his throat and every pore of his skin. He knew he should wash and get to the officers' mess for his dinner, but exhaustion made it pleasant just to sit in the lee of the hospital's sun-warmed doorway and smoke the cigarette passed to him by the stretcher-bearers as they headed out again for the long trip to the front.

The base hospital, to which he had been assigned since landing in northern France the previous autumn, was in a small village a few miles from the coast. It occupied an old winery, itself adapted from a medieval abbey. The ancient stone seemed to gather and radiate cold as the winter deepened, and the few windows let in little light, but at least the thick walls muffled the echoes of the big guns, which could be heard faintly to the east. Hugh had quickly found he hated playing the surgeon, making the morning rounds of the rows of the injured and indicating, with a crook of his finger, which cases he would take for the day. After a few weeks he had instructed his nurses that he would choose only three head-trauma cases a day. For the rest of his shift he was to be sent any case considered most pressing.

Hugh often lost track of his hours as he stood on a brick floor slick with blood and worked through an endless train of stretchers heaved on and off his operating table. He rubbed his hands together slowly, his fingers dry and sore from hot water, carbolic soap and the brush with which he cleaned his hands between patients. He never skimped on his hand-washing, even when the nurses were holding together ripped arteries, even when he could hear the patients breathing blood. He was deliberate in his movements, moderate in the tone of his commands and calm in the face of the most appalling injuries. This had earned him notice from his superiors such as he had long sought in his medical-school years, but he took no interest in their praise now. The dream of acclaim and fortune as a surgeon, with a prosperous practice and a tall house in Harley Street, had been rendered insignificant and empty in the face of the daily carnage. His calm was merely a numbness that saved him from insanity.

He drew one last drag from the cigarette, feeling it burn to his fingertips, and resisted the urge to let the flesh burn. He dropped the butt and ground it under his boot, which was caked in blood, dirt and great purple streaks of iodine. He stood up and stretched, moving his shoulders to slough off the twelve hours of hunching over wounded flesh in the shadows made by poor lamplight. The air was cold this

early evening in late February, but at least it was not raining. It seemed to be always raining in France, a particularly
spiteful gift from providence, never fierce enough to stop
the fighting but damp enough to make every day painful.

'Good night, Dr Grange.' A pair of nurses, swathed in
long wool cloaks and thick boots, passed out of the doorway. He found his throat too dry to answer so he merely
waved and watched their starched linen caps bobbing down
the road like two white doves, incongruous against the
bleak, muddy landscape. They had surprised him, the nurses,
with their quiet endurance. It was harder for the women.
Not because they were weaker, but because the patients,
seeing a woman's face, that halo frill of a cap, would so
often clutch for a hand and beg a momentary word of
comfort – a plea for pity that no man would impose on him,
the doctor. The job was hard enough encased in numbness
and ticked off on medical charts. How much harder must it
be to have that veil of professional ice pierced many times a
day by a dying man whispering a message to his mother?

'Mr Grange, I mean Lieutenant, sir?' The voice was familiar. 'Is that you, Mr Grange, sir?' The skinny private buried
in the collar of an oversized wool trench coat was leading a
rickety civilian cart pulled by a grey wolfhound with one
ear. The small cart was overloaded, its cargo securely roped
under a canvas tarp. It could not have looked less like a
proper military shipment if it had been covered by a circus
tent. The boy pushed back his cap, and Hugh's tired brain
slowly registered the angles of the face and the sharp eyes.

'Why, Snout, is that really you?' he asked. 'What are you
doing here?'

'I'm in the war, same as you, sir,' said Snout, grinning.

'I mean what are *you* doing *here*?' said Hugh, stepping forward into the road to shake his hand. 'I thought Colonel Wheaton's outfit was up north?'

'We were brought down to fill in some holes about twenty miles east of here,' said Snout. 'We've been a bit in the thick of things, sir.'

'Is my cousin with you?' asked Hugh, trying to appear casual but gripped about the heart by the sudden fear of a bad answer.

'Yes, sir, he's fine,' said Snout. 'They laugh at him for writing his poems while they're waiting to go over the top, but he's always first over when the signal comes.'

'And Harry Wheaton?'

'Got a piece of shrapnel in his arm and got promoted to captain,' said Snout. 'Confined to camp, but he's still giving orders, and I'm his batman; so here I am tramping the entire countryside on his say-so.'

'What's in the cart?' asked Hugh.

'Colonel Wheaton's after giving a regimental supper, and Captain Wheaton sent me out to procure the necessary fancy stuff, like ham and champagne and tins of something called "foyes grass",' said Snout.

'Foie gras?' said Hugh. 'You do not have foie gras on that miserable-looking cart!'

'I don't know as I do, sir,' said Snout. 'On account of I can't read the foreign writing on the tins. But the man I got it off swore it was, and Captain Wheaton'll have to make do. There's a war on.'

'Will you come back to my quarters and have some tea, Snout?' said Hugh. Snout hesitated, and Hugh added, 'Look, I know it's against regulations, but I'm so happy to see a face from home, and I have some biscuits I've been saving for just such a special occasion.'

'Come on, Wolfie, there's biscuits for us,' Snout said, tugging at the dog's harness. As Hugh fell in alongside the rather foul-smelling Wolfie, Snout turned to Hugh and broke into a large smile that showed he was still just a boy. 'Well, Mr Hugh,' he said. 'People seem to think they can ask an old Gypsy like me to go round the regs all the time. But no one ever invited us for tea, did they, Wolfie old boy?'

Hugh smiled back, suddenly ashamed. In the back of his mind he had planned to ask Snout to carry a note to Daniel, also against regulations. He had assumed like everyone else.

'I think I have some potted meat too,' said Hugh. 'If the wolf doesn't mind partridge.'

Hugh had planned to spend his two-day leave on the coast, where an officer who made it known that he was amenable to paying whatever the bill was might be sure of a plate of fresh oysters, a good roast dinner and a bottle of red wine unearthed from the hotelier's private cellar. How the hotels managed to produce their small luxuries in the midst of war was a mystery to Hugh, but on his last leave he had been brought almost to tears by the appearance on his plate of a chocolate truffle.

Instead of the coast, however, his meeting with Snout had prompted him to request a pass to tour the forward aid posts and inspect the transportation of the injured between the front and the hospital. A week later, pass in hand, he hitched a ride on an ambulance going east, hoping to reach his cousin's billet by nightfall if Snout's highly individual directions proved accurate.

'If you was to inspect us and find us wanting, do you think they'd have to send us home?' said the driver, a fleshy corporal with a stained jacket and an unlit cigarette, which he had stuck in his mouth as soon as they left the hospital checkpoint. He leaned forward to wipe the fog of condensation from the windscreen. Outside a misty rain added misery to the road's bleak landscape of mud, dead trees and apparently endless convoys of lorries, horses and men moving slowly in both directions.

'It's not really an inspection,' said Hugh, thinking that war seemed to consist too much of this endless parade of troops and vehicles forever marching somewhere else. 'It's just me having a look round, trying to get out of the operating room and get a better feel for how it all works.'

'He's just having a look round, Archie,' repeated the driver in a thick Cockney accent. 'A day trip, like?'

'We can give you the full tour, guvnor,' said Archie. 'With a stop at the souvenir shop on the way home, right, Bill?' They both laughed, and Hugh heard the insubordination but knew how they felt. His casualty station was always being visited by dignitaries – from senior-ranking army officers to the occasional lady journalist – who seemed to have no problem getting orders that allowed them to poke around and interrupt even the operating rooms with ridiculous questions and requests to review reports and logbooks.

'My only cousin is a lieutenant somewhere over towards the ridge there,' he said, nodding forward to the dim line of low grey hills in the distance. 'We haven't heard from him in a while, so I'm hoping to see him.' There was a small pause, and then the driver, Bill, spoke in a less jocular tone.

'Been a rough time up there,' he said. 'They had to call us in to help a few times, and we was piling 'em in, right, Archie?' Archie was quiet and looked out of the window. Bill fumbled in his pocket and produced a match, which he struck against the dashboard and used to light his cigarette.

'I'm sorry,' said Hugh.

'We lost two of our stretcher-bearers, and they lost more from who was up there already,' said Archie.

'Last week we seen a bearer come staggering out of the trenches, covered in blood,' said Bill. 'A shell took out his partner and half the poor sod they was carrying, and he was so gone in the head he didn't even notice.' He laughed and sucked hard on his cigarette.

'Is he going to be all right?' asked Hugh.

'We gave him a shot of brandy and a cup of tea and pointed him back in the right direction,' said Archie. 'Long as you got both legs and both arms, you're qualified to carry stretchers.'

'It's been a bit quieter since,' said Bill. 'Expect your cousin is holed up in a nice dry cellar, sir. Playing whist and eating mulligatawny.'

'I doubt that,' said Hugh.

'Some mix-up with the quartermasters,' said Archie. 'Sent this area twenty thousand tins of mulligatawny. Everyone's sick of it.'

'You can get two tins for a twist of baccy,' said Bill. 'Not that we would be trading government supplies, of course.'

'Of course not,' said Hugh.

'Locals are sick of it too,' said Archie. '"I say, got any pandy burr?" and they wave their hands about. "Non, non, pas di mully-tawnaay," they say.' Hugh smiled at Archie's phonetic approximation of the French *pain beurre*. It was surprising how quickly the British Tommies had adapted the French language for their own use, though their vocabularies seemed to cover only food, booze and swearing.

'I heard some enterprising lad pasted chicken soup labels on his mully tins and sold 'em to a local farmer for rabbits,' said Bill.

'I heard the locals been pasting on labels of everything from pâté to spotted dick and selling us right back,' said Archie. 'Somewhere along the line someone's going to get shot, if you ask me.'

'So are you fixing up the injured?' asked Bill. 'We just drop the poor buggers off and never get no reports of whether they live or not.'

'We have a good system now from the casualty station onward,' said Hugh. 'Of course some of them never get past us. If they are too far gone, we give them morphine and offer to pass on any messages to their families.'

'We got our own system,' said Bill. 'Anything more than three quarters of a man and we bring him in. Less than that, we give him a cigarette and keep his morphine for some other poor sod. Funny thing, but they don't seem to feel the pain when they're that far gone.'

'Funny business all around,' said Archie. 'Cigarette, guvnor?'

The ambulance let him off outside the ruins of a village that was little more than half a church and a huddle of cottages with all the thatch burned from the roofs. Beyond the village, shell-pocked woodlands rose gently to the low hills. An encampment of British army tents made a new village, clustered around a small barn on a riverbank.

Harry Wheaton looked up from a long trestle table and gave a shout of welcome as Hugh entered the barn. 'Good God, you're a sight for sore eyes, Grange,' he said. 'Any news from home?'

'I had some letters yesterday,' said Hugh. 'My aunt and uncle are doing well, but Miss Nash wrote to tell me, among other things, that your sister's nanny is leaving in rather a hurry.'

'Letters from Miss Nash, you sly dog?' said Wheaton, raising an eyebrow. 'So what does Miss Nash say about Fräulein?'

'Some whispers of suspicious activities and letters from Germany,' said Hugh, ignoring Wheaton's insinuations. 'Nothing proven, it seems, but enough fuss that your family found her a job in America and paid her passage.'

'Poor Fräulein,' said Wheaton. 'I told Eleanor she would put the poor woman in difficulties.'

'What has Eleanor to do with espionage?' asked Hugh.

'Nothing, nothing at all,' said Wheaton. 'Perhaps a few love letters. Perfectly harmless, but I told her she should not involve the German nanny.'

'I see,' said Hugh.

'Eleanor always does what she wants, as if no rules apply to her,' said Wheaton in a breezy tone. 'I'm glad she is safe, and I'm sure Fräulein will love America.'

'Have you had letters?' asked Hugh.

'Been a bit hairy up this way,' said Wheaton, indicating his arm, which sported a large canvas sling. 'Mail was the first casualty of the shelling. Still waiting for deliveries to resume.'

'Did a doctor look at it?' asked Hugh.

'Flesh wound,' said Wheaton. 'Not enough to win leave. The old man has me in charge of putting on a full regimental dinner, like I'm a factotum from Claridge's, but I suppose I should be grateful for the brief respite from the fire trench.' His face grew stiff and grey as he spoke, and Hugh could see that even Harry Wheaton could not pretend the front line was some sort of gentleman's adventure.

'How is the Colonel?' he asked gently.

'Between you and me, he's a bit old for this kind of war,' said Wheaton. 'Impatient with all the digging-in and wants to be in Berlin by Tuesday.'

'No one quite expected the efforts to bog down like this,' said Hugh. The battle lines, so fluid in the autumn, had gradually become fixed all over Flanders and northern France, and over the winter the armies had dug increasingly elaborate networks of trenches. It was a slow, grinding way to fight, and Hugh's hospital received a steady flow of the injured, not just from large offensives but from the snipers and shelling that made every day some middle ring of Hell.

'It's a new way of waging war, that's for sure,' said Wheaton. 'I had to explain to the Colonel that it is not unsportsmanlike to use the machine guns and barbed wire.' He grinned again and rubbed his cropped hair impatiently. 'Funny thing, when so many are worried about their husbands and sons, that I'm out here worrying about my father,' he added.

'Quite the HQ you have here,' said Hugh, looking around the dark barn, with its cavernous rafters, mud floor, and canvas tarpaulins screening a few stalls in the rear. There were piles of tables and folding chairs to one side and a heap of bunting waiting to be hung for the festivities. Two soldiers worked a large wooden box radio in one corner, and the smell of cooking came from a tented area beyond a side door. 'Where do you keep the regimental silver?' he asked.

'Silver and full dinner service is coming up from the coast by cart today,' said Wheaton, consulting some large plans spread on the trestles. 'Real meat is hanging in a cellar. Soup is in cans. The cooks are making some new dessert with surplus Christmas puddings, and we have champagne in the icehouse.'

'So much planning,' said Hugh. 'One wishes such detail went into our offensives.'

'An army marches on its stomach, and the senior officers like to be well fed,' said Wheaton. 'This could mean another promotion if all goes well.'

'I hear young Snout – Dickie Sidley – has been helping you?' said Hugh. 'Good of you to keep the boy back from the front line.'

'Scrappy sort of lad and a real nose for foraging,' said Wheaton. 'Sorry to say he got badly shelled last week.'

'Is he all right?' asked Hugh with alarm. He imagined the thin boy bloody and lifeless.

'He's fine, but his bloody dog ran off after the blast, and the boy keeps wandering off looking for it,' said Wheaton. 'I've been trying to make excuses for him, but any more and he'll get himself shot as a deserter.'

'May I take a look at him?' asked Hugh. 'We've been getting a lot of shelling victims who seem disoriented. I'm trying to document their symptoms.'

'I sent him up to your cousin in the trenches,' said Wheaton.

'But he's just a boy,' said Hugh, with horror.

'Exactly,' said Wheaton. 'I wasn't joking about the deserting. I thought the boy would be safer with Daniel. Less chance to wander off in a small trench.'

'I'd like to go forward and see them,' said Hugh. 'Can it be arranged?'

'They'll be down tomorrow,' said Wheaton. 'Perhaps you haven't heard, but Lord North has been made the new brigadier of this command.'

'You can't be serious?' said Hugh. 'Craigmore's father? The man's an ass.'

'He's coming to dinner with our regiment tomorrow, and there will be a full-dress drill and parade before the dinner,' said Harry. 'You are invited, if you're staying.'

'Thank you, I'd be delighted,' said Hugh. 'But I really would like to go up and see the conditions for myself. I'm sort of on an inspection tour.'

'Bloody unusual request,' said Wheaton. 'Most are asking to go the other direction. But be my guest. I'll have someone lead you up as soon as the evening bombardment is over.'

'Bombardment?' asked Hugh.

'Regular as clockwork, first thing in the morning and right after teatime,' said Wheaton. 'We pound each other to pieces for an hour or two, and then the rest of the day we wash our socks and play draughts.'

The walk up the lines was dark and treacherous. The smell of smoke and gunpowder hung in the mist, and fires burned in shell holes all along the low ridge where the sandbagged front fire trenches faced the German lines in the valley beyond. Long dark slashes in the earth showed the communications trenches zigzagging back towards the rear, where troops on duty might snatch a few hours of sleep in rotation. Further back more platoons were bivouacked in reserve in whatever shelter they could find. As Hugh was led up, parties carrying water barrels and food jogged up ahead and several teams of stretcher-bearers came down, carrying the injured and dead from the evening's action.

Hugh found Daniel settled in a stone hut, half built into the hill and providing stout cover from stray shells. His men were camped below the stone wall of a pasture and had fashioned shelter from blasted tree limbs and canvas sheets. Small fires were banked to boil water for tea, and as Hugh stood in the doorway of the hut, he felt the strange domesticity amid a hellish landscape. The door of the hut was covered with an old sheet. Hugh gave a loud cough, and a voice invited him to come in.

Daniel was reclining on a folding cot, reading a book by candlelight. A small fire burned in a stone hearth, and a pot of soup simmered. In a corner of the hut, the boy Snout lay asleep on a pile of straw, covered by a rough blanket. A second cot was empty. A couple of small watercolour sketches tacked to the wall and a bedding roll suggested that a second officer shared the cramped quarters.

'I must be dreaming,' said Daniel. 'My cousin Hugh on a rambling holiday through France?'

'Just passing by coincidence,' said Hugh. 'Smelled the soup.'

'It is mulligatawny,' said Daniel.

'I heard as much,' said Hugh. In a moment, Daniel was on his feet and he and Hugh embraced. It occurred to Hugh that in all the long years of affection, they had never hugged each other, or so much as slapped each other on the back, and he thought it sad and strange that it would take a war to wipe away the cold formalities of life.

'War makes our needs so much smaller,' said Daniel. 'In ordinary life, I never understood how much pleasure it gives me to see you.'

'You are too kind,' said Hugh. 'Have you heard from home?'

'Aunt Agatha has sent me many letters, Hugh,' he said. 'And I am trying to find the forgiveness within me to write back, but I have only burned many drafts.'

'I brought all my letters to show you,' said Hugh, taking a small oilskin package from his coat. He was disappointed in his cousin's stubbornness, but the evening was too precious to start an argument. 'Is that cot free for the night?'

'Yes,' said Daniel. He hesitated and then added, 'My old pal Worthington, from the Rifles, drilled through the head by a sniper two days ago. I must send his paintings to his wife.' Hugh did not know what to say, and Daniel jabbed a smoking log further into the fire.

'How is the boy?' asked Hugh at last, nodding to the sleeping Snout.

'All a bit too much for him, what with the shell destroying his cart and the dog running off,' said Daniel. 'No injuries we can see, but he is definitely a bit off his head. I'm trying to get him sent home, but it's not so easy, even though a fool can see he's not nineteen.'

'Does he fall asleep at strange times?' asked Hugh. 'Only we've been seeing cases of this sort of neurasthenia.'

'Hard to wake him up too,' said Daniel. 'You know there's something off when a boy sleeps through the smell of a fried breakfast.'

They drank soup, and a batman brought in a hunk of strong cheese and a fresh baguette. Where there might still be a local bakery producing bread, Hugh could not imagine, but the baguette tasted of peacetime.

'Something about fresh bread in this place makes you want to cry, doesn't it?' asked Daniel. He offered a flask, and Hugh took a sip of strong rum. 'I've been trying to explain in a poem, but I'm miles from capturing it; something about sun-warmed squares and girls giggling in other languages and friends walking through summer landscapes with a backpack and no responsibility . . . blah, blah.'

'Most of the hospital bread is mealy and tastes of the tin it came in,' said Hugh. 'Plenty of sustenance in the British army, but not a lot of taste.'

After their simple meal, Daniel offered Hugh a spare pipe from Worthington's bedroll and the two cousins smoked and tended the small fire.

'Is it that our needs grew smaller?' asked Hugh. 'Or is it just that the fear and deprivation makes one appreciate simple things more?'

'I think our ability to be happy gets covered up by the years of petty rubbing along in the world, the getting ahead,' said Daniel. 'But war burns away all the years of decay, like an old penny dropped into vinegar.' He paused and added more tobacco to his pipe, tamping it down slowly and relighting it with a stick poked into the fire. 'Here there is nothing but doing our duty; and when duty cannot turn aside the stray sniper's bullet, one gives up the hubris of thinking man can control his destiny.'

'War is truly humbling,' said Hugh. He thought of his early attempts to save those with the head injuries, and how his written notes became more hurried, and more bloody, and how he stopped taking notes at all because all the notes in the world could not change the truth that those with holes in their skulls mostly died and that he could save more people by operating on almost anything but the brain.

'It's a kind of freedom,' said Daniel. 'I am free, not from fear of death, but from believing I can control death.'

'The warrior poet speaks,' said Hugh. 'I foresee much rhyming of *mud* and *blood*.'

'You joke, but perhaps now I could really write about the *David*,' said Daniel, his face earnest. 'Not as a beautiful shepherd boy, but as a frightened young soldier who knew his duty.'

'David thought God protected him,' said Hugh.

'Which makes him no different from any soldier who goes over the top,' said Daniel. 'Pray to God and keep your knees bent!'

'I'll drink to that,' said Hugh, taking another swig of standard-issue rum from Daniel's flask. 'Good God, you could run a lorry on this stuff.'

'Good old Hugh,' said Daniel, laughing. 'You always keep me steady. No use talking poetry with you, although you might appreciate one or two limericks I've been collecting from the men.'

CHAPTER TWENTY-NINE

DESPITE BEING ONLY A couple of miles from the German lines, Colonel Wheaton had insisted on a full brass band to accompany the drill and parade. The regiment was hosting Brigadier Lord North and high-ranking officers from several other regiments, and no German menace could be allowed to diminish the prestige of the occasion. The Brigadier came with a small army of aides and, shackled in a wagon, a group of prisoners who had been court-martialled for various capital crimes but not yet shot. The executions had been delayed by a bureaucratic issue: the absence of a chaplain to offer them the required pastoral offices. Unfortunately, the Colonel was discovered to be importing a chaplain to lead the dinner's opening invocation, and so the festive occasion would be followed by firing squad at dawn. Neither the Colonel nor the chaplain, who had made the trip on the promise of a fine dinner and would now spend the night with the condemned, was happy.

A stage of wooden planks nailed over barrels had been erected from which the guests might enjoy a view of the parade. Horses had been groomed and beribboned, uniforms had been brushed, muddy boots scraped and polished, and every man had been harried and insulted by the sergeant majors until they and their equipment formed sufficiently presentable ranks. Those just down from the trenches were staged at the perimeter, where their dirtier uniforms might be less noticeable, along with the way they swayed on their feet with tiredness. Given past animosities, Harry Wheaton had made sure that Daniel's unit was well to the rear, away from the Brigadier's eye. In the front ranks, senior officers had unwrapped dress uniforms and swords, and the Colonel had imported, along with the regimental silver, the official regimental ram. The ram wore a scarlet coat trimmed with gold braid and gold tips to his curly horns. He maintained a grimace as disdainful as that of any general and tossed his head, pulling on his heavy brass chain whenever he spied a patch of grass.

As an unofficial visitor and lower-ranking officer, Hugh watched the stamping about and marching discreetly from a shady patch of ground to one side of the stage. It was surreal how similar the proceedings were to festive military parades at home, and Hugh almost expected to see ranks of ladies with sunshades and children waving flags as the units marched past the tiny stage. Only the occasional *crump* of unseen artillery reminded him that they were in an active theatre of war.

After the marching, the Brigadier and his entourage were invited to inspect the troops, and went slowly up and down the ranks with Colonel Wheaton leading them and Captain Wheaton bringing up the rear. The band took a break during inspections, and in the quiet, Hugh heard the flapping wingbeat of a lone crow flying across the valley. He had not seen many birds recently, as they seemed to have an aversion for the blasted landscapes created by men, and so he was busy watching as a commotion broke out in the cookhouse by the barn.

A grey form came cantering from the tents, and Hugh could see it was a huge dog with an immense joint of roast beef dripping in its jaws. The appetising smell of the hot beef caused many eyeballs to swivel in the heads of men frozen to attention. A piercing whistle from the ranks caused the dog to stop, turn and trot obediently towards one of the rearmost ranks, where it dropped its prize at the feet of Private Dickie 'Snout' Sidley.

'Bad Wolfie,' said a boy's voice, carrying across the open space as Snout caught the dog by the collar. 'Where have you been?'

'What is that scurvy animal doing on a British army parade ground?' growled the Brigadier, moving swiftly in Snout's direction.

'Sorry, sir, begging your pardon, sir, I'll take him away, sir,' said Snout, directing his plea towards Daniel as a child might turn to the adult he knew. He bent down and picked up the meat in his two hands.

'Do not speak unless spoken to, Private,' said Colonel Wheaton. 'And for goodness' sake, someone take away this beef.' One of the cooks, who had hurried from the kitchens, stepped forward with a dish and took the piece of meat.

'It's ruined, sir,' he said. 'Not fit for anything.'

'Can I have it for Wolfie, then?' asked Snout. 'He likes a bit o' beef.'

'Is the boy an idiot?' asked the Brigadier as the cook gave Snout a cuff around the ear and hurried away. 'Do we recruit imbeciles?'

'Captain Wheaton?' asked Colonel Wheaton.

'Lieutenant Bookham?' asked Captain Wheaton.

'With permission, sir,' said Daniel. 'The boy suffered in the shelling and the dog was thought lost. They are both recovering, sir.'

'Injured in the shelling, sir,' said Harry Wheaton.

'I am not deaf,' shouted the Brigadier. 'I can hear what the Lieutenant said.'

'Sorry, sir,' said both Wheatons together.

'Lieutenant, is this animal an officially registered military animal?' the Brigadier asked.

Daniel raised an eyebrow at Harry, who replied, 'No, sir, Brigadier.'

'Was that government supplies he was carrying in his mouth, Captain?' asked the Brigadier, turning to Harry.

'It did appear to be part of the regimental dinner, sir,' said Harry. 'Though to be fair, the dog and his cart were instrumental in Private Snout's duties concerning the procurement of many parts of the said dinner.'

'I want it destroyed,' said the Brigadier. 'It's a disgusting mongrel and a disgrace to the name of the regiment.'

'Yes, sir,' said Colonel Wheaton. Harry Wheaton looked upset but said nothing.

'Permission to speak, sir?' asked Daniel.

'Lieutenant Bookham – Daniel Bookham – I believe?' asked the Brigadier.

'The dog was sort of commandeered when Private Snout found him abandoned, sir,' said Daniel. 'He pulls a heavy cart, sir, and he has been rather useful.'

'Lieutenant, why does it not surprise me that you speak up for such egregious lapses?' said the Brigadier. 'The dog is a thief and his upkeep is a misuse of resources. We are not going to win this war without standards.'

'He's no thief,' said Snout, turning very red. The insult, thought Hugh, hit close to home for the boy. 'He's been lost for days and he was starving. He only eats scraps normally.'

'Destroy it now,' said the Brigadier, nodding to Harry Wheaton. He had already turned on his heel to move along when Snout dropped to his knees and flung his arms around the dog's neck.

'You can't kill him, you can't,' he cried. The dog licked his weeping face with an improbably large tongue. 'He ain't done nothink. He's just a dog.'

'Captain,' said the Brigadier. 'Destroy the dog and put the private on charges for disorderly conduct. Make sure he's thoroughly thrashed for his behaviour.'

'Sir, he's just a boy, sir, and he's been hit by a shell,' said Daniel.

The Brigadier turned back slowly, and a smile with no humour in it twisted his lips. 'Colonel, it appears your lieutenant wishes to be also brought up on charges,' he said. 'I would be delighted to accommodate him, but I am prepared to overlook his insubordination so as not to dampen the festivities.'

'Permission to remove the private, sir,' said Daniel, looking to Colonel Wheaton.

'Yes, yes, do it quietly,' said the Colonel.

'No, no, you shan't kill him,' screamed Snout as Daniel signalled two corporals to drag him away.

'Snout, do as I say, it's for the best,' said Daniel, coming close to the boy's face and placing a hand on the now growling dog. Whether Daniel had some plan to rescue the dog, Hugh could not say. He was hurrying around the edge of the parade ground, trying to get to Snout and Daniel in an unobtrusive manner, when Snout got an arm free and punched Daniel squarely on the jaw, sending him sprawling to the ground.

The Brigadier motioned to someone in his own entourage. 'Take the private into our custody and put him with the other prisoners,' he said. 'Striking an officer is a capital offence. Boy or man, he will answer for it at dawn.' The soldier assisted the corporals, and it took all three of them to drag the screaming, kicking youth away.

'I'm unhurt,' said Daniel as some of the men helped him up. 'It was just an accident.'

'What a pity,' said the Brigadier, coming close to Daniel and leaning in to lower his voice. 'Once again you cause the end of a young man's life.' He gave a short laugh and drew away to signal the Colonel.

'Harry?' said Colonel Wheaton, giving his son a nod. Harry drew his service pistol and walked over to the dog.

'Steady there, boy,' he said, and rubbed the dog's ears. To Hugh's surprise the dog stood very still, almost as if he knew, and Harry shot him cleanly behind the eye. As the grey body slumped to the ground, Snout, being dragged beyond the barn, let out a howl every bit as animal as a dog's and haunting enough, thought Hugh, to affect the hardest of hearts.

'Good,' said the Brigadier. 'Let's dismiss the men and get to our dinner, shall we?'

Daniel would have spoken again, but Hugh reached him in time to grip his arm very hard. Harry Wheaton holstered his pistol, his face a little pale but otherwise seemingly unperturbed.

'Best ask for any clemency after dinner,' he said. 'Pass the port and then ask your boon of the king, so to speak.'

'The men are our responsibility, Wheaton,' said Daniel.

'Standing in the breach is all very well,' said Harry. 'But do try to avoid getting cashiered or worse for insubordination, Bookham. I know you have past animosities with Lord North. Let's be jovial over the junket and I'll try and put the Brigadier in the mood to be merciful.'

'I'm not hungry any more,' said Hugh. 'You persuade the powers that be, Harry. I'll keep an eye on the boy.'

There were five prisoners in the old, roofless sheep pen. They were all so dirty and scabby that it was hard to tell their ages, ranks, or even that they were British. Each huddled alone, sitting with knees hugged to chin or lying curled in a ball, scratching casually at the lice that plagued most Tommies. They were not shackled, but their faces showed an apathy that suggested they were no threat to the two privates guarding them. One man had begged a cigarette, another example, thought Hugh, of how the lowly cigarette had become the last small flame of humanity.

'Medical inspection,' said Hugh, showing his large medical bag and hoping his rank and RAMC insignia would hide his lack of official permission to approach the prisoners.

'Yes, sir,' said the guards, stiffening into an apathetic sort of attention. Their salutes would not have passed muster with the Brigadier, and Hugh wondered if they knew how thin the line was between them and their prisoners.

'At ease,' said Hugh. 'Who are these prisoners?'

'Criminals, malingerers and deserters, sir,' said the shorter lad, who had a pimply face and a curling lip. 'All court-martialled and to be shot in the morning, sir.'

'Usually the Brigadier has 'em shot on sight, but he was coming here, wanted to make a bit of a show of 'em,' said the second guard. 'To boost morale in the rest of us or something, sir.'

'Have they had food and water?'

One guard looked blank and the other shrugged. 'We just took over, sir,' said the taller. 'We just watch 'em, sir.'

'They may be criminals and deserters,' said Hugh, 'but they are British soldiers and we are British soldiers. Perhaps you've heard our Brigadier insist that standards must be maintained?'

'Yes, sir,' said the taller one. The alarm in his face suggested he knew of the legendary wrath of the Brigadier.

Hugh decided he was the more amenable to orders, and he put on his best frown to speak. 'The condition of these prisoners is your responsibility, Private. Go to the kitchen immediately and fetch a billycan of tea and some bread and butter.'

'Yes, sir!' said the private and saluted briskly before jogging off.

'I'll be looking them over for injuries and any contagious infection,' said Hugh to the remaining guard. 'Do you need to escort me?'

'I'll be able to see from right here, sir,' said the guard. His lip lost its curl of disdain, and he looked suitably anxious. 'Contagion, sir? You be careful there, sir.'

Hugh made a cursory stop by two of the men. One had a nasty cut over his eye, suppurating at the edges. Hugh gave him a small bottle of iodine and a handful of gauze and told him to clean himself up. The soldier with the cigarette had trench foot as bad as Hugh had seen: strips of wrinkled white flesh peeling about the ankles, toes bleeding and black with broken scabs. A strong odour suggested the beginnings of gangrene. Hugh gave him a packet of morphine for the pain and a pair of clean wool socks to cover up the sight of the feet. If he were not shot in the morning, he would need a proper infirmary or risk losing his feet.

The other two seemed dirty but unhurt and were dozing comfortably, and Hugh moved on to his real objective, the corner of the pen, where Snout lay crumpled and unconscious in a patch of weeds. He had a black eye, a split lip and blood still seeped from his nose. When Hugh reached to turn him on his back, he groaned and struggled feebly.

'Keep still, Snout,' said Hugh. 'It's me, Hugh Grange. I'm going to clean you up.' The boy nodded his head slowly. He kept his eyes closed, but tears leaked from under the lids and down his bloody cheeks. Hugh felt for broken bones and checked the boy for internal injuries. He had taken one or two blows to the stomach, but there was no blood under the skin. The soldiers who had dragged him away had made the boy pay for his struggling and lashing out.

Hugh used gauze and water from his canteen to wipe off the boy's face and then dabbed his cut lip with iodine and gave him a water-soaked pad to hold over his bruised eye. Finally, he helped him to sit up, his bony back propped against the stone wall.

'They shot Wolfie, sir,' said Snout, his lip trembling. 'Is he dead, sir?'

'He's gone, Snout,' said Hugh. 'He went quietly, like a good dog. You should be proud of how you trained him.'

'It were all him, sir,' said Snout. 'I didn't do nothing but buckle him to his cart.'

'I'm sorry,' said Hugh.

'He made me feel brave, sir,' said Snout. 'The war is nothing like they say it will be.'

'I know what you mean,' said Hugh. 'It's not quite the glorious classic epic of Virgil, is it? But you needn't be ashamed of feeling fear, Snout.'

'Miss Nash gave me her own Virgil,' said Snout. Hugh closed his eyes a moment to better hold on to a fleeting image of Beatrice's face, conjured in a ruined sheep pen. 'But it got blown up,' he added.

'Right now, you are in a lot of trouble, Snout,' said Hugh, opening his eyes and doing his best to snap both of them back to the present circumstances. 'Do you know you hit Lieutenant Bookham?'

'Did I?' said Snout, looking astonished. 'He's a good man, the Lieutenant. Always gives Wolfie the crusts off his sandwiches.' The boy seemed to fall asleep, and Hugh shook his arm gently.

'I need you to understand what is happening, Snout,' he said. 'You need to be ready to face a court-martial in the morning.'

Snout's eyes opened and he smiled a dreaming smile. 'Thank you for having us to tea, sir,' he said. 'Wolfie liked it.' The boy fell fast asleep, and though Hugh shook him again, he would not wake up. Hugh laid him gently on the ground and took from his bag a small blanket, a paper bag containing a bread roll, and a canteen of water. He wrapped the blanket around the sleeping boy and tucked the supplies under it, hoping none of the other prisoners would notice. The boy breathed quietly, and his pulse was steady and strong. Hugh could do nothing more for the moment. Reluctantly he left Snout to sleep.

'The boy over there is underage and injured,' he told the guard at the gate. As they were speaking, the second guard returned with a large can of tea and a box of sandwiches. Hugh frowned at both guards. 'He has also not yet been court-martialled. If anything happens to him I will hold you both responsible and you will answer to the Brigadier. Are we clear?' He left both guards muttering and suitably cowed – but whether by Hugh's own authority or by the mere mention of the Brigadier, he could not guess.

Hugh was lying on the ground in Daniel's tent, trying to ensure his greatcoat stayed in place on top of his blanket and pulling extra socks over his gloves against the bitter cold, when Daniel came into the tent drunk and shouting for joy.

'The sentences are commuted!' he said. 'The regiment asked publicly to honour the occasion with clemency and the Brigadier did his full wise Solomon speech and got a standing ovation for his trouble.'

'I am so very relieved,' said Hugh. 'Is the boy free?'

'I expect there'll have to be a hearing in the morning,' said Daniel. 'But given the night's precedent, Harry has full faith we shall get him back in the ranks with a few weeks' pay docked for his impudence.'

'Who did the asking?' said Hugh. 'Not you?'

'Oh, I kept well out of the Brigadier's sight,' said Daniel. 'But Harry Wheaton actually took on the job. Threw in one or two entirely fraudulent Latin quotes and several metaphors involving fox hunting. God help him if anyone wrote it down – because I'm sure it would be unintelligible to those who were not drunk on champagne and good roast beef – but it did the trick.'

Dawn broke ugly and red in a sky swelling with dark clouds and so cold the mud froze in the rutted lanes and the water was solid in the washing jugs. Instead of birdsong, the boom of large artillery greeted the sun, and the encampment was soon full of urgent, shouting men, the stamping of horses and roaring engines. As the sound of exploding shells and smoke began to drift down towards the village, Hugh, hurrying to the barn headquarters, wondered if perhaps the parade, and in particular the brass band, had been such a good idea. The Germans seemed to have recalibrated the range and direction of their artillery, and already a shell had landed in the river and another whistled overhead to explode in the already-ruined church.

Inside headquarters, the Brigadier had a scowl on his face that implied a headache of monumental size. He was not inclined to be flexible in his plans when it was suggested he leave immediately for safer ground.

'We will not win this war if we duck and cower at every fresh bombardment,' he said. 'Let them understand that we are the oncoming tide and their efforts are no more than small boys tossing pebbles into the waves.'

'I would be derelict in my duty if I did not insist on taking appropriate measures to protect such a vital part of our command,' said Colonel Wheaton. 'You and your aides must be able to command from a secure place.'

The Brigadier was not entirely immune to flattery. 'Then let us adjourn to the cellar and make this quick,' he said. Tables and lanterns were quickly carried into the adjacent cellar, a small outbuilding half built into the ground, with thick stone walls and a roof of grass sod. Hugh moved quietly to where his cousin was standing with Harry Wheaton to ask what was happening.

'I'm afraid the Brigadier regrets the appearance of softness in offering clemency to the prisoners,' said Harry Wheaton. 'Since he cannot go back on his word to the regiment, he has decided to make an example of the one prisoner who has not yet been sentenced and therefore did not receive clemency.'

'He's going to court-martial Snout,' said Daniel, his face white.

'Small room, so let's limit the numbers,' said the Brigadier. 'You and I, Colonel, are technically enough to provide the necessary tribunal. I assume you have no qualms about dispensing discipline and seeing justice carried out?'

'No, sir,' said the Colonel. 'But perhaps Captain Wheaton can join us as well? I believe three officers are preferred if they are available?'

'Very well,' said the Brigadier, but he did not look pleased to be challenged. 'And you there, medical man,' he said, indicating Hugh. 'We'll need a medical man to examine the prisoner and to pronounce death after any execution.'

'I would like to speak for the prisoner, sir,' said Hugh. 'He is entitled to be represented.'

'If you wish to do so, you'll act as medical officer too,' said the Brigadier. 'Otherwise we have no room for you.'

'Very well,' said Hugh.

'The officer who was struck must come down,' said the Brigadier. He looked particularly smug as he pretended no personal recollection of Daniel. 'The chaplain can earn his keep, and my aide will take down the proceedings and fill out the papers. I think we are ready?'

Snout looked, if anything, younger than he had done in the early summer, when his biggest worry had been Latin declensions and money for sweets and cigarettes. He was thinner from the harsh winter, and his battered face had the lost expression of a child woken from sleep. His hands were bound with rope, and Hugh wondered that anyone could think it necessary to restrain this exhausted slip of a boy.

The Brigadier's aide sat the boy in a chair and removed his cap. Then he bound his ankles to the chair with a second rope.

'Sir, is that really necessary?' asked Harry Wheaton. 'He is no danger to us.'

'If the sentence is death, we shall carry it out immediately,' said the Brigadier. 'No sense risking a whole firing squad in this bombardment.' The chaplain disguised a choke as a clearing of the throat, and Daniel gasped, while Colonel Wheaton hurried to add, 'Nothing will be decided until we have heard the evidence, of course.'

'Merely a precaution,' agreed the Brigadier. 'Best to bind a prisoner while he's docile.'

The recitation of events was brutally swift, the Brigadier's reaction to mitigation equally concise.

'It matters not that you were unhurt, Lieutenant Bookham, or that you have a leader's natural inclination to protect your man,' said the Brigadier. 'He was seen to strike you, and to ignore the striking of an officer would be disastrous to discipline and possibly lose us the war.'

'I submit he is underage and should not have been allowed to serve,' said Daniel.

'Again, not an excuse,' said the Brigadier. 'You must agree with me, Colonel?'

'The boy volunteered with the full permission of his family,' said Colonel Wheaton. 'Else I would not have taken him. Were there a petition from them for his return, I would consider it, but . . .'

'But there is not, so we have no grounds to consider him protected from usual military regulations,' said the Brigadier.

'Sir, as a medical officer, I find the boy to be unfit to stand this tribunal,' said Hugh. 'I believe he is suffering from neurasthenia due to a blast from shelling.'

'If we excused the behaviour of every soldier who has had his ears rung by an exploding shell, we should have no army left at all,' said the Brigadier. 'I believe this anxiety has caused the boy to wander off several times?'

'It has, sir,' said Harry Wheaton. 'But he is a good lad and would not have gone if he had been in his right mind. We can all attest to his good character.'

'A deserter as well as a mutineer,' said the Brigadier. 'I'm sorry, but I find the evidence to be crystal clear in this case and the boy to be a malingerer and to be guilty of striking his superior officer in front of the ranks. He must be made an example of. Colonel Wheaton?'

'I very much regret that the boy's actions were so public as to be impossible to ignore,' said the Colonel. 'I agree he is guilty, but I do recommend clemency.'

'As do I,' said Harry Wheaton. 'The Brigadier's actions last night brought great honour to the regiment and boosted morale for all ranks. I trust the Brigadier will continue his wise and just course this grim morning.'

'So we are unanimous,' said the Brigadier. 'Unfortunately, the clemency last night must not be extended lest it become known as weakness. I must be responsible for the discipline of my command, and as such, I sentence this boy to be executed.'

'No,' said Hugh. 'It is monstrous.'

'Sentence to be carried out immediately, due to exigent circumstances.' The Brigadier looked to his aide, who was writing down the proceedings in an official log. The aide paused as if unsure how to document the sentence. 'Immediate,' confirmed the Brigadier. 'Get the boy some rum and let the chaplain speak to him.'

Snout had remained quiet through the proceedings, looking about him in a dazed manner. Now the aide brought him a flask and helped him to drink from it. He screwed up his face at the taste but drank with the greedy experience of a soldier who knows how the daily rum ration wards off the cold for a little while. The chaplain pulled up a chair next to him and began to speak a psalm in a quiet voice.

'You were very effective yesterday, Captain,' said the Brigadier quietly to Harry Wheaton. 'Would you volunteer? I will call together a firing squad if necessary, but to risk twelve men under this bombardment seems inefficient.'

'He put down a dog yesterday,' said Daniel fiercely. He did not address the Brigadier as 'sir', and he stepped towards him with a look of determination.

Hugh stopped Daniel with an outstretched arm.

'I beg you to reconsider,' said Hugh. 'The medical evidence is clear, and his age alone demands mitigation.'

'Not much difference between a dog and a traitor,' said the Brigadier calmly. 'Deserters, malingerers – they are rabid curs and must be put down before they infect the rest of the pack.'

'Have you no compassion?' asked Daniel in the strangled voice of a man swallowing a violent emotion. 'Must you strike at the boy to hurt me?'

Hugh stepped in front of Daniel and pushed him back by both shoulders. 'Shut up!' he whispered, his voice fierce. 'You will not give him the pleasure.'

'I'll ignore your lieutenant's insults because I don't have all day; I have a war to run,' said the Brigadier sharply to

Colonel Wheaton. 'Can the Captain carry out the sentence, or must we risk the lives of twelve men in a firing squad?'

'The boy asks for Mr Hugh,' said the chaplain. 'Is one of you Mr Hugh?'

Hugh gave Daniel a warning shake and went to Snout. The boy was weeping now, tears running silently down his neck. Hugh knelt and wiped his face with a handkerchief.

'I want my mama,' said Snout. 'I want to see my mama and my sister, Abigail, Mr Hugh.'

'I know, Snout, I know,' said Hugh.

'I just want to go home, Mr Hugh.'

'You will be going home, Dickie,' said Hugh, taking the boy's bound hands in his own. 'I think it will be just a moment and then you'll be walking down the hill to Rye and your mother and father will be waiting at the door for you.'

'Will Wolfie be there, do you think?' asked Snout.

'I know that dog will find you if he can,' said Hugh. 'I will be here with you, Dickie. Lieutenant Daniel is here. Captain Wheaton is here too.' Hugh looked up to see Daniel wiping his eyes and Harry looking away to hide his distress.

'That's enough,' said the Brigadier. Even he looked pale, as if either his conscience or his bilious stomach were bothering him. 'Perhaps the squad is the more appropriate way. I can see the Captain is overcome.'

'I'll do it,' said Hugh. Death was inevitable and to wait for a firing squad would be an agony. His heart threatened to break in his chest, but he had seen patients die every day. He knew what it was to prolong suffering, and he had learned when to just hold a hand and let a man go. 'I'm a medical doctor. It will be painless and quick.'

'For the love of God, no, Hugh,' said Daniel. He stepped between Hugh and Snout and pushed Hugh away with a roughness that sent him sprawling into some bags of potatoes.

'Oh, God, I hate these pals' battalions. Everyone knows each other and no one wants to shoot his neighbour's gardener,' said the Brigadier. 'Stand aside, gentlemen. I'll finish this myself.'

As he took his pistol from its holster, Daniel threw himself in front of Snout, and the Brigadier's aide ran to pull him away. They pulled at each other in the fierce, awkward way of real fighting in an enclosed space. Snout was toppled to the ground, still roped to his chair. The Brigadier stood waving his pistol, more in the direction of Daniel than of Snout, and Hugh cried out lest he shoot Daniel, by accident or design. The Wheatons, father and son, seemed mesmerised and unable to move, as if seeing the entirety of the impact this day would have on their future careers. At last Hugh was grateful to see Colonel Wheaton stepping in front of the Brigadier.

When the shell made a direct hit on the roof, Hugh was aware only of a blinding white concussion and a huge sound cut short by unconsciousness.

He didn't want to wake up. It was pleasant under the weight of the covers, and when he moved it hurt, so how much better to drop back into a deeper sleep. He moved again, and the covers seemed to smother him. He had dirt in his mouth and his nose. He coughed and spluttered and gasped for air. The air smelled of grass and wet earth and bonfires. It was harder now to stay asleep and yet so hard to wake up into pain and a buzzing in his ears.

Distant voices called him. Hands scrabbled at his chest. He surfaced, and all he could see were dark skies. Fat raindrops began to splash on his face. He remembered now that a shell had fallen on the cellar, and he tried to call out, but he had no voice. He could only open his mouth and feel the rain on his tongue. There was a lot of pain as someone lifted his shoulders, and then he could only slip away as many hands pulled him from the sucking earth.

CHAPTER THIRTY

THE CASUALTY CLEARING STATION was a chaos of stretchers piled in haphazard rows on the ground in the rain. Patients died before they could be assessed. It had been a large-scale bombardment, almost an offensive, and the casualties covered an entire wheat field. Hugh had woken up in a familiar ambulance to find he was not badly hurt. It was Archie and Bill's ambulance, and Archie had cheerfully cracked jokes about holiday trips to the seaside as he taped up a couple of broken ribs and patched a nasty cut on Hugh's head. He could do nothing about the infernal ringing in Hugh's ears. He had kept his boots in the blast, but somehow lost his trousers, and had been laid semi-naked on the stretcher. Archie had covered him with a blanket and made ribald comments. Now he sat on a box outside the clearing station and tried to clear his head enough to either offer his help or search the field of stretchers for his cousin and the others.

'Here's a pair of trousers and a cuppa,' said Archie. 'We have to go now, guvnor. Taking a load to the train station.'

'Did you see my cousin? Did they pull any others out of my hole?' he asked. He drank the scalding tea and felt the burn of it in his throat.

'Can't say for sure,' said the ambulance driver.

'I never imagined angels would look so ugly, but you were a sight for sore eyes,' said Hugh. 'Thank you.'

'Who you calling ugly?' said Archie. 'Must've damaged an eyeball, sir.'

Hugh held a hand to his painful ribs and walked as swiftly as he could bear up and down the rows of stretchers and clusters of wounded men sitting on the grassy field. He knew he had only a few minutes to search before someone would stop him, or before he would feel bound to step in and help the wounded. It was selfish to look for his cousin when so many other cousins, brothers and sons were bleeding and screaming, but he felt the urgency to find Daniel as a drumming in his head. He was driven along the rows by a horror that he must find him or never be able to face going home.

A loose tourniquet on a stranger stopped him at last. A soldier called out for help for his neighbour, and Hugh, seeing the spurt of an artery, ran to tighten the leather belt on the injured man's thigh and secure the dressing on his wound with strips torn from his own handkerchief.

'Thanks, sir, he was a goner,' said the soldier who had called out. When Hugh turned to speak to him, the soldier was already dead, eyes empty and a large bloody stain still spreading from a wound to his lower abdomen. Hugh closed his eyes and placed the man's arms across his chest.

He wished there was a cloth to cover his face, but he had to make do with placing the soldier's cap on top of his hands. In place of a prayer he made a decision to help Daniel by doing his duty to all the wounded.

'Where are the operating tents?' he asked a passing orderly. 'I'm a surgeon.'

He worked for ten or twelve hours, standing at a make-shift operating table and moving almost mechanically to staunch, stem and close whatever wounds appeared before him. His ribs hurt so much he sometimes had to stop and wait for a surge of nausea to pass, but he refused morphine in case it dulled his abilities. The orderlies could hardly boil instruments quickly enough to keep up with the flow of patients, and Hugh, looking up from pushing a lower intes-tine back through a gaping shrapnel hole, saw with a start that the nurse was not the same one from when he started. He had been unaware of them changing shifts and had just continued to hold out his hand for instruments and slap them back into a waiting palm when he had finished.

It was deep into the night when the flow of the injured finally slowed and Hugh, shaking his head to clear his vision, knew that he was no longer thinking straight. The deep ache in his ribs now brought tears to his eyes. His head throbbed and his fingers felt numb from the hours of prodding and sewing. He spoke to the nurse and left the tent. He washed his face and hands with strong carbolic soap and freezing water. He took a thick ham sandwich and a cup of tea from a woman running a canteen from the back of a grocer's van. He was handed a fresh pair of socks and put them on, almost crying with pleasure at the feel of warm, dry wool against his feet. He requisitioned a blanket, and though he was tired almost to collapse, he set out with a kerosene lantern. He walked with the hunched gait of an old man, shuffling through the serried rows of men laid out in tents and in the field, their white bandages bright in the frosty moonlight. He looked in their dirty, broken faces and thought them all his brothers and cousins. And though he asked God to watch over his cousin Daniel it was enough to be here among Daniel's fellow soldiers and to have done his best to help them all.

In a field containing hundreds of sleeping, or softly groaning, wounded, Hugh found them by the sound of Harry Wheaton loudly calling for a nurse to bring him a bottle of burgundy and a dozen oysters.

'The service in this establishment is perfectly rotten,' said Wheaton as the nurse hurried away. 'My friend will have the lobster.' Wheaton was objecting to the mug of oxtail soup and hunk of bread she had left him. He was propped up on a cot, his arm in a sling and his legs covered by a rubber tarp.

'Harry!' said Hugh. 'I've been looking for you all.'

'You've found us, what's left,' said Harry. 'Wake up, Bookham, your cousin is here.' Daniel was lying barely conscious on the next cot, his head heavily bandaged. 'They told me to keep him awake,' added Harry. 'But he's always been incurably lazy, haven't you, Bookham? Always looking for a nap.'

'Daniel, can you hear me?' asked Hugh. He crouched beside Daniel's cot and felt for his pulse. It was weak but steady.

Daniel's eyes flickered, and he licked his lips. 'Hugh, is that you?' he asked. 'I thought you were dead.'

'How do you feel?' asked Hugh. 'Can you move?'

'Listen to me, Hugh,' said Daniel. He raised a hand, and Hugh grasped it. 'You must get the boy home. Please promise me you'll get the boy home.'

'He means young Sidley,' said Harry. He nodded across the aisle, and Hugh went to peer at the boy, who was bandaged across the chest and breathing in irregular gasps. 'Got a piece of shrapnel in a lung, they said.'

'Snout, can you hear me?' asked Hugh. The boy opened his eyes and looked at Hugh for a long moment. Then he gave a small smile and closed his eyes again. Hugh hurried back to Daniel.

'I heard the doctors talking,' said Harry in a whisper. 'Those who can survive the trip get put on a list for the ambulance trains to the coast. Those that are too weak do not.'

'It's a new system,' said Hugh. 'It keeps the most people alive and saves the very ill from additional pain that will do them no good.'

'Daniel and young Snout are not on the list,' said Harry. 'If you have any authority, you had better do something fast.'

'Where are the others?' asked Hugh. 'Your father? Lord North?'

'Dead,' said Harry. He turned his head aside to hide any emotion. 'My father is gone, Hugh.'

'I'm so sorry,' said Hugh.

'We are the only survivors,' said Harry. 'As I told them – such a shame when the court-martial had just found the boy innocent and we were about to leave.'

'Thank you,' said Hugh. He clasped Harry by the arm.

'Of course your cousin had to go and add that the Brigadier threw himself on the lad as the shell was coming in,' said Harry. 'Always the weaver of stories. Now Lord North may become a national hero.'

The doctor in charge of the casualty station was inclined to be helpful.

'You did sterling work for us today, Lieutenant,' he said. 'I will add your cousin to the transport list and give you a pass to go with him to the coast.'

'And my cousin's batman?' asked Hugh.

'Sorry,' said the doctor. 'One officer added to the list is a courtesy; having other ranks jump the queue begins to look like disregard for the regulations. Believe me, we spend too much of our time already turning down impassioned petitions.'

'I appreciate your help, sir,' said Hugh. He knew better than to argue. He would have done the same if he were in charge and might even have denied Daniel priority. How different it felt, thought Hugh, to apply rules universally and then to apply them to one's own family. He thought of the efficient way he conducted his surgeries, patching as he could and trying not to care too much if the injured died. There were always many more waiting, and he could not afford to waste his time mourning.

As dawn was breaking, Hugh waited with Harry and Daniel for the fleet of ambulances to come for the next round of patients. He was delighted to see Archie and Bill coming up the field and waved them over. 'Can you take my patients?' he said.

'Delighted, I'm sure,' said Archie. 'No one cares who we take as long as you got the right ticket.' A green label attached to the jacket indicated a patient for transport.

'Take the boy instead of me,' said Daniel. He fumbled for the ticket on his chest. 'We'll call it an error and I'll find a place on the next convoy.'

'You need to go now,' said Hugh. 'No arguments.'

Bill raised an eyebrow, and Hugh took him aside. 'Is he badly off?' said Bill.

'Yes,' said Hugh. 'He has a hole in his skull, and that kind of injury just can't be properly cleaned or treated at the field station. If I can get him home, or even to the big hospital on the coast, he has a chance.'

'And the boy?'

'Also not very good,' said Hugh. 'The lung may get infected. He needs to be out of the cold and nursed intensively, but they've marked him to stay.'

'Look, the answer is that you take them both and I'll go on the next convoy,' said Harry Wheaton. He tried to undo his ticket with his one good hand.

'Everyone's a hero today,' said Bill. 'Upper-class toffs, outdoing themselves to be romantic, Archie.'

'Quite making me teary-eyed,' said Archie. 'Good as a play at the music hall.'

'Insolent little man,' said Harry.

'Well, if the arm is not infected,' said Hugh, 'I suppose there is no harm in Captain Wheaton's delayed removal?'

'Except it's not his only injury, is it, guvnor?' said Bill. With a flick of the wrist he threw off the tarpaulin from Harry's cot. Harry's left leg was gone at the knee, a bloody stump wrapped in such a thick layer of bandages that it looked like the pollarded branch of a tree.

'Good God, Harry, why didn't you say?' said Hugh. 'Amputation is a serious injury.'

'Didn't want your pity,' said Harry. 'Plenty of my own to keep me occupied.'

'You need a hospital too, Harry,' said Hugh. 'Gangrene is a real possibility if you stay out here.'

'All right, Archie, what do you say we do a sloppy job again and take an extra passenger or two with the labels mixed up?' said Bill. 'Not like we haven't done it before.'

'It'll be docked pay this time for sure,' said Archie. 'But it only gets them to the train.'

'So maybe we get lost along the way?' said Bill. 'Take them all the way to the coast?'

'Not like we haven't done that before neither,' said Archie. 'Double quick then, before the sergeant major catches on.'

At the port, the ambulance mingled with those from the train station and delivered Hugh's little party and four other men directly to the big hospital near the docks. Bill and Archie got a severe dressing-down for producing six patients with only five authorised sets of papers. Their artfully disconsolate faces and shuffling feet could not hide a certain eye-rolling sarcasm from the sergeant major at the loading bay. Had the need for their services not been acute, they might both have been thrown in a dungeon – of which the sergeant major claimed to have use – but he docked them two weeks' pay and sent them off on another run with no time off for dinner.

Hugh clasped their hands and tried to offer them money, but the two were scathing in their rejection.

'Keep it,' said Bill. 'Champagne and cigars cost a lot here in port.'

'Spend it on a woman, guvnor,' said Archie. 'Put a smile on that long face of yours.' They drove away, still exchanging rude comments on Hugh's personal appearance and general stuffiness, and he understood at last that such earthbound ruffians formed as indelible a part of England's fabled backbone as any boys from Eton's playing fields.

The hospital was also a collection point for patients bound for England, and the wards spilled into two warehouses on the docks, where patients were cared for and maintained until the arrival of a hospital ship to take them home. Organisation in these warehouses was slightly looser than in the main building, and Hugh was able to persuade several orderlies that Snout the batman might stay with his officer, Captain Wheaton. Once they and Daniel were settled together, Hugh told Harry Wheaton to look after them while he went to secure passes to England on the next ship.

'Not sure what I can do except watch them drool,' said Harry, who was busy trying to look brave and interesting for a pretty nurse in a starched white apron bringing tea along the row of beds.

'Make sure they keep drooling,' said Hugh. 'Just don't let them die while I'm gone.'

In a large open office on the docks, he found his surgeon, Colonel Sir Alex Ramsey, surrounded by two walls of filing cabinets and pressed into a corner by the desks of clerks and nurses, who had their own rows of filing cabinets.

Overhead, large green-painted metal lights cast an unhealthy pallor on the proceedings.

'As you can see, things did not turn out as we had intended,' said the surgeon. 'They have me running half the hospitals. I spend my days with a paper knife, not a scalpel.' He did not, however, look displeased with such an arrangement.

'I have been kept busy,' said Hugh. 'You did not mislead me as to the experience I would gain. It may have been at the expense of some poor souls who got me instead of the more experienced surgeon.'

'A head-injury hospital is still on the cards for next year or so.'

'I suppose that means the war will be going on a while, sir?'

'We are making plans to see it through,' said the surgeon. 'What can I do for you, my boy?' Hugh told him a brief version of what happened and begged him to assign his little group of three passes for the next ship to England. The surgeon, too, hesitated over the private.

'He's underage, sir,' said Hugh.

'Well, I suppose we must prove our commitment to the men and show we assign no preference to officers,' said the surgeon. 'I expect you'd like to accompany them?'

'I do have leave owed to me,' said Hugh.

'And will you be using some of that leave to pay a visit to my daughter?' said the surgeon. Hugh felt a throb of panic in his chest, which he pushed away. His sense of honour struggled for a moment with his need to see his cousin safe. He tried to conjure Lucy in his mind, but instead he could only see Beatrice Nash, laughing on his aunt's terrace, her hair coming down from its pins in a sudden breeze. He opened his mouth to speak, but the surgeon stopped him.

'I'll understand that as a no,' he said. 'A pity, but it can't be helped. She's taken up with young Carruthers, you know. He joined the Coldstream Guards.'

'I'm very happy for her,' said Hugh.

'You are the better surgeon,' he added. 'But you understand, it can't be helped. I'll have to take him in with me.'

'I do, sir,' said Hugh. He was relieved to see the redbrick house and the fine consulting rooms officially disappear from his future. He was happy to let go of the dream of being the renowned London surgeon, for he had no interest now in what seemed like the shallow trappings of fame and society. Instead he could only see the little red rooftops of Rye, all huddled under the church, and the broad green of the marshes at sunset, the dark bluff of the Sussex hills behind, and a small cottage on a steep cobbled lane.

'Ten-day pass,' said the surgeon. 'Best of luck to you, my boy.'

While they waited for a hospital ship, Hugh consulted with the other doctors, changed dressings himself and talked the nurses into bringing extra beef broth, extra butter, extra blankets. He used his credentials to be allowed to stay all day, and at night he slept on the floor by Daniel's cot, rolled in a blanket. If love and care could shepherd his cousin and the others safely home, he was determined to provide both.

But Daniel grew worse as the others grew stronger. He was intermittently subject to a high fever that left him shaking and covered in sweat. His skull had not been broken open, which would have been a sure mark of death, but his head wound did not heal as fast as Hugh would have liked, and he suspected his cousin's brain was swelling. Daniel began to be confused about his surroundings, and he called a nurse Auntie several times.

On the morning that the hospital ship appeared in the English Channel, Daniel seemed calm and strangely lucid after a night of trembling sweats.

'I am not going to leave this place, Hugh,' he said. 'All night I dreamed of Aunt Agatha and Uncle John's garden, and of you and me smoking on the terrace, and I knew I was sitting there for the last time.'

'Don't speak that way,' said Hugh. 'The ship is coming, Daniel.'

'I'm not afraid,' said Daniel. 'I think Craigmore is waiting for me. I am only sad to leave you all, and I don't want you to be sad.'

'The ship is coming now,' said Hugh.

'I need you to take care of the boy,' said Daniel. 'To get him home to his mother.'

'We will take him home together.'

'Is Wheaton awake?' asked Daniel.

'I would be sleeping if you weren't chatting like fishwives over there,' said Harry, his gruffness hiding his emotion.

'I'm so sorry about your father, Harry,' said Daniel.

'If you see him up there, smoke a cigar with him for me,' said Harry. 'Tell him not to come and rattle all the dressers when I borrow his guns for the shooting.'

'A lovely sentiment,' said Daniel. 'And I thought you such a brute, Harry.' He seemed cheered by such a spirited exchange, but his breathing was very shallow.

'You will come home with me,' said Hugh. 'I insist.'

'I need to give you my poems,' said Daniel. He reached with some difficulty under his pillow for his small black notebook. 'Lock them in a drawer if you must, but perhaps you will ask Beatrice Nash to edit them.'

'Not your friend, Mr Tillingham?' asked Hugh.

'No, no, he would edit them to death in his own image,' said Daniel. 'Your Beatrice has a light touch. If you wish to publish them, give them to Beatrice.'

'She is not my Beatrice,' said Hugh.

'Make her so, Hugh,' said Daniel. 'She is so obviously meant to put up with you.'

'Daniel, you must be strong,' said Hugh. But Hugh could feel a tear on his cheek. His vibrant younger cousin was so very frail; his skin seemed to have already assumed the strange, waxy translucence of death.

'Will you write me a letter, Hugh, as they do for all the boys who must leave us?'

'Of course,' said Hugh. He fumbled for a pen and found a blank page at the back of the notebook.

'Give my father the respects of his son and tell him I hope I have performed my duty,' he said. 'To my uncle John, write that I send all the love a nephew ever gave a loving uncle.' He paused to catch a fleeting breath and added, 'Tell Celeste she made me the happiest of men and restored my name and spirit with the gift of her hand. I hope she and the child will live a happy life.'

'And what message have you for Aunt Agatha?' said Hugh. Daniel did not reply. He seemed to be fading into sleep. 'Do not leave her unforgiven, Daniel. Do not leave her with anger, Cousin, for my sake if nothing else.'

'Tell her I always knew,' said Daniel faintly.

'That she loved you?' asked Hugh.

'Tell her I always felt her great love like a blanket around me. Now I am come to the edge of the place she feared' – he paused and seemed to stare as if at a new landscape – 'tell her I can better understand why she tried so hard to save me. I have caused her fear to come true.'

'It is not your fault,' said Hugh. 'You did your duty.'

'Oh, Hugh, she will be so unhappy,' said Daniel. 'Tell her I will die with her name on my lips.'

'You are half my life, Cousin,' said Hugh. He could barely write for the tears moistening the paper and smudging the ink. 'You can't leave me to go home to Sussex alone. Please don't go.'

'You are half my life too,' said Daniel. 'Live for both of us, Hugh. Love for both of us. And for goodness' sake, try to be a little less stuffy.'

'Am I writing that down too?' asked Hugh, smiling and crying at the same time.

'Yes, dear Hugh. It is the unexpected note that makes the poem. You, Hugh, are the unexpected note.'

CHAPTER THIRTY-ONE

She wrote to Daniel every day, setting aside the hour from ten to eleven in the morning to sit in her study and stare at the bare branches of the trees, and the frost under the hedges, as she composed her careful lines. It was a bitter winter, and the glass study was unheated. Jenny brought a hot brick for her feet, as usual, and she wore gloves with the fingers cut out, and the cold and the wisp of her breath added the proper dimension of penance to the ritual.

She did not beg him to love her again, or to forgive her for what she had done in her fog of anxiety and fear. She did not seek to burden him with her pleading. Instead she wrote a cheerful account of the small events that stack, one upon the other, to build an ordinary day. She wrote of Smith and the gardener hacking the last frozen cabbages from the ground. She wrote of having to speak sternly to Cook, who had discarded her boots, and wore only men's socks in the kitchen on account of her inflamed bunions. She reported in detail on Celeste's contentment and how determined she was not to let her increasing girth keep her from visiting the sick and her needlework. She had made lace for baby bonnets and donated much of it for other young mothers at the church, and she played the piano weekly at the hospital and the almshouses.

They were keeping chickens behind the stable house and were drawing plans to turn over the lawn in her private garden to plant vegetables in the spring. From a surfeit of caution, she was careful not to catalogue John's comings and goings. She referred to 'an uncle of yours' and reported on such interesting news as his being an absolute baby about having a tooth pulled at the dentist and his new interest in acquiring goats, goats offering milk and meat while being better sized for a large in-town property than a cow. Jenny and Cook, she reported, had baulked at the idea of eating goat, as if offered rattlesnake or crocodile, and 'an uncle of yours' was in complex negotiations to have the goats sent to a farm when the time came, to be exchanged for a smaller portion of a butchered lamb.

She did not ask him for anything in return. She begged no letters or poems. She did not include phrases that hoped to hear from him, or longed to see his face. She simply sent him her small, carefully described miniatures of his home in hopes he would be cheered by the portraits, and she kept private her secret hope that he would not wince to see her figure wandering in the scenes she described.

Agatha had stopped looking at the newspapers and the illustrated periodicals, the ladies' journals with their side-ways glances at the war. Every recipe for meatless pie or economical carrot Christmas pudding, every instruction for sock-knitting or notice of a bandage drive was a little stab in the heart, more painful than the daily bulletins of fact. She set them all aside and lived beyond the comfort of stoking and nursing and picking at her fear. The constant and patient performance of her duties was her new ritual, her book of hours. The writing of the letter in the morning, the visiting hours, the careful dressing for dinner, even when the dinner was meatless and she and Celeste sat at a card table in the drawing room to save lighting the dining-room fire. The winding of the clocks, the ordering of winter feed for the horse, the continued care for refugees, and the inspection of boots to send to the cobbler. She invested each with her full attention and left no room in her mind for the luxury of pain.

Christmas had come and gone with subdued warmth. Beatrice Nash and Mr Tillingham came to dinner. Agatha gave Mr Tillingham a small book of old Latin poems picked out at an antiquarian book dealer John favoured, just off the Charing Cross Road. Beatrice gave him an ivory book-mark that had been her father's, and Celeste made him an exquisite lace cloth for his spectacles. With some flourish, Mr Tillingham presented each lady with the same faux-shagreen glove box he had given his secretary. His frugality was expected, but his lack of concern to differentiate in any way among the ladies had been of obvious hurt to Beatrice. Agatha hoped her gift to Beatrice, of an old calf-skin-bound copy of Chaucer with colour illustrations, would offer some compensation. She and John had a letter from Hugh, stiff in the boy's formal way, and filled with positive tales of his lodgings and the efficiency of the hospital. He did not complain of conditions or tell what horrors he might have seen; for this Agatha was grateful. She read the letter aloud after Christmas dinner, and Celeste produced a postcard, all embroidered wool flowers and a printed sentiment, on which Daniel had scrawled brief Christmas wishes to all at home. The card was passed around, and Agatha took it greedily in her hands and traced the signature with her finger as if it might summon Daniel to the room.

The card rested on the mantel in Celeste's green room, and Agatha sometimes slipped in to pick it up again and look at the loop of the penmanship. If Jenny or Celeste came in unexpectedly, she would wipe a finger along the mantel and blow away imaginary dust before ordering a second dusting, or shake out the curtains and wonder aloud if they needed retrimming.

Today she wrote that the March winds had died down, and with the days growing lighter and the nights shrinking back from their winter dominance, the snowdrops and early daffodils were defying the frost to bloom in the south-facing beds. She did not draw any conclusion or hopes from these facts, she merely let them blossom across her thin letter paper in the loops of her pen. Despite the bare elm tapping on the glass of her study windows, and the frigid cold radiating through the glass, she could almost imagine spring in the sharp blue sky and the small sparrows fluffing out their wings and sharpening their beaks on the branches.

The telephone rang in the bowels of the house, and she blocked the sound from her mind. She was not to be disturbed during this particular hour, and Jenny would let the caller know she was not yet about. A tap on the door violated her careful arrangement and caused her pen to drop a blot on the page.

'I'm sorry, ma'am,' said Jenny. 'But it's Mr Kent on the phone, and he insists.'

The jolt of fear, the deep breath, the suppression of any visible trembling; Agatha rose slowly, blotted her letter on the mat, and placed her pen in its holder.

'Tell Mr Kent I'll be right there,' she said, letting the maid hurry down while she took off her gloves, and the woolly blanket she used as a shawl, and proceeded in a dignified glide through the upper hall and down the polished stairs. No point in running and perhaps slipping, twisting an ankle. No point in assuming her husband was calling from London with some emergency. Better to keep to one's carefully constructed life of patience . . .

'I got a coded telegram from Hugh's surgeon,' said John. 'Grange, Wheaton, Bookham, Sidley STOP Blighty bound STOP HS Folkestone 18:00 STOP.'

'Oh, my God, they're hurt,' said Agatha.

'I telephoned Major Frank at the hospital, and he's sending his ambulance. They're coming home, Agatha.'

'I must get to Folkestone,' she said.

'I'm taking a train in an hour,' said her husband. 'Let me handle this, Agatha. We don't know what we'll find.'

'I'm coming,' said Agatha. 'No force on earth will keep me from those docks.' She put the telephone back in its cradle and called wildly for Celeste, Jenny, Cook and Smith. The household came running.

Beatrice was leaving school to go home for her midday dinner when Agatha Kent all but overtook her on the street with no greeting.

'Mrs Kent? Agatha?' called Beatrice.

'I can't stop,' said Agatha. 'I have to get to Folkestone and of course the car was taken weeks ago and all the trains are hopeless these days so I have to find anyone with a car or a lorry.' Most of the private cars had been acquired by the army for war service, and the trains were so slow and full of troops that travel had become difficult.

'A pair of horses might get you there in a few hours,' said Beatrice. It was over thirty miles to Folkestone, but a horse might do the trip in four or five hours at a trot.

'But they would be spent and lame from the effort and I would not get home again.' She stopped and took a deep breath. 'The boys are on a hospital ship with Harry Wheaton and young Sidley,' she added, looking stricken. 'They may all be badly injured. We just don't know.'

'Alice Finch,' said Beatrice. 'We must find Alice Finch.' Alice had managed to get her motorbike grudgingly exempted as part of her beloved motorbike and bicycle messenger corps. The corps included certain stalwart ladies, some Scouts, and assorted amateur male cyclists too old or young for military service, who enjoyed the thrill of cycling through the dark, carrying messages between shoreline sentry posts.

'A motorbike?' asked Agatha. 'I don't know.'

'Nonsense,' said Beatrice. 'I only hope she can take both of us because I'm coming with you.' She gave no thought to her afternoon classes. An image of Hugh, bleeding and pale on a stretcher, was before her eyes as they hurried up the hill to Alice's cottage and rousted her and Minnie Buttles from their luncheon. Alice agreed at once to take them, and Minnie ran to find them goggles and a pair of motorcycle breeches for Beatrice, who would have to ride astride. The motorbike was dragged from the shed, and Agatha pushed and shoved into the sidecar, an extra can of petrol under her feet. Then Beatrice tucked the unfamiliar breeches firmly into her belt and climbed behind Alice. A running start, pushed from behind by Minnie, and the engine roared to life. Alice opened the throttle, and in a sight that brought shopkeepers to their doors and made the dogs bark, three ladies flew down the high street and away across the marsh, hair and hat ribbons flying in the wind.

The Folkestone docks were chaos to the untrained eye. Lorries and ambulances crisscrossed the yards with no apparent care for the processions of soldiers, stretcher-bearers and walking wounded, who marched like ants from warehouse to warehouse. A large, badly painted steamship was moored in the middle of the chaos. A red cross painted on the funnel was its only protection from the U-boats that patrolled the Channel. Men were unloading stretchers from the deck and a lower cargo door, while those who could walk hobbled down the gangplank as best they could. Many were on crutches, some wheeled in bath chairs. Several men were carried down by orderlies, sitting on regular metal chairs.

From the steep hill above, Alice quieted the engine to say, 'Looks like they have the perimeter guarded. I'll try to use my credentials to get you as close as I can.' As Alice's credentials consisted of a certificate she and Minnie had printed up in their studio and handed out to all members of their messenger corps, Beatrice had no comfort that they would be allowed anywhere near the ship.

Fortunately, the brand-new private on the smallest checkpoint was already overwhelmed in managing his rifle and a clipboard while having to raise and lower the heavy barrier.

'Motorbike Brigade, transporting nurses,' shouted Alice as they approached. 'Can't stop in case the plugs give out.' She pulled a certificate from her coat and gave it to him as she continued to coast the motorbike forward slowly with her feet. 'Open up sharpish, lad,' she barked. 'Don't want to decapitate two matrons with the barrier, do we?'

'No, ma'am,' he said, and though his eyes widened at the incongruity of women in trousers and oily goggles, he ran to raise the barrier and wave them through, his rifle falling off his shoulder and hanging at a dangerous angle from his elbow. Alice drove all the way to the gangplank to park the motorbike among a row of waiting ambulances.

As they watched, the crowd began to seem less random. Beatrice detected patterns in how the injured were moved: some to ambulances, some to a makeshift hospital building. She could see several men with clipboards and lists giving directions as the stretchers came off the ship. Nurses moved up and down the rows of men, checking their injuries.

'We should ask a man with a clipboard,' said Beatrice. 'They have the lists.'

'No, they will surely have us escorted away,' said Agatha. 'See where they are keeping families behind that fence?' Back towards the main road, a small group of people waved and called out. But they were too distant to hear anything or make themselves heard. 'We should ask a nurse.'

She stepped from behind the ambulances and consulted a nurse in a severe navy blue uniform and frilly cap under a scruffy man's greatcoat. The nurse looked around and nodded. Then she went over to a man with a clipboard and asked him a question. While he was consulting his papers, Beatrice scanned the myriad faces for Hugh's. It was alarming how many men looked, at first glance, as if they might be him: a similar turn of the head or line of jaw, a pair of grey eyes under a heavy bandage, a hand reaching out from a man whose face was burned beyond recognition. For a moment she feared she had forgotten what Hugh looked like. Perhaps he had faded from memory as her father's face kept doing this winter. Fading so she had to stop, sit down and will back every feature, every quirk of the eyebrow, until she had his face again for immediate conjuring.

She saw John Kent first, walking from behind the last ambulance in the row, speaking to the driver. Agatha saw him too, and began to run towards him. Beatrice turned to follow, but Hugh's face appeared in her path. She did not see from where he came. She felt her heart leap as she looked him up and down for injuries. She did not bother to be shy; there were too many hurt to consider one's manners.

'Beatrice,' he said. She ran into his arms, and he embraced her hard, his head sunk on her shoulder and his shoulders shaking as he tried not to break down.

'Are the others with you?' she asked, her face pressed to his hair. 'Daniel?'

'Daniel is gone,' said Hugh, his voice hoarse. 'I could not bring him home, Beatrice.'

'I am so sorry,' she said. As she comforted him, she saw Agatha struggling to look in the back of the ambulance.

Her husband pulled her away and spoke in her ear. As he held her tight, her knees buckled and she threw her head back in a low cry that seemed to come from the deepest core of pain.

'We must go to your aunt,' said Beatrice, and Hugh hesitated for a moment, as if unwilling to let her go. But then he put his chin in the air, pretending that he could see perfectly well out of eyes blurry with unshed tears, and they hurried to help John and his distraught wife.

It was bittersweet to follow the ambulance home to Rye, to see it draw up outside the Wheaton home and to see Lady Emily and Eleanor sobbing with joy and pain, cradling Harry Wheaton in their arms. Agatha climbed from the front seat of the ambulance as if she had become a hundred years old in the journey of a few miles. John supported her arm. She could only shake her head slowly at Lady Emily. And Lady Emily could only kiss her cheek, as if both ladies had been struck dumb by death. Hugh helped unload the stretcher cases as Major Frank examined the patients' labels and directed their disposition about the hospital.

'This one doesn't belong here,' said the Major. 'He's a private, and this is an officers' hospital.'

'He's a local boy, Major,' said Hugh. 'Served as batman to both Harry here and my cousin, Daniel. It was my cousin's last wish that we see him home.'

'Understand the sentiment entirely,' said Major Frank. 'But can't be done. No mixed wards, you know? Have to send him on by train to Brighton.'

'No, you can't,' said Hugh. 'He'll never last the trip, and besides, his family doesn't have the money to traipse to Brighton to care for him.'

'My hands are tied,' said the Major. 'From the shape he's in he probably should never have made the Channel crossing.'

'You'll put him in the private wing of the house,' said Harry Wheaton. His voice was slurred from exhaustion and pain. His stump oozed at the edges of the bandage, and he was obviously in more agony than he was showing. 'Put a cot in my father's study. Easy for the nurses to get to and his family can come and go through the garden doors.'

'Harry, you'll not put the farrier's son in your father's study,' said Lady Emily. 'How could you think of such an insult to your dead father?'

'Not his study any more,' said Harry.

'I beg your pardon!' said his mother.

'I beg yours, Mother,' said Harry. 'But my father, the Colonel, took care of his men, and I should do the same.' He gestured to the orderlies holding the stretcher on which Snout lay unconscious, his cheeks flushed and his chest wheezing with each breath. 'Chop, chop. In the study, if you please.' As the stretcher was carried in, Harry added, in a low voice, 'Perhaps if I had stood up for the scrawny little blighter earlier . . .'

'I'll let his parents know,' said Alice. 'And I'll take Miss Nash home.'

As Beatrice climbed into the sidecar, hitching her baggy breeches up once again in full view of a puzzled Lady Emily, Hugh came to grip her hand in his.

'Once again duty divides us, it seems,' he said. 'I must make sure Snout is settled and then go to my aunt and uncle.'

'Do not feel any concern for me,' she said. She returned the pressure of his hand. 'I am so grateful you are here to help them. Daniel is an unbearable loss, Hugh.'

'When I have seen to both, may I come to you?' he asked.

'I would be happy,' she said. 'I will wait up for you.'

'I may not leave you again,' he said. He squeezed her hand fiercely. 'I know now that I am home.'

'I will not let you go,' she said, and felt no blush of hesitation as she looked into his face. As Hugh left, Alice fired up the engine and walked the machine forward until it caught.

'I'll be sending Minnie round for a midnight chat with her father,' said Alice. 'Someone'll need the Vicar first thing in the morning.'

Beatrice went home and lit a fire in the grate and under the kettle in her small kitchen. She took her meagre dinner, left out under a damp towel, and shaped it into the semblance of a cold supper. She unearthed a bottle of sherry, given her by a pampered boy whose leg was now blown off. When the kettle sang, she took it to her basin and scrubbed the dirt and day from her body. Dressed in a loose gown, her hair brushed and down around her shoulders, she barred the doors to her landlady's rooms and sat in the dark firelight, nervous but not afraid, to wait for Hugh. This was the confusion of war, thought Beatrice. That some should sit mourning in a drawing room, or smoothing the brow of a dying boy, while in a cottage on a cobbled street, two young lovers could only choose to stand against the shocking burden of death and loss with their love and their passion.

Hugh and Beatrice were married the next day, walking together to church on a morning unexpectedly mild, as if to celebrate the vernal equinox, when the world balances perfectly between light and dark, and spring signals fresh life. The war seemed to have swept away and rendered useless all the normal etiquette of mourning and marriage. Hugh telephoned his uncle in the early hours but gave him every option to remain at home. They came to church, the Kents, and Celeste; and though they were swooning with their grief, they offered no remonstrance but only tender words of affection and happiness. Alice Finch and Minnie Buttles came out to sign the register for them, and the Vicar made the ancient ritual short and simple, unadorned by superfluous hymns and prayers.

The boy, Snout, lingered for a week, his lungs succumbing slowly to pneumonia brought on as a corollary to a trench fever unrelated to his later wound. Hugh spent long hours with Dr Lawton at the boy's bedside and consulting with the hospital doctors. Snout's family was a constant at the Wheaton house, going silently in and out of the garden. His invalid mother was carried in every morning and seemed to grow stronger as she fought for her son's life. His great-grandmother came in with herbs and teas, foul-smelling concoctions that eased his breathing but could not defeat the infections. She rubbed his chest with salves and made such prayers and incantations that the hospital nurses, gliding in and out, whispered of witchcraft.

Such is the slow accumulation of sorrows in a long war that the requests for memorial services begin to outweigh the marriages and the parishioners begin to keep their black coats brushed and hung at the front of their wardrobes. The church bulletin, hand-delivered on Tuesday, announced that Sunday's communion service would be another memorial for two officers fallen and buried overseas: Colonel Archibald Preston Danforth Wheaton, commanding officer, Second Battalion, Fifth Division, Royal East Sussex, of Wheaton Hall, Rye; and Lieutenant Daniel Sidney Bookham, also of the Second Battalion, Fifth Division, Royal East Sussex, of Rye and Lansdowne Terrace, London. The bulletin highlighted KILLED IN ACTION, an enticement to attend not dissimilar to the greengrocer's sign announcing 'fresh from Devon' or 'picked today'. But first there was a boy to bury.

The funeral service for Richard Sidley was on Saturday. Beatrice felt guilty that she faced the sombre ritual with the warm heart and flushed cheeks of a newly wedded woman. She and Hugh had lain in each other's arms to the last moment that morning, watching the clock's hands and finding excuses, and shortcuts to their dressing, so they might snatch an extra few moments away from the world.

Now they stood in the cobbled street outside the church and waited for the funeral cortège to arrive. Agatha had insisted she was well enough to attend and stood between her husband and Celeste, her face white and old against her black coat. Celeste, too, looked older than her years, but she held up Agatha's arm with quiet strength, and it seemed to Beatrice that she had already acquired the resilience of a mother in these past days.

Much of the town seemed arrayed on the narrow pavement; even the Mayor and his wife had come, and he was sombrely dressed with the mayoral chain of office tucked inside a dark greatcoat. Many of Snout's schoolfellows stood scuffing their boots against the kerbs. Some of them looked sheepish, as if they were visited by every taunt and shove they had inflicted on the poor boy. And now the coffin came slowly up the street, borne on the undertaker's best dray and covered with the Union Jack and the town flag with its prancing lions. Behind the coffin, Snout's mother rode in a pony cart, his father leading the stout pony by the head. Beside him, Snout's sister, Abigail, carried an armful of lilies and, somewhat strangely, a large jar of coins tucked under her arm.

A stir among the crowd of townspeople greeted the turning in to the street of Snout's great-grandmother, driving her barrel-topped caravan and wearing a scarlet coat fastened with gold sovereigns and a heavy black skirt stiffened by many black-and-red petticoats. Her grey hair was braided about her head and a top hat perched above, covered with a long black lace veil. The wagon was bright with new paint, its wheels picked out in red and gold. The horses in the shafts pulled together, their flowing manes and the feathers on their feet brushed to silk and streaming in the breeze. The harness jingled with bells, and the leather shone with waxing.

Behind the caravan, a line of Gypsies, gathered from all over the county, marched. First a young boy leading a riderless horse, a pair of boots tied across its back. Then the men walked, with grim faces, their black coats bright with red scarves, flowers and gold buttons. Behind them came carts with floral tributes, wagons filled with elderly women and children, and in the rear, young Gypsy girls and their mothers, each in her best dress with hair braided and tucked under a dark shawl or mantilla. The men remained outside the church, a dark army silent and severe. Only the occasional whinny of an impatient horse, the tossing of its head and harness, broke the quiet of the street. Beatrice saw some of the good people of Rye melting quietly away, too proud to share the sanctuary of the church with the Romanies. Others hurried in, and Beatrice watched idly to distinguish who was there to mourn, who to be seen by others, and who was chiefly anxious to have the service done, so they might spread the story of the Gypsy mourners to all their friends.

The church's familiar liturgy covered Richard Sidley in the comforting blanket of conformity, and he was laid to rest in the churchyard on the hill with all the usual solemnity and respect due to a fallen soldier and a local boy. Mrs Stokes stood with Snout's father, her grandson, at the graveside, both as still and erect as the stone angels on the neighbouring monuments, and her people stood apart from the graveside and were as silent as the cemetery itself. Beatrice tried to remain as steadfast. But at the Vicar's recitation of John 14:2, 'my father's house has many rooms', she leaned against Hugh's strong arm and wept into his sleeve for a boy who gave his young life for a country and a town that did not always know his value.

Later, as the mourners were leaving, Beatrice saw Mrs Stokes embrace Agatha. The two women spoke quietly, and Agatha kissed the old woman again on the cheek.

'It's always us old women who must bury our children,' said Mrs Stokes. 'Why does the good Lord not take us instead?'

'Why indeed,' said Agatha. 'We are not as strong as He thinks.'

'When I see Him at last, I shall give Him a piece of my mind,' said Mrs Stokes. 'Be it into the pit with me, I shall have my say.'

The evening light slanted across the flat marshes, and the cold of dusk was a reminder that summer was still far away. It was less than a year since Hugh Grange had first gone to the station to meet Beatrice. Now, coaxing the pony trap out across the marsh, he looked at the curve of her cheek and the way her hands folded across her lap, and he could not believe that she was his wife. The price of their happiness had been steep, but not enough to extinguish their hopes. He would have to return to the front in a few days, and they could not be sure his name would not one day be listed with the fallen. But today and tomorrow he was married and in love, and he would live each moment as if it were a year.

'Do you hear the lark?' she asked. A trembling song rose and fell above the grass, a sound he might have missed against the ring of horseshoes on the road. 'They will be thick in the air again, when summer comes. An *exaltation* of larks, they call it.'

'I will be home again,' he said. 'We shall lie on our backs in the fields and count birds.'

'I don't think trying to count them is quite in the exalting spirit,' she said, and though she smiled, her chin trembled for the sadness of the day.

At the shore, they climbed hand in hand across the dunes to find Mrs Stokes's family and friends gathered on the beach below. Aunt Agatha, Uncle John and Celeste stood with Abigail on the edge of the crowd, and his uncle carried a small bundle in his arms. Hugh had helped him collect the items this afternoon: a book of Longfellow, much written in the margins and stained with the wine and late-night suppers of a college poet; a favourite velvet smoking jacket patched at the elbows and frayed at the sleeves; his army cap, which Hugh had carried home. They had not included any of Daniel's poetry, it being valuable to the wider world, they hoped, but Aunt Agatha had sacrificed a precious cardboard folder filled with Daniel's childhood writings. They were gathered to say goodbye to Richard Sidley in private, away from the prying eyes of the town, and Mrs Stokes had honoured Hugh's aunt and uncle by including them in the ritual.

Uncle John stepped forward to climb the wooden steps of Maria Stokes's caravan and place his bundle inside the open door next to her great-grandson's small collection of clothes and possessions. Abigail then ran to add the precious jar of coins, and her father took a basket of sweet herbs and wildflowers from his wife and tucked it inside.

'He was my son,' said Snout's father. 'He was a scholar and a soldier and a good son to his mother.' He took a brand from the fire and held it high. 'And underneath he was one of us, a proud Romany man.' He tossed the brand inside, and the caravan, fresh with paint, caught like a torch and was soon consumed in a ball of fire and smoke. The smoke, in defiance of the war, climbed high into the sky and the caravan burned like a beacon. Men with a violin and accordion set to playing a low, wailing tune. And so they stood, as the light drained from the sky behind the town of Rye, and the crescent moon grew brighter in the dark, and the ceaseless waves ignored the small rituals of mankind to run up on the shore and withdraw again, under the strange regular hand of gravity.

EPILOGUE

'Come with me,' he said, 'and I will show you
where your son lies.'

RUDYARD KIPLING, 'The Gardener'

IN THE HIGH SUMMER of 1920, Beatrice and Hugh accompanied Aunt Agatha to the Continent. The fields of northern France and Flanders had already grown new coats of grass and hay to cover the mutilated nakedness of the battlefields. The first new crops had been planted in the less damaged areas, and red poppies nodded again in fields of wheat. All the hotels and guesthouses were full and festively decorated with fluttering pennants and bright awnings, and ladies dined under the awnings in the breezy, loose-fitting dresses that celebrated a new, more liberal era.

It was all the rage to visit the dead, scattered over the countryside in small-town cemeteries or patches of woodland, or often in what had been a field outside a clearing station. There was to be no repatriation of bodies. Instead, dignified new cemeteries were planned. In London, as in Rye, the talk was of new guidebooks and of finding just the perfect little *pension* from which to tour the battlefields.

'Vieux Jacques and his wife took such care of us at *Pension* Michel,' Bettina Fothergill had repeated around town. Her only nephew, Charles Poot, had managed to acquire a government post in London and so sit out the war in comfort, but she had been to visit the grave of her husband's cousin's nephew, several times removed, and made up for her lack of proximity to sacrifice by asserting herself as an expert on the logistics of the visit. Beatrice noticed that those who had lost more were quieter about their pilgrimages, slipping away unannounced and coming back with a photograph of the gravesite taken by some enterprising local photographer. Now that she was in France, she had more sympathy for the opportunistic locals, with their photographic services and their shrapnel souvenirs, and their farms turned into makeshift *pensions* – for in the shattered lands, it was still a scramble to make a living and feed a family through the winter.

Hugh left his patients to the retired Dr Lawton, whose practice he had taken on. Some grumblings were to be heard around Rye, for though they admired the decorated young surgeon who had chosen to give up his London ambitions to live as a quiet country doctor, they were selfish beings, and were inconvenienced by his taking his young wife away for a much delayed July holiday. Beatrice had been kept on at the school through the end of the war, teachers being in short supply, but as a married woman she was gently sent home at the armistice. She devoted most of her time to her writing now. Her small edition of Daniel Bookham's poems, with a gentle introduction extolling his passion for platonic ideals and his two great loves, for his friend and for his wife, was well received and took its place amid the many volumes of poetry from poets who now lay beneath the fields of the Continent. She was also working on her novel, having received a small advance from her father's publisher in gratitude for her work on Tillingham's book. Uncle John had not accompanied them to France. Troubled with sciatica these days, he stayed behind with Celeste, who had become too much like a daughter, and her small son a grandson to let her leave England when her father hurried away at the end of the war.

Beatrice rose early this morning, as was her routine, and sat by the window of their room at the *pension* to try to write a few lines. But she found her attention torn between the splendour of the morning light on the fields and the splendour of her young husband, lying sprawled in a tangle of sheets. She could not have imagined how marriage would enlarge and perfect the other pleasures of her life. To share books, to talk over one's work, to write letters and to see life reflected in another's eyes had brought a deep sense of satisfaction. Under her happiness ran a thin vein of sorrow that millions like her would feel down the years. It did not stop their feet from walking, or prevent the quotidian routines of life, but it ran in the population like the copper wires of the telephone system, connecting them all to each other and to the tragedy that had ripped at their hearts just as it had ripped at the fields outside her window.

Thanks to the influence of Uncle John and Mr Tillingham, Daniel had been among the first to be moved from his makeshift wartime grave and laid to rest in one of the new, experimental cemeteries, not yet finished. Mr Tillingham had arranged for them to visit privately and would meet them at breakfast. He had capitalised on his refugee work to claim a position on the Imperial War Graves Commission, where he joined the literary voices among a group of cemetery designers that included Britain's finest architects, landscape designers and engineers. A knighthood was the very least he hoped for from his labours. He was spending much of the summer in the area, where he could shuffle among the plots, providing daily supervision of the work and expanding his influence beyond anything asked of him.

Agatha was already at breakfast when Beatrice and Hugh came down. A plate of poached eggs and fruit sat untouched before her. She was drinking a cup of tea, holding the cup in both hands, paused as if lost in the chattering of the sparrows in the flowering window box.

'Good morning, Aunt,' said Hugh, and he kissed her cheek. She closed her eyes at his touch. It seemed to Beatrice that Hugh's presence brought Agatha great joy and great pain all at once, and she feared that his aunt might never see him without the ghost of his cousin standing at his shoulder.

'Good morning, all,' said Mr Tillingham, entering the breakfast room with the expansive cheer of a monarch sweeping to the throne. The old waiter bowed, and the kitchen girl rushed in with his thick toast and his soft-boiled egg; he was a regular and a procurer of many guests, and they leaped to his every need. 'A fine day for it, no doubt,' he continued. 'We will keep the gate locked until you are done, dear lady, but we should get an early start.'

So saying, he sat at table and took a great deal of time to chew his way methodically through his breakfast.

Under a blue sky, with the sound of birdsong in the poplars and a light breeze glittering through the leaves, the cemetery looked almost painfully beautiful. It was set in a plain rectangular garden wall, not so high as to hide the glory of the countryside all around. The gravestones of English Portland stone, brought from Dorset, were planted in uniform rows on either side of straight grass paths. A cross at the gate and a monolith at the far end provided weight and spirituality. But to Beatrice's eye, the beauty lay in dozens of pink rosebushes, lying about in great heaps, and a gardener patiently planting them between the gravestones so that the dead might sleep in a pretty, tidy English garden.

They descended from the carriage and Mr Tillingham stopped to speak to a watchman at the gate. Hugh helped Agatha up the pathway and they assembled on the steps of the monolithic Stone of Remembrance while the watchman went to consult the gardener about the gravestone they had come to see.

'The inscription was Kipling's choice, a little obvious perhaps,' Tillingham said, pointing to the heavy chiselled statement, THEIR NAME LIVETH FOR EVERMORE. 'I told them we should remove the 'for' as superfluous, but it being from the Bible, he and the commission were rather sticky about keeping the usual wording. Let me give you a brief overview of the meaning behind the Cross of Sacrifice and its bronze ornament . . .'

But Agatha Kent went forward to meet the watchman and the gardener, who were coming towards them, and they spoke to her in French and pointed halfway along the sleeping rows.

'Will you excuse us a moment?' said Hugh. 'I think my aunt would like to go forward alone.' He looked to Beatrice for permission, and she gave him a smile and a nod. In proximity to grief, she was little more than a tourist compared to her husband and his aunt. She would wait patiently with Mr Tillingham, and he would have to jingle his watch chain and peer from a distance, and they would both have to examine their own irrelevance to the story unfolding in this little garden.

As Hugh held her arm, Agatha turned left into a row and slowly, so very slowly, walked along. Beatrice could tell she was reading each name, whether to defer the agony or in the hopes that such an incantation might wipe Daniel's name from the pale limestone, she could not say. But the stone was found and the sound of her single sob carried down the rows to where they stood together.

'It's always the mothers,' said the gardener.

Beatrice opened her mouth to correct him, but it was suddenly as clear to her as the blue sky above that of course he spoke the truth.

After a moment she dared to peek at Mr Tillingham. His face was as greedy as that of a glutton before the feast. She knew then he was thinking of how to use Agatha's secret tragedy, imagining a famous story to gild his reputation and surround himself with a new aura of exquisite compassion. She did not know how he could continue to just take the souls from people he knew and mix them about on his palette like a rude painter. For now it seemed to her that all his novels were filled with people he knew and had betrayed. He must have sensed her looking at him. He coughed and shuffled his feet, and then he turned his weak grey eyes to her and said, with a half-apologetic air, 'One is always careful to change the names, of course. It's only courteous.'

She walked away from him to stand and mourn alone, in a scene she knew no writer would ever capture well enough that men might cease to war: Agatha half-kneeling on the grass, Hugh bending in silent grace to comfort, the milk white of the gravestones and the pink roses vivid against the new-cropped grass. Overhead, a single lark spilled its praise into the blue dome of the sky.

ACKNOWLEDGEMENTS

WHEN WORLD WAR ONE ended at 11 a.m. on 11 November 1918, many young poets, including Rupert Brooke and Wilfred Owen, had died for their country. The work of the war poets is as enduring a remembrance of the conflict as the red poppy…

Writers and poets are at the heart of my novel and it is perhaps no accident that the most renowned Sussex- and Kent-connected authors, who inhabited a special shelf in the Rye bookshop when I was young, all lived in this time period: Henry James, E. F. Benson, Radclyffe Hall, Vita Sackville-West, Rudyard Kipling and Virginia Woolf. Edith Wharton was also on the shelf, as she would regularly visit Rye to take her friend Henry James out in her large car. Alas, the bookshop is gone, as are the used book dealers where I spent my Saturday job money on dusty hardcovers of these authors' books, but their work and lives continue to inspire me.

A novel with a historical setting is a great challenge. Among the many books, websites and other sources I read in preparation for writing *The Summer Before the War*, I must mention a few standouts. *Agatha Christie: An Autobiography* and Vera Brittain's *Testament of Youth* showed me young women coming of age in this tumultuous period as the rigidity of their upbringing was swept away by the tumult of war. *Myself When Young*, edited by Margot Oxford, featured famous women of Britain recalling first-hand their Edwardian girlhoods and provided a wealth of detail. *Henry James at Work*, by his longtime amanuensis Theodora Bosanquet (edited by Lyall Powers), not only showed an intimate portrait of the Cher Maître, as he liked to be called, but, more important, gave me insight into Theodora's life as an independent unmarried woman who went on to a literary career of her own after James' death.

Military history can be dry, but *Europe's Last Summer*, by David Fromkin, gave me a clear day-by-day run-up to the declaration of war, so I knew what Uncle John was up to. In *Boy Soldiers of the Great War*, by Richard Van Emden, I was shocked to find out that more than 250,000 underage Richard Sidleys might have enlisted in Britain's military services. The Bryce Report, a 1915 British government report similar to that which Mr Poot works on, described atrocities in Belgium and was dryly hilarious in its refusal to describe some atrocities because they were too atrocious. Not funny at all was its finding that rape, though widely reported, was probably not officially forbidden at the highest levels and therefore not to be classified as an official war crime. War diaries, photographs and records were found on many websites, including 1914-1918.net and firstworldwar.com, which both feature enthusiasts doing stellar work in collecting and preserving information. I must pause to acknowledge Google for the miracle of being able to search any idea mid-sentence.

My depiction of life in Edwardian Rye was informed by a series of booklets called *Rye Memories*, the result of an oral history project by pupils of my old school, Thomas Peacocke (Rye Grammar in 1914 and now Rye College), and local seniors. Thanks to Mrs Jo Kirkham, MBE, former Mayor of Rye, and town historian, who founded this project and who advised me many times on additional information about the town's history. The *Bexhill Quarterly* newsletter from 1914 was a plum find at Rye Library and landed Bexhill a cameo role.

The more I researched my British Romanies, the more ashamed I became of my own lack of awareness of the international plight of the Roma people, a UN-recognised ethnic minority against whom racism and prejudice have persisted unbroken for over a thousand years. I would like to thank Professor Ethel Brookes of Rutgers University, an international expert on Romani studies, for introducing me to Ian Hancock's *We Are the Romani People* and for her guidance and openness in discussing my research.

All research errors are my own, but expert advice on Vergil (the original spelling) and Latin came courtesy of author Madeline Miller. My poetry may owe more to *The Pickwick Papers*' 'Ode to an Expiring Frog' than to the indelible legacy of the British war poets, but my prosody was expertly dissected by the Whiting Award-winning poet Professor Julie Sheehan of SUNY Stony Brook Southampton (hello to all at Southampton). I would be remiss if I did not also thank the places that make research and writing possible – libraries. The New York Public Library at 42nd Street, and its books, represent the marble halls of civilisation to me. The British Library Newspapers at Colindale gave me access to large leatherbound books of original newspapers and magazines from 1914, which I read for hours at a huge slanted oak desk. The division is now closed and these original periodicals restricted for preservation. Alas, microfilm and searchable digital content cannot replace the thrill and serendipity of reading a full newspaper just as my characters would have done. The branch library at Rye, with its shelf of local history resources, was a joy to work in, as was the Rogers Library in Southampton, New York, where I took refuge to finish this novel in several long shifts.

I can attest that a second novel is harder to write, not easier, than the first and I have many people to thank for supporting me in my creative struggle. Let me begin by thanking my agent, Julie Barer of The Book Group, and all her colleagues, including Anna Geller and Meg Ross – with a grateful nod to Barer alums William, Leah, Gemma and Anna W. At my very first meeting with Julie, I slowly understood that this extraordinary agent was willing to take me on and secure me some small place in the great community of writers. As I stepped from her office into a busy New York street, it seemed that the landscape of my second novel spread out before me as I stood on a Sussex hilltop with Agatha Kent. I nearly got run over by a cab, but this novel was born then, in a moment of pure exhilaration.

My enduring thanks to Susan Kamil, my editor at Random House, for taking a chance on an unknown debut novel and supporting me all through the writing of my second. Her edits always pierce to what is true. Her laughter is infectious. The entire team at Random House is amazing: Thanks to Gina Centrello, Avideh Bashirrad, Sally Marvin, Andrea DeWerd, Robbin Schiff, Benjamin Dreyer, Evan Camfield, Jennifer Garza, Leigh Marchant and Molly Turpin. Also thanks to Caitlin McCaskey and Lisa Barnes at the Penguin Random House Speakers Bureau.

My wonderful UK publishing house, Bloomsbury, offered invaluable British editing assistance. Much appreciation to Alexandra Pringle, my editor, and to founder Nigel Newton, who shares a fondness for Sussex. Thanks also to Antonia Till, Alexa von Hirschberg and Angelique Tran Van Sang. Warmest regards to my British agent, Caspian Dennis, of Abner Stein, whose kind words sustained me during the saggy, baggy times. Gratitude to

Patrick Gallagher and Annette Barlow (Australia), Maggie Doyle and Katel le Fur (France), Annette Weber (Germany), and my other fine editors and publishing houses around the world.

The writing life can be frustrating and lonely, and it is friends and family who sustain me but who also give me the well-deserved eye roll, and kick in the pants, when I need it. Thanks to writer friends Mary Kay Zuravleff, Susan Coll, Michelle Brafman and Cindy Krezel. Thanks to Lisa Genova and Tim Hallinan for your long-distance advice. Brooklyn friends, I thank you all, especially Susan Leitner, Sarah Tobin and Leslie Alexander, who have known me since before I ever picked up a pen, as have Joe Garafolo and Helena Huncar and her family.

Last but first is always family. To my parents, Alan and Margaret Phillips, who left Sussex for an exciting new life in southwest France and who were loud in their opinions that my novel needed no editing whatsoever, thank you for the unconditional love! Appreciation also to my father-in-law, newspaperman David Simonson, whose stalwart care of my elegant and gracious mother-in-law, Lois Simonson, in her declining health was a lesson in love and family for all of us. Thanks to my sister, Lorraine Pearce, and her family for keeping us connected to Sussex and invited to family gatherings.

A special thank you to Ian Simonson, elder son and computer engineer, for web design help and for rescuing the chronology of my story at a critical juncture. Jamie Simonson, younger son, went to study abroad during editing, perhaps to avoid having his considerable writing skills pressed into service! It has been our greatest joy to watch the world through our sons' eyes as they have grown up into fine young men. They are an inspiration, even when they are mercilessly teasing me about my writing!

And always there is my John, my love, my best friend and my husband of some thirty years. That the years have been swift only means they were happy. Here's to taking the future at a run.

ALSO AVAILABLE BY HELEN SIMONSON

MAJOR PETTIGREW'S LAST STAND

THE INTERNATIONAL BESTSELLER

Major Ernest Pettigrew is perfectly content to lead a quiet life in the sleepy village of Edgecombe St Mary, away from the meddling of the locals and his overbearing son. But when his brother dies, the Major finds himself seeking companionship with the village shopkeeper, Mrs Ali. Drawn together by a love of books and the loss of their partners, they are soon forced to contend with irate relatives and gossiping villagers. The perfect gentleman, but the most unlikely hero, the Major must ask himself what matters most: family obligation, tradition or love?

Funny, comforting and heart-warming, *Major Pettigrew's Last Stand* proves that sometimes, against all odds, life does give you a second chance.

'Words can't convey the slow-burning pleasure of this novel'
THE TIMES

'A charming, funny and absorbing debut'
WENDY HOLDEN, DAILY MAIL

'Refreshing in its optimism and its faith in the transformative powers of courtesy and kindness'
ALEXANDER McCALL SMITH, NEW YORK TIMES

ORDER YOUR COPY:

BY PHONE: +44 (0) 1256 302 699; **BY EMAIL:** DIRECT@MACMILLAN.CO.UK

DELIVERY IS USUALLY 3–5 WORKING DAYS. FREE POSTAGE AND PACKAGING FOR ORDERS OVER £20.

ONLINE: WWW.BLOOMSBURY.COM/BOOKSHOP

PRICES AND AVAILABILITY SUBJECT TO CHANGE WITHOUT NOTICE.

BLOOMSBURY.COM/AUTHOR/HELEN-SIMONSON

BLOOMSBURY